CAROLINE

ALSO BY SARAH MILLER

YOUNG ADULT NON-FICTION

The Borden Murders: Lizzie Borden and the Trial of the Century

YOUNG ADULT FICTION

The Lost Crown

Miss Spitfire: Reaching Helen Keller

CAROLINE

LITTLE HOUSE, REVISITED

SARAH MILLER

WITH THE FULL APPROVAL OF
LITTLE HOUSE HERITAGE TRUST

WILLIAM MORROW
An Imprint of HarperCollins*Publishers*

HarperCollins books may be purchased for educational, business, or sales promotional use. For information, please email the Special Markets Department at SPsales@harpercollins.com.

A hardcover edition of this book was published in 2017 by William Morrow, an imprint of HarperCollins Publishers.

FIRST WILLIAM MORROW PAPERBACK EDITION PUBLISHED 2018.

Designed by Bonni Leon-Berman

Library of Congress Cataloging-in-Publication Data has been applied for.

ISBN 978-0-06-268535-3

23 24 25 26 27 LBC 8 7 6 5 4

None knew thee but to love thee,

Thou dear one of my heart,

Oh, thy memory is ever fresh and green.

"Daisy Deane"

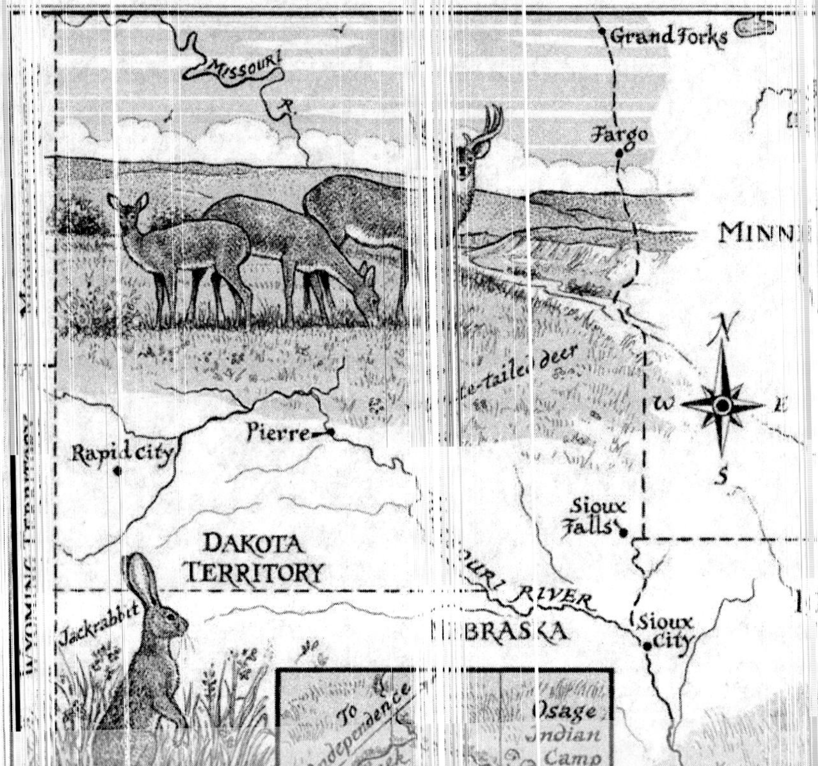
Grand Forks
MISSOURI
Fargo
MINNE
N
W
E
S
Pierre
Rapid city
Sioux Falls
DAKOTA TERRITORY
Jackrabbit
NEBRASKA
Sioux City
To Independence
Osage Indian Camp
Walnut Creek
Onion Creek
Ingallses' site
Closer view of Ingallses' home area
COLORADO
KANSAS
Omaha
Boston's Ferry
Atchison
Junction City
Topeka
Lawrence
Pawnee River
Arkansas River
Dodge City
Wichita
Verdigris River
Neosho R.
Independence
Ingallses' site
Coffeyville
NEW MEXICO TERRITORY
UNORGANIZED TERRITORY
TEXAS

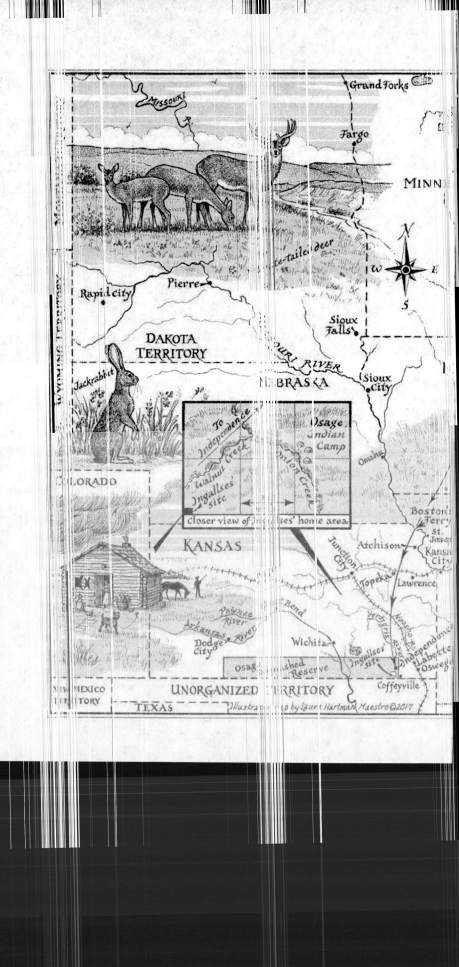

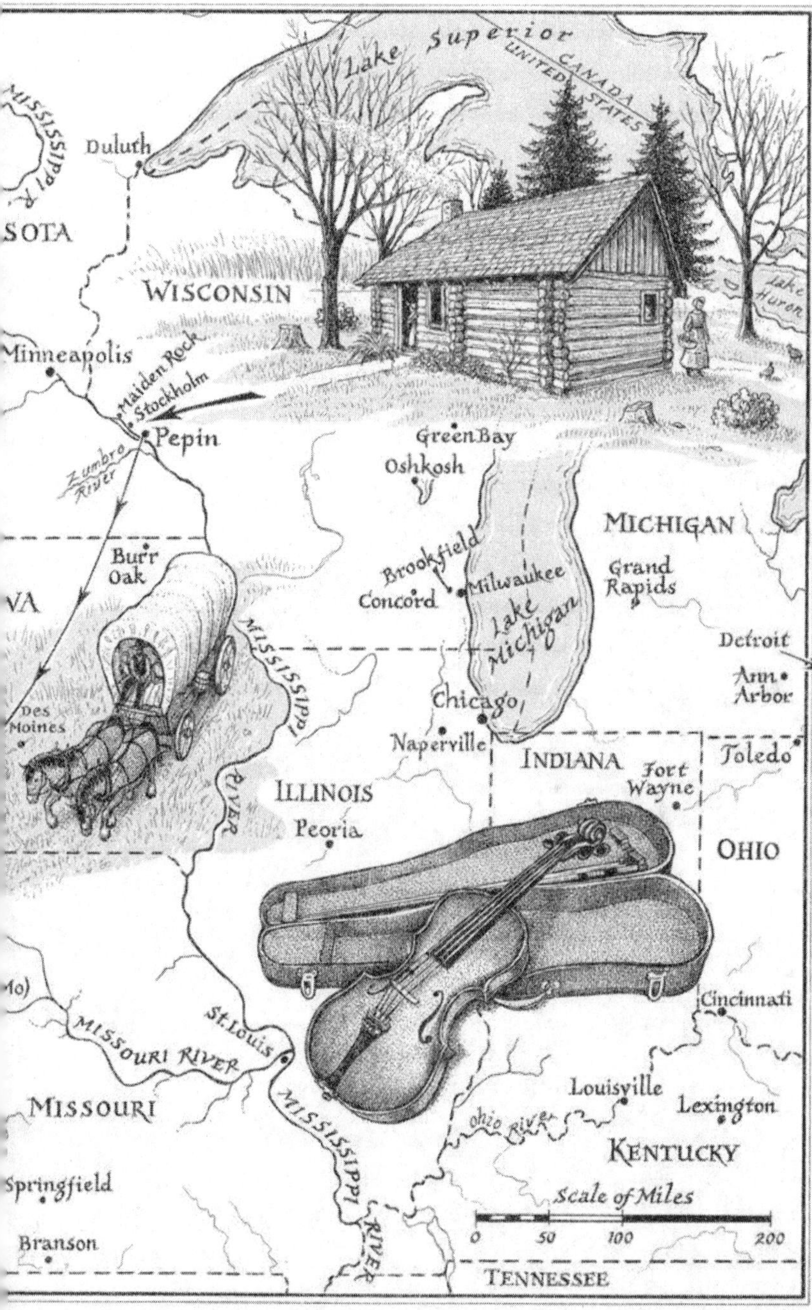
Lake Superior
UNITED STATES
CANADA
MISSISSIPPI R.
Duluth
SOTA
WISCONSIN
Lake Huron
Minneapolis
Maiden Rock
Stockholm
Pepin
Green Bay
Oshkosh
Zumbro River
MICHIGAN
Burr Oak
Brookfield
Concord
Milwaukee
Grand Rapids
VA
Lake Michigan
MISSISSIPPI
Detroit
Ann Arbor
Chicago
Des Moines
Naperville
INDIANA
Fort Wayne
Toledo
ILLINOIS
RIVER
Peoria
OHIO
Mo)
Cincinnati
St. Louis
MISSOURI RIVER
MISSISSIPPI
Louisville
Lexington
MISSOURI
Ohio River
KENTUCKY
Scale of Miles
0
50
100
200
Springfield
RIVER
Branson
TENNESSEE

One

CAROLINE'S WRIST TURNED and flicked as the steel tongue of her crochet hook dipped in and out, mirroring the movement of the fiddle's bow. With each note, the white thread licked a warm line across her finger. Her pattern had just begun to repeat, chorus-like, as the tune ended. She smoothed the frilled cluster of scallops against her cuff and smiled. So long as she could keep ahead of the mending, a pair of lace wrists would freshen her second-best blue wool before snowmelt. There would be no time for a collar—once the trees began to bud, she must turn her hands to the tedious seams of a new set of diapers, bonnets, and gowns.

Charles rested the fiddle on his knees and primed himself with a breath.

"What is it, Charles?" Caroline asked, plucking a slouching festoon of thread into place.

"I've had an offer for this place," he said.

Caroline's hook stilled. "An offer?"

"Gustafson's agreed to pay one thousand twelve dollars and fifty cents for our half of this quarter section."

The sum swept her mind clean as a gust of wind. "My goodness," she said. One thousand twelve dollars. And the delightful absurdity of fifty cents besides, like a sprinkling of sugar. They could use it to buy a week's worth of satin hair ribbons for Mary and Laura. "Oh, Charles." Caroline clasped her hands before her lips to hide their eager trembling. "And the same for Henry and Polly's half?"

Charles grimaced. "Gustafson can only afford eighty acres. Your brother isn't going."

Going. The image her mind had already begun to embroider unraveled. Such foolish greed; she had let herself imagine that money as though it were sitting in her lap, beneath this very roof—not as the lever that would pry her loose of it.

She need not ask where they would go. All winter long Charles had talked of Kansas: the free, level land and bountiful game. Even Mary and little Laura could repeat his reveries of the mighty jackrabbits and treeless acreage as easily as the words of "The Gypsy King." The West was a song Charles wanted a hand in composing.

A subtle tightening, as though she were taking hold of the cabin and everything in it, passed over her. To move westward was nothing new, but always, she had traveled from the sanctuary of one family to another: from Ma and Papa Frederick's house in Concord to Father and Mother Ingalls' farm, and from there to this quarter section they had bought together with Henry and Polly, just seven miles east of the Mississippi.

And yet beneath that apprehension, a twinkle of excitement. Caroline remembered the thrill, after three years of married life spent under others' roofs, of buying this place and making of it a home all their own. Within six months she had been pregnant. How might it feel to do the same on land that bore no mark of another family? Such a place would belong more thoroughly to them than anything had before.

"We stake our claim, make improvements on the land while Gustafson makes his payments, and by the time the Indians move on we can clear the mortgage on this place and preempt a full one hundred sixty acres with upwards of five hundred dollars left to spare," Charles went on, pulling a blue handbill from his pocket. "The settlers put up such a fuss that the government's finally reneged on the railroad interests. The Indian Territory is there for the taking—a dollar and a quarter an acre. We only have to be there when the land opens up. The sooner we arrive, the sooner we've put in our fourteen months' residency." He leaned forward for her reply.

The arithmetic alone spoke for itself: twice the acreage, none of the debt. Cash in hand, where before they had banked with pelts and crops. She should not hesitate at such a gain. Yet how to weigh that against losses that could not be measured? Departing before the Mississippi thawed would not leave time enough to bid her own mother goodbye. She did not answer yes or no. "We will have an increase in the family well before then," she said instead.

Caroline tucked her lips together. She had not intended to tell him for another month yet, not until she was certain the child was safely rooted. But Charles looked at her as though it were the first time, and she went rosy in the glow of his happiness. "When?" he asked.

"Before harvest."

He combed his fingers through his whiskers. "Should we wait?"

Her conscience rippled. She could say yes, and he would give her the year at least, restaking himself to this land without question or complaint. Another year with her sisters and brother, with Mother and Father Ingalls, with plenty of time to visit Ma and Papa Frederick one more time. One final time. Were she to answer on behalf of the coming child, it might even be an unselfish thing to ask. Yet she'd had no sense of its presence—only the absence of her monthly courses coupled with an unaccountable warmth in her hands and feet—nothing to signal it as separate from herself.

Caroline's eyes roved over the place where her china shepherdess stood gazing down from the mantel. The silken glaze of her painted dress and body seemed at once so hard and smooth as to render the little woman untouchable. If she indulged herself by claiming this time, Caroline thought, Charles would treat her with almost unbearable awe and deference. No matter that carrying a child made her feel no more fragile than a churn full of cream. Staying would only make for a year shadowed with lasts—one vast goodbye shattered over innumerable small moments. "Better to travel now," she decided. "It will only be harder if we wait."

He leaned back, grinning, until the chair was on tiptoe. Her news had dyed the fabric of the coming year twice as brightly for Charles. He took up the fiddle and played softly, so as not to wake the girls.

There's a land that is fairer than day,
And by faith we can see it afar.
For the Father waits over the way,
To prepare us a dwelling place there.

Caroline laid her morsel of lace aside and rocked herself deeply into the long notes.

Two

"LONG AS THOSE hickory bows are curing, I might as well make a trip into town," Charles said, shrugging into his overcoat. "We still need oakum to caulk the wagon box and canvas for a cover."

"Get a good heavy needle and plenty of stout linen thread," Caroline reminded him. "And check the post office," she added, silly as it was. The letter she'd sent into town with Henry the week before could hardly have reached her mother in Concord by now. Charles winked and shut the door, whistling.

Caroline stood in the middle of the big room with a burst of breath puffing out her cheeks. Charles always saw the beginning of a new start, never the loose ends of the old one that must be fastened off.

The cabin had not seemed overlarge before, but it was more than would fit in a wagon box—the straw ticks alone would fill a third of it. Every object she laid eyes on suddenly demanded a decision of her. To look at it all at once made her mind swarm. *One thing at a time,* Caroline told herself. She pulled the red-checked cloth from the table, and the shepherdess from the mantel. Some few things, at least, there was no question about.

IN THE BEDROOM, Caroline opened her trunk and lifted the upper tray out onto the bed. In one of its shallow compartments lay the glass ambrotype portraits from their courting and marriage, and her three schoolbooks. She opened the reader. Its cardboard cover shielded her certificate of good behavior and the little handwritten booklet of poems she'd sewn together as a youth. She slipped a fingernail between its leaves and parted the pages. "Blue Juniata" stood out in Charles's writing. She smiled, remembering the cornhusking dance where she had first heard Charles play the tune. He had not sung the words correctly, and she had been so bold as to tell him so. "That's the way we Ingallses sang it back East," he'd said, and his eyes twinkled at her. They'd twinkled again when she asked him to inscribe his version in her booklet. "Now no matter which way I sing it, it'll be by the book," he'd teased.

She did not hear Mary and Laura come pattering down from the attic until they stood in the doorway.

"What are you doing, Ma?" Mary asked. "Can we help?"

"May we," she reminded, secreting the fragile booklet back into the reader.

"May we, Ma?"

Laura was already peering over the rim of the trunk. A tongue of frustration licked at Caroline's throat. She could not let children of five and three pack her best things, yet they would make themselves busy getting underfoot if she did not give them something to do. She smoothed back a sigh. "Very well. Mary, please bring me the scrap bag, and Laura, you may fetch the newspapers."

INTO THE BOTTOM of the trunk went her books, together with the family Bible and the volume of Sunday school lessons her mother had given her. The lap desk just snugged in beside them. Caroline slipped the ambrotypes beneath the trunk's lid and cushioned them with a length of flannel Mary fished from the scrap bag.

"Now, Laura, we must fill the cracks and corners with newspaper. Pack them tightly, so nothing can wiggle."

While Laura crumpled and crammed newsprint into every cranny, Caroline showed Mary how to roll the silver spoons up in squares of felt. The girls occupied, she packed a sturdy cardboard box with her thin china teacups, leaving a hollow in the center for the shepherdess. When Laura finished, Caroline folded her wholecloth wedding quilt with the red stitching and squared it over the layer of books.

"Now Mary and Laura, please bring me the good pillows." She let them put one at each end of the trunk, then nested the box of porcelain amongst the goose down. Her pearl-handled pen and the breast pins she slipped into the red Morocco pocketbook before tucking it into the lid compartment.

The delaine, shrouded in soft brown paper and tied with string, came last of all.

"Please, Ma, can't we see the delaine?" Laura begged. Her mouth fairly watered for its strawberry-shaped buttons.

Caroline could not help remembering her mother's broad hands sewing those buttons onto the rich green basque by lamplight. Just now, she did not want to unwrap that memory any further, even for her girls.

"Not today."

"Aw, Ma, please?"

Caroline raised an eyebrow. "Laura." Her tone dwindled the child into a half-hearted pout.

Over it all Caroline smoothed the red-checked tablecloth, then lowered in the tray and latched the lid. *Tck* went the latch, and the band of tension broke from her chest. "There now," she said, and felt herself smiling. "Thank you, Mary and Laura." With such things out of sight, she could begin imagining them elsewhere and other people's possessions in their places.

BY THE TIME Charles came back from town, she had packed one of their two carpetbags tight with trousers, calico shirts and dresses, sunbonnets, and cotton stockings. At the bottom waited her maternity and nursing corsets with the baby gowns Mary and Laura hadn't worn out. The other would hold their spare sets of woolens, along with their nightclothes and underthings. At the sound of Charles's boots on the floor, the girls abandoned their half-folded pile of dishcloths, napkins, and towels and scampered to him for their treats.

"Sweets to the sweet," he said, handing them each a sugared ginger cookie. "And something for your ma." A quick little inhale betrayed Caroline's hopes for a letter. She looked up eagerly as Charles flopped a drab bundle tied with twine from his shoulder onto the bed. The *whoosh* of its landing fluttered her stacks of linens.

"There you are, Caroline—thirty yards of osnaburg canvas and the stoutest thread goods in Pepin."

She sat back on her heels. "Thirty yards!"

"Fellow in the dry goods shop said four widths ought to be enough to stretch over the wagon bows, and it'll have to be double thick. Need extra to double-sack all our dry provisions besides. How long will it take to make?" Charles asked. "Lake Pepin's solid as a window pane, but the cold can't hold out too much longer."

Three doubled seams more than twice as long as she was tall, plus the hemming and the sacks. If each stitch were a mile, her needle could carry them to Kansas and back dozens of times over. Caroline's fingers cramped to think of it. "No longer than it will take you to bend those hickory bows and fit up the wagon," she told him.

He chucked her under the chin. "Got some extra crates for packing, too," he said.

ON MENDING DAY, she gave herself over entirely to the wagon cover. Laid flat, it stretched from one side of the big room to the other. In the time it took Caroline to fetch her papers of pins, Laura had already taken to tunneling under the carpet of canvas.

"Mary, be a good girl and take Laura upstairs to play with your paper ladies," Caroline said after she'd scolded Laura. "There isn't space to have you underfoot down here. If you play nicely until I've finished, you may cook a doll supper for Nettie on the stove tonight."

Mary needed no more enticement than that. She took her sister by the hand and marched Laura to the ladder. Caroline straightened the lengths of fabric and settled down to her long chore. With every stitch she pictured the journey in her mind, envisioning the views the hem now before her would soon frame.

When the pads of her thumb and forefinger grew rutted from the press of the needle, Caroline laid the canvas aside to dip the steel knives and forks in soda water and roll them in flannel to keep against rust, or to melt rosin and lard together to grease the outside of the bake oven, the iron spider, and Charles's tools. With the leftovers she would waterproof their boots and shoes.

By noontime the close of the center seam was less than an arm's length away. She might have finished it before dinner, if not for a burrowing sensation low in her middle that would not be ignored. Caroline pinned her needle carefully over her last stitch and stepped out from under the stiff blanket of fabric. Her forearms were heavy with fatigue from holding the everlasting seam at eye level.

"Girls," she called up the ladder into the attic, "I'm going to the necessary. Keep away from the fireplace and cookstove until I come back."

"Yes, Ma," they sang out.

It took longer than she intended; where before the slight pressure of her womb had driven her to the chamber pail three and four times between breakfast and dinner, now the child had taken to making her bowels costive.

She could not hear the girls' voices overhead as she stripped off her shawl and mittens in the narrow corridor that led in from the back door. A twist of unease tickled the place she had just voided. "Mary? Laura?" she called. Giggles in return, muffled. Caroline cocked her head, not entirely relieved. "Girls? What are you up to?"

She strode into the big room and stopped short. Her rocking chair stood twisted halfway around, bare of its canvas cloak—they'd dragged the wagon cover over the table and benches and made themselves a tent of it. Her needle dangled in a widening gap that formed the flap of their door.

Caroline threw up her hands and dropped into her rocker. *A woman can resolve that whatever happens, she will not speak till she can do it in a calm and gentle manner,* she recited to herself as she waited for the flare of temper to ebb. *Perfect silence is a safe resort, when such control cannot be attained.* "Come out of there, the both of you," she said evenly after another moment.

They crawled out on hands and knees. "We're playing 'going west,'" Laura explained. "I'm Pa, and Mary's Ma, and this is our wagon." Laura was so earnest, Caroline pinched back a smile in spite of herself. Mary stood by, sheepish.

Caroline made herself sober. "You know better than to tangle with my mending," she said, mostly to Mary. "Our wagon cover must have good strong seams to keep us safe and dry. You may not play—"

"Aw, Ma," Laura mourned.

"Laura. It's very rude to interrupt. You will have more than enough time to squander it when we go west." She looked again toward Mary. "There will be no doll supper tonight."

"Yes, ma'am," Mary said.

"And no bedtime stories from your pa," she told Laura. Caroline stooped and gathered up the span of canvas. "Now set the table for dinner and sit quietly in your places while I repair this seam."

Caroline felt as though she needed a good stitching. Dinner had not been started, the wagon cover still lay in pieces, and already her body simmered with exhaustion. Well, there was no great loss without some small gain—at least she would not have to hover over the cookstove with Mary and her pattypans.

"READY?" CHARLES ASKED.

Caroline nodded. Together they leaned over the sideboards of the wagon and took the corners of the folded sheet of canvas from Mary's and Laura's outstretched hands, pulling it square over the hickory bows.

"Best-looking wagon cover in Wisconsin," Charles proclaimed. He tossed Laura and then Mary up over the tailgate and cinched the rear flaps down so tightly they could barely peek through. "There we are—snug as a tent!"

Caroline could not deny it was handsome, all clean and close-fitting as a new bodice. It was easily the largest thing she had ever sewn. And yet it looked to have shrunk. All that canvas, which inside the cabin had seemed vast enough to set a schooner afloat, now enclosed an area barely the size of the pigpen. "I declare, I still don't know how it's all going to fit," Caroline said as the girls ran whooping up and down the length of the wagon box.

"I'm whittling a pair of hooks for my gun. Tell me how many you need, and I'll make you enough to hang anything you like from the bows."

"That will do for the carpetbags, but we can't hang the bedstead and straw ticks."

"I'll lay a few boards across the wagon box to make a loft for the straw ticks right behind the spring seat," Charles said. "The girls and the fiddle can ride there, with the extra provisions stowed underneath."

But there was still the medicine box of camphor, castor oil, laudanum, and bitter herbs. The willow-bough broom, sewing basket, scrap bag, sadirons, soap and starch; the kerosene, candles, tinderbox, and lamps; the chamber pail. The whole of the pantry must go into the wagon, from the salt and pepper to the churn and dishpan. Always there was something small and essential turning up that must be wedged into a box—packets of seeds, scraps of leather and balls of twine, the little box that held Mary's rag doll and paper ladies, the matches screwed tightly into a cobalt blue medicine bottle. And yet there must be room for Charles's things: chains and ropes and picket pins, the metal tools and traps, his lead and patch box and bullet mold. It was a mercy the buckets and washtub could hang outside the wagon.

"Don't worry about the furniture," Charles added. "We'll leave all that. Once we get settled I can make more."

Caroline pulled her s[illegible] her chin, stricken. Over and over again she had imagined her th[illegible]anged in the new place Charles would build, until the picture fe[illegible]iar, almost beckoning. All at once there was no place to spread th[illegible]checked tablecloth, nowhere to prop the pillows in their embroide[illegible]ms. Even her cozy vantage point—her rocker before the hearth[illegible]anished from the image. "That will help," she said weakly.

Charles loosened the [illegible] stuck his head inside the wagon. "Any Indians in here?" he call[illegible]ary and Laura. Caroline measured the wagon one last time wi[illegible]eyes, then left Charles and the girls to their play.

The cabin still smelle[illegible] linseed oil she'd used to cure the canvas. Boxes, crates, and b[illegible] leaned in the corners, encroaching on her sense of order no ma[illegible]w neatly she stacked them. Turning her back to the disarray, Ca[illegible]went to the hearth and lowered herself into the embrace of the r[illegible]ing chair, listening for the accustomed sigh of the runners across th[illegible]oards. Charles had fashioned this chair for her of sugar maple ju[illegible]e Mary was born. In the last days before the birth, its sway had so[illegible]er nerves as much as it soothed the baby afterward. Beside it sat C[illegible]s own straight-backed chair and Mary's and Laura's little stools, [illegible]wooden family. Charles had built them all, and he would build n[illegible]. Caroline stroked the arms of her rocker. Her fingers knew the g[illegible] their curves as well as they knew the coiled knot of her own h[illegible]he work of Charles's hands might make a new chair familiar to he[illegible], but it would not be the same.

Three

IN THE GRAINY dark before dawn, Caroline woke to the pull of her stomach drawing itself taut. Before opening her eyes she resigned herself to it; better to let her muscles express her dread of this day than give voice to it.

Already the room had changed. Neither Charles's clothes nor his nightshirt hung on the nail beside her own, though the usual sounds of him putting on his boots and taking up the water pail came from the back door. She lay still a moment more after the door shut, letting herself collect the feel of the roof and walls around her one last time before kneeling alongside the trundle bed to pray.

As she fastened her corset, Caroline marked the faint rise of her waist, like the dome of a layer cake peeking over the pan. The quickening would follow before long. She was more impatient for it this time than she had been even with Mary. After spending weeks packing boxes and crates, it was disquieting not to have felt her own body's cargo. Caroline flattened her palms below her ribs and drew a breath. Not a flicker, yet the steady press of the steels along her core eased the quiver of her nerves. With each successive breath she stretched her lungs deeper still, until she was nearly within reach of her accustomed cadence.

Caroline took her dress down from its nail and the bedroom turned gaunt—stripped and scoured down to the last bare inch. Vinegar still stung the air, sharpened by the cold. It crowded out the familiar traces of Charles's shaving lather and rosemary-scented bear grease. Caroline washed her face, then with her damp palms smoothed the length of her braid before pinning it carefully up. Last of all she dipped the comb into the basin [illegible] water and slicked down the loo[illegible] between her forehead [illegible] nape of her neck.

A fre[illegible] half-melted snow already wa[illegible] the cookstove for her. [illegible] stoked up the fire and set [illegible] deftly as Charles [illegible] his fiddle. She filled the coffeep[illegible] skillet with snow, draped [illegible] underthings over the back of th[illegible] to warm, then went to [illegible] the last of the salt pork.

At th[illegible] of the newly emptied pan[illegible] hesitated. A score of years [illegible] since she'd faced such a bar[illegible] shelves, yet the sight w[illegible] to waken the old tremors [illegible] The few things she had [illegible] able to make room for—th[illegible] half-dozen jars of preserv[illegible] eggs in their big barrel of salt[illegible] water—beckoned to be p[illegible] persistently as the bedstead and [illegible] chair. Tightly as they'd [illegible] the wagon, Caroline could not h[illegible] wondering if hunger would [illegible] place to lodge among the crates a[illegible]dles.

Caro[illegible] herself free of such thoughts. [illegible] morning at least, they w[illegible] their fill of eggs and empty [illegible] jar of tart cherry jelly o[illegible] cornbread.

As s[illegible] milk into the cornmeal, he[illegible] counterclockwise. [illegible] meal in this cabin, Carolin[illegible] remembered, she had nearly [illegible] she'd forgotten the sugar—some[illegible] forgotten it entirely when th[illegible] packed the wagon with their share [illegible] provisions at Father a[illegible] Ingalls's house that morning. [illegible] just pressing the cornbr[illegible] the pan when she'd realized.

Ch[illegible] looked at her, with her hands [illegible] cornmeal and her face o[illegible] verge of falling, and said, "I don't s[illegible] sugar could make that c[illegible] any sweeter than the prints o[illegible] hands already have." That n[illegible] bed, he'd kissed her palms inste[illegible] cheeks.

On[illegible] salt pork was parboiling and th[illegible] cornbread was in the oven, s[illegible] her hands and went in to wak[illegible] and Laura. Caroline s[illegible] she crouched beside the trun[illegible] at the harmony of thei[illegible] beneath the patchwork quilt [illegible] nudged them from their dreams, then sat back on her heels to watch for the moment she delighted in, when their faces seemed almost to shimmer as their minds began to stir. And then the way the girls looked first at each other, as though the sight of the other was what made the world real to them.

When both had taken their turns with the chamber pail and washbasin, Caroline led Mary and Laura to the stove. They yawned and rubbed their eyes as she buttoned the bands of their flannel underwear over their stockings and layered them with woolens. She combed their hair until it lay straight and soft as corduroy, then sent them back into the bedroom to put their rolled-up nightdresses into the carpetbag and pull the linens from their bed while she finished breakfast.

Charles stepped in. "Anything to take out yet?"

Caroline split an egg against the lip of the skillet and opened it onto a saucer. Still fresh, though its white was tinged pink from the preserving barrel. "The second carpetbag is packed," she said. "As soon as the girls have stripped the trundle bed the straw ticks will be ready. The chamber pail and basin may both go once they've been emptied and rinsed. And my trunk." She dropped the eggshell into the teakettle to take up the lime, wondering aloud how long it would be before they would have eggs again.

"Indian Territory's swarming with prairie hens," Charles promised.

Caroline's fork jittered in the skillet. "I wish you wouldn't call it that," she said as gently as she could manage.

"What?"

"Kansas. Indian Territory." She pricked at the curling strips of pork as she spoke. "I don't like to think of the Indians any more than I have to. I saw enough of them in Brookfield."

"The Potawatomis never did your family any harm."

"Just the same, I've had my fill. I'll be thankful when they've moved on."

Around the edges of the skillet, a dribble of egg white was beginning to form a skin like the rim of a pancake. Caroline's stomach [illegible]uddered as the smell suddenly u[illegible]d, thick and brown, saturat[illegible]g her nostrils.

"Are you all right?" Charles aske[illegible]

She swallowed hard, remembering [illegible] she had not taken her usual [illegible]ss of warm water to insulate her [illegible] against the skillet's odors. [illegible] will pass if you'll fill a mug from [illegible] kettle for me, please." Caro[illegible]e dragged the skillet to the side [illegible] stove and scraped the crusted [illegible]embrane of egg loose before sinking [illegible] to the bench.

Charles held the steaming mug [illegible] as Caroline hooked her [illegible]gers through its handle. She lean[illegible] the vapor and drew its blank [illegible]nt through her nose and mout[illegible] [illegible]ately the steam began to [illegible]lt her queasiness like a breath ag[illegible] frosted windowpane.

As each sip expanded her throat [illegible] became aware of Charles [illegible]nding over her, silent but breath[illegible] [illegible]ly. He had seen her ill this [illegible]y before, yet the pitch of his an[illegible] was keen enough to draw [illegible] girls from the bedroom.

Caroline raised her eyes over the [illegible] of the mug. All three of them [illegible]ood posed before her, waiting, [illegible] suddenly she understood that [illegible]thout a word she could stall the[illegible] A simple shake of her head [illegible]uld send Charles to unload th[illegible] But it was not going she [illegible]eaded—only leaving. Waiting [illegible] the dread more tightly. [illegible]nce the break was made she wo[illegible] all right. She held them with [illegible] silence a moment longer before [illegible] "Thank you, Charles." And [illegible]en with a nod toward the bedro[illegible] way where Mary and Laura [illegible]vered, "Go on with the packing [illegible] manage breakfast with the [illegible]ls' help."

[illegible]HILE MARY AND Laura wiped t[illegible] [illegible]kfast dishes, Caroline packed [illegible] coffee mill and the tin dredging [illegible] of flour, salt, and pepper into [illegible] open crate with the iron spider [illegible] oven. "Put these where we [illegible]n reach them easily," she told Ch[illegible] "The skillets and other things [illegible]ay go anyplace you can fit them, [illegible] room for the dishpan."

Caroline emptied the dishpan into the snow, then lined it with a towel and collected one tin plate and cup at a time from Mary and Laura. Through the window, they heard the jostle and clang of Charles fitting the crates into the wagon. They finished just as he returned. "This is the last," Caroline said, untying her apron and folding it into the top of the dishpan. She held the door for him, then turned to face the naked room.

The bare hearth and table, the cooling cookstove—the bedstead, peeled of its mattress. They had not left, yet this place was no longer their own. Only the calico edging on the curtains and the coats and hoods on the line of pegs by the back door had the look of home about them. Without Charles's fiddle box or her mending basket close by, even the chairs looked as though they might belong to anyone. There was more comfort in going than staying, now.

In the middle of it, the girls stood looking at her. Mary hitched Nettie up close to her cheek. Laura seemed stranded, as though she were understanding for the first time all that "going west" meant. A tumble of sympathy rolled across Caroline's breast. Like her pa, all of Laura's visions of the West had begun with the journey, not the departure.

Piecing together a smile, Caroline held out her hands for both Mary and Laura. "Come along, girls," she said. "Pa and the horses will be waiting." Laura took hold of her arm with both hands. Mary ducked beneath Caroline's elbow and leaned her head into the cinnamon-colored folds of Caroline's skirt. She felt a smudge of tears on Mary's cheek, but did not scold. Her own eyes threatened to swim as she shepherded her girls past the empty cluster of chairs before the hearth.

Mary and Laura did not speak as they bundled each other into their coats and rabbit-skin hoods. Caroline's fingers stumbled over her shawl pin until a little berry of blood ripened on her fingertip, bright as the girls' red yarn mittens. She winced and licked it clean.

"I wish Nettie had a shawl, too, Ma," Mary said.

"I am sure there is something in the scrap bag that will do," Caroline said as she tucked Laura's [illegible] collar under her hood. "When [illegible] all settled into the wagon, [illegible] may see. Hold Nettie close for now [illegible] she will not feel the cold." [illegible] herself would have liked to take [illegible] of the girls up and tuck th[illegible] inside her wraps. The steadiness [illegible] so firmly for the children's [illegible] was forming a brittle shell around [illegible] and Caroline wished to [illegible] with their softness. Instead, she [illegible] back and looked the[illegible] "You look very nice," she said, and [illegible] toward the door.

THE HORSES GREETED [illegible] and the girls with billowed [illegible] as they rounded the corner [illegible] cabin. Although her fingers k[illegible] each stitch of its skin and its [illegible] protected every portable scrap of t[illegible], the wagon did not beckon [illegible] Caroline as she had hoped. The s[illegible], full and waiting, only [illegible] worry for the weight and space [illegible] presence demanded — [illegible] burden added to the load. Im[illegible]ly a ribbon of guilt ran do[illegible] Caroline's back as she imagined tha[illegible] rubbing against the bu[illegible] living freight she herself carried.

Before she could re[illegible] herself of the absurdity of such [illegible], Caroline stopped short. [illegible] trunk stood on the ground below [illegible] gate. All her best things [illegible] in the snow, and the wagon [illegible] to the bows. The finge[illegible] pricked with her shawl pin thro[illegible] dropped Mary's and La[illegible] hands, afraid that they might feel [illegible] rush of her pulse.

"Charles?" she calle[illegible]

What would she say [illegible] were no room for it? Nothing [illegible] essary could stay behind [illegible] place, yet he might as well [illegible] as that trunk.

His boots sounded [illegible] the planks until he stood hunch[illegible] braced on his thighs, a[illegible] of the wagon box. Caroline wa[illegible] the brim of his hat dip [illegible] from her face to the trunk.

"Didn't want to cha[illegible] lifting it by myself," he explained, [illegible] himself down into the [illegible]. "It's the size, not the weight. [illegible] help me get it on board, I can slide it up the aisle all the way to the front, under the straw ticks." Caroline closed her eyes, unable to hide her relief in any other way. Charles paused. "You didn't think . . . ?"

A lie would have been simpler, but she could not make room for the weight of it. "I'm sorry, Charles," she admitted. "I wasn't thinking."

With a nod, she was forgiven. Caroline wished now and again that he were not so quick at it; Charles's good nature hardly left her time enough to reap the satisfaction of repentance.

As they bent to grip the leather handles, a chain of sleighs came hissing across the north field from Henry's place. Spokes of light from their pierced tin lanterns sliced through the air. Mary and Laura clapped their mittens, prancing on tiptoe as they named one face after another: Grandpa and Grandma Ingalls with Aunt Ruby and Uncle George; Uncle Henry and Aunt Polly; Aunt Eliza and Uncle Peter, and every one of the cousins.

Caroline braced herself to greet them. She could not let them see how much she craved and dreaded this moment.

One by one, Charles's and Caroline's brothers and sisters lifted their little ones down into the snow. Caroline watched Peter hold his hands up for her sister Eliza, brimming with her fourth child, just as Charles always did for her. She loved to see the ways their families mirrored each other. With three marriages between them, the Ingallses and Quiners were interwoven close as tartan—first Caroline's brother Henry had married Charles's sister, and then Eliza had married one of his brothers. Their children were double cousins twice over.

"Morning," Charles said to the whole company of them.

No one answered; they had not come to say hello.

Apprehension feathered through Caroline's stomach to see all of them together, yet so tight with quiet. The wagonload of family that had come to tell her own ma of her father's drowning in Lake Michigan had been muffled by the same sort of silence.

"Here, C[illegible]," Henry said, taking hold of one [illegible] of her trunk. "Let me." P[illegible]d George both stepped forward [illegible] the wagon box after [illegible] suddenly all the men were insp[illegible] lashings and harnesses.

The wom[illegible] before the wagon as if it were [illegible] grave, their noses pink [illegible] cold and the labor of not crying. [illegible] children, made skittish by t[illegible] parents' restraint, collected in shy [illegible] around their mothers.

Practical[illegible] Caroline's tongue loose. "[illegible] anything you can use from [illegible] and the attic," she told Eliza a[illegible] Mother Ingalls.

Polly t[illegible] a handful of brown paper pac[illegible] tied with black thread. "See[illegible]," she said. "The best of my pumpkin[illegible] tomatoes, and those good [illegible] cucumbers. And don't you try t[illegible], Caroline Ingalls."

Caroline [illegible] smiled. Thank goodness Polly [illegible] always Polly. She could not h[illegible] it if her brusque sister-in-law [illegible] soft with her today. Caroline [illegible] obeyed and tucked the packets into [illegible] pocket.

"Write," [illegible] asked. "We can't send the circ[illegible] until we hear where you'[illegible]ed."

"Charles [illegible] handbill from the land office in M[illegible] County. He's told [illegible] to send the next payment th[illegible]." Caroline trailed off.

Mother [illegible] handed Caroline a jug of maple [illegible]. "You won't find this [illegible] for anything like a reasonable [illegible] it or trade it—whichever [illegible] brings you the most sweetness," she [illegible] with a wink.

"Thank [illegible]" Caroline said. "I wish there was ro[illegible] your sleigh for my rocker," [illegible] told Eliza.

"Hasn't [illegible] bought your furniture?"

Caroline [illegible] across the press of Eliza's bel[illegible] kissed her sister's cheek. "I [illegible] keep it in the family," she whis[illegible]. "Promise me you'll take [illegible] can contrive a way to get it h[illegible]."

"Of course." Horses' hooves crunching across the snow interrupted her. "Oh my land," Eliza said.

Caroline turned, and there was Charley Carpenter's sleigh coming over the hill, with her sister Martha beside him. Martha's oldest boy, Willie, jumped out to help his mother climb down over the runner so Charley could lower a bushel basket swaddled in woolen veils into his wife's arms.

"Martha," Caroline gasped. "Oh, Martha, you shouldn't have, not so soon."

"I know it," Martha said, trying to laugh, "but that can't be helped." Her voice knotted. "I had to see you, sister, and you had to see our Millie."

"Martha Jane Carpenter, you don't mean to say you brought the baby?" Mother Ingalls said.

"Oh, pshaw. She's snug as a dumpling. My Charley made a nest of buffalo robes down between our feet for the basket, and I put two hot flatirons under her pillow. Look and see, Caroline."

Caroline pared back the layers of veils. Wreathed in flannels and goose down lay her niece, a wren-faced little thing, still ruddy with newness. The warmth of the baby's breath moistened the air around her. "Three weeks old yesterday," Martha said.

"I'm glad you came," Caroline said, though they'd only made it harder. The longer she looked at the child, the more the membrane holding back her tears thinned.

"You'll come to our place and warm up those flatirons before you go," Polly told Martha. "You'll all come."

The image of all of them crowded into Henry's cabin burned Caroline's throat like hot maple sugar. All at once, there was no more to be said but goodbye.

The men embraced briefly, a mittened clap on the back signaling the moment to break away. Caroline hugged her sisters and Charles's as long as she dared, tightening her clasp as she felt the flutter of emotion rising arms then thrusting herself apart [illegible] kiss. Eliza clung to her a moment too long. "Write," she said ag[ain.] Caroline forced herself to [nod.] Something like a wad of wool had [lodged] behind her tongue.

[Mo]ther Ingalls saw her struggling [and] said not a word, simply to[ok] her by the shoulders for a good, [lon]g squeeze as they pressed their cold cheeks together. The older [wom]an's firm smile tightened [illegible] at the seams, so that when [illegible] reached the men Caroline [f]ound herself able to do for them wh[at] Mother Ingalls had done for her. She would not have them shame [them]selves with tears on her account.

"Look in on Ma and Papa Frederic[k] [if] you can," she asked her brother. "I wrote to tell them." Henry [nod]ded. A flash of heat stung the rims of her eyes and nose. She had not [men]tioned the coming child, had not told them that if it were a boy, he [wou]ld be called Charles Frederick, for her husband and her stepfathe[r]. "There hasn't been an answer. I never expected them to come, not with the way driving pains Papa Frederick, but I had hopes for a letter," [she] confessed.

"There could be one waiting by now. [If th]ere isn't, I'll send Ma's reply to you when it comes," Henry p[romis]ed. "You know they would be here if they could."

"Kiss your cousins," Polly comma[nded] her brood. "You might not ever see them again." So the children s[olemn]ly kissed and hugged Mary and Laura like little ladies and gen[tlemen], performing a soundless little dance.

"You first, Caroline," Charles said [in the] long pause that followed. "I'll hand the girls up after."

With Charles at one elbow and H[enry] bracing the other, Caroline stepped up onto the doubletree and t[hen] to perch on the edge of the footboard. She grasped a bow and sw[ung her] legs over the wagon box. Inside it smelled of hemp, pine pitch, [and lin]seed oil.

"Upsy-daisy," Charley Carpenter [said as] he scooped Mary up by the underarms. Her feet scrabbled i[n the air un]til her toes found the sideboard. Caroline steadied her with a smile and a pair of firm hands around Mary's waist.

Before Mary's shoes were on the floor, Laura was climbing between the spokes and the singletree. "I want to do it myself, like Ma did," she insisted.

"You're not tall enough to reach over the sideboards, little Half-Pint," Charles said. Only the tips of her mittens peeped stubbornly over the edge of the box. Caroline could hear her shoes scraping at the boards for a place to grip. "Maybe by the time we get to Kansas you'll be big enough," Charles teased, hoisting her up.

Caroline settled the girls onto the straw tick with the old gray blanket as Charles shook his father's hand and clambered in over the jockey box. With a lurch, he dropped down onto the spring seat beside her. Father Ingalls handed up the reins.

Charles cleared his throat. "All ready?" he called over his shoulder.

"Yes, Charles," Caroline answered softly.

Father Ingalls tipped his hat and stepped from sight. Caroline craned forward, but the wagon's canvas bonnet beveled out overhead, blocking her view. They had already said goodbye, Caroline reminded herself as she straightened her shawl and folded her hands into her lap. They were her mother's hands, nearly as broad as a man's. Like her mother, she kept them always folded, the long fingers tucked neatly into her palms.

Charles released the brake lever and the wheels hitched forward. The snap of movement loosed Caroline's grip on herself. A sob juddered halfway up her throat before she could clasp it back.

Charles looked at her, the tears in his eyes only adding a luster to his excitement. Caroline tightened her cheeks to echo his smile as best she could.

Those she could not bear to leave sat close around her, yet as she looked backward through the keyhole of canvas at the blur of waving hands, Caroline could not help but wonder whether Charles and the girls would be enough.

Three

THE TOWN WAS m[illegible]te[illegible] snow. A steamy chill hung in th[illegible], as though the drifts w[illegible]re [illegible]g. Charles drove past McIl[illegible] and the Prussian dry-go[illegible]ds [illegible] to the Richardses's storefront. [illegible]ys one of them willing to [illegible] b[illegible]gain," Charles said. Caroli[illegible] not answer. Her back w[illegible]s [illegible] th[illegible] aches. The wagon rolled t[illegible]p, and her body swaye[illegible] w[illegible] A[illegible] the seven miles down into [illegible] he had held herself tau[illegible] ag[illegible] [illegible]e slope of the land. Now the le[illegible] of the road left her u[illegible]nc[illegible] [illegible]s though the steadying pull of [illegible] the cabin could no longer r[illegible]r.

CAROLINE HELD [illegible] [illegible]he h[illegible]p and Mary by the hand [illegible] les and the two youn[illegible]er [illegible]d [illegible]rothers piled provisions [illegible] the counter. To the fo[illegible]d [illegible] [illegible]ad[illegible]ed painted canvas tarpauli[illegible] ten-gallon water keg, a[illegible]d a [illegible] collapsible gutta-percha bucke[illegible] [illegible]ed more powder and c[illegible]ps [illegible] [illegible] shot, too," he said.

"What kind of fi[illegible]ear[illegible] [illegible]rying?" Horace Richards a[illegible]

"Rifle," Charles [illegible]nsw[illegible]

"That old single [illegible]ho[illegible] [illegible]oader?" Linus Richards said[illegible]

Charles bristled. "O[illegible] [illegible]s always been plenty for me."

Linus Richards [illegible]u[illegible] [illegible]d [illegible] up his hands. "I'll be the l[illegible] to impugn your aim, [illegible]ga[illegible] [illegible]dy trades more bear pelts here[illegible] you do." He glanced at [illegible]ar[illegible] [illegible]d [illegible]e children and dropped his [illegible] only low enough to mak[illegible] h[illegible] [illegible]h[illegible] [illegible]ear toward the men. "S[illegible]all[illegible] [illegible]ild animal's one thing—a[illegible] [illegible]ed brave with a full quiver and [illegible] besides is quite another. All I'm saying is, I wouldn't take my little ones into the Indian Territory without a decent pistol to level the field."

Caroline felt Mary's grip tighten as Horace Richards pulled two snub-nosed guns from under the counter. "We've got Colt army-model percussion revolvers and one brand-new Smith and Wesson Model Three top-break cartridge revolver."

Dry at the mouth, Caroline put Laura down and guided both girls toward the row of candy jars. "You may each choose a penny's worth," she said. The girls looked up at her, their astonished eyes like blue china buttons. "Go ahead. You're big enough to choose for yourselves. Any one you like."

From a neighboring shelf, Caroline gathered castor oil, ipecac, paregoric, rhubarb, and magnesia while the men haggled and the girls pored over the sweets. "Let's get two different flavors," she heard Mary tell Laura. "I'll give you half of my stick, and you give me half of yours. Then we'll both have two kinds of candy."

Caroline smiled. "That's my smart girl," she said.

ELISHA RICHARDS STOOD at the till with his thumbs hooked into the pockets of his vest and his nails scratching beneath them as though he were tallying the Ingallses's account against his flanks. With every undulation of his fingers, the sum mounted in Caroline's mind, until her head seemed to teeter on her neck. The expense was well within their reach, yet she could not keep hold of the numbers any more than she could take her eyes from the storekeeper's vest. It was cut from a rust-colored paisley that swirled her senses in a way she could not describe. Charles began to count one bill after another into Elisha Richards's palm, peeling the wedge of cash like an onion, and the movement of gray-green against the paisley field made the room roll around her.

It struck her that her body was behaving as though she could taste that vest and feel the pattern augering into her stomach. Caroline balked at the s[illegible]ness of it, she would not let su[illegible]g as a swath of cloth take [illegible] of her. She set her jaw, refu[illegible] acknowledge the saliva [illegible] under her tongue, but the quea[illegible] that had overcome her befo[illegible] was already at her throat[illegible] or not, she must put [illegible] between her eyes and her st[illegible]

“[illegible] La[illegible], it's time for dinner.” Th[illegible] turned, reluctant to obey[illegible] they wanted to stand at [illegible] to see their two stic[illegible] paid for, but that could not[illegible] It did not matter now [illegible] looked at. Another minute [illegible] would be sick where she [illegible]. She swept forward and took [illegible] the wrists. “Come, girl[illegible] will bring your sweets.”

[illegible] the wagon, she unwrapped the [illegible] of bread and plunged her [illegible] slice as the girls gawked[illegible] The first bite worked qui[illegible] sponge. Her stomach grumble[illegible] It was not garish sm[illegible] that set her senses raving, [illegible] realized as she parceled [illegible] portions of bread and molasses [illegible] and Laura, but hunger[illegible] would have to guard against that [illegible]road.

[illegible] stiffened the molasses so that it [illegible] to their teeth in thin stra[illegible] Laura slipped a fingernail unde[illegible] a brown festoon and tri[illegible] it loose from her slice.

“[illegible],” Mary said with a shake of he[illegible].

“[illegible] like lace,” Laura protested. “I[illegible] pretty to eat.”

[illegible] melted on Caroline's [illegible]. They had never noticed [illegible] the care she took drizzlin[illegible] molasses. Perhaps for a tr[illegible] would try spelling out their n[illegible] She imagined her wrist gu[illegible] graceful flow of the syrup, [illegible] of her daughters as th[illegible] their names drawn out in [illegible] sweetness. It was the ki[illegible] frivolity her own mother coul[illegible] spare time nor money fo[illegible] practical, too—it was high tim[illegible] of them began learning th[illegible].

“[illegible],” Mary insisted, pointing at Laur[illegible]

[illegible] hand blanketed Mary's. “I[illegible] rude to point,” she reminded. "Now finish your dinner nicely, girls, so you may have your candy," she said.

The back of the wagon jolted under a hundredweight of flour. "All stocked up and cash to spare," Charles announced. "Where are all those empty sacks, Caroline?" he asked, shifting through the crates and bundles.

"Leave that to me, Charles," Caroline said. "You must have something to eat before loading all those provisions."

Too eager to sit, Charles leaned over the front of the wagon box, joking with the girls while Caroline unrolled the sacks and threaded her stoutest needle. She slit open the unbolted flour, cornmeal, beans, and brown sugar and filled a ten pound sack from each to round out her crate of daily supplies.

When the corners were sewn shut again she held the canvas mouths of the biggest sacks wide for Charles to lower the dry goods in, then quickly folded the edges together and basted each one shut. Mary and Laura knelt backward on the spring seat, watching as they sucked their sticks of candy. Their curled fists were like bright berries in their red yarn mittens.

"Did you get the pepper and saleratus?" Caroline asked.

"In my pockets," Charles said. "Bought myself a gutta-percha poncho," he added as he heaved one hundredweight and then another of cornmeal. "There's bound to be rain somewhere between here and Kansas." Caroline nodded. "And the Colt revolver."

Her mind veered around this news, as though she might avoid the logical progression of thoughts: *The pistol could not have cost under fifteen dollars. Charles would not have spent such a sum without a reason.*

"Caroline?"

"Whatever you think is necessary, Charles."

CHARLES CINCHED THE wagon cover down in back, leaving only a peephole against the cold.

"Have all you need, [illegible] Elisha Richards asked, stepp[illegible] the hitching post to help [illegible] the horses' nose bags.

"And some to spare," [illegible] answered. "Anything else, Ca[illegible]" She shook her head. The [illegible] box was packed tight as brow[illegible]. Anything else would hav[illegible] ride in their laps.

"Good luck to you, [illegible] has been my pleasure trading wi[illegible]." Caroline ventured a gla[illegible] the storekeeper's vest as the [illegible] shook hands. Her eyes [illegible] had no appetite for it, but the [illegible] claimed no sway over [illegible] of her. Richards nodded at Ca[illegible] Charles swung himself u[illegible] the wheel. "Take care of yours[illegible] those fine girls."

The compliment to[illegible] Caroline squarely at the base [illegible] throat. A small rush o[illegible] ironed out her shoulders and [illegible] down her core. She [illegible] hands together in her lap, [illegible] they might catch the [illegible] Behind them, a whorl of wa[illegible] braced her womb—not [illegible] child, but the space it occupied [illegible] making itself known. I[illegible] enough to remind her that she w[illegible] than a passenger.

"Thank you, Mr. Ric[illegible]," she said.

THE ROAD RAN straig[illegible] onto the lake, narrowing betwe[illegible] of slump-shouldered [illegible] drifts. Away from the plowed track [illegible] looked tired, blotched [illegible] here with a sweaty sheen wh[illegible] had melted.

"Charles?" Caroline [illegible] a hand on his wrist.

He stayed the team. "[illegible] mind to the snowmelt," he sai[illegible] be at its thickest here, [illegible] the snow's been plowed, so lon[illegible] kept it bare all winter." [illegible] stood up to survey the track. [illegible] two miles distant seem [illegible] more than waist high. "Looks [illegible] as I can see." He gave th[illegible] a gentle slap, and the wagon [illegible] the creaking snow.

The horses' shoes s[illegible] the ice road as though it were th[illegible] a drum, and their ears pricked at the sudden sharpness. Through the plank of the spring seat, Caroline felt the wheels grind like sugar under a rolling pin. The sound made her shoulder blades twitch. She turned her attention to the rhythm of the team's gait. They had not sped up, but they raised their feet more quickly, as though they too mistrusted the sensation of metal meeting ice.

The flash of their shoes lifted a memory in Caroline's mind of the circus that had once passed along the road by the Quiners' door back home in Concord. Caroline smiled to think how she and her sister Martha had laughed at the great gray elephant delicately putting one foot and then another on the first log of the corduroy bridge spanning the marsh.

For all its bulk, that timid elephant must have been on firmer footing than this wagon and the supplies newly added, Caroline realized: hundredweights of cornmeal, unbolted flour, salt pork, bacon, beans, and brown sugar; fifty pounds of white flour; ten of salt; fifteen pounds of coffee and five of tea; the feedbox brimming with corn. Better than three thousand pounds of horseflesh pulling it all. Surely that corduroy bridge had been thicker than a plate of ice nearing the edge of spring.

Suddenly Caroline did not want her girls boxed in like cargo behind her. "Mary, Laura, come here and see the lake," she said, beckoning them over the spring seat. Mary settled onto Caroline's lap, big girl though she was, while Laura stood solemnly at her pa's elbow.

Charles halted the team. The lake lay like a mile of muslin, seamed by the ice road with the sheared hilltops of the Minnesota shore binding the distance. Sounds from Pepin's banks seemed to bob in the air alongside them, small and clear as a music box.

"See that, Half-Pint?" Charles asked. "That's Minnesota."

"All of it?" Laura asked, poking her mitten toward the opposing shore.

"All of it," he answered. "Wisconsin's already a mile behind us now."

Mary huffed at Laura's pointing, but Caroline had no voice to settle her. It was too much to hold in her mind all that was behind them, be-neat[illegible] before them. A lump thi[illegible]'s egg blocked her [illegible] if she so much as swallowed, it [illegible] shatter.

T[illegible] horses fidgeted. Their scra[illegible] sent unwelcome ting[illegible] Caroline's underbelly and [illegible] of her thighs as tho[illegible] poised at the edge of a pre[illegible] breath was coming [illegible], as it had at her parting fro[illegible] they did not move for[illegible] surge of emotions would over[illegible] all sides.

C[illegible] her cheek to her daug[illegible] Mary's candied [illegible] ked her nose with sharp, s[illegible]. It was a summer scen[illegible] he last sip from a pitcher [illegible]. First her mouth and [illegible] eyes watered with the memo[illegible] taste.

I[illegible] saw her striving to keep hold [illegible] she did not know it. [illegible] him chirrup to the tea[illegible] the horses leaning into [illegible].

T[illegible] gated, then skidded in pla[illegible] jerked her head up [illegible] see Laura grab hold of Cha[illegible] to keep from pitc[illegible] floor.

"[illegible] Laura," Charles said, and s[illegible] reins. The traces we[illegible] the horses' energy seemed [illegible] further than the wa[illegible].

"[illegible] not be sharp enough," [illegible] as their hooves lic[illegible] "Didn't expect we'd nee[illegible] their shoes for one cro[illegible]

[illegible] around. "Nettie's all alo[illegible]

[illegible] her fast. "Nettie is as saf[illegible]," she said, but she hea[illegible] in her words. Looseni[illegible] Caroline shifted Ma[illegible] lap and motioned Laura i[illegible] them near, but no[illegible] against her that her own [illegible] touch them. She th[illegible] arms loosely around thei[illegible] to snatch them clo[illegible], and let her nervous han[illegible] their wraps. "Now let'[illegible] so Pa can drive."

[illegible] mouth was folded so deepl[illegible] sternation that the whiskers beneath his lower lip bristled outward. He slackened the horses' lines so that all their effort would travel straight into the singletree. The strain stood out on the animals' necks as their legs slanted under them. Watching them, Caroline felt her own sides clench.

"What's wrong with the horses?" Laura asked. "Is the wagon too full?"

"Ben and Beth are strong enough to pull us across," Caroline assured her, "once they find their footing." It was the strength of the ice that worried her, with the two horses prying forward like great muscled levers. Beth snorted and stamped a hoof. Caroline winced at the impact. They were a mile from either shore.

No matter how strong the road might be, the ice would be at its thinnest here in the middle of the lake. It was one thing to pass steadily across the surface—quite another to linger prodding at this frailest point. Could not a deft stroke, like the blows she delivered to the rain barrel's thick winter skin, open a split down the center?

Caroline looked over the girls in their hoods and mittens and flannels. Together they were lighter than a single sack of flour, but the drag of so much sodden clothing would carry them straight under if the wagon broke through. Her eyes traced the cinched canvas brow overhead. They were hardly better off than kittens in a gunny sack.

If the wagon did not budge in the time it took to pray Psalm 121, Caroline decided, she would lift the girls down and lead them across on foot. Even if she had to carry Laura, the three of them could slip over the mile of ice light as mayflies, leaving the team's burden nearly two hundred pounds the lighter.

Caroline prayed, and still the wheels had not moved. Nor could she. The psalm had given her imagination time to extend beyond the relief of reaching solid ground—to turning, safely hand in hand, to face Charles stranded on the lake behind them. What could she do for him or their daughters, clutching their small mittens on the opposite bank of the Mississippi, if the wagon rolled forward and the ice opened—

With a rasp, one metal [illegible] shoe bit into the surface. Carol[illegible] her breath for the collaps[illegible] a muscled jolt inched the [illegible] ahead. She felt herself lea[illegible] toward the team, as if her own momentum could coax th[illegible] forward.

Once more the iron ti[illegible] over the ice, this time the [illegible] as welcome as the snap o[illegible] box. Laura clapped her han[illegible] cheered the horses until th[illegible] hauled up onto the Minnesota [illegible] Mary slipped out of Caro[illegible] and burrowed under the spri[illegible] to scoop up Nettie. "I wo[illegible] alone again," Caroline hea[illegible] promise the doll.

"Those horseshoes mak[illegible] ice skates," Charles procl[illegible] "but I don't believe I'd lik[illegible] a pair nailed to my feet." Ma[illegible] Laura giggled. They coul[illegible] the chagrin behind the boo[illegible] voice. He would not say [illegible] his fault for stopping the [illegible] but Caroline knew he wo[illegible] discussing such a situation wit[illegible] unless he'd felt a scorch [illegible]

"Go on with Mary," Ca[illegible], nudging Laura over the sea[illegible] air rushed silently in and [illegible] chest. She was shaking, now [illegible] was over. Relief saturate[illegible] there was no lightness in it. [illegible] she was salted down wit[illegible] that she should be so thankfu[illegible] Wisconsin behind them.

"Good thing Ben and [illegible] pulled through," Charles said, [illegible] again. Caroline had not [illegible] control over her breath t[illegible] at his pun. "Would have [illegible] portage all this equipment on foot."

Something in his voic[illegible] between her tremors and tur[illegible] head. "Charles?" she ask[illegible]

He cocked a smile at [illegible] half-turned up.

One look at him and [illegible] did not need to ask wheth[illegible] thought about the ice. [illegible] of fear so much as brus[illegible] whiskers.

Perhaps the threat sh[illegible] only been another queer sp[illegible] she'd had in the store. It was as though a single droplet of any one sensation had the power to soak her through. The notion left her lightheaded, as if she had no traction on the world. Caroline pulled her shawl across the points of her shoulders and elbows, wishing for a sturdier veneer.

Charles's brow had begun to furrow. He was still waiting for her to speak. "We should make camp soon," she said, "if supper is to be ready before dark."

"The Richardses said there'd be a place along the shore just north of the crossing," he said. "Little spot the lumber men use in season. It's out of the way a mile or so, but I figure you and the girls would rather spend our first night out under a roof instead of around a campfire."

A house. The very thought lifted Caroline's cheeks and smoothed her forehead. "Yes, Charles," she said. "In weather like this it will be a mercy to have one more night of shelter."

IT WAS A bunkhouse, wit[illegible]ng the walls like shelves. [illegible] [illegible]lling by the hearth, a stu[illegible]r. Nothing more.

"Looks like you won't [illegible]ok out tonight, Caroline," [illegible] said.

Caroline's lips smil[illegible]d, [illegible]eks did not follow. Alread[illegible] herself shrinking from th[illegible]s confronting her. The wago[illegible] cramped and chill, but [illegible] this empty room it was [illegible] their own.

Mary snugged Nettie [illegible]ld of her elbow. "It isn't [illegible] inside," she ventured.

"It will keep us warm [illegible] Caroline said, speaking as [illegible] herself as to Mary, "and t[illegible]y to be thankful for." She [illegible] narrow bunks.

"I'll bring the big stra[illegible]or you and the girls," Charle[illegible] "Best if I sleep out with th[illegible]nd team."

She could not allow he[illegible]nsider how it might feel to s[illegible] this place without him—[illegible]as to get supper before da[illegible] line swallowed twice to s[illegible]muscles in her throat. "And t[illegible] crates of kitchen things, [illegible]ares."

First he brought her tw[illegible]now and an armload of w[illegible] cooking firewood from th[illegible]side the door—mostly p[illegible] some maple mixed in. S[illegible] hardwood aside and laid [illegible] cookfire with the res[illegible]. T[illegible]blazed up merrily, the warm[illegible] nishing her cheeks.

"We will need mo[illegible]e h[illegible] bank the fire for the nigh[illegible]," line said when he came in with the crates. "The pine hasn't enough pitch left to burn through until morning." She hated to ask him after all he had done this day, but already the dry pine was burning too hot and fast to trust with a pan of cornbread. Charles only nodded and buttoned up his overcoat.

With her own things in her hands, Caroline warmed to her tasks. She melted a kettle full of snow to a simmer and dropped in as much salt as she could pinch between her thumb and the curl of her first finger. The evening had the thin sort of chill that made her hunger for a pot of bean soup. Instead, hasty pudding would have to do.

She had hardly pulled her wooden spoon from the crate before the girls came rushing to help. Caroline met Laura with the broom and set Mary to straightening up the straw tick. Before long they were whinnying in circles around the bed, the broom held between them as though they were a team of ponies. Caroline let them run—they were restive from travel, and hasty pudding would demand more attention than she could share out if she were not to burn their supper.

The bag of cornmeal was chilled to the core. After the texture of the road, Caroline welcomed the even grit sifting through her fingers. Her hands moved in tandem, one sprinkling, one stirring. As the grains melded with the salted water, a sweet, starchy scent reached upward. Sometimes she crouched and sometimes she bent over the kettle, easing the long sinews in her back and calves by turns while the spoon droned its low swirling song against the iron kettle. Slowly the room behind her began to warm, as slowly Mary and Laura's play wound down into the rhythm of her stirring.

Caroline's hands were thankful for the movement, and her mind content with the stillness of hovering over the bubbling pot. If a thought began to stray back across Lake Pepin or ahead to the night to come, her tempo faltered and the hasty pudding bubbled and whined, calling her mind to attention.

By the time Charles came in with the carpetbag and another pail of snow, she ha[illegible] her misgivings to the kettle's [illegible] chamber pail was [illegible] under his arm. He set everything [illegible] the hearth to warm and sq[illegible] alongside her, tilting his palms [illegible] "Smells fine," he said.

Caroline [illegible] "It's nearly ready."

"Ma?" Ma[illegible]. "There's no table."

"That's be[illegible] we're camping now," Charles said. "[illegible] and get your plates, [illegible] and I'll show you how it's done." [illegible] paused, hooked his fi[illegible] through the loop of Mother Ingalls' [illegible] and lifted it from the box [illegible] dishes. "What's this?"

"Maple sy[illegible]," Caroline said. "Your mother [illegible] trade, she said [illegible] she trailed off. His palm was [illegible] jug's belly.

"Isn't that [illegible] Ma," Charles mused. His [illegible] over his crimped lips, [illegible] Caroline saw the clutch of his thr[illegible] opened his mouth and dr[illegible] breath, holding it for a moment. "[illegible] maple syrup on hot [illegible] pudding," he said to Mary and L[illegible] the cork loose. It [illegible] with the sugar maples of W[illegible] nearly in sight, but [illegible] had been sharp in so many ways [illegible] could not refuse th[illegible]ness.

They at[illegible] their laps, hunched along the ed[illegible] bunks. Caroline [illegible] of the hasty pudding [illegible] line down her [illegible] warmth gathered steadily in her [illegible] seeped outward [illegible] chill from her skin.

They di[illegible] as they were and spread [illegible] wall with nothing but [illegible] room before them. Caroline [illegible] imagine how it would [illegible] with a man sleeping on every shel[illegible] would be little better [illegible] pantry stocked with lumberja[illegible].

Darkness [illegible] around them before they fin[illegible] waited without a[illegible] turn for a drink, only to op[illegible] mouth and yawn mightily [illegible] the tin cup when Mary passed [illegible].

"It's be[illegible] little girls," Caroline said. Her [illegible]ids were thick at the ri[illegible] shoulders grainy with fatigue.

Their nightgowns were still cold red bundles in the carpetbag. Caroline draped them over the broomstick handle and propped it before the fire like a fishing pole. She had Laura's shoes off and her dress half unbuttoned before Mary said, "I need the necessary, Ma." Caroline nodded toward the chamber pail at the edge of the hearth. Mary shook her head. "The necessary."

Caroline pinched off a breath. A ring of exasperation burned below it, but it was her own fault. She had not thought to ask before undressing them. "Go and get your wraps, then, and Laura's," she said, walking her fingers back up the row of buttons.

Charles pocketed a pair of matches and put on his overcoat. "I'll light a lantern in front of the outhouse door," he said, and left them to bundle into their mittens and hoods.

Caroline went down on her knees to help Laura thread her toes into her shoes. "Ma," Mary said again, this time with a keener edge. Caroline looked up, primed to urge patience, and saw the grimace on her face.

"All right, Mary," Caroline said. She hoisted Laura to her hip stocking-footed and slung her shawl across the both of them while Mary scurried to open the door.

The necessary was a four-holer, clean enough, but scaled for grown men. Laura and Mary both sat leaning forward with their palms braced against the plank seat, as though they were afraid they might tumble down the latrine pit if they let go. Neither could they reach the strips of newsprint dangling from a quartet of bent sixtypenny nails on the facing wall. They waited for Caroline to finish her own business and hand them their paper.

Laura melted like a rag doll into Caroline's chest as Caroline fastened Laura's drawers and lifted her from the wooden bench. She blanketed Laura with the shawl and rested her cheek against Laura's forehead.

Outside, the glow of the two bunkhouse windows pointed their way back down the path. The little room had warmed since they first walked [illegible] door, and Caroline found [illegible] had warmed toward it as [illegible] were the girls' nightgowns [illegible] cely by the fire and [illegible] hasty pudding to welcome [illegible] Caroline hummed a low- [illegible] as she helped Mary and [illegible] their nightclothes, for [illegible] trust her lips with the wor[illegible]

[illegible] my vow and lock'd embrace,
[illegible] parting was fu' tender,
[illegible] pledging aft to meet again,
[illegible] ourselves asunder.

[illegible] just settled them under the [illegible] when Charles brought in [illegible] box. Laura's drowsy eyes sp[illegible] awake at the sight of it.

"[illegible]night, Half-Pint," Charles s[illegible] tuckered out. But you [illegible] can keep the fiddle warm [illegible] night, can't you?" He [illegible] snugged the case under the [illegible] of the straw tick at their [illegible]

"[illegible]," they said solemnly. Cha[illegible] up at Caroline. She [illegible] explanation. It was not the [illegible] wanted shelter for, but [illegible] He had seen him tuck t[illegible] of their cash—just [illegible] by her figures—beneath its [illegible] ing.

"[illegible] you're plucking the strings [illegible]es," he teased, and [illegible] their hair goodnight.

[illegible] the girls cuddled down to sle[illegible] smoothed the left- [illegible] pudding into a bread pan [illegible] it with a dishcloth [illegible] overnight. For breakfast the[illegible] the fried mush, and [illegible] rest of the cold white brea[illegible] molasses would serve for [illegible] dinner.

[illegible] by the hearth, she heated [illegible] the dishpan and wiped [illegible] clean. Into the kettle she [illegible] a half dozen scoops [illegible], then covered them with [illegible] put the mixture to [illegible] of the fireplace to soak.

She was unpinning her hair when Charles came in to pocket the two flatirons she had laid on the hearth to warm for him. "Asleep already?" he whispered, pointing with his whiskers toward the girls.

Caroline nodded.

"Good. Come on outside. I want you to learn how to load that Colt."

A wrinkle traveled up her spine. Caroline gave herself a moment to mute the sensation against her shawl, then followed him out.

The wooden box lay open beside a lantern on the wagon tongue. Compartments lined with red felt surrounded the revolver and its accoutrements. "It's an 1860 army issue—the same as your brother Joseph would have carried at Shiloh," Charles told her, as though she might be afraid of it. She was not frightened of the thing itself; she was only afraid of needing it.

"It's not so much different from the rifle. Tip the powder flask to measure out a charge, then pour the powder into the open chamber on the right. Drop a bullet in on top. No patch cloth. Last comes the cap." He pinched a bit of brass shaped like a tiny dented button from a tin with a green paper label. "This fits over the percussion nipple at the back of the chamber. Now watch." Charles pulled the hammer to half cock and twisted the cylinder so that the loaded chamber rested above the trigger. Then as if husking an ear of corn, he pried a lever loose from the underside of the barrel and bent it back until it clicked. "This tamps down the loaded charge in place of a ramrod," he said. "And that's all there is to it."

Charles let the hammer down softly before handing her the pistol. Caroline stripped off her mittens and tucked them under one arm. The revolver was cold in the places he had not touched, and heavy as the family Bible. "Go ahead," Charles said.

She could not push the latch of the loading lever straight down as Charles had done; it bit into the tips of her fingers until she rotated her grip and pulled it free of the catch from below. "That's fine," Charles said when she finished. "You'll need two hands to fire it—hold your arms out straight ahead, and lay your fingers around the stock the way you do to pray." Caroline's tongue rose to object to the [illegible], then halted. If ever she had cause to fire this gun, there would indeed be a prayer behind it.

"That's right," Charles said, "steady and even, just like that. We'll only keep five of the chambers loaded with caps while we're traveling. Safer that way. Just remember to twist a loaded chamber up to the barrel as you cock it."

Caroline cupped her elbows beneath her shawl as he packed the pistol away again and climbed up over the sideboards. "It'll ride in the box, under the seat," Charles said. "I'll still use the rifle for hunting. With any luck that's the last time we'll need to open the box." He sat facing her with his hands laced between his knees.

She handed him the lantern. In the instant before he blew it out, the glow framed him in a halo of canvas. Firelight from the cabin's windows dusted over them. "Will you be warm enough?" she asked.

He patted his coat pockets. "I'm snug as a tent in here with the canvas cinched down at both ends, and these flatirons all to myself." His eyes slid down the curving length of her braid. Caroline felt the pink rising in her cheeks and lifted her shawl over her head. She could not bear to put his hands to her hair. This was neither time nor place for what would surely follow.

"The bundle of extra quilts is at the foot of the small straw tick," she told him. Still his eyes stayed on her, asking her to do no more than fill his gaze. He could make her feel full as the moon, looking at her that way, and she was too [illegible] to allow herself to melt into it. The [illegible] of heat were already drifting along her edges.

Caroline rustled her [illegible] softly between them. "Charles?"

"Hmm?"

"Will you reach the [illegible] for me, please?" she asked, [illegible] the moment short.

He got to his knees on the spring seat, leaning so far to reach the bag on its peg that he ought to have pitched over. It was thick through the middle and nearly as tall as Laura. Caroline shifted the bundle to her hip and reached one hand up to the lip of the wagon box. He took her hand in his, kneading her palm with his thumb. "Call if you or the girls need for anything," he said. "I'll be sleeping with one ear open."

Her smile crept into the dark. "Rest yourself, Charles." She felt the brush of his whiskers against her fingertips before he floated her hand back down to her. The wisp of movement carried her back to the bunkhouse without another murmur.

The girls did not stir at the clack of the latch. Mary lay with her rag doll up under her chin, her arms folded close as hens' wings around her calico darling. Caroline let her shawl back down to her shoulders and carried the scrap bag to the bunk nearest the hearth. Loosening the drawstring, she unfurled the bag into her lap. It was not a sack, but rather a circle of denim that would spread itself flat with the cord fully unlaced. Seven deep pockets, each holding one color, pinwheeled from a center humped with plain cuttings of flannel, buckram, and the like. Caroline chose two remnants of muslin to veil the windows, then felt her way into the pocket of browns until she found a swatch of felt, small and nearly triangular. A few nips with the scissors would turn it into a shawl for Nettie. She laid it on a bunk with their wraps, then bolstered the fire with slim maple logs before finally undressing.

She found herself standing before the hearth in the place where her rocking chair would be, were this their own fireplace. Without it she was not sure how to settle the day's many layers into herself. She turned to the straw tick, hunkered on the floor like a patchwork raft. The coverlet puffed softly up and down over Mary and Laura. Caroline watched them as she had that morning. Their tempo was so like a hymn, a strand of scripture encircled her.

[illegible] thy presence; and take [illegible] Spirit from me.

With [illegible] travel had wrought, [illegible] days still to come [illegible] she had never felt so [illegible] to the Lord's [illegible] knelt where she stood [illegible] down to meet [illegible]

No [illegible] Eyes closed, she was [illegible] taper until [illegible] words of praise or [illegible] fragment of the 24th [illegible] her voice.

[illegible] the hill of the Lord? [illegible] his [illegible]

[illegible] hands, and a pure heart; [illegible] up his [illegible] nor sworn deceitfully.

[illegible] blessing from the Lord [illegible]

Carol [illegible] wed and her heart [illegible] as she pledged [illegible] clasped hands. It [illegible] shape of a prayer, [illegible] binding; she would [illegible] to keep [illegible] sight of Providence.

The [illegible] around her as [illegible] tufts of fragra[illegible] into place beside [illegible] the anonym[illegible] ding smelled more [illegible] cabin itself had [illegible] ene and rosemary [illegible] thing so famili[illegible] not name it. Caroli[illegible] it was the girls [illegible] She had not slept alongside [illegible] daughters since Lau[illegible] their nearness satur[illegible] comfort.

Her [illegible] the covers and [illegible] of her navel. [illegible] burbles turned beneath [illegible] her supper [illegible]. No swish or flutter [illegible] could not yet fe[illegible] ture inside, she need [illegible] whether it was sen[illegible] wagon or the flood [illegible] tions.

Within its cushion of waters, perhaps it felt nothing at all. Caroline shut her eyes and imagined herself enveloped in such a warm and fluid cradle—every sound and movement diluted, graceful. If she could not shelter herself from this journey's vagaries, there was some satisfaction at least in knowing she was a shield for the budding child. Beside her, the rise and fall of her daughters' breaths led her gently toward sleep.

A SOUND LIKE the crack of gunfire shot through Caroline's consciousness. Motionless in the vibrating air, Caroline groped with her senses for her bearings. Nothing fit. The ceiling above her was peaked rather than flat, the bed too near the floor.

The tiny muscles along her ears strained into the silence. Only the dwindling embers whispered to themselves. No voices. Not a whicker from the horses; no movement behind her makeshift curtains.

Another shot brought her to her elbows. The sound seemed to cleave the air. It stretched too long and deep for the pop of a bullet, yet she could make room in her mind for nothing else. Caroline sat up and patted her hands across the straw tick, searching for the fiddle box. "Charles?" she called in a whisper. Beside her, Laura stirred.

The latch rattled. Caroline froze. Bolts of alarm unrolled into her thighs and down the backs of her arms.

The door seemed to peel open. "It's the ice cracking on the lake," Charles's voice said. Thankfulness loosened her so thoroughly, she could do nothing but spread herself back over the mattress. Charles came to the hearth and nudged another length of hardwood into the fire behind her.

"Are you warm enough?" she asked.

With a creak of leather, he squatted down and leaned over to kiss her, whiskers softly caressing her skin. "That'll help," he said. He stood and went out, easing the door shut behind him.

Caroline laid her forearms across her ribs. Each crack of the ice scored a cold line across the hollow places in her body, like a blade that [illegible] not cut. The sharpness [illegible] almost tickled down in [illegible]

At the next report, Laura [illegible] Caroline rolled to her should[illegible] Laura's eyes were casting abo[illegible] desperate to light on so[illegible] thing she recognized. Carolin[illegible] to her view. Their gazes m[illegible] Caroline saw her daught[illegible] with comfort. A pool [illegible] opened behind Caro[illegible] she watched. She glided [illegible] over the peak of La[illegible] The baby roundness that [illegible] from Mary's face still li[illegible] Laura's.

"Go to sleep," Caroline soo[illegible] It's only the ice breaking up." La[illegible] fast to Caroline's gaze u[illegible] crack snapped her eyes sh[illegible] Caroline cupped her palm o[illegible] stroking the little g[illegible] with her thumb. Laura [illegible] drowsily.

There is a happy land, far, [illegible] Caroline hummed. Her te[illegible] with the effort of h[illegible] quiver from her chin. Th[illegible] traveled hardly ten miles [illegible], but in a heartbeat the bre[illegible] of the ice had driven a we[illegible] wide into the distance back[illegible] own little cabin.

Under her fingers, Laura's [illegible] slowly quieted into a beat [illegible] kisses. Caroline drew [illegible], making a nest of hers[illegible] Laura was too big now to fit [illegible] she once had, but her brea[illegible] tinged with maple sugar, [illegible] spaces between them.

Six

BY MORNING, CAROLINE'S hip and shoulder could feel the floor through the straw tick. Soreness warmed the backs of her thighs when she rose. She rubbed the heels of her hands down the muscles along her backbone and winced. There was only so much she could blame on the spring seat. The rest was her body retaliating for being kept so tightly clenched the day before. Caroline closed her eyes and released as much of the lingering tension as she was able. Today there would be no more goodbyes, she reminded herself, no reason to hold herself so rigid. Today they could go cleanly forward.

To her hands, the morning was hardly distinguishable from any other. Caroline dressed and washed, laid the girls' clothes to warm before the fire, put fresh water over the beans, and swung the kettle into the heart of the fire. She fried up a dozen strips of bacon, then laid four thick slices of chilled mush into the drippings. The edges crisped like cracklings in the grease.

Charles came whistling in to his breakfast, as he so often did. His tune tickled her. A perfect match to the day, as usual. "Wait for the wagon! Wait for the wagon! Wait for the wagon and we'll all take a ride!" he sang for Mary and Laura.

His cheeks gleamed from the cold, and their eyes were bright with excitement. In the pan the fat popped and sizzled merrily around their breakfast. The whole morning was beginning to shine.

"Wouldn't wonder if the ice broke up today," Charles said to Caroline. He doused his mush with syrup. "We made a late crossing. Lucky it didn't start breaking up while we were out in the middle of it."

Caroline ope[illegible] and then closed it. Ha[illegible] him only now? S[illegible]elp herself. "I thought [illegible]-day, Charles," sh[illegible]

He looked at [illegible] he had spotted her [illegible] with his shaving [illegible]ry, only puzzled by wh[illegible] might have fo[illegible]

Laura's fork ha[illegible]ing. A long bead of syr[illegible] her chin and o[illegible]oline could see the ter[illegible]-ening behind he[illegible]es's words sank in. "Y[illegible] somebody, Charl[illegible]ured.

He hugged La[illegible]his side. "We're across[illegible]" he sang out as th[illegible]ust now stepped from [illegible] you like that, [illegible]sweet cider half drunk[illegible] going out west [illegible]ve?"

Caroline win[illegible]he stoke Laura's eager[illegible] would be smoki[illegible]ty by the time they r[illegible]-tory. If the weste[illegible]as bold as Concord's P[illegible] eagerness woul[illegible]. A brush or two wit[illegible] might have nip[illegible]ite in the bud, but the[illegible] mercifully fre[illegible]ers.

"Yes, Pa!" L[illegible]e we in Indian countr[illegible]

Caroline ste[illegible]ation with a low, stead[illegible] country' is a l[illegible] We must drive acros[illegible] Iowa, and Mis[illegible]aid, making the name[illegible] foreign. "It wil[illegible] we see the Kansas lin[illegible]

"Oh." Laura [illegible]and poked at her mush. [illegible] barrassed, as th[illegible]e something wrong b[illegible] stand what. Ca[illegible]faltered. She had not [illegible] Laura quite s[illegible]oline dismissed her s[illegible] and tried agai[illegible] all finish our break[illegible] "the sooner we[illegible]."

CAROLINE CHECKED OVER the room one last time. Nothing showed that they had been there except for the neatly swept floorboards and a few lengths of leftover maple added to the kindling pile. She opened the door to go.

Outside, the air was poised on the edge of freezing—moist, as though the lake had spent the night exhaling through the cracked ice. Charles's voice boomed out to greet them:

Where the river runs like silver, and the birds they sing so sweet,
I have a cabin, Phyllis, and something good to eat.
Come listen to my story, it will relieve my heart.
So jump into the wagon, and off we will start.

Laura let go of Caroline's hand and ran ahead to be swung up into the wagon box. Mary waited while Caroline carefully latched the bunkhouse door.

"I don't like riding in the wagon very much, Ma," she said. "Can't we stay and make this house pretty?"

Caroline held out her hand. "Pa will build us a pretty new house in Kansas."

Mary lingered. She seemed anxious, as though she did not like the feel of disobeying yet could not bring herself to move. Caroline reached into her pocket for the little triangle of brown felt. "See what I've found for Nettie to wear? A traveling shawl."

Caroline helped Mary wrap the fabric over the doll's shoulders and lap its ends together. "Nettie says thank you," Mary said. A flush framed her polite smile, as though she were suddenly feverish. "Ma?"

Caroline squatted down and touched her forehead. No warmer than a blush, but Caroline knew something was wrong. Mary had not resisted like this in leaving their own cabin behind. "What is it, Mary?"

[illegible] did not look at her. Her [illegible] came out in a hot, high-[illegible] little wail. "Nettie doesn't [illegible] lakes."

[illegible] a splash of relief. Caroline [illegible] "You tell Nettie she has [illegible] to worry about. There are [illegible] to cross." Mary took [illegible] and squeezed. A soft litt[illegible] yet the depth of reassur-[illegible] contained watered Caroline[illegible] Caroline gave a gentle press [illegible] and together they walked to the [illegible].

"[illegible] Nettie's new traveling shaw[illegible]," Mary said. "Ma made it."

"[illegible] traveling shawl I ever s[illegible]" [illegible] said, and hoisted Mary [illegible] the sideboards. *Traveling shawl.* [illegible] to Caroline.

She felt her cheeks dimple and p[illegible] finger to her lips.

[illegible] O'CLOCK? OR maybe half [illegible] Caroline guessed by the thin-ning of the light between the everg[illegible] her breasts throbbed [illegible] wish it were later. They [illegible] tender at this stage, but [illegible] was something altoget[illegible].

This morning she had left the to[illegible] of her busk unfastened, [illegible] sometimes did at home, to [illegible] breasts the pressure. By [illegible] Caroline had promised her[illegible] not make that mistake [illegible] Each frozen rut, each icy [illegible] shattered under the wag-[illegible] weight sent an unwelcome [illegible] juddering through them. [illegible] embrace of her corset [illegible] been so much the better. [illegible] last hour or more she had [illegible] arms folded tight beneath [illegible] breasts, bracing against the jol[illegible].

"How far have we come today?" [illegible]

"[illegible] fifteen, sixteen miles," Ch[illegible].

It did not seem far enough [illegible] before they had managed [illegible] all that time at the store [illegible] But Caroline was tired and [illegible] and with supper yet to fix. [illegible] was just beginning to [illegible] itself. "It will take better [illegible] hour to lay a fire and finish [illegible] chores," she said.

"[illegible] there," Charles called to [illegible]

The wagon jerked to a halt. Caroline winced. Everything was instantly quiet. Behind her the girls' heads popped up like two rabbits peeking from their burrow.

"In that case, we'll camp right this minute." Charles scanned the roadside and shrugged. "It's as likely a place as any. There's enough snow, we won't want for water no matter where we stop." He turned to Mary and Laura. Their mittens made a dotted line across the back of the spring seat. "Unless you girls think we should keep on?"

"No, Pa!"

EVERY STEP ACROSS the board floor made Caroline's numbed toes feel bigger than her shoes. Corners of crates and boxes poked into the aisle, catching at her skirts as she brushed past. Most all of her neat stacks had jiggled into raggedy looking piles.

Caroline did not stop to set them right. She went straight for the kitchen crates and fished out one spongy wedge of dried apple from the sack. The water in her mouth began devouring it before her teeth had bitten it through.

Outside, Charles cleared a place for the fire and hammered the irons into the ground on either side. While he laid the sticks Mary and Laura brought him, Caroline strung the crosspiece and chain for the kettle.

It was an unruly little fire that flashed hot as sunburn on her face and hands, and no further. Her apron was warm to the touch when she tucked her skirt between her knees to stir the beans, but the heat did not penetrate. Everything from her earlobes back was left chill and clammy.

Caroline circled her spoon through the mass of warming beans. The way some of them struck the wood made her wonder if she had waited too long to stop for supper. They had soaked all night and all day, with a parboiling at breakfast and another at noon, and still they were not soft. Some had not even split their skins. Caroline reached for another stick of wood, then changed her mind. The flames already stroked the bottom of the kettle. [illegible]'s fault, then—it was h[illegible] had not accounted [illegible] at the open air would [illegible]

Caroline listened to [illegible] harles's shovel as he du[illegible] pit and pinched her p[illegible] teeth. He would be hu[illegible] much hacking at th[illegible] th, and there was nothi[illegible] do to hurry the be[illegible] ing them.

Charles stowed [illegible] wagon, lifted the sprin[illegible] and set it down be[illegible] stood no higher than [illegible] Caroline made a litt[illegible] the edges of the po[illegible] sitting. The last thi[illegible] those boards across [illegible] thighs again.

Charles sat dow[illegible] ounce. His knees slop[illegible] than his hips, so h[illegible] is legs and propped th[illegible] boots—one, two—[illegible] He inhaled deeply and [illegible] would not rush her [illegible] she knew he was hung[illegible] ing. Her own stom[illegible] rough the apple slice.

She spooned up [illegible] tasted them. None were [illegible] One, the largest, [illegible] nter like a fresh pea. Sh[illegible] over the edge of the [illegible] were watching her, eager [illegible]

Caroline wavere[illegible] on the hearth a bean li[illegible] give up its bone in [illegible] it in the open with uns[illegible] pine, there was no [illegible] longer. It was either t[illegible] with guesses or s[illegible] beans now. Neither pr[illegible] her, but eating no[illegible] a hardship than waiti[illegible] that might not imp[illegible] She swirled a drizzle of [illegible] the pot, then dish[illegible] ls.

They ate with th[illegible] faces, trying to keep [illegible] inconspicuous. Ch[illegible] his plate without ask[illegible] ond helping. "That [illegible] supper," he said.

Caroline flushe[illegible] Charles always meant [illegible] he said—but if sh[illegible] nce on a blackboard, [illegible] connect to *hot* an[illegible] was not quite a bad m[illegible] ought to have had better—a meal with more virtues than its temperature. She would rather do without any praise at all than be complimented for not failing completely.

She scrubbed the dishes clean with hard fistfuls of snow, thinking of her stove. Her stove, with its four round lids and good steady oven. Beside it, the neat stack of dry seasoned stove lengths. Every bean she baked in it came out a soft nugget of velvet. Caroline smiled a little at herself. It felt good to miss that stove, good as a long hard stretch. That was one thing she could let herself miss. It did not sting like other, dearer things.

CHARLES CLOSED DOWN both ends of the canvas tight as knotholes.

The wagon had a new odor with all of them sealed inside it: the moist, vinegary musk of skin encased all day long in woolen wrappings, their sweat chilled and thawed and now chilling again. And Charles had hung the new poncho up on a hook alongside his rifle. It added a dry, rubbery tang.

Mary and Laura watched Charles roll up the small straw tick from the pile of bedding and push it onto the floor at the front of the wagon.

"Where do we sleep, Ma?" Laura asked.

"Right down here," Charles said, "where the spring seat was. Just like the trundle bed."

The space was narrow, even for the small tick. Its edges curled against the sides of the wagon box and made a little nest of it. Their two pillows bunched together where the sides met in the center.

Caroline nestled one hot flatiron in each corner to warm the foot of the small bed while the girls stood on the big straw tick to be undressed. She worked their red flannel nightgowns quickly down over their red flannel underthings and tied their nightcaps fast under their chins.

First Mary, then Laura hopped down into the nest of straw. Both of them grinned through chattering teeth at the novelty.

"Snuggle up close, now." They scooted together. Caroline laid two quilts [illegible] the third she tucked down in [illegible] boards and [illegible] crimping the edges tight a[illegible] around her daught[illegible]

Ma[illegible] shivered gratefully under [illegible] blankets. [illegible]ched them, so tired yet s[illegible] that they [illegible]. She remembered how [illegible] settled down [illegible] drowsy in the lig[illegible] bunkhouse [illegible] before, and her breath h[illegible]

S[illegible] not [illegible] to look even tha[illegible] forward. On th[illegible] had been simple. All day [illegible] the road reach[illegible] thought herself steadily forw[illegible] vague, brigh[illegible] the new land, the [illegible] child. Now [illegible] but the long still nigh[illegible] to cast [illegible] a blank wall of canva[illegible] toes.

N[illegible] closer yet than that, Caroline [illegible] Charles undre[illegible] straw tick was longer [illegible] box was wide[illegible] was folded under its[illegible] she lay diagonal[illegible] middle of the mattress, Ch[illegible] with his knees [illegible] Caroline was not sure she could [illegible].

S[illegible] across [illegible] the side nearest th[illegible] crimp hersel[illegible] like a triangle to lea[illegible] could for Ch[illegible] it was cold. Cold filled [illegible] beneath her. [illegible] each down for the [illegible] knew was some[illegible] the [illegible]y stretch of muslin, b[illegible] ted and pulle[illegible] close to guard its own [illegible] would have liked [illegible] Mary and Laura's little [illegible] drawn up a[illegible] ger all around.

Ch[illegible] quilts and a fresh rush [illegible] with him. He [illegible]y in beside her, closing [illegible] them—his [illegible] into [illegible]rs, her seat in his lap [illegible] at the crow[illegible] The cold from his nightsh[illegible] through her back [illegible] his arm under hers, set[illegible] heart.

The gentle pressure of his hand melted her as though she were made of wax. One tear and then another burned across the bridge of her nose. She had kept her sadness so carefully lidded these last two days that it had thickened into a stock so rich she could smell the salt before she tasted it. Caroline's throat narrowed so she could scarcely draw breath. Only a long thin note, too high to hear, seeped steadily through to warm the roof of her mouth.

IN THE MORNING, a thin frost rimmed the underside of the wagon cover—their breath, adhered to the canvas.

Caroline's nightdress had climbed past her stockings, leaving her kneecaps bald to the chill even under the quilts. Charles's space beside her was empty; she could hear kindling just beginning to snap to life outside. She leaned to peek at Mary and Laura, trying not to stray outside the warm outline her body had made in the straw. Only the white crowns of their nightcaps were visible.

Caroline's breath hissed out in a pale cloud as she laced her corset. It was likely only her imagination, but it seemed she could feel the frigid lines of the steels through the heavy cotton drill. Her body warmed her dress, and not the other way around—that she did not imagine. She gathered Mary's and Laura's clothes and put them under her quilts. Perhaps the little heat she had left behind would warm them.

A rind of ice topped the water in the washbasin. Caroline broke it with the handle of her toothbrush. Charles came in just then with a pail of water steaming softly in his hand.

"Morning," he said, and, "here," as he poured the warm water into the basin. Caroline stood over it, not moving. The moist steam on her cheeks was heavenly.

"Are you all right?" Charles asked.

Caroline's toothbrush quivered with one last shiver as she nodded.

"Are you sure?"

Her reflection in the water showed a nose already pinking from the [illegible] as though she'd been crying. [illegible] led and dabbed it with [illegible] handkerchief. "It's only the cold."

[illegible] NOT believe it was only the [illegible] when she fled from the pan [illegible] to retch into the snow [illegible]. Nearly. If she had not [illegible] hungry for warmth, she [illegible] realized the fire was too [illegible] their breakfast was indeed [illegible]. Never mind that she had [illegible]—what? Stubborn? Proud? [illegible] the better judgment of [illegible] body.

[illegible] nose had caught the first wh[illegible] thing barely beginning to [illegible] quicker than quick she [illegible] meat. Every strip turned [illegible] as Laura's hair ribbon against the cast iron. Caroline stood [illegible] pan with the fork in her hand [illegible] her overactive senses. [illegible] was that a child in the belly [illegible] woman's nose into a verita[illegible] [illegible] fying glass, she would ne[illegible] d. *They that dance must [illegible] fiddler*, she reminded herself.

That was all the time it took for [illegible] drippings beneath a twist of [illegible] to singe in earnest. Caroline's [illegible] flared in warning at the [illegible] scent, but it was too late. All [illegible] gut rippled and her jaw [illegible], and still she held her ground. [illegible] would not be sick, she in[illegible] to herself, any more than she [illegible] Charles and the girls [illegible] meals in succession. Ca[illegible] the bacon to the edges [illegible] iron spider and tried to whisk [illegible] drippings apart with the [illegible] of the fork until a wave of heat [illegible] able. By the time she [illegible] the pan was smoking.

"It was the cold," she made excuses [illegible] Charles could ask. "I might [illegible] ed in time if not for the cold."

[illegible] through her watery eyes she [illegible] the dubious cast of his [illegible] Charles did not argue. [illegible] his handkerchief and [illegible] backward through his weath[illegible] "Another week or two at [illegible] these temperatures'll be [illegible]," he promised.

Seven

A WEEK, CAROLINE soon concluded, is too cumbersome a thing to count—or to be counted on. Even an hour was a deceitful measure. An hour might thin itself over three or four miles of level roads or be filled to bulging by one scant mile of sandy incline. An elusive ford or a single mudhole placed just so could swallow a whole string of hours right from the middle of a day. Time, Caroline decided, could be trusted to measure the distance between meals, and nothing else. But a mile was always a mile, no matter how long it took to traverse. Days spent on the road were best measured in miles.

Eighteen one day, just over twenty the next. Now and then a good long stretch of twenty-four, twenty-five miles. On the road a week became plain arithmetic: a hundred and ten, a hundred and twenty miles, or maybe only ninety-five.

No cycle of washing, mending, and baking marked one day out as distinct from another. Each day formed the same narrow circle; six of them stacked together earned a Sunday. Only the Sabbath, immune to the tally of miles, managed to keep its identity.

Three things governed their moods: the quality of the road, the disposition of the weather, and the supply of fuel and water. Any one out of balance, whether leaning toward good or ill, left a mark in her memory.

First was the morning when the washbasin did not freeze. Her mind preserved other, earlier days, but that morning always stood out of its proper order. The water had been cold enough to sting her teeth, but it was not frozen. Close beside it was the night the knot in the wagon cover came [illegible] girls woke to find their [illegible] hes sugared with sn[illegible].

Most of the [illegible] made were not worth the [illegible] re-call them: salt p[illegible] cornbread in the [illegible] then bacon, [illegible] Ordinary mainstays that [illegible] simple to prepa[illegible] cooking became a sta[illegible] self and the fire.

One could le[illegible] ment of a stove or [illegible] pa-tience and d[illegible] ir most fractious m[illegible] each new cook[illegible] itself a stranger, and [illegible] that did not req[illegible] ampering. Rain meant [illegible] and the delay [illegible] wood dry enough to b[illegible] winds necessitated [illegible] ole and hunching ov[illegible] there was no[illegible] than weeds, she su[illegible] and poured [illegible] cakes into the iron [illegible] frustration [illegible] Mother Ingalls's maple s[illegible]

Her triump[illegible] er; nothing, down [illegible] tea, tasted quite [illegible] cooking. The water [illegible] imposed its [illegible] y, sudsy, sulphured [illegible] that did not [illegible] arried the faint too[illegible] powdered al[illegible] ify each day's supply [illegible] ter. Some b[illegible] bornly to their du[illegible] carefully sh[illegible] liment. Dusty wat[illegible] so much to [illegible] t parboiling the sa[illegible] a bucket left [illegible] f grit behind to gr[illegible] teeth. More [illegible] thought it would b[illegible] ing to Minn[illegible] llands to fill the t[illegible] pure clean sn[illegible] would be seasoned [illegible] ber by the ti[illegible] out of the spigot. [illegible] least—she d[illegible] with stove black [illegible] on top of her ot[illegible].

EVERY DAY, WHILE the spring seat squeaked against the wagon bows and Charles fidgeted and whistled beside her, Caroline wrote letters in her mind.

To Henry and Polly she described the lay of the land, its prospects for crops and husbandry, and its yield of game, as though her words might lay a path for them to follow. She wished she could put to paper the queer thrill of driving headlong into spring instead of waiting by the fireside for winter to melt and trickle away from them. The weeks seemed to warp and ripple beneath the wagon wheels. It made for such a pleasant sort of bewilderment.

For Ma and Papa Frederick she saved the news of their smaller travails, for her mother would neither believe nor enjoy a letter without some trouble in it. Things like the pheasant that somehow eluded Charles's good aim, the quick spattering of hail that woke them their first night inside the Iowa line. She left out the occasional roadside grave markers, only hinting at them by mention of the picked-over piles of iron hardware showing the places where abandoned wagons had rotted down to metal skeletons. They passed by enough ox bones leftover from the gold rush days, she mused, to fashion a bushel basket full of crochet hooks, buttons, and the like.

The truest of them went to Eliza. To Eliza she could confess how keenly she felt the want of walls and doors—something solid to partition themselves from the space around them. The arc of canvas left her always penetrable, never fully sheltered from wind, or sun, or temperature. Caroline did not know whether Eliza would understand that, but there was no one else she wanted to try to explain it to. Perhaps Eliza would not even fully understand the elation she had felt over the first good dinner she had fixed. Caroline doubted she could adequately convey it without sounding like a hedonist.

They had camped late that Saturday night along a riverbed, in the shelter of a clump of shagbark hickory. The campsite alone was enough alf-giddy: good hard … ter in plenty, both … ach.

… oline went to start br … rning, there was a … catfish dangling fro … Charles, grinning … They were lovely little … white bellies, and … backs lustrous in the … traced her finger … oth whisker.

… before daybreak," Ch … I shouldn't have, … bath, but I tell you, C … feel a bit like work."

… laughed out loud. She … had not even felt it … the way those eyes … He looked as though … fish had already do … good as a full day's … gleamed brighter yet a … of her laughter.

… we've both got somethi … now," he teased … ged her cheeks. She … to bat playfully … they had played too … here would be ev … wer for if Mary and La … behaving this way … morning. "Charles Ing … death of me," she … She lowered her eyes … give her that look … one that followed it— … his smile crinkled … kers—she never could …

… the good hickory … bright and steady … campfire ring the te … on the fringes … es. Now and then a … t nothing strong … le with the fire. Ca … dozen delicate … white flour and fried … golden brown … e beside the skillet … dried apples with … and cinnamon. The f … h snapped in the … the apples bubbled … cooking at h … gan.

… butter, no light bread, … serves, and yet the … avor of a true Sunday … s thin skin crac…

led and its moist white flesh flaked apart on her tongue. Caroline ate until her belly was more than filled, and still her mouth wanted to keep hold of that fish. *Sinfully good,* Charles had said with a wink.

If she wrote it all down and sealed it in an envelope, Caroline wondered, would the humor keep fresh long enough to reach her sister? She liked to think their heartstrings were so closely interwoven that they might still share such moments in spite of the distance. And yet she could not blot out the worry that the months between the happening and the reading would only stale the story and leave Eliza too shocked to laugh.

How many miles had they come? Less than halfway, and already Caroline had the sense that a separation such as this could put more than miles between folks, could right this minute be working changes she might not be entirely conscious of and might never realize at all unless she and Eliza saw each other again.

Caroline gave her chin a little shake and smoothed her hands into her lap. Such far-off things did not bear worrying about. Not when there was one fact this journey did not change, one fact that did deserve more than idle concern. But those uneasy thoughts Caroline could imagine committing to paper for no one, not even herself.

When she tried to think of the coming baby, the pictures formed in the back of her mind instead of stretching out before her. She could see herself only in the rocker where she had nursed Mary and Laura, with a hazy-faced bundle in her arms and Black Susan purring at her feet. Out on this widening land there was no frame to hold new scenes of rocking and feeding. Was that the reason the child had still not quickened—because her mind had not made it properly welcome? Or had her body already communicated to her brain that there was no need to imagine such things for this baby? If there were no life in it, Caroline tried to reassure herself, her body would have expelled it by now. Wouldn't it? That was such cold comfort, it made her shudder. The days were so full of jostles and bumps, she told herself, how could anything so small possibly make itself fe[illegible] d felt both Mary and Lau[illegible] were smaller yet.

Only a little m[illegible] was the matter of who [illegible] when it came time [illegible] child. Even a stillborn ba[illegible] hands to catch it. [illegible] needed to explain. [illegible] ask Charles to r[illegible], and he understood.

Always it had be[illegible] the foot of the bed, Polly, [illegible] so stolid that Carol[illegible] consider quailing a[illegible] was the one thing s[illegible] herself to try imagi[illegible] ent face looking up [illegible] her knees, different ha[illegible] where none but Po[illegible] before. Worse yet wa[illegible] of no one at all.

Caroline knew [illegible] would look for in land[illegible] water, timber, and [illegible]. Not one of those [illegible] could be sacrificed [illegible] need of a claim alo[illegible] bor with a wife, an[illegible] these thoughts to hers[illegible] made another small [illegible] gap between them [illegible]

NIGHTS, SHE AND [illegible] to sitting before the [illegible] Or rather, Charles [illegible] Caroline concentrated [illegible] mending.

"What's that?" C[illegible]

Caroline held a [illegible] up before her. Some[illegible] a set of threadbare [illegible] caught her eye in the [illegible] spare moments she [illegible] seams and joined [illegible] long stretch. "A [illegible]. "To go under the [illegible]

"Looks fine. I'll [illegible] the morning."

Caroline smoot[illegible] across her knees. "[illegible] blanket stitch the [illegible]"

Charles smiled [illegible] half a shake. "Here," [illegible] handed her his mitt[illegible] of them hinged backwa[illegible] a row of finger gus[illegible] them on, only the tip[illegible] gers were left exposed. He watched her adorn a few inches, then said, "Wherever we are, you'll always contrive to make it look like home."

Caroline's breath caught. For a moment she thought the baby had given a little flutter, but it was only a quick beat of delight at his compliment.

"Thank you, Charles," she said.

He balled his fists into his pockets and tipped his head back to look at the sky. "If I could build a roof so fine and high as that, I'd never want to move again."

Caroline watched the firelight stroke his whiskers. He was a man in love with space. Every mile they traveled seemed to loosen him. How, she wondered, could she learn to find such ease in being wholly untethered?

"Charles, tell me how it will be in Kansas." Like a child asking for a bedtime story. "Not the giant jackrabbits and horizons. Tell me how we'll live this first year."

"Well, I figure we ought to save all the money we can toward preempting our claim. For a quarter section at $1.25 an acre we'll need $200 plus filing fees, and the land office won't take pay in pelts. So I'll hunt and trap this winter and trade furs for a plow and supplies enough to last until Gustafson's payments arrive. Should be plenty of game to see us through until spring. Then I'll plow up a plot for sod potatoes and another for corn. Land won't raise more than that the first season. The next year we'll sow fields of wheat and oats and anything else we want."

"I've brought seeds from our garden," Caroline said, "and Polly's. She sent me with the best from her pickling cucumbers." Those cucumbers would be like a little taste of Polly herself—crisp and sharp with vinegar.

What, Caroline wondered, would make the home folks think of her? When they wanted for music, even the music of laughter, they would pine for Charles, of course. What taste, what sound might make their [illegible] "Caroline?" Perhaps [illegible] fragment of red [illegible] scrap bags.

[illegible] swallowed hard. *Forward,* she [illegible] *Not back.* "And [illegible]"

[illegible] so thick out there, [illegible] carve up the [illegible] bricks. Makes walls [illegible] Keeps them [illegible] summer and warm in the [illegible] there's no end of [illegible]

[illegible] Not a soddie?" A house [illegible] crumbly and [illegible] She shuddered as though [illegible] had reached out [illegible] back.

[illegible] consternation, then, "I'll [illegible] say."

[illegible] regretted the sound of [illegible] she'd heard [illegible] half-wincing smile and [illegible] this time. [illegible] of anything but good [illegible]

[illegible] what we'll have," he said [illegible] as ever. "I [illegible] won't be so big as [illegible] have to start [illegible] see his mind pacing [illegible] space beyond [illegible] One room, say twelve [illegible] fireplace at [illegible] ows east and west. [illegible] good slab roof [illegible] tar paper and shingles, [illegible]" His voice [illegible] away as he plotted [illegible] Caroline's nee- [illegible] to him. "Dunno i[illegible] fieldstone for [illegible] parts. I halfway [illegible] rather patch a [illegible] chimney now and then [illegible] thirty years [illegible] of my fields."

[illegible] focused on a spot just [illegible] The depth [illegible] made it seem as though [illegible] were no more [illegible] into something real [illegible] fancied she [illegible] through it and touch her hand [illegible] She joined [illegible] spot testing the fee[illegible] quickened. [illegible] had a destination as much [illegible] the taste of Polly's pickles. Kansas was too vast a thing to pin herself to, and Montgomery County only an empty square on Charles's map, without a single dot of a town. Caroline could not conceive of the infinitely smaller speck she herself would make on that map.

Real or imagined, she needed some mark to aim toward, and what better place than a house? A home. She wanted to be able to see it in her mind, to picture herself inside it as she had not dared to do since Charles informed her they would be leaving the furniture behind. If she could do that, Charles might stop the wagon anywhere he pleased, and she could pin that vision of home to the map.

Caroline's hands toyed with her thread as though it were a latch string. It was risky, fashioning another such reverie with no firm promise that the reality would match. She looked again to Charles. The image he'd built was still before him, solid as though he'd made it out of boards. Perhaps yoking her vision to his would secure it somehow. Caroline gripped the leather latch string in her mind, and pulled.

The room that opened before her was so new she could smell the freshly hewn logs, yet immediately familiar: a straw tick snugged into each of the corners beside the hearth, her trunk beneath one window, the red-checked cloth on the table and the bright quilts on the beds. Without looking she knew Charles's rifle hung over the door. Even the curtains she recognized—their calico trim from a little blue and yellow dress of Mary's that Caroline had loved too much to tear into rags.

The whole house might as well have been standing there finished.

"Will that suit you?" Charles asked. His voice was so near, it was as though he were standing beside her in the imagined doorway.

Caroline whispered, "Yes, Charles."

Eight

CAROLINE HELD THE vision before her all the way to the very [illegible] Kansas—the Missouri River.

It bore little resemblance to the map. On paper it was a thick [illegible] squiggling between Missouri and Kansas, as though it were caught [illegible] crimping iron. Creeks and streams veined the map with blue.

This river was less than [illegible] across and so yellowed with [illegible] it looked as though it had been [illegible] with mustard powder. [illegible] opaque water did not seem to flow but to roll. It carved steadily [illegible] own banks, paring away [illegible] slices of earth that crumbled, [illegible] sugar-like, into the water.

They waited almost three hours to cross at Boston Ferry and gave four dollars from the fiddle box for the privilege. Ferries farther [illegible] stream in St. Joseph were apt to charge as much or more, Mrs. [illegible] said, and their lines were sure to be longer. "Why, by the time you get there you might not even cross today, and those that run their boats on the Sabbath aren't the sort I'd trust with all my worldly goods."

That settled that. Charles could not keep himself confined to the wagon long enough for dinner, much less another full day, not with [illegible] as in plain sight. He stood and paced along the bank, hardly remembering to eat the wedge of cornbread and molasses Caroline put in his hand. Caroline considered the opposite shore. No pattern, texture, or [illegible] marked the Kansas side as distinct from Missouri. Yet there Charles stood, looking as though he were about to step from burlap to broadcloth. That land called to him, and he could scarcely wait to answer.

Mary did not like it, not from the moment she spotted the ferry [illegible] opening up a hatch to shovel water from the hull. She spent the last half hour before their turn to cross scooted in close to Caroline, with Nettie clamped under one arm and her fingers woven into Caroline's shawl, while Laura asked Charles a dozen questions. *What's this do, Pa?* and *What's that? What makes it go, Pa?* and *Why does it go sideways?* Charles named the stob and pulleys and cables for her, and tried to explain how the ferryman slanted the oar board against the current to trick the water into pushing the raft across instead of downstream, but it was more than either of the girls could grasp. For Laura it was enough that her pa understood how it worked. Mary was not comforted.

Caroline ran her hand over Mary's hair as Mary struggled to make sense of it. Barbs of chapped skin snagged the fine golden strands. On either side of the part, Caroline could see the lines the comb had scored that morning. All of them needed a good soak in the washtub. At home their hair would have been glossy by week's end. Now it was only dusty and lusterless, the part faintly gray instead of white.

The wagon gave a little jolt and Mary startled. The ferryman was signaling Charles onto the raft. "I don't want to see anymore," Mary said. "I want to go back on the straw tick."

Caroline put her hand to Mary's knee. "Stay here where I can reach you until we reach the other side."

"I don't want to." She was beginning to flutter with panic as the raft loomed nearer. Caroline pressed more firmly. "Ma? I don't want to."

Charles heard and slowed the team. The ferryman waved again. "Move ahead!" he called out.

The wagon stayed in place. Caroline could feel both Charles and the ferryman turn toward her. She must appease the child or scold her, and fast. The quickest would be to let Mary go and burrow under the gray blanket. But this was no two-mile ice crossing. The child had watched the ferry shuttle more than half a dozen wagons safely from shore to shore. She could not let Mary's fear keep cutting itself larger and larger patterns.

Ca[illegible] swift. "Mary, we mus[illegible] things we d[illegible] Yo[illegible] may be afraid, but yo[illegible] ur fear chase[illegible] wh[illegible] must be done. This [illegible] ft, and it wil[illegible] he[illegible] side if we all sit still a[illegible] nan do his jo[illegible], n[illegible]w, and don't keep the f[illegible] g." She gave [illegible] rch[illegible]ef and faced herself for[illegible]

"A[illegible]

Ha[illegible] nod[illegible]ded pertly to Charles[illegible] olled. Mary [illegible] tly beside her. Each littl[illegible] Caro-line's [illegible] had been sure of herself [illegible] e, but how [illegible] rig[illegible] thing if it left the [illegible] nging? Carol[illegible] he tiniest shake. Sh[illegible] erself such t[illegible] n[illegible] ke that had no servic[illegible] he did not bl[illegible] vou[illegible] d circle her mind, sea[illegible] So she began [illegible]

[illegible] he [illegible] iver,
[illegible] th[illegible] shore,
[illegible] e b[illegible] arman,
[illegible] bea[illegible] us o'er.

All [illegible] up[illegible] at that, even the imp[illegible] nd it cheere[illegible] it. She matched her temp[illegible] nging of the [illegible] on [illegible] he boards, and so sh[illegible] slow-ing ne[illegible] the ferryman motioned C[illegible] loser, closer, [illegible] e f[illegible] ont of the raft. As the [illegible] o tilt towar[illegible] e r[illegible] ver Mary closed her [illegible] ashes all but [illegible]

Car[illegible] ur[illegible] ge to pull Mary onto [illegible] rom-ised th[illegible] safe where she sat and mus[illegible] ng to contra[illegible] nade herself as still a[illegible] y to be, except for her toes, which slid forward to brace against the wagon box. Laura leaned back and gripped the edge of the spring seat and asked, "Why, Pa?"

"The logs at the ends of the ferry boat are cut at a slant like the blade of my ax," Charles said. "That makes them fit snug to the riverbank's slope under the water. The ferryman can't move us unless we help tip the logs off the bank. Watch him, now."

Behind them the young man—Mrs. Boston's son, judging by the look of him—unfastened the mooring rope and sank a pole into the water between the raft and the bank. He pried upward against the hull until with a sandy scrape the ferry came loose. Then with a leisurely swoop he leapt aboard.

"Center them up now," he instructed Charles.

Ben and Beth found level, and Caroline felt herself lift as though the water had unhitched her from her own weight. "Oh!" she said. Mary and Laura and Charles all looked at her. "It's so light." She did not know how else to explain. Her own bed was not half so yielding as this river. There on the hard spring seat her whole body felt as though it were suspended in that soft space between wakefulness and sleep. She leaned back and let the swaying, swishing current rise up through the logs, the wheels, and the boards to rock her.

This was altogether different from tiptoeing across the brittle Mississippi. This river was a living road. It opened itself for them, made room for them to settle into its waters, beckoned them with the tug of its current. This river would not crack behind them.

Just over halfway across the ferryman cranked the windlass and the ferry's nose swung around to angle downstream. "Back them up a couple of yards now, if you please," he said to Charles.

With his hand on the brake Charles persuaded the team backward. One step at a time the front of the raft began to edge out of the water. Mary's breath hissed in and no further. She did not breathe, but she sat there with her hands folded just like Caroline's, a perfect little statue of obedience and bravery. Pride buoyed Caroline up so light, she was still floating as the ferry docked and the wagon pulled off down the road.

Charles was jubilant. "Kansas!" he said, and that was all for nearly a mile. He was so lost in his own satisfaction. Then his toes began to bounce. Next thing Caroline knew, he was whistling "The Campbells Are Coming," and then he was grinning too broadly to whistle. He slapped his knee and chortled instead.

"Charles?" Caroline said. Her own voice curled toward laughter. His eyes did not twinkle—they shone. Charles bellowed out:

The Ingalls are coming, hurrah, hurrah!
The Ingalls are coming, hurrah, hurrah!
The Ingalls are coming to Indian Territory,
All the way 'cross the Missouri!

All the way 'cross the Missouri. Caroline traced the map in her mind as she figured the sum. Some four hundred twenty-five miles they had come. Four hundred twenty-five miles, with still two hundred more down into Montgomery County—Indian Territory. She did not like to call it that, but that is what it would be until the Indians moved on. It gave her a sort of flutter inside to imagine what this land might be holding in store for them. Caroline shivered a delicious little shiver. She had felt this eager, frightened tremor only twice before: stepping up to the justice of the peace with Charles on their wedding day and again five years past with the first tentative pangs of Mary's birthing. Crossing the wide Missouri was the same sort of threshold, Caroline realized. Like those other times she must go ahead uncertain of whether the world was about to open or close around her.

Nine

"WHAT WOULD YOU say to stopping early, Caroline?" Charles asked.

"Now?" She did not know what else to say. It was only midafternoon; they were not ten miles inside the Kansas line.

Charles nodded. "I don't like the look of that sky."

Caroline turned westward. The horizon was like a pan of dishwater. A rumble, faint as a cat's purr, ruffled the air. "Well, I'd be thankful for rain enough to fill the washtub and the time to use it before Sunday," she said.

Charles's mouth hooked into half a smile as he unfolded his map. The points where the creases met were wearing thin as the elbows of his red flannel shirt. "I'd stop right here if the ground were higher."

Caroline scanned the landscape. They stood in a gentle hollow, broad and shallow as the center of a platter. The slope was so gradual she had not felt it.

"We can't be but a few miles from the Saint Joseph and Western line as the crow flies," Charles said. "Ought to be some good level stretches along the railroad bed. First likely place I see, we'll make camp." With that, he eased Ben and Beth due south. The edge of the wind angled across Caroline's face as they turned off the road, flapping her bonnet brim eastward. The wagon cover gave a shiver as the same stiff breeze strummed its ribs.

Caroline let her core ease as the wheels sighed into the spring-softened earth. Already the smell of rain dampened the air. Caroline smiled to herself. Even a fleeting thundershower might grant her enough rainwater [illegible] stockings and drawers. [illegible] the crust [illegible] a's cuff.

Alongsi[illegible] Caroline watched the br[illegible] through th[illegible] blades whispered, then [illegible] the wind t[illegible] belly.

They ha[illegible] mile before the storm [illegible] roundhous[illegible].

Rain sta[illegible] though it were intent on [illegible] cover, whi[illegible] it against the canvas [illegible] scattershot

"Jerusal[illegible] thundered into the [illegible] saw a storn [illegible]"

Ben and [illegible] chins to their collars, [illegible] from the sa[illegible] grab the gutta-perch [illegible] peg and be[illegible] toward his shoulder, searc[illegible] He had not [illegible]

"Charles [illegible] top"

"Ground[illegible] can't keep on, we'll [illegible] minute. Be[illegible] walk it out. Here," [illegible] her the rein[illegible] find my way into thi[illegible] lines in her [illegible] could feel the forward s[illegible] hooves that [illegible] "Go on back with th[illegible] dry as you [illegible]

Caroline [illegible] the spring seat and straw [illegible] Standing on [illegible] had only begun to feel [illegible] ward pull o[illegible] the moving wagon, [illegible] between her [illegible] her feet as she fough[illegible] Staggering, [illegible] to the tailgate and [illegible] ropes, closi[illegible] keyhole. Still the wet [illegible] and snapped [illegible] bows.

She turne[illegible] against the provision[illegible] were damp [illegible] tugged, but the crate wo[illegible]

pinched by the boxes of kitchenwares crowded around it. Caroline snatched up the dish towels and blanketed the bags of flour and meal.

With a sound like a spank, the wind broadsided the wagon. "Ma!" Mary and Laura wailed.

Behind her, rain was hissing up over the sideboards to spit at the girls.

They had left too much slack between the bows; the row of knots along the wagon's sides were not drawn fast enough against the weather.

Two solid feet of boxes and bundles stood between Caroline and the sideboards. She hinged at the waist, putting her hands out to catch the wooden lip.

From either side of the bows, the wagon cover bellied toward her. Caroline tucked her cheek to her shoulder and thrust one hand down between the wagon box and the cover, searching for the rope. A whiskery wet knob of jute met her fingers. The knot was already so fisted with water and wind, she could not feel its loops and strands, let alone part them. Every crack of the canvas kicked a spray of rain into her face. Defeated, Caroline shifted her weight to the heels of her hands and vaulted herself backward.

She stood panting a moment in the center of the wagon, mopping her face in the crook of her arm while lightning flared and Charles shouted calm to the horses. Then without a word to the girls she stripped the gray blanket from their knees and began bunching it into the gaps as best she could.

With every ram of the blanket she upbraided herself for being so ill prepared. She had known it must rain. Of course it would. On the trek she and Charles had made from Jefferson County to Pepin it had rained every afternoon for a solid week. As she sewed and oiled this wagon's cover she had thought of little but the wind and rain and sun that would strike it.

But she had not considered all the ways in which a storm such as this could reach beneath it. Thunder vibrated the boards at her feet.

[illegible] it the canvas as tho[illegible] wick of a kerosene la[illegible]

[illegible] of it all, the girls [illegible] nd of the straw t[illegible]k h[illegible] kittens. Mary [illegible] frightened herself to b[illegible] to her sister.

[illegible] them, Caroline felt [illegible] wagon cover. No mat-te[illegible] tried to put herself [illegible] ls and the storm, she w[illegible] able keep its rag[illegible] h[illegible]m. She wished she c[illegible] them both close [illegible] one, as she had when th[illegible] bies. The soft thunde[illegible] had been enough to s[illegible] then, but she could no[illegible] ear enough to hear it [illegible]

[illegible] know which of them [illegible] t. She had not arms e[illegible] shelter them both at once [illegible] still so little, but Mary [illegible] mothering in her own [illegible] not seem fair that each c[illegible] half of her, nor that [illegible] ould favor one side of h[illegible] since Laura was new [illegible] Caroline felt so keenly th[illegible] not be mother enough [illegible] soon there would be a[illegible] thought made her want [illegible] her own ma.

[illegible] the vanity of new [illegible] Caroline realized, she had g[illegible] thought to Mary and [illegible] she agreed to go west. S[illegible] them into the wag[illegible] ets and sheets. Now s[illegible] for it.

[illegible] though she was, C[illegible] apart from them no l[illegible] faces were unth[illegible] Whatever thin com-f[illegible] offer belonged to the[illegible] but the press of her d[illegible] assure her she was [illegible] task.

[illegible] her way onto th[illegible] put her back to the [illegible] "Come here my girls," [illegible] broke loose from e[illegible] came skittering tow[illegible] eagerness that spread [illegible] her heart.

[illegible] Laura huddled so clos[illegible] sides, the tips of her steels dug at the soft flesh under her arms. At once Caroline saw that it did not matter what she did, so long as she was there for them to cling to. Their trust in her was built of thousands upon thousands of moments already past. She was *Ma,* and that in itself was enough. Just pressing against her seemed to sand away the edges of their fear, and Caroline's own flesh yielded to welcome them.

Thoroughly bolstered, Caroline swaddled her shawl around their shoulders and shielded their laps with a quilt. With long circles, she passed her hands slowly up and down their backs, kneading their taut spines with her knuckles. Cold needles of rain struck the back of her neck as she stroked. Caroline let them melt into her collar; she would not break her rhythm to slap them away.

Lightning slashed through a clap of thunder, and Mary's body recoiled from the sound.

"There is nothing to be frightened of," Caroline soothed. "It is only light and air bumping together."

But the next crack sounded so near, it tingled the pit of her stomach. Reverberations cored through her arms and legs. Caroline cupped her palms over Mary's and Laura's ears and rocked the girls from side to side, tucking her chin close to their heads as she began to sing:

Wildly the storm sweeps us on as it roars,
We're homeward bound, homeward bound;
Look! yonder lie the bright heavenly shores:
We're homeward bound, homeward bound;
Steady, O pilot! stand firm at the wheel;
Steady! we soon shall outweather the gale;
Oh, how we fly 'neath the loud creaking sail!
We're homeward bound, homeward bound.

"I want to go home, Ma," Laura said. "Can't we go home?"

All Caroline's self-assurance washed straight down her throat. Lightning cut [illegible] the sky again before she could [illegible] cause belongs to [illegible] on now. We had storms in the [illegible], Laura. This one [illegible] ferent." If she pulled the truth [illegible] would tear. Th[illegible] storms—storms that struc[illegible] walls made of logs [illegible] the middle as Laura hers[illegible] the cabin the tree[illegible] the raindrops and combed [illegible] narrow strands. [illegible] were neither out nor in, the[illegible] er than a hat.

"Is M[illegible]

Caro[illegible] and pushed her lips into a [illegible] once she would [illegible] for her tears. The child [illegible] amed as she was [illegible] line could feel Mary's hot [illegible] her side.

Laur[illegible] oss to pet her sister's arm. [illegible] and ventured t[illegible] her face.

"I'm [illegible]," Laura said.

Caro[illegible] Mary wipe her cheeks [illegible] hand. Their fi[illegible] st as corset strings over Car[illegible] ghtning scratch[illegible] the sky and both girls ducked [illegible] to smile she epis[illegible] her before chancing a glan[illegible]

In th[illegible] Caroline's love for them [illegible] surface of her [illegible] child inside could not feel [illegible] on of its sisters' [illegible] ing overhead, she hoped [illegible] affection might [illegible]

The [illegible] seemed to float with her, [illegible] corner pitched [illegible] was not more than [illegible] er body tipped [illegible] water with all her muscles [illegible] level.

"Ch[illegible]

He [illegible] to the team. The wagon [illegible] rd, then dropp[illegible] re[illegible] snapped like thund[illegible] wagon leaned [illegible] less sharply this time. Ca[illegible] ch of the horses [illegible] the strain so strong her sho[illegible] alongside her ea[illegible] release. They had not move[illegible]

"Charles," she called again.

"That's it," he barked over his shoulder. "We're stuck."

She heard the reins strike the floorboards before the spring seat bounced up, knocking the top rungs of her spine. Charles was on his feet, cinching down the ropes at the wagon's mouth. It was dim as the inside of a flour sack.

"I've got to unhitch the team, chain them to the leeward side of the wagon," Charles said. He stood mopping his face and whiskers in the crook of his elbow. "Caroline, I need your help managing the canvas so I can get the harnesses under cover." The girls' heads tilted up at him, their bodies furrowing against this news. "You girls will have to sit tight," he told them.

"Are the horses scared, Pa?" Laura asked.

"No, Half-Pint, but they're colder and wetter than they've ever been before. I haven't got a chance of rigging a tarpaulin up in this gale," he said to Caroline. "The best I can think to do is get them out of the wind. I need you to stand inside and hold the canvas closed while I unbuckle the lines. I'll shout for you to open up when I'm ready to hand the harnesses in."

"All right, Charles." Caroline unwedged herself from the girls and unwound her shawl. She folded it into a neat triangle and laid it between them. "Mary, Laura, will you please keep this warm and dry for me?"

They nodded, hunkering protectively over her shawl, still crouched with fear, yet unwilling to cave to it.

"That's my brave girls," she said, and it starched them up some to be called so.

Caroline eased herself over the spring seat, where Charles stood waiting, and tucked her skirts back between her calves.

"All ready?" Charles asked.

She nodded and reached for the ties.

"Not yet," Charles said. "I'll cinch them up behind me from the outside and hand them in." He turned up his collar, screwed his hat nearly eyebrows, and tipped his ... out into the storm. The ... k like a knothole ... in his fist full of rope ... between the canvas and ... box.

Caroline crouched down and ... the ties from him. Each ... er shoulders as the wind ... let the canvas from the ... For forty beats the st... its rhythm through her ... e she heard Charles's ... through the wet canvas. ... burned across the palm ... loosened her grip, and ... is and traces came ... them in one-handed ... into the corner, a ... for the rope she had ... planed across her face ... ear. Then came Beth ... er doughnut heavy with ...

"Close up," Charles shouted.

She had not the muscle to ... canvas tight again, so ... rope twice around her f... braced her heels. "Mary ... b...," she called.

"Why, Ma?" Mary asked.

"Get *back*," she said again, ... cocked and loaded, ... elf backward into the ... The twists of jute ... on the back of her hands ... wagon clamped its mou... was like driving ... ways, holding those ... ed so insistently, the ... of her fingers scr... another. Before she could ... her grip, she felt the ... ground and Charles ... n. She stood and threw ... e, opening the wagon's ... half of the tack ... I'll be in soon as I've ... chained to the feedbox." ... uted. "Can you hold ...

Caroline's pulse th... the pads of her thumb ... ed up a shout and ... "Yes, Charles." ... herself backward and ... shrank shut.

In a moment the girls ... sound of the chains ... jockey box and th... ing. Then Caroline fe...

jounce and knew Charles had climbed to the doubletree. His boot heels knocked against the falling tongue, and then his hands were parting the canvas.

"Give me some slack," he called, and Caroline let loose the ropes. With a gust of wind the wagon cover seemed to inhale, raising Charles to his toes. "Great fishhooks," he cried.

Caroline grabbed for the canvas flapping below his fists, and together they tugged it back down.

"Reel one end of the rope in taut and stand on it," Charles yelled to her. "Clamp it under your heels."

As soon as Caroline had done as he instructed, Charles tumbled in with the other end. He crouched on the floor and knotted his length around hers. Then he hooked the pair of horse collars onto his elbow and heaved them over. "Step back," he said, and wound both ends of the rope through the collars until they were secure. When he let go, the wind pulled the knot tight against the weight of the collars.

Charles sank down into the bramble of wet tack. "Caroline, how did you ever hold against that wind?"

"I don't know, Charles," she admitted. She looked at him, and the girls. "I only knew that I had to." She was so rigid with tension, she could not even shiver. "Girls, my shawl, please, quick."

The fabric was warm as they were. Caroline swathed it close around herself and stroked the rain from her face with its ends. Wet streaks of hair channeled rainwater down her temples and neck. With her fingers she pried the strands from her skin and combed them into place.

"I tell you, that rain is falling every which way but down," Charles said. He took hold of his whiskers as though he were about to milk his chin. With a twist, he wrung a fistful of water onto the floor.

Laura giggled first, then Mary.

"Think that's funny, do you?" He did not quite snap at them, but all the expression seemed to have vacated his voice. The girls pinned their lips together.

Caroline could not [illegible] so she frothed up her [illegible] with cheerfulness. "Charles [illegible] those wet things," she [illegible] a layer of his [illegible] peel away with the [illegible] "[illegible] Laura, find Pa some dry [illegible] carpetbag and make [illegible] on the straw tick while [illegible] per."

Caroline spread the [illegible] spring seat before [illegible] way to the back of the [illegible], she unswathed the [illegible] picked over the provisions [illegible] the bake oven half-full of [illegible] bread, but that she would [illegible] eakfast, to warm over [illegible] they must have a cold supper [illegible] decided, she would [illegible] of it—crackers and cheese [illegible] pples—though what [illegible] most just then was a mug of [illegible] a king of light bread [illegible] to melt butter.

To distract herself from [illegible] ting, Caroline fanned [illegible] of apple quarters like a [illegible] 's and Laura's plates. [illegible] long yellow strips from the [illegible] cheese and layered [illegible] between the apple petals. A [illegible] of cheese brightened [illegible] of each plate, and a wh[illegible] rs framed it all. For Charles [illegible] made no such dainties [illegible] of apples and crackers, [illegible] cut of cheese thick enough [illegible] her wince as the kni[illegible] pressed into her rope-rough[illegible]

"What happened to your [illegible] Charles said as she pass[illegible] plate and a mug of water. [illegible] from shouting.

Pink welts striped [illegible] side. "Only a bit of [illegible]" she said. "Nothing that [illegible]"

Charles put down his [illegible] ched for her wrist. "I [illegible]

He would blame him[illegible] them—no matter [illegible] not the one who had [illegible] round her hands. "It'll [illegible] Charles," she insisted. "[illegible]

A sigh hissed between his [illegible]

"Your cornbread won't [illegible] sweet for it," she v[illegible] tease. *I never ask any other sweetening,* he'd said since that first supper in Pepin, *when you put the prints of your hands on the loaves.*

A short snuffle—almost a laugh—escaped his nostrils. "All right, Caroline," he said.

She saw from the way his movements loosened when he bowed his head to pray that it had been levity enough to oil his hinges. He cleared his throat for the blessing and winced.

"Rest your voice, Charles," Caroline said. "I think Mary is old enough to say grace for us. 'For what we are about to receive,'" she prompted.

Mary straightened up and refolded her hands primly. "For what we are about to receive," she repeated and then took a careful breath, ". . . may the Lord make us . . . ," another breath, ". . . truly thankful." Her eyes popped open, looking to see if she had done right.

"Very nice," Caroline praised her. Mary puffed up like a vanity cake, muddling Caroline's pride. Had she sown the wrong kind of modesty in that child? From the day Mary was born, Caroline had known that warding off vanity promised to be the greatest task in raising her. She had felt it welling in herself as she gazed on those delicate blue eyes and stroked the first golden wisps of Mary's hair. How, she wondered then and ever after, had she made anything so beautiful?

Laura sat in awe of her sister. Caroline watched her fork a crumb of cheese from the center of her plate and taste it carefully, as though the food might be sauced with a new flavor after being blessed by Mary's voice. Caroline sat down beside Laura and smoothed her little brown braids. They were so waxed with the week's dust and oil, they would likely hold their shape without ribbons.

Once again there would be no Saturday bath, Caroline realized, just as there were no fresh loaves of light bread. At this hour the inside of their cabin would be fleecy with yeast and the breath of bathwater—unless Mrs. Gustafson, being a Swede, did her baking and bathing by a different timetable. Caroline scanned the dim expanse of the wagon.

She [illegible] the girls' small white b[illegible] yellow firel[illegible] warm snowmelt [illegible] the [illegible] feathery feel [illegible] hair. Buttoned into fr[illegible] gowns, they [illegible] knees to have their [illegible] damp to m[illegible] Sunday. The little hou[illegible] Caro-line's [illegible]

Sh[illegible] her dinner while [illegible] their ears, [illegible] the fruit and che[illegible] than pine [illegible] her. But Caroline [illegible] oughts conf[illegible] wagon. Often Saturday nigh[illegible] time to read [illegible] the fire while her own [illegible] pots and [illegible] easing herself into [illegible] und of Char[illegible] whittling knife. Tonig[illegible] do but wipe [illegible] bed, and she sai[illegible] lected their [illegible]

M[illegible] ne's cuff. "Where a[illegible]?" she whis[illegible] over Mary's hea[illegible] har-nesse[illegible] space.

"I [illegible] small tick, sleep in th[illegible] aisle [illegible] bed.

"I [illegible] you a mug of tea for [illegible]

Ch[illegible] "It'll pass."

Ca[illegible] crumbs from the pl[illegible] hcloth and f[illegible] the crate while th[illegible] aisle with [illegible] They brought Caroli[illegible] she rinse[illegible] with water from [illegible] polish, spend[illegible] on such things with [illegible] down on th[illegible] tussle with the w[illegible] til the wind [illegible]

Ch[illegible] chamber pail back to t[illegible] on the m[illegible] Caroline readied the [illegible] the pillo[illegible] wagon would tug [illegible] than the [illegible] nightcaps close und[illegible]

Perched on the edge of the tick, they watched Charles unfold a tarpaulin the length of the aisle and lace a slender rope through the line of metal rings that bordered its edge.

"What are you doing, Pa?" Laura asked.

"Got to be ready—" He cleared his throat and shook his head.

"Pa is preparing a shelter for Ben and Beth in case the rain doesn't stop," Caroline explained as she folded the girls' dresses and petticoats and tucked them into the carpetbag.

"Oh, Pa, do you have to go out in the rain again?" Mary asked.

"The horses must stand in the weather until Pa can cover them," Caroline said. "Ben and Beth have brought us this far, and we must take care of them." She paused with Mary's blue wool half-folded against her chest, thinking what it would mean if either of the horses took sick. "Now let Pa work so he can rest."

When he was done Charles rolled the tarpaulin up like a rug and doubled it in the middle. He carried the bundle to the tailgate and propped it alongside the kitchen crates.

"It's time little girls were asleep," Caroline said when he lifted the lid from the chamber pail and began to unbutton. "Let me hear your prayers."

Mary and Laura got to their knees at the head of the aisle and latched their folded hands under their chins. Their two voices chorused *Now I lay me,* drawing the day closed like two ends of ribbon weaving a bow.

"And God bless Ben and Beth," Laura added as a little flourish. Caroline smiled. All finished, they scuttled under the quilts and reconciled themselves to sleep. Caroline salved her sore hands with the softness of their hair and kissed them both goodnight.

Charles did not undress. He laid the small tick down in the aisle and wedged himself into the narrow trough it made. His shoulders were straightjacketed by the sides of the ticking, and his calves extended beyond its edge.

"I should wake you if I hear the wind calm?" Caroline asked.

[illegible] nodded. Sh[illegible] hande[illegible] [illegible] quilts, and he cl[illegible] [illegible] without another word be[illegible] [illegible]

[illegible] expected sen[illegible] [illegible] round Caroli[illegible] [illegible] [illegible] herself and u[illegible] [illegible] her shawl a[illegible] [illegible] Mary's and La[illegible] fee[illegible] how, to join t[illegible] covers in spite [illegible] he [illegible] the wind and [illegible] into a curta[illegible] [illegible] nothing she ne[illegible] nothing she co[illegible] lo[illegible] [illegible] Charles and [illegible] not found a m[illegible] [illegible] rself since Wi[illegible] ness within the wagon [illegible] ghts from the [illegible] consequences, [illegible] Car[illegible] the quiet spac[illegible] [illegible]. Tomorrow [illegible] they would n[illegible] the weath[illegible] [illegible] er a complete [illegible] h she'd been [illegible] n's worth of [illegible] momentum. [illegible] exhale that [illegible] unfastening [illegible] d why, she w[illegible] she always in[illegible] ngs in the mor[illegible] s freest to expand. [illegible] only be still, [illegible] id, Caroline t[illegible] ngside Mary—*B[illegible] that I am God.*

"[illegible]INE?"

[illegible] ine felt her eye[illegible] rise [illegible] of light met t[illegible] on an elbow. "[illegible]

[illegible] wind's died d[illegible] rig somethin[illegible] o shelter B[illegible] Caroline broad[illegible] to the sou[illegible] sky still wr[illegible] , but she c[illegible] way the rain [illegible] The drops f[illegible] sidelong ag[illegible] western fla[illegible] Charles asked.

[illegible] t up and le[illegible] pat her ha[illegible]

[illegible]"

He beckoned for it, and his boots. She lifted the garments gingerly over the girls. Dirt crusted the soles of the boots. "Do you need help?" she asked, reaching for her shawl.

Charles shook his head. "You stay in with the girls. The noise is likely to wake them." He shouldered the rolled-up tarpaulin. A rope dangled from either end.

Caroline followed him down the cockeyed aisle, hearing more than seeing him secure one of the ropes to the tailgate latch, then loosen the cover and lean out to boost the rolled-up tarpaulin onto the roof. It landed with a thump, sagging the canvas and jostling the hickory bows. He hesitated. "I may need you to open the front of the wagon cover so I can tie a rope inside."

Caroline tested her fists. The palms were tender yet, but so long as the wind did not wrestle with her as it had before she would manage.

"All right, Charles."

The girls stirred as Charles threaded himself through the opening and into the rain. All Caroline could see of him were the toes of his boots as he strained to push the tarpaulin farther across the roof. In a moment a whiplike *crack* snapped overhead—the other end of the rope, landing halfway across the roof. Then it hissed against the canvas as Charles reeled it back for another throw.

Mary bolted up on her hands and knees before Caroline knew she was awake. "Ma?"

Caroline waded back through Charles's bedding to reach her. "It's only Pa, making a tent for the horses."

Mary crawled into her lap and augered herself close against the soft new curve of Caroline's belly. "I don't like it here," she said in a pouting tone Caroline would have corrected under any other circumstances. "Where are we?"

"We are in Kansas," Caroline said.

"I don't like Kansas," Mary declared.

Again the *crack* came, this time farther toward the front of the roof.

The wa... the wagon as Charles ju... ground. A fe... hea... then the front of the wa... with his foot... he falling tongue then... singletree to d... bo...d.

"... ng the tarpaulin acro... Caroline said... wagon's spine, bumping... the bow to th...

"... aura," Caroline told M... tarpaulin flatt... them. "Be a good b... her if she... help now."

C... limbed over the spring s... damp agai... re the poncho ha... count of how... hoisted her legs over... board this day.

C... se collars and crouched... ropes that... wagon cover shut. With... driving them... apron strings. Charles p... in line taut... re it to the nearest bow.

"... e up the cover and go... Caroline... ere."

... er the spring seat and... where she... ura did not like Kansas...

"... "We should all be asleep... noth-ing... and felt no movement... that the... spicuous. The girls did... Caro-line... apprehension as... d. No harm... Charles, but surely... have hap... s as though he were... still in the... ticked against the can... until it s... ust be wrong. His na... her mo... now whether she might... more by... by leaving the silence... then

Charles's voice pricked the sidewall, so near to her pillow that Caroline's shoulders flinched at the sound.

"Caroline?"

She closed her eyes. "Yes, Charles."

"Lean up close to the sideboards and talk to the team," he said. "I'm afraid it's going to startle them something awful when I unroll the tarpaulin."

Once more Caroline peeled herself from her covers to creep down the small hill of the straw tick, clucking her tongue. "Here, Ben; here, Beth," she crooned, "poor wet things. Steady now. Easy." Mary and Laura inched up on their bellies to whisper sweetly to the team. There was a snuffle and a nudge at the canvas. Laura flattened her palm against it.

"Ben's nose," she said. "I can feel him breathing."

"How can you tell it's Ben?" Mary whispered.

With a flap like a clothesline full of sheets, the tarpaulin unfurled down the side of the wagon. The horses' chains hummed tight, jerking the wagon bed upward as Ben and Beth tried to rear back from the crashing canvas. Laura snatched her hand away, tumbling backward in her surprise.

Caroline listened to the chain links clinking, the horses' heavy breath steaming from their nostrils. "Steady," said Charles's voice, "steady now," and Caroline felt her own breath slowing at his words, whooshing softly over her upper lip.

Charles reached in over the tailgate and clattered through his toolbox. Caroline heard him lever out the iron stakes that held her pots over the campfire, and then he was gone. In a moment the clang of his hammer rang out shrill in the dark as he pounded the stakes into the ground.

As she settled Mary and Laura back to bed, Charles tugged the tarpaulin's corners down to the stakes, gently rocking the wagon. The girls were asleep again by the time he came in over the tailgate and st... lifted to hold the drenc... of his poncho away fr... y.

... the weather ... t fo... he said.

... ded. Like a pi... e ... dou... pan, Charles ... expand to fit ... ver ... demanded of him. ... ed to thank him fo... such ... he felt so rounded ... at she did not ... ove ... shook him by the ... k.

... ded him his night... irt ... . "Drape your wet ... crates," she whispered. "... in the morning." ... meant to watch. F... n he ... was only his out... ped off his rain g... ar an... his clothes, threads of ... spiderweb in sunlight. ... off his shirt, and ... silvered his wet shoulders ... ing his spine. As ... his trousers the ... sed ... of his belt buckle ... note in the darkness and ... ed, turning half... t of the wagon.

... her, running her fingers ... the way he did ... ngry for her? That was ... wanted now, and ... ed her palms again... the ... She wanted only to ... stood, so bar... capa... dusting of light. ... of such breadth ha... cho... he seemed to de... narrowness, Caroline co... When she had ... his wife, his first ... ndul... not been a kiss. He ... hed out to place ... han... another around her ... bsent at her ... and ... watched the pleasure ... his face. "A perfect ... t," ... warmth of his ... her skin and ... ed ... deepest recesses of ... now she wondered whe... decided to kiss ... r se... up on tiptoe ... lips to him.

... straightened his back, h... ... chilling upward, ... heard the sound of his fi... ... thrumming through his scalp. She smiled to herself. The one thing Charles could never do was tame that hair of his. With a shrug, his nightshirt snuffed out his nakedness and Caroline closed her eyes, penciling the shape of him onto her dreams.

SHE WOKE WITH Mary's cold toes knuckled into the crook of her knees. On her other side Laura had screwed herself into a little knot.

Caroline sniffed the air. A dull, almost meaty smell tinged the wagon—the pile of damp harnesses. The storm's temper had eased overnight, but the rain had not abated. Streams of it sluiced off the canvas, striking puddles in a way that made her bladder tingle. She had not emptied herself all night. Caroline looked toward the rear of the wagon. Charles and his narrow bed filled the path to the chamber pail.

Gripping against the downward press of her water, Caroline deliberately rustled the carpetbag as she dressed. The damp had reached into everything. Her dress and drawers were clammy and seemed to have thickened, like drippings in a cooled skillet. Even the good stockings she saved back for Sundays still held the shape of her feet. Nevertheless, the left one hugged her shin too tightly where the beginning of a bruise shined her skin. She put on her second-best navy wool with the black braid, never mind that there was no call for it. It would be at least as warm as her everyday, and she wanted to feel a touch of fineness.

The wagon's pitch tugged insistently at her bladder, forcing her to draw her belly upward until she felt as though she stood on tiptoe. Caroline nudged a toe under Charles's pillow and whispered his name. He opened one eye at a time and looked up at her. She nodded toward the tailgate.

Charles stood and they minced a half pirouette in the straw tick so that she could pass.

The rear of the wagon was in disarray—Charles's poncho drooping over the churn dash, his shirt and trousers splayed nearby. Beside the chamber pail was the drying puddle where he had come in from the

rain, its edges curl[illegible]es. Caroline lifted [illegible]
A skin of mud [illegible] they had stood.

All of those [illegible] tomorrow.

She need attend [illegible] her little brood, C[illegible]
as she held the [illegible] deluge. Runoff lick[illegible]
her cuffs and [illegible] elbows before she p[illegible]
back under the ca[illegible].

Behind her, C[illegible] his bed and dressed [illegible]
best—more be[illegible] dry than for Sunda[illegible]
line supposed [illegible] the tailgate with [illegible]
feedbox flapped [illegible] were awake. Almo[illegible]
their tempers beg[illegible] quibbled over who [illegible]
to the chamber p[illegible] should button up wh[illegible]
voices sharpening [illegible] Caroline's patience.

"Girls, please," [illegible] more a request than a [illegible]

"I only have [illegible]," Mary said. "Lau[illegible]
mine first."

"Mine's all ope[illegible] wait," Laura prot[illegible]

Caroline hesita[illegible] poised at the tip of h[illegible]
did not want to soil [illegible] the sound of her [illegible]
yet this time they [illegible] asked. She closed [illegible]
leveled a silent [illegible] swiveled Laura b[illegible]
and buttoned her [illegible].

"The water's co[illegible] protested again as Ca[illegible]
behind her ears.

"It is the best [illegible] said, "and we can b[illegible]
not frozen." Laura [illegible] up to her earlobes

Mary joined in, "We'[illegible] even Ben and Beth, [illegible]
complain." She fair[illegible] periority.

Mary turned to [illegible] tantly. Caroline did [illegible]
Mary had said noth[illegible] Caroline could not help [illegible]

her own sentiments dressed in a smaller size—but it troubled her that Mary took such care to polish her tone to a gleaming point. Vanity again, buttered with virtue. *Virtue is the purest kind of beauty.* Hadn't she always impressed that upon her daughters? Only just now, watching Mary, it did not feel true.

"Forty-three degrees," Charles said as he came in, noting it in his weather journal. "And I'll bet it's not much warmer in here."

Caroline wished he had not announced it. She herself was not cold enough to shiver, but the chill was so embedded in her clothes that her skin resisted touching the fabric. Pinning a number to the cold only made her more sensible of it.

"Everybody taken their turn?" Charles asked, hefting the chamber pail by the handle. He opened the rear of the wagon cover and flung the contents out into the rain. "Tried to dig a latrine pit under the tarpaulin but it'll likely be full of water by the time anyone needs it," he said as he swirled the pail full of rinse water and cast the swill out again. "It's like digging at the bottom of a well out there. I left a bucket hanging below the feedbox to bail it out."

Charles sat down on a crate and scrubbed his sides with his fists. "Sore," he said. "Had to lean backward stiff as a rafter to hoist the tarpaulin onto the roof."

"We'll all rest ourselves today," Caroline said, tying on her apron.

"Is it Sunday again, Ma?" Laura asked.

"It is," Caroline answered. Laura knew better than to scowl, but the news swept down her face like a sadiron.

"Are you too tired to drive, Pa?"

"I am, Half-Pint," Charles said, patting his knee for Laura to climb aboard. "And it's a good thing, because Ben and Beth are too tired to pull."

Laura wilted onto Charles's shoulder and buckled her lips over a sigh. "Why doesn't Sunday ever wait until *I'm* tired?" she lamented.

Ca[illegible]oli[illegible] w[illegible]ned with a laugh [illegible] A still and [illegible]ny [illegible]nt [illegible]t any three-year-[illegible]d's [illegible] none so so[illegible]ly [illegible] th[illegible]e way she took a[illegible]er [illegible]

La[illegible]ra [illegible]ou aren't too tir[illegible] [illegible]t, are you, [illegible]a?

Th[illegible] [illegible] co[illegible]l not bite back a[illegible] [illegible] Caro-line, [illegible]e's [illegible]ing that's allowe[illegible] to [illegible]ay—a ston[illegible]h," [illegible] Hi[illegible]mbl[illegible]ng laugh wa[illegible] [illegible]

CHA[illegible]LES [illegible] thro[illegible]gh his we[illegible]the[illegible] [illegible]roline scra[illegible]l t[illegible] [illegible]nolasses from the [illegible] Hasn't been [illegible] rai[illegible] [illegible]s," he said. "Not [illegible]"

S[illegible] fol[illegible] [illegible] the kitchen cra[illegible] [illegible]gth of the [illegible] go[illegible] [illegible]led every edge o[illegible] her [illegible]ll the big [illegible]aw[illegible] [illegible]ayed back and th[illegible] [illegible]neath Mar[illegible] nd [illegible] not, the bed mus[illegible] be [illegible]e four of th[illegible] [illegible] [illegible]ere to sit. Carol[illegible] [illegible] to the aisle. [illegible] sheet from the [illegible]att[illegible] [illegible]hes lit the b[illegible]ks [illegible]

"M[illegible]ry, [illegible]n the bed and h[illegible] [illegible]." She hand[illegible] M[illegible] [illegible]egan backing do[illegible]n [illegible]other.

"I [illegible]ant [illegible]!" [illegible]ura insisted, graz[illegible]ng [illegible] shin to re[illegible]h f[illegible]

S[illegible]ene[illegible] as [illegible]aroline's elbows [illegible] [illegible]undle away [illegible]ro[illegible] [illegible]s. "Climb up be[illegible]ide [illegible] one of her [illegible]ne[illegible] [illegible] her. "There isn't [illegible] here."

Ca[illegible]oli[illegible] [illegible] to heat the back of [illegible] stood idle, [illegible]ait[illegible] [illegible] negotiate who s[illegible]oul[illegible] [illegible]. She woul[illegible] ha[illegible] [illegible] fold it herself in [illegible]pit[illegible] [illegible]an let this [illegible] [illegible] n her morning.

"I[illegible]ne'[illegible]," [illegible] said.

"I[illegible]ne, [illegible]

Caroline's elbows went slack. Her end of the sheet brushed the aisle. "The weather makes everything feel damp today, girls. It can't be helped. Now please, help me fold this sheet up nicely."

"No, Ma," Mary said.

The contradiction came within a hair's breadth of lighting Caroline's temper by the wick. She opened her mouth and found she had no words to parry such bald-faced disobedience—especially from Mary.

Mary climbed down and held up her corner. "It's wet. See?" It was. Not clammy with cold, but more sodden than freshly sprinkled laundry.

"Is the bottom sheet wet, Laura?"

Laura tugged it up into her lap. "Yes, Ma."

Caroline stifled a groan. She skimmed her hands across the mattress. All along the west end, the cover was heavy with moisture. Practically wincing with reluctance, she unbuttoned one corner and fished out a handful of damp straw.

Baffled, she touched the canvas wall above it. Dry.

"How in the world?" she wondered aloud, and then she saw. A tongue of the gray blanket had lapped out into the rain. Caroline pulled it, black and drooling, back under cover. In the places where the two abutted, the ticking had spent the night supping rainwater into itself silently as a cat at a saucer.

Caroline's sigh formed a small gray cloud as her whole morning deflated under the weight of one soaked blanket.

With Charles's help she spread the sheets, one over each side of the aisle, to dry as best they could. The gray blanket Charles strung from the front bows with its wet hem drooping, frown-like, toward the floor. The entire wagon dimmed. Caroline pulled the end of the straw tick across her lap and resigned herself to plunge her arms in to the elbows. At least it was soaked only at the foot, where she could sift out the wet straw without emptying the entire mattress. For that small mercy she managed a pinch of thankfulness.

...not last long. Each stiff ... straw stabbed at her sore ... cold and pain numbed her ... they became insensible ... her fingers could not ... difference between ... between nutmeg and ...

... it back and balled the ... her arms. Two pillow- ... of straw slumped beside ... yet to come. "I declare," ... know what to do with all th... whether it would soon ... the pillowcases than ... could not bring her- ... toss it out into the ... *waste not, want not,* her mother's ... , but what earthly use ... for wet straw? ... as well empty it out ... boards before the spring ... the muck from their ... they came in from the ... And then how long ... began to smell ...

... cocked her head. "Ch... do any good to spread ... the tarpaulin for Be... ... question brought him to ... slap of reins. "Would it ... hurt." He clucked her ... way past. "Leave it to a ... woman," he said.

... SATURATED ... ALL ... noontime. They ... the utmost center of ... mattress, hitching the- ... from its edges— ... knew would not dry ... half ...

... girls were sullen and peeki... not complain, but Ca- ... their moods ... slightest provocation and ... foam. Charles was ... with his compass ... as though every ... backward footstep. ... known a man ... the moment his ... stilled. He had ... , she noticed, on the ... of the wagon, as though ... the eastward pull of ... wheel.

Caroline drew her shawl to her earlobes and exhaled down into her collar, warming her neck and the underside of her chin with the feeble cloud of warmth. Cold limned her nostrils and fingertips. All the heat she could muster had settled at the back of her throat—two little burrs of it—and these she tried to smother. What glowed inside them did not belong to the Sabbath.

This was not the sort of stillness she had craved, with every inch of her laboring to rest. The energy her body needed to resist the cold tightened her muscles until they begged to be moved. Her mind itched just as badly, piling up a stack of undone tasks: the balding fabric at Charles's elbow, the molasses piping on Laura's sleeve, the thinning heel of her own stocking. A little droplet glimmered at the tip of Laura's nose, winking in and out. The hot pinpricks in Caroline's throat gleamed brighter with every breath Laura took. How long could the child leave it dangling there? As Caroline reached for her handkerchief, Laura's mitten swiped the dribble free.

Caroline's temper tried to rear, but there was not spark enough in it to burn past the chill. "Laura, please. Use a handkerchief," she said, blotting the soiled wool. "We don't know how long it will be before I can wash these mittens again."

The scratch and hiss of a match interrupted her. Caroline and Laura both looked up. A tiny flame cored with blue lit Charles's face, then dipped into the bowl of his pipe. He puffed, then exhaled a soft column of smoke. Caroline did not protest. Behind the blaze of sulfur, the pipe's sweet smell ached of home. Charles lay back on an elbow and blew a languid ring for the girls. Laura reached up and tickled it into wisps.

"Don't, Laura," Mary said.

Charles blew one afresh, and then another. "There's one for each of you to do as you like with." Mary's floated over Caroline's head. She imagined drawing her number fourteen crochet hook through it, whisking its rims into latticed garlands—like the scalloped wrist, lying half-finished in her work basket. Its curves and lattices looped through her thoughts. She clos[illegible] and let her threadl[illegible] fing[illegible] the pattern.

"I can't sit here like t[illegible]ger," Charles said. "I[illegible] goi[illegible] see the lay of the land."

Caroline straighten[illegible]s weather?" He did n[illegible]t ans[illegible] leaned to tug on hi[illegible] dro[illegible]. She tried again. "Charles[illegible] stay in and play us [illegible] hym[illegible]ddle?"

"This kind of weath[illegible] the fiddle than it [illegible] for [illegible] keep it warm and dry i[illegible] Won't hold its tune anyw[illegible] would you like to fetch [illegible]cho, Half-Pint?"

"Yes, Pa!"

Caroline sat help[illegible]ess [illegible]tfulness as Laura scramble[illegible] past her. He knew Lau[illegible]t refuse, just as he knew [illegible] herself would not contr[illegible] tell Laura to stay p[illegible].

"Here, Pa," Laura sai[illegible] was nearer. She thanked La[illegible] lifted the poncho from [illegible]ched arms. Moisture still c[illegible] sweat to its shoulders.

"It's wet yet from las[illegible] told Charles.

Charles took the pon[illegible]. "I've got enough impatien[illegible] ing in me to dry it from [illegible]ut," he said as he threaded [illegible] through.

Impatience—the ver[illegible]y had not lost a minute of [illegible] Mired or not, they wou[illegible]ted early and spent this day [illegible]r the Sabbath. Ye[illegible] he [illegible] himself out into the weath[illegible] clothes soggy as day-old [illegible]—as though they had not p[illegible] our hundred miles behi[illegible]ess than two months' time.

"It's Sunday, Charles," [illegible]ed him.

"It's not work, Carolin[illegible]ed his collar up to meet th[illegible] of his hat. "Taking a walk[illegible]k the fourth command[illegible]

Caroline's lips flitted [illegible]. A tart *Whatever you think* [illegible] might give him pause if [illegible]her words just so. But the[illegible] not room in the wagon f[illegible]y at each other this way.

Sunday, and with the girls underfoot. Better to have him doused and satisfied than dry and sullen in such small quarters. Caroline balled her fists inside her pockets and said only, "Be careful."

He took his gun from the hook and ducked around the gray blanket. The wagon jerked like a slammed door as he jumped to the ground.

Caroline followed to tie the cover down behind him, then paused a moment behind the blanket-curtain. The muscles lining her backbone and the spaces between her ribs were weary of bracing against the tilt. Lately when she tired it was a bubbling sort of exhaustion, as though her muscles and joints were stewing in ammonia. She arched her back and spread her arms wide. The fringe of her shawl brushed the sidewalls. Caroline yanked her hands right back. Not even the canvas could leave her be.

Caroline unlocked her jaw and rolled it from side to side so that her ears crackled. One long inhale, then another, chilled her mouth before she went back around the blanket and over the spring seat to the girls.

Their faces as she settled down beside them plainly said, *Well?*

Caroline's jaw bulged anew. Why must they always *do* and never simply *be*? Charles might have his solitary tramp, but there would be no respite for her. The children were like little tops that must be kept spinning, always spinning. And on Sunday they must spin slowly, quietly, without tipping.

"Why won't the thunder stop?" Mary asked. "It makes my ears tired."

"You must not complain," Caroline retorted. Vinegar flavored her voice, and she knew by Mary's sour look that she had tasted it, too. Caroline pulled another cooling breath across her tongue. If she were going to let her vexation flare outward, she would have done better to put her foot down with Charles than singe the girls. Then at least it would have served some purpose. Nor could she simply swallow her ire and leave the child beneath her apron to pickle in such brine. She had charge over their moods, and she would not squander it.

Caroline tuned herself to the rumble of sounds from outside and began [illegible] Charles had been [illegible] ining the [illegible]

"That is [illegible]," he explained. "There is [illegible] nearby. I shouldn't [illegible] rain has flooded it."

[illegible] they lay down [illegible] ed at her [illegible] the row of jet buttons [illegible] Caroline's [illegible] them the story of [illegible]

"[illegible]," Laura droned. "Pa [illegible] Beth, and Mary [illegible]

"[illegible] boy, to make it right."

"[illegible]"

Mary [illegible] glared at Laura. "I don't [illegible] boy."

"You can [illegible] Adam, so you have to [illegible]

Mary [illegible]

Caroline [illegible] Everything pressed [illegible] canvas [illegible] leaning on either side [illegible] child motion [illegible] belly. If she didn't get [illegible] it, even [illegible] would vanish under the [illegible]

"I am going [illegible] my necessaries," she said [illegible] shawl over her head [illegible] reluctantly before [illegible] seat. It would be [illegible]. "Do either of you [illegible]"

Laura [illegible] Mary seemed to consider [illegible] Caroline silently [illegible]

"Not now," [illegible] decided.

"Very well. [illegible] here until I come [illegible]."

Caroline [illegible] from the handle [illegible] and hunched [illegible] The rain fell straight [illegible] the sky. [illegible] tongue, she lowered [illegible] she were [illegible] water. The mud enveloped [illegible] Step by step, [illegible] through the [illegible] the tarpaulin.

The [illegible] depression, less th [illegible]

skirts clutched in one fist, she bailed a bucketful of rainwater from it, then straddled the hole.

Ben and Beth eyed her. Their fetlocks were curled and pointed with mud. She was near enough to Ben to touch the steam from his nostrils. It did not seem fair that she should foul the horses' ground, but that could not be helped. Caroline turned her head and let go her water. It made no sound over the unfaltering beat of rain.

The moment she sat down on the spring seat the girls peeped around the gray blanket and watched her peel off her shoes. Her stockings had kept dry, but her shoelaces were so caked they must be put to soak before they stiffened into twigs. There was nothing to do for the shoes themselves but wait for them to dry enough to scrape clean.

"Your shawl's dripping, Ma," Mary said.

"I shouldn't wonder," Caroline answered. She swung herself out from under it. An arc of brown droplets struck the floor. More mud. At least she had kept her second-best skirt clean, Caroline thought as she flopped the muddied fringe out into the rain to rinse, then strung the shawl across Charles's gun hooks to drip dry.

Colder now than she had been before, Caroline sat down on the straw tick and pulled a quilt over her shoulders. Again the girls served her those expectant looks. This time Caroline refused to meet their gaze, looking instead to the diamond-patterned mesh of the shawl hanging behind their heads.

It shamed her to realize that the rain had not put out that spark of selfish ire. In her own way she was no less impatient than Charles—only better able to hold herself outwardly still. How childish, to think herself above him rather than admit her envy that he could escape. Caroline let her eyes rest on Mary and Laura. Of the four of them, only the girls had acted their age, bearing the day's trials with as much grace as could be expected from such young children. They deserved something of a treat.

Caroline reached for the work basket and cut a length of red worsted. She tied its ends together and strung the yarn over her hands.

"Oh, Ma!" Laura clapped. "Can we [illegible] cradle on Sunday?"

"[illegible] Laura. And no, you may [illegible]. [illegible] watch, girls, and listen." [illegible] dipped in and out of the loops [illegible] over the strings like a [illegible]. It had been years since she [illegible] figure, but the pattern [illegible] like a childhood tune.

As she [illegible] the string, she told the girls the story of Jacob, who slept [illegible] for his pillow, and dreamed of a ladder filled with angels [illegible] and descending from heaven.

"[illegible] whiskers," Mary said when Caroline [illegible] the middle of the [illegible].

"[illegible] not interrupt, Mary."

[illegible] flourish Caroline twisted [illegible] and Jacob's ladder [illegible] a mosaic of red triangles [illegible] her hands. The girls' [illegible] popped open in delight.

In their moment of wonder Caroline said, "And, behold, I am [illegible], and will keep thee in all places whither thou goest, and will [illegible] again into this land; for I will not leave thee, until I have done [illegible] I have spoken to thee of. And Jacob awaked out of his sleep, [illegible] 'Surely the Lord is in this place; and I knew it not.'" Her [illegible] as she said the words. [illegible]

[illegible] her gaze lift to the arch [illegible] bows framing her [illegible]. The rain still fell and [illegible] beyond a creek still [illegible] warm shiver fanned across [illegible] down her arms.

"[illegible], Ma, please," Laura begged.

[illegible] listened. Had the girls felt [illegible]? But Laura was looking [illegible]. Caroline smiled and shook her head. To do it again [illegible] into play. "But if you want [illegible] what's special about a [illegible]," she conceded, "I will show you how to make one from the [illegible]."

"[illegible] laid her baby in the manger," [illegible] clapped.

"[illegible] smart girl," Caroline said.

THEY WERE TAKING turns with the yarn when Charles climbed inside and stood dripping in the space before the spring seat as though it were a porch. Water rained from his hem into a ring on the floor.

"Creek's about half a mile from here," he said. He took his hat by the crown and flapped it. An arc of droplets spattered the canvas wall. "Flooded so high I can't even tell where the blasted banks ought to be."

"Charles, please," Caroline said, her hand at his elbow. She could not have his oath fraying the peace she had somehow spun out of this day.

"I know it. And I'm sorry, Caroline." He dropped his hat onto the spring seat and flopped down beside it. "But we're stuck here and that creek is only the half of it. There isn't but a hand's breadth of daylight between the mud and the front axle." Great clods of mud rolled from his boots as he shucked them off. "Ben and Beth can't hardly lift their own feet, much less pull. This ground'll rust their shoes and rot their hooves if we leave them standing, even if we empty the whole straw tick under them."

She looked at the limp socks slouching past the ends of his toes. "Are your feet dry?"

"I haven't the foggiest. I'm too wet everywhere else to know the difference." Beneath the poncho's seams his shirt and pants were dyed dark with streaks of wet.

She pulled a pair of his winter socks from the carpetbag. "Here. They're not clean, but they're dry. For now, at least." Charles took them without a word.

Though his mood was no brighter, all the sharpness had gone from it. He was only cold and wet and disappointed. Caroline watched him pull the socks from his wrinkled white toes, and all her sympathy reached for him. If her shawl were dry, she would have liked to drape it around his shoulders. The quilts would do just as well for warmth, but they would not enfold him in the same way. Instead she finger-combed the fringe of damp whiskers away from his neck.

"You were right, Caroli[illegible] [illegible] shaking off a shiver. [illegible] hou[illegible] h[illegible] gone out."

"Just so you're here, Ch[illegible] [illegible] clothed, blotting his [illegible] lar[illegible] a[illegible] wel. "I only wish I cou[illegible] [illegible] a hot meal for you." [illegible] e ga[illegible] l[illegible] ing thought to heating [illegible] [illegible] lantern for tea.

"[illegible] l warm soon enough, [illegible] [illegible] ain can't reach me." [illegible] e loo[illegible] it[illegible] le girls stringing yarn [illegible] [illegible] gers and cocked an [illegible] bro[illegible] [illegible] line. She only smiled a[illegible] [illegible] toward them. "Tell P[illegible] ha[illegible] [illegible] ed from that yarn toda[illegible]

"While Mary and Laura to[illegible] [illegible] out the manger and [illegible] lad[illegible] [illegible] line considered the pro[illegible] [illegible] the cornbread ran [illegible] t i[illegible] [illegible] occurred to her that nea[illegible] [illegible] food they carried, [illegible] om[illegible] [illegible] pork to the flour, was ra[illegible] [illegible] sixty-odd dollars [illegible] ing[illegible] [illegible] box, they could not aff[illegible] [illegible] making whole meal[illegible] cra[illegible] [illegible] cheese, and dried apples [illegible] [illegible] nough flour to fill a [illegible] shba[illegible] [illegible] more water than she cou[illegible] [illegible] she could not bake [illegible] mu[illegible] [illegible] umb. As a child, she co[illegible] [illegible] imagined such a cor[illegible] dri[illegible] [illegible] had been want back h[illegible] [illegible] the spare times in [illegible] onc[illegible] [illegible] was many a day witho[illegible] [illegible] better than breadc[illegible] nbs[illegible] [illegible] sugar water—but neve[illegible] [illegible] had she gone withou[illegible] r ne[illegible] [illegible] a cookfire.

Caroline tied on her apron [illegible] as though the garm[illegible] its[illegible] [illegible] tell her what to do. If [illegible] [illegible] ould speak, it woul[illegible] sure[illegible] [illegible] her mother's voice. She [illegible] [illegible] Ma would think t[illegible] ee h[illegible] [illegible] stock-still among sac[illegible] [illegible] thinking she had [illegible] thir[illegible] [illegible] Ma, who had fed a w[illegible] [illegible] of children, sometim[illegible] dow[illegible] [illegible] last pinch of dust from [illegible] [illegible] rel. Her mother wo[illegible] hav[illegible] [illegible] joy to see crates half [illegible] [illegible] pork and bacon, [illegible] onl[illegible] [illegible] mouths to fill—just as sh[illegible] [illegible] the stranger who [illegible] e ha[illegible] [illegible] of flour on credit. Ca[illegible] [illegible] nger recollected his [illegible], b[illegible] [illegible] el stood like an altar [illegible] [illegible] ery. All of them ha[illegible] kne[illegible] down on the spot to thank Providence for it; she could still feel the kitchen floorboards under her knees.

Caroline grasped the knife and carved the cheese into chunks large enough to fill their hands. They would eat it in spite of the expense, and give thanks for their plenty.

THE GIRLS NUDGED closer as she lay down beside them, seeking her warmth. Their teeth had clinked like china as they shrugged out of their coats and hoods and into their cold nightgowns. The best she could say for the sheets was that they were no wetter than anything else by the time she tucked them back over the limp ticking.

Now Caroline felt a thin layer of herself rising through the quilts to shelter her girls, as she always did when they were so near. Even when they were not seeking protection, Caroline could not help making a shield of herself between them and the world.

Their warmth was welcome, yet Caroline wished Mary and Laura could sleep in their own place, that it could be Charles alongside her instead. With Charles she could release that motherly hovering and settle fully into herself—and into him. To lie fitted side by side, bolstering one another without a word. That was all she wanted. Even after ten years of wedlock, Charles treated her touch, her very presence, as something he must earn. When she could give to him unasked, his deference became a gift to both of them. It would do them both a world of good after such a day as this had been. A man so chilled and stymied should not have to huddle alone on the floor. Yet tonight they must be *Pa* and *Ma,* not *Mr. and Mrs. Ingalls.*

Ten

"PACK UP a fe[illegible] f provisions, Caroli[illegible]," [illegible] through th[illegible] car[illegible] und a place to camp. [illegible] south."

Caroline [illegible] the tailgate. Some[illegible] rain had st[illegible] ghter, too, with the s[illegible] against the [illegible] enough still that she [illegible] at her colla[illegible]

"Charles[illegible] she [illegible] n't mean to leave [illegible]

"I can't s[illegible] it. Guess I'll have to [illegible] any worse [illegible] st couple nights. Just give [illegible] together a [illegible] he untied the ropes [illegible] awning. "H[illegible] asked.

"Come i[illegible] breakfast first," she i[illegible] he hoisted hi[illegible] a kiss good morning [illegible]

Caroline [illegible] dry oats into ea[illegible] kled them w[illegible]

"Like the [illegible] asked.

"Eat that [illegible] strong enough to pull [illegible] said. His ow[illegible] before Caroline sat [illegible] soon as I've [illegible] up," he said. He pull[illegible] from his poc[illegible] bedding in the big str[illegible] loft boards t[illegible]

The roar [illegible] Caroline's ear[illegible] the kitchen [illegible] essentials. Thank[illegible] not prod at her a thousand times over as the storm had. Without the rain-beat constantly delineating the canvas's perimeter, she noticed, it seemed as if the wagon had expanded overnight. She paused to consider the space around her. Cramped as it had felt the day before, the wagon would likely dwarf whatever shelter Charles was "lashing together" out in the open. Caroline's next thought pinched at her: Kansas promised Charles a boundless horizon, yet they were hardly inside the border and already her own meager territory was shrinking.

It would not be forever, she reminded herself. Only until the creek went down. In the meantime they all must have hot food and flatirons to warm their bellies and their beds.

Caroline licked her lips and released the bitter little cloud. "Selfish," she murmured, and shook her head. Always, it was selfishness that blighted her. What business did she have brooding over elbow room—as though Charles would do any less than his utmost to shelter them? As though he had ever done anything other than his level best for them.

Caroline pulled her mixing bowl and cutting board back out of the crate. She must do no less to keep them nourished in both body and spirit. If she sliced the bacon and measured out the beginnings of corn dodgers right here, dinner would be ready for the fire the moment she arrived at the camp.

In her vigor, Caroline knocked the floor through the bottom of the cornmeal sack with her enamel mug. The sound startled the girls. They came running up the aisle to peer down into it.

"Is that all we've got left?" Mary asked.

"There is another great big sack under the loft," Caroline said. That was so, but it was not full. By now it had likely thinned worse than the straw tick. Before they moved on she would have to gauge Charles's map against what remained.

Caroline tipped her bowl and brushed the meal back into the sack. She reached for Mary and Laura's tin cup and began again. Until she knew how [illegible] delay would consume, [illegible] with the smaller [illegible] much distance [illegible] to traverse.

[illegible] saleratus went into [illegible] Caroline covered it [illegible] and took stock of the [illegible] in her kitchen [illegible]

[illegible] box and the flour [illegible] than half-full. [illegible] them through when [illegible] out. And there [illegible] The time they must [illegible] let her make [illegible] beans at last. The [illegible] molasses had not [illegible], but that deprived only [illegible] At least in this [illegible] not have to worry about [illegible] up.

[illegible] another matter. She [illegible] to scrape the [illegible] the rain, and in the [illegible] stubble of mold [illegible] and mossy. Caroline [illegible] and shaved the [illegible] The salt pork had long ago [illegible] pink to a soapy [illegible] between yellow and gray [illegible] matter. Salt pork [illegible] in a pantry as in a wagon [illegible]

[illegible] cornmeal, Caroline [illegible] make do un[illegible] week without pulling [illegible] beneath the loft. [illegible] the crate with her apron [illegible] girls from the [illegible] it up, pillows and all.

[illegible] NOT count how many [illegible] Charles to ferry the [illegible] and supplies to the [illegible] horseback. Each [illegible] space inside the wagon [illegible] she hated even [illegible] leaving it. Then he [illegible] that formed [illegible]

[illegible] Charles levered them [illegible] them out while [illegible] silently folding her [illegible] again. That small [illegible] had let her mind [illegible] box into three [illegible]—one for traveling, [illegible], and one for [illegible]

Until now, they had been only paused. But with their living space dismantled and their things strewn between the wagon and the campsite, the sense that they were stranded rushed in to fill the empty places.

Only one thing appeared unmoved—her trunk, standing off to one side. The moment her gaze fell across it Caroline steadied. She had not seen it in weeks.

Caroline waded through the sacks to spread a hand over the peak of its belly. A picture of what lay inside built itself layer by layer in her memory. Everything rich and fine and delicate, all of it sleeping beneath her palm—untouched since Wisconsin.

"Mary, hand me my work basket, please." With one hand still on the lid, Caroline fished into the compartment that held her steel crochet hooks and pulled out the key to her trunk. There was no reason to open it, except that she wanted to. Caroline turned the key and lifted the lid no wider than a slice of bread. The smell of newsprint, dry and crackling, met her nose. Caroline inhaled softly. That reassuring scent and all the others behind it unfurled into her lungs. It was like stepping back across her own threshold—*home,* packed tight and snug and waiting.

There was no more she needed to take from the trunk than that. Caroline latched the lid and slipped the key into her pocket.

"Aren't you going to put the curtain in?" Mary asked.

"It would not fit," Caroline said.

"You didn't try," Laura said.

"You must not contradict, Laura," Caroline said as she lifted the girls onto the lid. She stood by a moment, held by their upturned faces. It made such a pretty picture—all the precious little things she loved best in the world, stacked together.

"IT'S NOT FAR, but the first half mile isn't fit for you and the girls to walk," Charles explained. "Ground down here's so waterlogged it'll swallow you to the knees if you step in the wrong places." He lifted one [illegible] to show the sl[illegible] [illegible] his calf. "Ben and [illegible] back and forth en[illegible] the shallowest route [illegible] [illegible]d. If you ride wi[illegible] [illegible] both horses and [illegible] [illegible] on my arm."

[illegible], Pa," Laura [illegible] [illegible] carried."

[illegible]ura, be still," Ca[illegible] [illegible] not care for Cha[illegible] [illegible] more than Laura d[illegible] [illegible] that matter, who sil[illegible] [illegible]ed her reluct[illegible] [illegible] of her mitten. [illegible] [illegible]zed back, disg[illegible] [illegible] as reassurance.

[illegible]ere was no other [illegible] [illegible] out one saddle, [illegible] [illegible] ride Beth astr[illegible]de [illegible] [illegible]ing hold of both [illegible] [illegible]ddle horn. She lif[illegible] [illegible] leveled her chin. If [illegible] must be done, th[illegible] [illegible]it.

[illegible]roline let go o[illegible] M[illegible] [illegible] up the front of [illegible] [illegible]ng to a wago[illegible] b[illegible] [illegible] right foot for th[illegible] [illegible] her heel snug[illegible] [illegible] loop she eased he[illegible] [illegible] back. The horse'[illegible] [illegible] wide wedge of spac[illegible] [illegible]ees. Caroline's [illegible]

[illegible] right?" Charl[illegible]

[illegible]roline nodded, an[illegible] [illegible] Mary into her lap. H[illegible] [illegible] knuckles turne[illegible] pa[illegible] [illegible] the saddle horn.

[illegible]roline put her [illegible] [illegible]t. Her other han[illegible] [illegible] saddle horn. Wi[illegible] [illegible] hugged Beth's flanks, [illegible] [illegible]ighs against M[illegible]ry.

[illegible]h's not going [illegible] [illegible] Charles warned both [illegible] may lurch and [illegible] [illegible]." He caught Carol[illegible] [illegible]ldn't put eith[illegible]er [illegible] if I didn't trust [illegible] [illegible] not. She knew hi[illegible] [illegible] know that. Still, he[illegible] [illegible]ased her mind eve[illegible] [illegible] her grip. "You be [illegible]

[illegible]ld fast," he sai[illegible] to M[illegible]

[illegible]y nodded, hu[illegible]dli[illegible] [illegible] handhold.

[illegible]arles crooked his a[illegible] [illegible] Laura. "Climb on, H[illegible]

"Please, Pa?" Laura asked, looking longingly at Beth. "I won't be scared."

"Makes no nevermind who's scared and who isn't. I can't lead Ben and Beth and carry more than a little half-pint of sweet cider half drunk up."

Laura obliged. Charles shouldered the tailgate back into place and cinched down the canvas one-handed before clucking the horses forward. Beth began to walk, her careful gait rocking Caroline from the hips.

Behind them the wagon stood beached like a small ark. Caroline wished she could have sewn a keyhole or a latch string into its cover. Anyone who happened by might untie the ropes and see plain as plain what they carried. All that remained of their provisions, her trunk, the fiddle. *Good heavens,* Caroline thought—the fiddle box and its secret lining of greenbacks. If anyone helped themselves to that it would leave them doubly bereft.

"Charles," Caroline called, her voice pitched high enough to stop him midstep. "The fiddle box?"

He patted his breast pocket. Caroline nodded, only partially eased. Her shawl slipped with the movement. Every step tugged it a little lower. It was not pinned high enough, but she could not let go of Mary to adjust it.

"Wait, Charles."

Caroline let go of the saddle horn to unpin her shawl, opening it wide. "Lean back into me, Mary," she said. Mary hunched her spine backward, still clinging to the saddle. Caroline put her palm to Mary's chest and hugged her gently in. "Let go now," she coaxed. "Hold on to me instead." Mary uncrimped one fist and latched it to Caroline's arm. Then the other.

Quickly Caroline swathed the long ends of the shawl around her, bundling Mary close. She anchored the knot with the pin and said, "All right, Charles."

Again h ... ’s steps. Secu ... tension le ... the terrain beg ... Mary butt ... a pair of har ... prayer.

How lo ... e last held M ... The shawl, ... l body finding ... of it carrie ... winter with M ...

Those ... re the fire, h ... doubled ... ing her and the ... familiar w ... ped around the ... new to be ... d begun to be a ... hers, and o ...

She look ... w. Such a b ... enough to ... nest of red ... *shall bind ... heaven.* She ... her cheek ... head, wishing ... hair meeti ... the rabbit-fur ... child came, ... erself, she wo ... these same ...

Somewh ... water that c ... The farther ... deeper the sa ... it be eno ... nall being w ... her, to giv ... vitality? Caro ... ness from t ... e and stirrups, ... Mary’s bac ... could sense ... weight, ... le poised ab ... more.

Carolin ... tment. Mary ... space it m ... with the so ... Not even ... ady the child ... its sisters ... Mary right th ... line consid ... calmed, and ...

ing that same calm herself. Their comfort spiraled one into the other, as it always had. From the very first, she found she could not suckle her baby girl without feeling nourished herself.

It was a kind of sorcery: What her girls believed of her, they made real, and in so doing fed back to her. Every day it happened, though never with the magnitude as it had during the storm. Their faces cried out for a refuge, steady and serene, and that is what she had become, lifted from her own doubts by the sheer force of their need.

Caroline closed her fist over Mary's bare fingers. The palpable warmth she passed into those cold little hands left her wondering: How much of what they loved in her was real, and how much was fashioned from what they envisioned her to be?

AT THE LIP of a small rise, a stand of trees cupped a plot of open ground. There Charles had fashioned an open-ended lean-to of branches and canvas. Two forked boughs stood on either side of the entrance with a third strung between them—very like the stakes and spit that held her pots over the campfire. Two more slender poles angled backward from the forks, forming supports. A tarpaulin made the roof.

Beneath it, Charles had laid the boards from the wagon loft over a crisscross of limbs to raise a floor a few inches above the spongy ground. The platform was just larger than the big straw tick.

It was as she had expected: small, sturdy, and adequate. With the time and means available, he could have built nothing more elaborate.

Charles halted the horses and looked back for her approval. His face pained her. He so wanted to please her, and this was all he had to offer.

Caroline did not have so large a thing as a smile to give in return, but she would not let him be disappointed. There was something smaller and truer she could offer.

"You've done well, Charles," she acknowledged. Saying the words broke a little path through her resignation. Again that ray of thankfulness shone out for a man who so rarely failed to furnish their needs.

[illegible]ill [illegible] ish the thought o[illegible] little thing. [illegible]Vel[illegible] ll she would do — [illegible] not live in it.

C[illegible] Laura inside the sh[illegible]lte[illegible] d up for Mary. "I'll [illegible] nd a trench for run[illegible]ff [illegible] ir comes again. [illegible]Ve[illegible] eek than the wago[illegible] won't want for [illegible]ate[illegible]

T[illegible] t Caroline could hea[illegible] th[illegible] ning louder yet [illegible]an[illegible] h[illegible] ounds of it she m[illegible] fy every bucket [illegible]ith [illegible] i[illegible] e filtered water b[illegible] fit for drinking [illegible] put that task to [illegible] mind. The tea [illegible]us[illegible] w, and she needed [illegible] bacon and corn [illegible]dg[illegible]

C[illegible] h[illegible] re so high, the sou[illegible] was like horses [illegible]allo[illegible] a[illegible] w pages from the [illegible]ack [illegible] her journal for [illegible]ndl[illegible] t[illegible] The flames roast[illegible] eeks deliciously [illegible]nti[illegible] s a potato skin. H[illegible]ow[illegible] relish a potato! [illegible]irst [illegible] ing through the sk[illegible]n, [illegible] into the pow- [illegible]ery [illegible] t as steam turned [illegible] lid[illegible] the world filled [illegible]cc[illegible] tato. She could fea[illegible] al[illegible] ted potatoes— [illegible]ota[illegible] lices of white bre[illegible] butter. Perhaps [illegible]ven [illegible] milk, hot from th[illegible] meal would be [illegible]elv[illegible] g after all these wee[illegible] cornmeal.

C[illegible] h grumbled at her, a[illegible] work. She fried [illegible]aco[illegible] ling. Hot pinprick[illegible] o[illegible] her hands, and [illegible]e [illegible] f[illegible] n them. The iron s[illegible]ide[illegible] e spooned corn [illegible]dg[illegible] pings. Her mouth w[illegible]ate[illegible] s she craved the [illegible]ee[illegible] her mind, she cou[illegible] of her imagined [illegible]ast[illegible] ls and sounds befo[illegible]

I[illegible] ng the food she ste[illegible]pe[illegible] mugs of tea for [illegible]ers[illegible] Each golden swa[illegible]ow[illegible] throat with its [illegible]arr[illegible] nd Laura there w[illegible] plain hot water. [illegible]lle[illegible] he kettle their tin cup[illegible] their hands as well as their mouths, so they squatted patiently beside it and took turns blowing ripples across the steaming surface. Such good girls. Caroline wished again for milk, to cool their cup and treat them to cambric tea.

It did no good to warn them of the bacon, nor Charles. Sparkling hot, the strips of meat branded their mouths and salved their chapped lips with fat. Mary and Laura grinned at each other as their tongues juggled the hot meat. Caroline felt her own smile glistening as she watched. What potato, what bread could fill her as much as the sight of them all warm and dry at last? Caroline set her plate aside and stretched out her legs to toast the soles of her shoes.

"I'M LEAVING THE Colt with you and the girls," Charles told her. "Under the carpetbag. You remember how to fire it?"

Caroline nodded.

"Good. If you need me for anything in the night, fire a shot," he continued. "But don't worry if you hear the rifle before daybreak. Going to see if I can find us some fresh game."

Caroline raked the last flatiron from the coals and wrapped it in flannel for him. He pocketed the hot bundle.

"Good night," he said.

She did not reply.

Charles took her softly by the shoulders. "Caroline?"

Her eyes flickered away from his face. What might he ask that she could answer? If it were all right for him to leave them without door or walls? If she were frightened? True or false, she could not answer him. She could barely smooth the trembling from her lips. There were tears gathering uninvited, tears she could not press back alone. Before she shamed herself Caroline looped her arms under Charles's, laying her palms over his shoulder blades, and pulled herself into his chest.

His hands slid down her sides. Those broad firm hands that had once spanned her waist. Could they feel the laces at the base of her maternity corset now? As if his touch melted through the knots, her body gave [illegible] a shiver, then slackened. [illegible] pulled in a breath. Nothing [illegible] its way. Her chest fell [illegible] though from crying, but the [illegible] had gone.

Not a word passed between [illegible] stood with the crown of her [illegible] tucked under his chin. [illegible] Her chest rode his inhales [illegible] back his exhales.

[illegible] moved one hand up [illegible] the [illegible] of her neck. Caro- [illegible] heartbeat deepen as [illegible] brushed her chignon.

[illegible]," she whispered. [illegible] head to meet his gaze and [illegible] coil of her hair [illegible] palm. He kissed her [illegible] in the space between [illegible] the warm print lingered af- [illegible] had left her skin, [illegible] whatever fears might reach [illegible] the night.

[illegible] brought her palms [illegible] and gently eased herself from [illegible]

"Good night," she said.

[illegible] lifted the blanket flap [illegible] Mary and Laura lay at her [illegible] the quilt's red binding [illegible] over their noses. She knelt [illegible] of them as Charles [illegible] undressed, [illegible] her [illegible] and lay down beside th[illegible]

[illegible] SHOT woke her. [illegible] Charles came over the rise [illegible] bird dangling from [illegible] had smoothed her hair and [illegible] fee pot on.

[illegible] goose," Charles said. [illegible] straggler, it's so late in the [illegible] maybe it got caught [illegible] storm. Should I fetch the tin [illegible] from the wagon?"

[illegible] thank you, Charles. I'll [illegible] for breakfast."

[illegible] better still than the [illegible] day before, rich and fresh [illegible] with juice. A hint of [illegible] made the savory flavor [illegible] her mouth.

[illegible] lifted her drumstick [illegible] last shreds from the bone [illegible] "Look, Pa."

Caroline looked up as well, ready to address Laura's manners. Little though she was, Laura never would have flaunted her table scraps that way at home. But Charles and Laura's attention was not where Caroline expected to find it. She looked beyond the bone in Laura's fist and saw a man on a black pony emerging from the trees. Charles rose, plate in hand, as the rider approached.

Caroline sat still as a rabbit poised to run, watching. The stranger was strung together like a ladder—perfectly straight up one side and down the other. His horse was lightly built, slender through the back and face. "That your wagon down there in the dale?" the man asked.

"Certainly is," Charles said. He handed Caroline his plate and propped his fists at his hips. "This your land?"

"Nearly."

Caroline blanched at the two plates in her hands. Not only had they set up camp on another man's stake, but their mouths were half-full of his game. Quietly she stacked the dishes onto her lap and swallowed.

"We're only passing through," Charles said. "Be on our way just as soon as I can dig out and ford that creek."

The man swiped a hand through the air. "You're welcome to camp as long as you need. I heard a shot this morning and thought I ought to make sure there wasn't any trouble. The name's Jacobs," he said to Charles, then "ma'am," with a nod to Caroline and a glance that traveled down to her lap.

Caroline could not tell whether it was the plates of purloined goose or her own form that drew his attention; she was rounded enough at the navel now that anyone who chanced to look might notice. Either way, his eyes did not linger.

Charles extended his hand to Jacobs. Caroline folded her fingers inside her palms to hide the lines of grime under her nails. "Ingalls," Charles said. "Headed down into Montgomery County."

"Looks like you've come a distance already."

Caroline would have liked to whisk a sheet over the camp at that.

Anyone wou th t g bonds, with their ha ke

and sogg y wr s the tarpaulin ropes. T is r

black beard t m r nd neat it lay flat as o

first tim she not C arles's hair had grow

own nec k it f it had strayed into h co

"Left Pepi Co in, nearly five weeks ag

"That so?" is attention was on B

line marked them. If he had looke at h

she wou d no hav a gentleman. "Fire,

got there," t

"That the are"

Jacobs ve ure t is, I've been on he

pair of draft or and a half years in

section east mption filed on this one.

section, $5.

Char les g the price—better t

they hoped pa

Jacobs no dec. w it. One fine crop w

arm's re ach pa t at is, if I can clear enc

in time I w ider a trade?"

Charles g . She said nothing. "

on your off"

Jaco s lo s horse, then back to Ch rle

in a differe measured Ben and Be

much longe t, she would be com

stand besid her I offer my matched pair

cobs said at her twin sister."

Car line y. Where Ben's and B

outwar d, all and sleek. Not m

teen h nds stance that belied h

so brig ht a bl g at her gave Caro in

"Th oth this summer, so the

bargain," Jacobs went on. "I've had a look over your wagon, and there's nothing in there the pair of them can't pull as far as the Territory."

Had he inspected the wagon with the same intensity that he scrutinized everything else? Caroline did not like to think so.

"Guess there's no harm in going for a look," Charles said.

"WHEN WILL WE have dinner, Ma?" Laura wondered again. She had been promised dumplings and gravy, and though breakfast still filled her belly, her mind was already hungry with the thought.

"Not until after Pa comes back," Caroline answered. She laid her dish towel over the iron spider to keep the flies from the drippings. The plates were wiped and the camp tidied, and still he had not returned. A pot filled with the remains of the goose simmered at the edge of the fire.

Caroline brushed her hands on her apron. The calico was tacky with the week's grime. More than a week. Here it was already Tuesday—another washing day come and gone—and she could not leave the girls alone with the fire to haul water for laundry. And there would be no mending, for her work basket was down in the wagon. There was not a lick of work she could do until Charles returned. Yet she could not sit idle. If she did not busy her hands somehow, her thoughts would begin to chase in circles. Charles had not been gone long, not really, but he had already taken more than enough time to ride half a mile and see a horse.

Beth nickered and tugged at her picket pin. Caroline went to her and reached up to rub the long white blaze on her forehead. "Easy now, Beth," she said. "They'll come back. Your Ben and my Charles, they always come back." Beth shook her head, tinkling the iron ring on her picket pin. Caroline rubbed Beth's nose and scratched under her chin. She had not known Beth to be nervous before. She half wondered whether the animal could sense what Charles was contemplating on his errand.

"...a, don't," Mary s[illegible] ...aroline turned. Laura ha[illegible] ...stick from the kin[illegible] ...on the ground. "You'll ge[illegible] ..."

...ine looked at Laura's [illegible] ...ggles and zigzags and he[illegible] ...lightened. "Mary and [illegible] ...," "how would you lik[illegible] ...to write your names?"

...'s nose gave a dub[illegible] "In the dirt?" she asked.

...only a single b[illegible] ...Caroline did not [illegible] ...itled to that. Fe[illegible] ...if she said so, but such a ...child was not always [illegible] What did Mary expect? She ...r slate nor pencil. Al[illegible] ...and paper but for Charles's ...journal were buried [illegible] ...of her trunk. Still, the[illegible] ...something she could [illegible]

...oline went to the kitche[illegible] ...opened the sack of meal. He[illegible] ...easured the scant depth[illegible] ...not be waste if it fed [illegible] ...she decided, and pulle[illegible] ...to sprinkle onto a clean [illegible] ...e

"...a dish?" Laura asked.

"...and see," Caroline s[illegible]

...h the handle of the wood[illegible] ...e traced an *L* in the grit.

"...aura," she began.

...en years had passed [illegible] ...been anyone's teacher, yet the ...of excitement it gave h[illegible] ...as ever. She had not be[illegible] ...more than a girl herself [illegible] ...Caroline remembered how the ...coax a pupil to the thres[illegible] ...standing. Then that breath... ...—waiting, watching, [illegible] ...to reach forward and gra[illegible] ...had shown Mary how [illegible] ...ear, and both of them w[illegible] ...ring a growing list of lit[illegible] ...tasks, but this was differen[illegible] ...was real learning. And th[illegible] ...own two girls.

Both of them were s[illegible] qu[illegible] ...Caroline's pride and pleas[illegible] ...ed inside her. Eac[illegible] str[illegible] ...poised for the next like the ...wobbling steps forward.

Mary frowned at her work. "I want it to look like yours, Ma."

Caroline lavished them with her best praise. "You have both done very well."

"I mean when you write letters on paper. It's prettier, all long and fine."

"Like ribbons," Laura agreed.

"Our letters look like sticks," Mary said.

"This is called printing. Once you have learned to print each letter nicely, I will teach you how to write."

"Show us, now, Ma," Mary begged. "Please."

Caroline gave the plate a shake, then drummed the underside with her fingertips to even the surface of the meal. She eased a hairpin from its nest and began to trail it across the tin, taking extra care with the flourishes and gracefully knotting the cross of each *t*.

> Dear Ma and Papa Frederick,
> The girls have asked me to write a few lines. Though these words will not reach you, I hope that you are well and not worrying yourselves on our account.

Beth whinnied, and there was Charles coming up over the rise. A bulging flour sack rode on his back as though he were Santa Claus. Suddenly self-conscious of what she was doing, Caroline shook her letter from the plate and quickly threaded her hairpin back into place. "Well, Charles?" she asked before he had one foot out of the stirrups.

He swung down from the saddle and tossed the sack into the shelter. "Straw," he said. "Jacobs spared us some for the tick."

"Charles! You didn't ask him for such a thing?"

"Pshaw. You know me better than that. He offered. Said he'd seen the straw on the ground by the wagon and figured we'd have use for some fresh."

Caroline did not know how to greet this news. She could not fault the ... generosity, but there seemed ... about them that ... escape ... 's notice. If they must ... wished he would ... do ... of leaving something ...

... good piece of land up here ... squatting ... inside the bake oven ... its to trade. ... The ... many trees to clear ... stumps any- ... thi... be out of the Big ... should have ... an... ff."

... ?" Caroline prodded softly ...

... fine-looking pair ... were woven ... out ... the way he keeps them ... so eager to ... get ... started on his acreage ... both teams ... down."

... generosity. It was ... almost too close ... to ... nothing in her wanted to ... give herself a ... the decision in her ... as though it's ... proposal," she allowed. ... and Beth how ... own claim?"

... the fading Montgomery ... bill from his ... passed it to her. Its corners ... wear. "Wide ... Dollar and ... Quarter ... ted. "Where ... won't need draft horses ... Anyhow, place ... flooded with folks coming ... long. Plenty ... to trade for a bigger team ... n't up to the ... 'll save us a week's work ... some. Mus- ... like draft horses. They'll ... grazing, and ... barn. I can't think ... refuse."

... us. Charles—"

... how he can. A thief has ... if he wants to ... law. Man's got a ... a one of them ... cod. There's a spanking ... and a pair of ... the kitchen. That ... ched into his coat pocket and pulled out a bundle made of a blue-checked napkin. "Mrs. Jacobs sent a fresh baking of light biscuits."

They were warm yet. Caroline untied the corners of the cloth. A moist, yeasty cloud filled her nose. "My land," Caroline said. She sat slowly down on the spring seat and tapped the golden bottom of one biscuit with her fingernail. The light hollow sound set her mouth swimming.

"There's just something about them, Caroline," Charles continued. "I know Ben and Beth'll pull us anywhere I point them, but this pair seems to *want* to move. Their feet are as itchy as mine." The spark in his eyes told her the deal was as good as done, but still he looked at her, asking.

Caroline chalked out her thoughts one last time. Aside from bumping into her pride, Jacobs himself had done nothing to arouse ill ease. That alone was not ample reason to doubt him at his word. Yet it did not seem prudent to entrust their team to a perfect stranger with nothing to back his end of the trade. Caroline drew a breath to speak, and the scent of the warm bread in her lap beckoned to something beyond prudence.

"If you think it's best for all of us to trade, well then, we'll trade," she consented.

Charles slapped his knees and sprang up. "I'll take Ben and Beth over to Jacobs's place right this minute. Do them both a world of good to be under a solid roof for a while."

Laura trotted alongside Charles to Beth's picket pin. "Where are Ben and Beth going?" she asked.

"They're going to stay with Mr. Jacobs's horses in his stable."

"What about us?" Mary wanted to know.

"We're going to wait right here until the creek goes down and the mud dries up."

"I'd rather stay in a stable than any old hut."

Caroline's voice whipped out sharp. "Mary!"

...rupted. "Jacobs did offer ..." He spoke low and ... talked to the horse— ... herself spoke when ... to moderate his voice ...

... much. She gentled her ... her sentiment. "W... sleep in the hay ... has made us a good ... here."

... stayed in a stable," Mary ... and her baby, too."

... up her hand. "Mercy ... at Charles's coattails ... to see his ladder.

...

... Half Pint?"

...er."

... great laugh rang out ... As quickly as she ... Mary, Caroline put ... Try as she might ... close, she felt her ... into her cheeks. It ... Providence were walking ... is a mister," Mary ... didn't have misters ...

... call him mister," Laura ... shoes, and Charles ...

... shook her head. C... their notions. What ... le—Mary, with the ... and straight as hems, ... a tangle of fancies. ... of them Caroline ... find her footing ...

... brushed her collar ... slipped down to her ... smile turned over ... She looked for ... when without a song ...

... right, Laura," Caroline ... I'm pleased to see you ... your Bible stories ...

... up. Caroline nodded ... truly, that nod said ... Laura's smile, and ... at the power these ... her to render th...

THE CREEK NEEDED only a few days to calm; the soggy ground lingered for a week. One solid week they were neither wet nor cold nor moving. Every day Charles dug at the mired wheels. Every evening Caroline soaked and scrubbed his mud-stiffened trouser legs in buckets by the fire. For a day or two Caroline reveled in the motionlessness, then the camp blurred like the road—all bean porridge, backache, and lye.

Not one thing in the camp, not the bed, the cookware, nor the spring seat, stood taller than knee high. The wagon's low cover had only made her imagine she was forever stooping. Out here, her body quickly informed her of the difference. Caroline did not allow herself to complain in words the girls might hear, but her hunched and crouching muscles cursed freely.

By the time Charles declared they would strike camp the following morning, Caroline was ready to welcome road and wagon both. Their drawers and socks were clean, if dingy from the creek water, and she had gotten ahead of the mending. She had nothing else to show for it.

CAROLINE CLIMBED INTO the wagon behind Mary and Laura. Beneath her steps the boards rang out solid and even as she straightened the crates and squared the sheets over the straw tick. The clean white walls spread over her, smelling of sun-bleached cloth. Pleased, she took her seat. Up off the ground she felt lofty as a ridgepole.

"Come here, girls," she said, patting the board beside her, "and let me tie on your sunbonnets. Then we will be all ready to go when Pa comes with the horses."

Laura spotted Charles and Jacobs first, each leading one black mare down into the hollow. A brindle bulldog trotted along behind. "It's Pa!" she said.

"Those aren't Ben and Beth," Mary said. "Are they, Ma?"

"But that's Pa," Laura insisted.

"You are both right," Caroline answered. Neither was satisfied, and they peered out across the grass.

…e … nice ponies, … r. Jac… …id politely as th…
…he f…lling tong…
… ar it, Miss Ingal…," Jac… …ing one right up …
… because they're …our…
… to be addresse… so … dropped from …
… aned out over t… fr… …n tiptoe. "Lo…
… y …ies, Ma!" To C…arle… …at's their names…"
… es tossed their …eads … …eir feet, preeni…
…t—in the sun t… … …lack backs had …
…k.
… till, watching Ja…obs … …aura were allow…d
… et noses and rec… … Pet and Patty. …
… le… uche… her, made … …e. Eager as he … s
… he …ad traded … way … …and beautiful to …
… ould not hide th… loss.
… ure … the trade …d no… … girls until Cha… s
… hit…hing the … … n. For that mat…
… real to Carolin… unt… …men tightening …p
… bell… bands and … …e smaller anim…
… en and Beth?" …ary …
… ing …ere to hel… … …his fields," Char…es
… l around. "Ma? Her …
… her …ace and n… dded. … …ura looked at each
… as qu…ickly looke… straig… …oline did the sa…
… ing s…he could sa… Her … …ssed. She could …ot
… ters' faces rippl… and … …g more to see th…
… rave… than it wo…ld … …y.
… st th…e girls tha… thr… …mposure. Ben and
… sto…k, but she …nd … …d those horses …
… ad …ad Mary a…d … …r acre, mile u…on
… been a good, s… … was grateful to

them in a way she did not know how to express, and now, she realized, she would not have the chance to try. To drive away without giving them so much as a pat goodbye was nearly like leaving home all over again.

Caroline's eyelids burned. Her hand darted into her pocket and clenched her handkerchief. There had been no tears leaving Pepin. How absurd to think of crying now, over horses. Everywhere she tried to pin her gaze made the burning worse. Then her eyes found the bulldog. He was already squinting up at her, and with some suspicion. His jaw was thrust out, the lower teeth denting into the upper lip like pinking shears poised to snip. The black folds of his nose quivered in Caroline's direction, then he snorted, twice. He seemed vexed, as though something clouded her smell and would not let him scent her properly. He sniffed instead at Charles's ankles, then circled the wagon once, twice, three times. On the third pass Caroline heard him wetting on one of the wheels. Then he trotted back to the mustangs' heels, plunked himself down, and licked his nose.

Jacobs buckled the last mud strap and ran his hand over the mare's flank before extending it to Charles across the wagon tongue. "Good luck to you," Jacobs said. He tipped his hat to Caroline and the girls.

"And the same to you," Charles said.

Jacobs took a single step back, as though trying out the feeling of turning his team over to Charles. Charles waited, respecting the man's last opportunity to change his mind. All the heavy straps and buckles that harnessed the animals to their wagon did not matter. For as long as Jacobs cared to linger, the mustangs still belonged to him. Slowly he put his hands into his pockets, and Caroline knew his mind had made the break. Only his gaze seemed unable to let the beautiful little creatures go.

Caroline said, "The light biscuits Mrs. Jacobs sent were a treat after so much travel. Please thank her for us."

Jacobs turned his face gratefully up to her. "I'll do that, Mrs. Inalls." He gave a [illegible] nal, then turned and [illegible] astward.

The bulldog [illegible] sat completely un[illegible] ng Jacobs go.

Charles climb[illegible] pring seat and still [illegible] udge. "Charles," [illegible]

Charles called [illegible] o whistle for your dog?"

Jacobs half tu[illegible] ng away as he spoke. [illegible] vants to follow [illegible] Otherwise, he's all y[illegible] ure that fella ba[illegible] beef. He's taken a shine to [illegible] angs like you've [illegible] ir life. I guess you could [illegible] of them were p[illegible] far as he's concerned [illegible] ponies. You and [illegible] n of them."

"That so?" Ch[illegible]

Jacobs slowed [illegible] keep from shouting [illegible] between them [illegible] a fact. He'll let me take [illegible] a time anywhere [illegible] e minute I start hitching [illegible] of them, he's w[illegible] wagon like a sentry. I [illegible] never seen the [illegible] n't want for a better [illegible] he sees you're t[illegible] e of those mustangs [illegible] stitch you've go[illegible] hildren like his own."

"What's his n[illegible] ed.

"He answers [illegible] 't think he'll much [illegible] him, so long as [illegible] es. Good luck," Jacobs [illegible] his shoulder.

Charles shrug[illegible] rruped to the mustangs [illegible] thrust forward [illegible] ed rumps rounding. W[illegible] the wagon came [illegible] umped up to level. Ch[illegible] horses sharply [illegible] heels from sinking into [illegible] bounded the bu[illegible] between the wheels to fo[illegible]

"Well I decla[illegible]," [illegible]

For a little w[illegible] olled along flat and sm[illegible] earth, then began the long climb toward the road. Caroline craned into the slope, curious how these small horses would take the load. Where Ben and Beth had only to lean ever forward to make the wagon follow, this team strove ahead, truly pulling. Caroline could see the effort of it flowing under their hides with every step. At the lip of the road the mustangs touched noses, the gesture like a wink between them, as though they knew their labor made them even more beautiful.

Charles laughed.

Caroline blushed. Perhaps she had spoken the thought aloud. "What is it?"

"I don't know," Charles said. "I just feel like laughing. Maybe it's the horses."

"They are lovely to watch," she mused.

"It's something more than that. Feel them," he said, handing her the reins.

She took the lines firmly in her hands. In only a few steps the team's eager rhythm loosened her wrists, traveling past her elbows and into her shoulders. It was like dancing, with the leather straps a line of music running from the horses into her palms. Caroline's breath lifted, light and airy, into two soft notes of laughter.

Charles grinned. "Feel it?"

Caroline nodded.

"I don't know when I've run across a finer matched pair than these," Charles said. "Tell you the truth, I don't know how we'll tell them apart after the one foals."

Caroline studied the rounded sides of the mare in front of her—the one Mary named Pet. "She can carry that colt, and the wagon, too?" she asked.

He raised an eyebrow at her.

She flushed more deeply and gave him half a smile in return. "I'm not pulling the wagon, Charles."

He laughed again and took the reins.

Eleven

KANS[illegible]

Th[illegible] lar[illegible] m[illegible], to breathe all a[illegible]

It [illegible]s [illegible] ot [illegible]id of trees, as C[illegible]ol[illegible] [illegible] from the g[illegible]nd b[illegible] ar[illegible]'s handbill. But th[illegible] im-ber d[illegible] n[illegible] la[illegible]scape as they did [illegible] ne-sota. [illegible]hey [illegible] n[illegible]m the edges of [illegible] [illegible]hey had t[illegible] n[illegible] Missouri. Here o[illegible] [illegible]ered mod[illegible]ly i[illegible] a[illegible]s along creek be[illegible] [illegible]ark the p[illegible]ces [illegible] r[illegible]wed, fringing Ca[illegible]s of gree[illegible].

Ju[illegible] g[illegible] th[illegible] prairie made her [illegible]ger, fulle[illegible] Ca[illegible] ot[illegible]own they could h[illegible] [illegible]nce. With[illegible]ut [illegible] as[illegible]lls there was not [illegible]g to fool [illegible]r [illegible] i[illegible]t some arbitrary [illegible]gh a lid h[illegible] su[illegible] f[illegible] the world. Car[illegible] see-ing [illegible] [illegible] the sensation of it [illegible] from taki[illegible] in [illegible] u[illegible] of separate pieces [illegible]tion. Clea[illegible]r, [illegible] T[illegible] world ceased to be [illegible] be-came on[illegible] [illegible]e thing.

I[illegible] [illegible]ou[illegible] [illegible] well. Always th[illegible] had come from [illegible] th[illegible] the leaves and t[illegible] Here it w[illegible]sp[illegible] h[illegible] so that its voice [illegible] the gro[illegible]d. Sh[illegible] ar[illegible]eat sweeps of it pa[illegible]ing [illegible], lift-ing [illegible]d fa[illegible] vi[illegible] breath. Here the [illegible] was visi[illegible]. Th[illegible] in[illegible]grass made it so, a[illegible] Caroline saw that the wind was not composed of one single movement—it fanned with hundreds of fingers through the tall blades all at once, stroking ruffled, swirling patterns all over the prairie.

Charles was smitten. She had not seen his face so soft with wonder since the day Laura was born, had never in her life seen him so at ease. The constant rushes of motion around them worked a kind of magic on him, appeasing the restlessness he'd always battled. Caroline herself was not sure whether he was driving more leisurely, or if the way the grass seemed to dash alongside the wagon had altered her own sense of speed.

They breasted a roll of prairie, spring green and golden. The sky was sudsy with clouds. Before them, the sun was sinking between the hills like a coin tucked into a pocket. Light melted into the hollows and dales. From where she sat high on the spring seat, Caroline fancied she could feel the very curve of the earth.

This was to be home, she told herself. This was where her child would be born. She hugged her folded hands around the small hill that was her belly. Her own roundness mirrored the abundant swells before her, making her welcome.

All her life she had been accustomed to making do with little if any to spare. *We must cut the coat to fit the cloth,* her mother had so often said, and by mimicking the careful movements of Ma's broad hands Caroline had learned well how to stretch every thin scrap of food or fabric or fuel she was given.

On this wide teeming land life could be different. She could smell it in the moist soil, feel it in the way the waving tufts of grass seemed to brush at her heart. Caroline looked again at Charles. He was aglow. Simply aglow. You could not sit beside him without feeling it. But it was in her, too. Seeing the spread of this country opened her somehow, broadened her so that it seemed her expectations stretched out not just before her, but all around her in a way she had never felt before nor could quite describe. Perhaps, she thought, this was what Charles [illegible] time back home [illegible] ward reaching. [illegible] le so often sang [illegible] hout horizons. Th[illegible] only part of him [illegible] onstricted by wall[illegible] trees.

[illegible] pathy for him [illegible] chest. So much [illegible] llen in love with [illegible] en for vibrancy a[illegible] uth been frustrat[illegible] she'd only now [illegible] and. Perhaps if sh[illegible] ind of woman, [illegible] tward more ofte[illegible] might have recog[illegible] Were she not car[illegible] s fleck of him insid[illegible] red, would she ha[illegible] it at all? Carolin[illegible] net brim aside to [illegible] s was already a fin[illegible] and could only ch[illegible] tter. Almost agains[illegible] thought rippled i[illegible] he change so full[illegible] no longer recog[illegible] ssured herself, tha[illegible] le. This place wo[illegible] but give him roo[illegible] himself. Sudden[illegible] imagine how muc[illegible] and and father he [illegible] that he would n[illegible] ing up against th[illegible] like the honeybee[illegible] o their cabin on[illegible] into exhaustion [illegible] k out through th[illegible]

[illegible] SOUTH they d[illegible] landscape opene[illegible] it opened the m[illegible] pondered its pos[illegible] as a place made f[illegible] as Charles. Farme[illegible] pper alike could [illegible] the land alone. C[illegible] surely be in hig[illegible] ng. He could defi[illegible] he liked, or no[illegible] d. If he so chose [illegible] mself to any bu[illegible] for instead of co[illegible] a livelihood piec[illegible] this lay as an in[illegible] es to reap as mu[illegible] —whether from [illegible] land itself or from those who would settle it—with nothing to hamper his reach.

Charles knew it better than she, had likely reckoned it would be this way since before they crossed the Mississippi. He was so happy it was comical, very nearly indecent. Caroline had never seen him look at her so boldly—boldly enough to make her flush to the tips of her ears and turn her head so that her bonnet hid her face from him. Only the girls in the wagon box and the baby already in her womb kept his gleeful hands from straying from the reins to the delights of her body. After a mile she chanced a peek at him and noticed that whether he was looking at her or the prairie his expression did not change. Caroline sensed then that the two of them were curiously tied in his mind. He did not know how else to show his burgeoning love for Kansas, and so he wanted to do with her what he could not do with the land.

Caroline slid closer to him, so that their hips touched. She could give him that much, at least. Pleased, he shifted the reins to one hand and with a glance that said *May I?* laced an arm around her waist. His warm palm rested softly on her flank. Caroline laid a hand over his and wished again that the child would move, for both of them.

If she bore a son, she mused to herself, what a gift that would be to all of them in this vast place. A set of footsteps to follow Charles along any path he settled on, another pair of hands to share out the labor. And if it were a daughter, what then? Her mind flipped like a coin at that. It would be harder, without her brother Henry's help, for Charles to manage a full quarter section alone, no matter how amenable the land.

Caroline blinked. She was thinking of this child as if it were a tool, an instrument to help them stake their claim. What of the child itself, the person it could become? Beyond the near certainty of blue eyes, she still could not make her mind form a picture of this baby, nor the life it might lead. Caroline felt her thoughts taking that peculiar shift backward as though she were trying to remember the child rather than imagine it. Bac[illegible] ds a[illegible]d the familiar in[illegible] her rocker befo[illegible] Sus[illegible] purring at her [illegible]t.

None of it w[illegible] y w[illegible]ld be born not [illegible] the coattails of [illegible] e w[illegible]ods, but on the [illegible] would be no c[illegible] ter[illegible] arth, no rocki[illegible] gazed out over [illegible] ass, [illegible]ying to pictu[illegible] house Charles [illegible] re [illegible] campfire, w[illegible] low calico curt[illegible] it [illegible] inside that [illegible] two, but three [illegible]

That was a [illegible] toge[illegible]er. All in one [illegible] same vastness [illegible] pro[illegible]ise for Charles [illegible] line how small [illegible] belong to her a[illegible] by comparison [illegible] of the imagined [illegible] turned edges [illegible] sharper, narr[illegible] house in the Bi[illegible] cramped, but [illegible] great dark tre[illegible] vi[illegible], Caroline und[illegible] insignificant it [illegible]

She turned [illegible] Mary and Laura, [illegible] ing on the str[illegible] place, yet, for [illegible] find room to [illegible] this—no chur[illegible] no community [illegible]f. [illegible]t even the narr[illegible] of kin.

One day, if [illegible] the land would [illegible] cultivation of [illegible] at fed more tha[illegible] then, Mary's [illegible] wo[illegible]d be confined t[illegible] than their own [illegible] them needed m[illegible] only to look at [illegible] Mar[illegible] was already t[illegible] too spirited t[illegible] tha[illegible] promise. For th[illegible] not root herse[illegible]

Caroline sa[illegible] have an educa[illegible]n."

"Hmm?" C[illegible]

"The girls [illegible]tion," she said again.

He nodded without looking away from the horizon. "That's so. Any time you judge them ready."

"Mary is nearly ready now. I hate to make her wait."

"Why wait?" And with a wink, "Seems to me you were a schoolteacher once."

It was the wink that did it. Caroline saw no room for teasing in this; the breadth of their daughters' learning could not ride on something so light as a wink. A wind rose up in her, strong enough to form a shout. For a moment Caroline could not think sensibly. It was all she could do to grip the rush of anger and rein it back. She would not let it go racing out at him. Her body went stock-still with the effort of speaking quietly. "Two terms, Charles. I taught just two terms and then I was married. That's been better than ten years ago. Mary and Laura will have more capable instruction than that."

She could hear the muscled quiver in her voice. It pulled Charles's eyes from the scenery and his arm from her waist. She felt the hard set of her face as his eyes met hers, saw it bewilder him so rapidly that he nearly looked hurt. "I've never known you to be incapable of anything," he said.

Caroline sat dumb. A compliment. Of course. He had no end of them—if not completely true then always sincere. Usually it was the sincerity that disarmed her.

Not this time. Yes, she could teach them all she knew, but her learning was a decade old. She would not let her own limits be imposed upon their daughters.

"Promise me, Charles," she said. "No matter where we settle, Mary and Laura will have a formal education."

He slowed the mustangs to study her. She watched the small muscles around his eyes contracting as he searched for something that would tell him what he had done to light such a flare between them. When he spoke the words were stripped bare. "Caroline, I swear to you—"

Caroline's breath hissed back from the word. Even this was not wo ... ith ... "Please, Charl... said. "C...

"... ur ...ildren will have ... broke her ... to sweep his eye ... "All of ...

... "All right," she said, ... own aga...

... and changed ... she mig... last thrash of ... that, and ... Grateful. Reli... proud. ... little flick and ... Caroline wa... to carry them ahead, ... then croo... the crease of his elbo... steady hers... apologize. He ... side, forg...

NEXT D... as ever. Caroline ... that she ... and to find limits ... A pale ... years, she thought ... that left ... the bottom of the ... it was ... Never mind that she ... to climb... She still could not lo... with ... it could satisfy ... like Char... everything the world ... until the ... That alone was ... his grow... arred by want.

Sh... grudge him his ... little like ... beside him with ... as the ra... Beautiful as it was, ... in the sa... the more he f... Caroline ...

W... nonsensical, she scolded ... been

taken from her. Nothing tangible would be denied her. Yet it pinched ever so slightly to watch Charles unfurling like a beanstalk beside her, knowing that Kansas offered her no similar satisfaction, no chance to reach beyond what she had been for the last ten years: *Mrs. Ingalls, Ma.* She could stretch forever toward that horizon and grasp nothing new.

As if it had grown out of her thoughts, a dull ache meandered across her right side and descended into her belly. Caroline followed it with the heel of her hand, but the narrow cord of pain was too deep to reach. The only part of her that could be counted on to expand in this place was her womb, she thought, and even that was half Charles's doing.

Caroline moved to fold her hands together again and found her left had formed a fist in her lap. She had fairly balled herself up with envy. Envy, of all things, when everything they shared was bound to increase. And after she had vowed in the bunkhouse that first night to do all she could to keep her family worthy of Providence's care. She wiped the damp palm across her skirt, uncrossed and recrossed her ankles. It helped some to break that selfish thought up and brush it away, but she did not know what to do with her hands, did not like the empty feel of them, or trust them not to clench up again. They needed something of their own to hold besides themselves, the way Charles had his reins and the girls their playthings. But what? She did not want to sit there with a wooden spoon or a skein of yarn in her lap. Her books and slate came first to mind, but they lay at the very bottom of her trunk, and anyway, she was not a teacher anymore and never would be again. Perhaps if she had never taught school, Caroline thought, never held an envelope filled with dollar bills she had earned herself, she would not feel so empty-handed now. Not even Mary or Laura would fill that space in the way she wanted.

Seeds. The little packets of seeds she had saved from the garden, and Polly's, too. Those belonged to her in a way that nothing else inside the wagon did. Only she could not very well go digging through the crates to find them now. There was no call for it, no way to explain [illegible] wanted them. The be[illegible] sh[illegible] in out the handfu[illegible] [illegible] envelopes in her [illegible] how the seeds fo[illegible] [illegible] would feel thro[illegible] Th[illegible] were the wink[illegible] [illegible] that were turnips [illegible] the cucumbers, [illegible] and onions with their [illegible] the flat squash see[illegible] [illegible] fingernails; the tiny [illegible]. They had reach[illegible] [illegible] the Wisconsin ground an[illegible] spring she would work the [illegible] Kansas soil so they c[illegible] [illegible] lacy tendrils, fi[illegible] [illegible] finest crochet thread, [illegible] through the dirt u[illegible] [illegible] something to grasp [illegible] firm. Seeds alwa[illegible] [illegible] down before reaching [illegible]

[illegible] was comfort in that.

Twelve

THE WILLOWS ALONG the Verdigris River traced a soft green line over the prairie. Their trunks were slender, and their young leaves not thick enough yet to provide much shade. Through the haze of yellow-green, Caroline could make out the tops of a few dozen haystacks on the opposite bank. They seemed to stand in crooked rows and squares.

"Must be the outskirts of Independence," Charles said.

Town. Caroline's heart began to patter.

Laura pulled herself up by the back of the spring seat. "Where, Pa?"

Like Laura, Caroline wanted to stand up in her seat to see this town, this place so fresh it had not earned itself a spot of ink on the map. Caroline had only half believed it would be here at all. She took hold of the outermost wagon bow and stretched her tired back out long and tall, tipping her chin toward the horizon. The smell of the river skimmed past her nostrils, a clean, silvery scent.

Somewhere just beyond the river were people, supplies, news. Perhaps, Caroline thought breathlessly before she could help herself, perhaps a letter. There had been waysides and whistle stops all along the road, but all that had mattered about them was how much they charged for feed, or how many miles' travel they signified.

"This is the last town before the Indian Territory?" Caroline asked.

"So far as I can tell. Map's no help for that anymore. I expect it'll be the last town between us and the Territory, anyway," Charles said.

She had known the answer before asking. Today or tomorrow they would drive past the rim of the nation. No matter how far beyond Charles drove, this town would belong to them, and they to it, and so

Caroline was anxi[illegible]us t[illegible] [illegible] what kind of a place it wa[illegible], [illegible] of people inh[illegible]bite[illegible] it. [illegible] the wagon bow anothe[illegible] ge[illegible] craning as far as s[illegible]e [illegible] those haystacks with[illegible] her impatienc[illegible]. Th[illegible] she [illegible]ld not mind strange fa[illegible]es [illegible] her. What wo[illegible]ld they se[illegible] [illegible]e wondered, what wo[illegible]ld the [illegible] of Independen[illegible]ce e[illegible]pect [illegible] come to claim a q[illegible]rter [illegible] with her husb[illegible]nd? Perha[illegible] [illegible]ld surprise them. Perha[illegible]s [illegible] surprise herse[illegible]f.

The Verdig[illegible]is w[illegible]s [illegible] lap at the undersid[illegible] of the [illegible] bed, but calm [illegible] [illegible] the river easily. With [illegible] splash from P[illegible] and Pat [illegible] emerged from the [illegible] lows and the weste[illegible]n [illegible] to view.

Had she be[illegible]en [illegible] would have sat rig[illegible] bac[illegible] again. The haystac[illegible]s [illegible]—little half-breed b[illegible]ldin[illegible] ber on the bo[illegible]tom [illegible] larger than sheds. Ca[illegible]oli[illegible]e [illegible] wagon bow sli[illegible] thr[illegible]ugh [illegible] she sank into the she[illegible] of he[illegible] How could an[illegible]one [illegible] this place a town?

Charles pul[illegible]ed u[illegible] be[illegible] the hay shanties. A fad[illegible] sig[illegible] announced *Br[illegible]ad an[illegible] P[illegible]* [illegible]. Caroline winced a[illegible] th[illegible] a[illegible] This place wa[illegible] not [illegible]

Charles du[illegible]ked [illegible] door and in a few mi[illegible]u[illegible]es [illegible] out a loaf wra[illegible]ped [illegible] of newsprint. "Here's a [illegible] Caroline. Lig[illegible]t br[illegible]ad."

It felt a trif[illegible]e he[illegible]vy [illegible] lofty name of light bre[illegible]d, [illegible] warm and sm[illegible]led [illegible] unwrapped it and slice[illegible] it [illegible]

"'Immigrat[illegible]on [illegible] pour in,'" Charles [illegible] paper as she w[illegible]ite[illegible] [illegible]s to find its way from [illegible] the jug. "'As many [illegible] have been taken in [illegible] one day. At th[illegible]t r[illegible] will have an occupa[illegible] [illegible] His face sober[illegible]d so[illegible] [illegible] we didn't get here an[illegible] better inquire at th[illegible] [illegible] the best prospects."

He did not wai[illegible] to [illegible], but drove with his [illegible] hand and the reins in the other past the clusters of hay-topped sheds toward what Caroline had taken for a house and barn from the riverbank. They stopped between the two, and she saw that the pair of buildings comprised the whole of Independence's business district. A double-log structure, the hotel, proclaimed itself the Judson House. The store with its sawn-board walls and shingled roof looked like it might just fit inside their house in Wisconsin. Size notwithstanding, it was by far the neatest, most sturdily built place in town, and it bore its few months' weathering almost boastfully. The proud little building was already the matron of Main Street, Caroline mused, a grande dame in her graying boards and shining glass windows.

It was a fanciful idea, something like Laura might come up with, and Caroline felt it nudging her impressions of Independence into a more charitable light. The town was undeniably raw, but it did not intend to remain so. This was a place still becoming itself.

"Huh," Charles said, looking the street up and down. "Maybe the land office is sharing quarters with the store. Ought to stock up either way," he said. "I'm short of tobacco and I better get more powder and shot while I have the chance. What else do we need?"

Caroline weighed each dwindling sack in her mind. "We still have plenty of beans and dried apples. The cornmeal, flour, and sugar are all low, especially the meal. Coffee. Some fresh salt pork or bacon would be nice. Molasses. And maybe, if they have any—" she stopped. "No, never mind that." He had already treated her to the light bread.

"What? There can't be a thing in this town that's too good for you." His eyes twinkled, and Caroline felt the quick bloom of pleasure warm her face. She wished she were not so prone to blushing at his flattery. He could turn her ears halfway to red talking that way, and he knew it. "Tell me or I'll have to guess," he teased, and Caroline's earlobes tingled. The man had no mercy.

If she told him now it would sound silly. And if she did not, Caroline knew he would buy her something far too extravagant. Tins of oysters or a yar[illegible] of [illegible] to ma[illegible] over her old apro[illegible]. She [illegible] her fol[illegible] h[illegible]ds. "[illegible] Ju[illegible] a small jar of cuc[illegible]mber[illegible]."

"Pic[illegible]les," Charl[illegible] r[illegible]peated. "That's it?" Caro[illegible]ine n[illegible] very m[illegible]ch t[illegible] wri[illegible] fr[illegible]m under the bemu[illegible] [illegible]. "Laura, [illegible] me t[illegible] b[illegible]." He pocketed a t[illegible] went in[illegible]ide. [illegible] Caro[illegible]ine could wipe the cru[illegible] fr[illegible] Laura's mou[illegible]s, [illegible] a[illegible] back a[illegible]ain.

"Nob[illegible]dy [illegible]," [illegible].

"Wh[illegible] do [illegible] ou m[illegible], Charles?"

"She[illegible]ves a[illegible] f[illegible] g[illegible]ds, but there's not a sou[illegible] inside." [illegible] and wa[illegible]ked [illegible]ro[illegible] [illegible] toward the hotel.

Caro[illegible]ine [illegible] the brightly polished win[illegible] could a [illegible] kee[illegible] [illegible] l and spotless wit[illegible] n[illegible] o[illegible] [illegible].

A so[illegible] of [illegible] from under the wagon. [illegible] Carolin[illegible] [illegible] familiar sound registere[illegible]. [illegible] every b[illegible] as [illegible] t[illegible] c[illegible]dren as Jacobs pro[illegible]ised [illegible]. She loo[illegible]ed [illegible] of [illegible] wagon and saw [illegible] with a [illegible] ke [illegible] shoulder was nearing. The [illegible] rake ag[illegible]inst [illegible] of [illegible] store in a way t[illegible] sug[illegible] line tha[illegible] he [illegible] before approaching [illegible] fella," [illegible] sai[illegible] a[illegible] ed d[illegible]wn with his palm open [illegible] assess. [illegible] t[illegible] " A[illegible]d then to Carolin[illegible] w[illegible]en [illegible] him wi[illegible] a [illegible]rt [illegible]g to stock up, ma'am?"

"Yes, sir. [illegible]y h[illegible]—" [illegible]e did not want to s[illegible]out [illegible] girls lo[illegible]king [illegible]. "[illegible] th[illegible], headed for the [illegible]?"

The [illegible]an [illegible] loc[illegible].

Cha[illegible]es [illegible]ne[illegible]. "[illegible] ou[illegible] place?"

"Tha[illegible] it [illegible]. I'm [illegible]. Sor[illegible]y to keep you wait[illegible]ng. I [illegible] two of [illegible] th[illegible] re[illegible] w[illegible] got so busy raking [illegible]ay we [illegible] pull up. It's [illegible] m[illegible] for [illegible]aymaking, but co[illegible]e wi[illegible] excuse [illegible] b[illegible] ho[illegible] f[illegible]er [illegible] this country."

"A s[illegible]und [illegible]," Charles said, so grave[illegible] that [illegible] hear a joke coming behind it. "Whatever your stock doesn't eat, you can likely sell as roofing."

Wilson laughed. "That's a fact. The Indians call it Hay House Town." Chuckling, the two men headed together through the doorway. Their boots were ringing on the board floor before Wilson turned and asked, "Will you come in, ma'am?"

There was nothing she wanted more just then than to go into that store. The reflection of the wagon cover had filled its windows so that from where she sat Caroline could only just see the shelf tops. Since the wagon stopped her mind had been fleshing them out with neat rows of provisions in their sacks and cans and jars, polished tools, bright bolts of cloth. Her eyes would be so grateful for such plenty—not only the quantity, but the color and variety. Even the crisp black words printed on the labels would be a treat. Most of all, she wanted to stand inside those square board walls with a straight, solid roof over her head. Caroline grasped the wagon bow, this time to offset the way her balance shifted now when she stood, and realized just in time.

It was no longer seemly for her to be in public. How many weeks had passed since any man but Charles had seen her? Three, and Mr. Jacobs had likely suspected even then. She glanced up and down the street. There was no other woman abroad, much less one in her condition. Sitting still up on the spring seat it was not so plain, but if she stepped from under the wagon's cover, the outline of her dress would make her instantly, doubly conspicuous.

Still, she hated to say no. There was a thin, wheedling feeling taking hold of her throat that would not let the word pass. It was such a rough place, she argued with herself, and men would not show their disapproval with the same sidelong glances as women. No, men would self-consciously look away, not knowing how to speak to her—or whether to speak to her at all—and that would be every bit as bad. Worse. Wilson himself might blush to the collar if she stood.

Caroline let go of the wagon bow and the spring seat gave a tiny sigh, [illegible] disappointment had made [illegible] was no business of [illegible] diminish whatever propriety [illegible] had managed [illegible] by indulging herself [illegible] you, no. The [illegible] I will wait in the wagon."

[illegible] sounds that drifted out [illegible], and the [illegible] [illegible]-and-forth of two voices [illegible] and clearer: "[illegible] pound for white sugar? [illegible] war's over?"

[illegible] heard right? They had [illegible] such prices in [illegible] Caroline held her breath [illegible].

[illegible] voice rose slightly to [illegible] tone stayed [illegible] "You'll find there's not [illegible] gar out here, [illegible]

"[illegible] n't think so at those rates." [illegible] her preempt [illegible] and than twenty ounces [illegible]

[illegible] pound. It staggered [illegible] anyone in these [illegible] paying that kind of money [illegible] luxury. Pres[illegible] himself would have to [illegible] he would put [illegible] on her table at that [illegible] things they [illegible] —the brown sugar, cornmeal, [illegible] arithmetic was [illegible] the swelling figures painful [illegible] contemplate. If all [illegible] prices were so steep, by [illegible] ng but green [illegible] the fiddle box.

"[illegible] can't expect Mississippi [illegible] Verdigris," Wil[illegible] went on. A flare of anger [illegible] mental arithme[illegible]. Of course they had expected [illegible] approached [illegible] but three and four times [illegible] thing else al[illegible]. From the way Wilson was [illegible] could guess [illegible] had reacted no better. [illegible] sounded as [illegible] were backing away from [illegible] he slid across [illegible] seat to listen more closely.

"[illegible] so much the goods as the [illegible] ained. "Look, [illegible] branch of the Union [illegible] as near as the other side of Labette County. I'm paying them top dollar to get it that far, plus another $2.25 per hundredweight on overland freight to Independence. I promise you, these are the fairest rates I can afford. If you want anything like back East prices, you're welcome to make the drive out to Oswego or Fontana yourself, and no hard feelings."

The names of the towns were not familiar to her. Perhaps they were not on the map. How far, then? Caroline wondered. And how much cash did they have, how long would it last? Always the same questions, since she was a child: *How much? How far? How long?* The stack of bills had seemed almost too much when they left Pepin—enough to stock the wagon and secure just over one hundred acres besides. Still, she had never expected all of it to last as far as Kansas, not with paying upward of forty cents a bushel to keep Ben and Beth warm and hale until the snow broke. That constant nibbling had taken a greater toll than the bridges and ferries, Caroline realized. If only she'd paid more attention, kept better count.

Her mouth was open now, the breath coming in spurts. Silently, Caroline brought her lips together. She pulled an unbroken stream of air through her nose and held it. One small crack and the old fears came tumbling in. Quickly, methodically, she sealed off her mind with calm thoughts. They had made it safely to Montgomery County. Right this minute there was food and money in the wagon. She could go and touch the crates and sacks if she wanted to, slip her fingers under the lid of the fiddle box and feel the crisp edges of the bills. She had her seeds, and Charles his gun. They did not owe a cent to a soul in all the world, and the government would not require payment on a preemption for nearly three years. And there was Gustafson, she remembered. That was enough to let her breath out smooth and warm. The Swede owed five hundred and six dollars. The fiddle box had only to hold out until Gustafson's next payment. There could be a letter waiting now.

Caroline half stood to peer through the doorway for any sign of a postal cabinet behind Wilson's counter. Beneath her, Jack rumbled [illegible] her man, this one [illegible] was [illegible] pproaching th[illegible] sto[illegible] t down again [illegible] nd [illegible] [illegible] ide of the spring s[illegible] easure. The f[illegible] llow [illegible], too preoccu[illegible] ied [illegible] y notice her, t[illegible] ppi[illegible] [illegible] past. [illegible] he men's voic[illegible] s r[illegible] [illegible] eeting and in[illegible] rod [illegible] ine permitted hers[illegible] [illegible] hs. Charles w[illegible] uld [illegible], with men to [illegible] alk [illegible] ed to revel in [illegible] he [illegible] ce around hi[illegible], th[illegible] [illegible] that came a[illegible] ive [illegible]. As he cast a[illegible] out [illegible] Caroline cou[illegible] m[illegible] tra flourish of [illegible] veli[illegible] [illegible] had not hear[illegible] it o[illegible] weeks. It was goo[illegible] [illegible] what the pa[illegible] per [illegible] ion? Twenty [illegible] lain [illegible] iled?"

[illegible] ays it sure feel[illegible] lik[illegible] [illegible] aid. "Other d[illegible] ys [illegible] ould mow an [illegible] cre [illegible] ng a custome[illegible]."

[illegible] d I'd better c[illegible] eck [illegible], see where [illegible] try is. Which [illegible] f th[illegible] [illegible]?"

[illegible] isn't one."

[illegible] 's voice splutt[illegible] red, [illegible] e got a hand[illegible] ll r[illegible] [illegible] ontgomery C[illegible] ount[illegible]."

[illegible] ay be so, but the[illegible] [illegible] ng press in t[illegible] s t[illegible] [illegible] over a month [illegible] go. [illegible] 've seen'll ha[illegible] e c[illegible] [illegible] vego, same as [illegible] ny [illegible] arch."

[illegible] Caroline had time [illegible] e bulldog sta[illegible] ked [illegible] r the wagon, poi[illegible] and growled. She [illegible] d such a gro[illegible] l fr[illegible]. It was a lo[illegible] sa[illegible] prickled all d[illegible] own [illegible]. Gingerly, sh[illegible] lea[illegible] d the canvas to see [illegible] im. Across th[illegible] st[illegible] dians were ey[illegible] ing [illegible] heir own pon[illegible] s. I[illegible] locks striped the[illegible] the shoulde[illegible] s of t[illegible] rk vests. Tufts of [illegible] ms of their le[illegible] gin[illegible] e flattened h[illegible] r b[illegible] ng seat. Her [illegible] kin[illegible] strangely light, as though every hair on her body were lifting to reach out, whisker-like, in anticipation of danger. Something about them frightened her, something deeper than Jack's ire. She did not want them to see her looking at them again, so she closed her eyes and waited for their image to flash against the darkness of her eyelids.

Three sleek black scalp locks glinted in her memory. That was all, and it was enough. She remembered now, and understood: in Wisconsin, the Potawatomis dressed their hair that way only in preparation for war.

"What's Jack growling at?" Laura asked. She was starting to climb over the seat.

"Stay back, Laura." There was no tone in her voice. Caroline did not hear how loudly or softly she spoke and did not care so long as Laura obeyed. Her ears had room only for her own racing thoughts.

How near to let them come before calling for Charles? If they meant no harm and she created a scene there would be trouble, worse trouble maybe than if they had some kind of malice in mind. It was broad daylight, in the center of town, such as it was. All they had done was turn their heads.

But those scalp locks. Everything in her told her not to ignore them as the sound of unshod hooves striking hard-packed dirt came steadily nearer.

Jack growled again, so long this time Caroline thought he must be scraping his lungs raw with the sound. Then he snorted and strutted back under the wagon. Caroline sat quite still a moment, then leaned out from under the canvas. On one side, the Indians were riding away up the street, and on the other was Charles, heading out of the store with Wilson just behind him.

"I'd head into the southern or western townships if I were you," Wilson was advising. "There's still good land open in Rutland, Caney, and Fawn Creek. Just don't be surprised if the Osages come calling." He paused to give a wave to the departing Indians. Two of the three riders raised an a[illegible] [illegible]e've got in the habit of collecting five dollars from ea[illegible] as they see it."

Five dollars [illegible] 'Do they always—'" [illegible] tered, knowing [illegible] would sound coming from [illegible] fresh from the [illegible] always dress their hair that [illegible]

Wilson gave [illegible] than she expected. "More often [illegible] They mostly [illegible] th[illegible] coaches for special occasions."

Caroline did [illegible] herself with the tenor of the [illegible] er's reply. The [illegible] sinking sensation had vanished from [illegible] skin, and her se[illegible] the heat back into her body. [illegible] there was a vag[illegible] came from knowing [illegible] relied upon to in[illegible] tribes had no [illegible] the Osages.

Charles ha[illegible] pound sacks of meal and [illegible] and unbolted [illegible] Edwin brought out two bushels of oats and one of sh[illegible] the feedbox. No meat.

"I couldn't do i[illegible]" [illegible], "not at these prices. [illegible] us plenty of game, [illegible] for Pet and Patty. [illegible] the pound here, [illegible] would have bought myself [illegible] but I couldn't afford [illegible] shot. The heavier the g[illegible] the more they cost. [illegible] I treated us to [illegible] beans instead of gr[illegible] add on for freight, [illegible] isn't any bargain [illegible]."

No great loss [illegible] Caroline thought, though [illegible] the gain was so [illegible] almost spiteful. That was [illegible] fault, though, so Ca[illegible] into the shape of a smile. [illegible] will be nice." And then, [illegible] No letters?"

Charles shook his [illegible] any post office yet. Letters [illegible] with riders from Oswego [illegible] over. Costs ten cents [illegible] collect them." He [illegible] up and frowned. "Fontana's [illegible] hundred miles north [illegible] Scott. Oswego's [illegible] but if it's the other side [illegible] Pacific's south branch [illegible] a good thirty miles east." He took up the reins and turned the mustangs westward.

His plans had not changed, then. Caroline folded her hands and pointed her bonnet brim straight ahead.

FOR THE FIRST time since Wisconsin, Caroline felt a pull from behind. Every mile that spread between them and Independence tugged at Caroline as though her corset strings were looped over the hitching posts. It was not so much the town itself calling to her, Caroline reckoned, but the notion of a town—a link to the society of others, however rudimentary it might be. The farther Charles drove, the more tenuous that join became.

So Caroline was not as startled as Charles when they found themselves suddenly at the edge of the wide cut in the earth. The feeling of an approaching rim had held her poised, leaning slightly backward these last ten miles. And now there was the very break she had sensed, inches from the mustangs' noses. Perhaps it was not the line between Kansas and the Territory—perhaps they had already passed that boundary—but this cleft in the prairie's flesh, with the slender vein of creek flowing through its bare red bluffs, spoke to her as the Missouri had spoken to Charles. Life on the opposing shore would be measurably different. How many more wagons must follow them across that creek, Caroline wondered as Charles frowned at his map, before the seam it embodied drew tight and disappeared?

Down into the bottomlands the mustangs went, not pulling now, but pushing to hold the wagon from skidding down the steep grade. Caroline held her spine rigid as the brake lever and angled herself backward, and still she could not fully resist the steady downward momentum. This land was uncanny, she thought as the wagon slid lower and lower, the way it managed to make her body enact the shapes of her emotions.

Between the hot red cliffs the bottomlands spread out still and smooth as the first page of Genesis. Across the creek grazing deer stood em, utterly unco[illegible] presence. The world unto itself [illegible] by the wind. [illegible] trampled the grass [illegible] the horses to [illegible], felt suddenly [illegible] leveled. [illegible] currents pulled [illegible] this sheltered [illegible] ing to feel but herself [illegible] hands and [illegible] sides, gauging herself [illegible] within.

[illegible] palms warmed the dusty [illegible] then slowly [illegible] et and chemise to [illegible] the gentle [illegible] the pulse of each finger [illegible] softly. Some-[illegible], Caroline hoped, [illegible] the creature [illegible] same calm throbbing [illegible] signaled wel-[illegible] ow how much longer [illegible] the answer-[illegible] ws, knees, and heels [illegible] something [illegible]

[illegible] toward her, drawing [illegible] as if to speak, [illegible] and looked back to the [illegible] Caroline fitted her [illegible] stormed knot and [illegible] high," he [illegible] can make it all right." [illegible] old wheel [illegible] rding place—two [illegible] up neatly [illegible] What do you say, [illegible]

[illegible] off an unexpected [illegible] Close be-[illegible] er awareness rising of [illegible] as it had at [illegible] s of the street.

[illegible] before her had changed [illegible] the least [illegible] ed. Puzzled, she [illegible] and down, [illegible] er it was that might [illegible] on guard. [illegible] nd deep, as Charles h[illegible] had known [illegible] o. The swath of [illegible] its middle [illegible] he looked at the [illegible] pointed out. If [illegible] of the other [illegible] last seven [illegible] ould not say how.

Caroline closed her eyes as she had done on the street in Independence. This time nothing leapt out at her in warning. The creek flowed no differently, no more menacingly in her mind. She opened her eyes. Charles was looking at her, waiting. Still she did not speak. The cold liquid feeling remained lodged in her middle, though there was not one thing in the scene before her that she could blame for it. It was as placid a spot as could be, with the soft green willow boughs swaying lazily above the surface of the creek.

Caroline thought again of the Indians and their scalp locks. She had not been fully right about them, but neither had she been fully wrong. In Wisconsin the flutter of apprehension they had triggered might well have saved her life. Here it had only made her look foolish and fearful. She squirmed inside, remembering how Mr. Wilson had looked at her when she asked about the Indians' hair. The storekeeper could think her a silly woman if he liked, but Caroline could not abide the thought of her husband giving her that same look. She wished Charles had not asked.

There.

The little swell of recognition momentarily pushed her fear aside. That was it—not the creek at all, but the question itself. It was not like Charles to ask such a thing. Always he consulted her before deciding when and where to camp, but the roads with their forks and fords and bridges, those were his business. If the route confounded him somehow, he muttered only to himself over the map.

There was no mistaking his wariness now. It wafted from him like a scent. He was not just taking in the scenery as Pet and Patty drank, but scrutinizing it. Caroline watched him look at the horses, then at Jack, searching for a reaction to link with his own. Something, some tiny thing, must have whispered at him not to cross, so faintly he could not make it out.

Did you hear that, too? That was the question buried under what he had asked. She had not, and so she did not know what to say. She could [illegible] yes and did not want to [illegible] she could think to do wa[illegible] permission to [illegible] as he [illegible] t.

[illegible]line spoke low and firm [illegible] alone would sound flippan[illegible] were not careful. "He m[illegible] trust embedded in them [illegible]ever you say, Charles."

[illegible] a long pause. Even Pet [illegible] stopped drinking to listen [illegible] heard the water dripp[illegible] their noses, the l[illegible]ping o[illegible] tongue as it poked in and [illegible] creek.

[illegible] tie down the wagon cov[illegible] decided.

[illegible]. The word flashed throug[illegible] body, bright and sizzling [illegible] Then, with a shudder, it fl[illegible] air. Charles had jumped to [illegible]und, leaving the springs [illegible] back and forth behind him. [illegible]ked at the canvas straps [illegible] that Caroline could hardly [illegible] hold of her thoughts with [illegible] shuddering around her. He [illegible] being careful, she told [illegible], securing the cover so tightly. [illegible] never in his life knowing [illegible] danger. She must trust [illegible]tion as she had trusted [illegible]

"[illegible] may have to swim, [illegible] middle," he said as he sat [illegible] beside her again. "But we [illegible] right, Caroline."

[illegible] her pinprick of increase [illegible] her body recoiled ever [illegible]ly from the will of her [illegible] had not asked for reassur- [illegible] could only be himself [illegible] reassuring, and it had not [illegible] Everything about him [illegible] taut as the wagon cover — [illegible]th, the grimacing muscle[illegible] his eyes. He had the reins [illegible] so firmly around his f[illegible] the skin stand out in little [illegible] between the leather. Ca[illegible] again at the line of [illegible]its. [illegible] painted so clearly into the [illegible] could be no questioning [illegible] ford.

[illegible] wheels dropped into [illegible] piped up behind them, "I [illegible] Jack could ride in the wagon [illegible]."

[illegible]ra took to the new baby [illegible]kly as she had taken to that secondhand bulldog, Caroline thought, she would count herself lucky. Charles did not answer. Had he even heard?

"Jack can swim, Laura," Caroline said. "He will be all right."

One by one the mustangs' legs cut into the flowing water, carving wide V shapes across its surface. Then came a little sideways tug as the creek began wending its way between the spokes of the wheels like a needle pulling a thread through cloth. Charles slapped the reins again and the team continued gamely forward.

Caroline watched the water lap gently at their bellies with a sympathetic shiver. It crept steadily up the horses' sides until their wet black backs shone patent leather smooth in the sun, then disappeared altogether. Beneath her, Caroline felt as much as heard the creek sloshing now and then at the underside of the floorboards.

They were already nearly halfway across. Charles leaned back a little and the rigid angle of his elbows eased. He smiled bashfully at her, a smile like that of a boy suddenly no longer frightened of the dark. Caroline unclenched herself and felt the gentle hug of her corset welcoming her back. Then the reins drooped. The mustangs had hesitated, their ears swiveling upstream.

There was no time to ask what or why. A gush of water came splashing at the sideboards. It hit with a jolt that jostled Caroline's jawbone, then pushed its way under and around the wagon box. The furrows around Pet's and Patty's necks melted away as the current scooped them up. The wagon gave a funny sort of dip and then they were floating, horses and all.

Instinctively Caroline scooted inward, lifting her feet from the floor, but no water breached the seams. Only the churning of the mustangs' hooves reverberated through the water and up the wagon's wooden tongue into the box. Caroline felt the faint echo of their chugging in her chest as though a steam locomotive were passing.

"Gee!" Charles called out, and Caroline's attention expanded out-

ward. He was h ing with the reins, tr
mustangs tow he r

Upstream. It vrong. They always so that the hor it the current, not ine searched th bearings. Not pposing set of ts, have been a diff gether. Even the the shore hunched s though they C ne realized, n he creek itself at h gh to catch hold heir lowermos boughs downstre

Caroline looked ses' heads. The lready some u ere it had been v oments befor The ed them past in onds. Caroline over her mou lace began sl her.

The wagon no rudder or oars b ponies. Pet and atty addled mightily ent, but it was d the wagon i moment they he sound of the side of the Quiet opened up l them. Caroline ach plummeted nd stopped sh

They had fal Caroline thought derstanding her w whose dept of sounding. came an alm tremor, and was on its wa marshaling itse gathering rush

Caroline sp ter must not would pull the the willow bough ready crouched but Laura sa blue eyes viole oline's mouth breath. There could shield the

"Lie down, girls," she commanded. They dropped as though her voice had knocked them over. It was not enough. She whipped the gray blanket down over them. "Be still, just as you are. Don't move!"

The current came at the wagon in a great, muscular arm, caught hold of the back of it and swung it like a pendulum. The shore went swinging with it, out of sight until there was nothing but water before them. Caroline flattened herself backward against the spring seat. The whole of the creek was coming at her as though it would leap straight into her lap. It crashed and foamed against the boards, inches from her knees. Dark drops of spray shot up and dotted her skirt.

The water reared the mustangs backward, straining the pole straps that bound them to the neck yoke. They snorted and kicked and pulled, their noses inching nearer and nearer the narrow pole that joined them to the tongue. Then with a whinny the creek forced them up again. Caroline gasped and gripped the seat as the front of the wagon tipped upward, pried by the tongue.

The leather straps and steel rings would likely hold, but the wooden yoke? Caroline flinched at the thought. With the weight of two horses yanking each of its ends backward even a good hickory pole might snap like a twig broken over a man's knee. The long tongue was only a little less vulnerable. If either of them splintered, the mustangs would come crashing into the wagon box. They must keep fighting the current, Caroline realized, if only to keep the wagon intact. *Swim,* she willed them, *swim.* But Pet and Patty were as frightened as she was. The creek had them in a chokehold. Their necks straightened, their noses pointed to the sky. Caroline could see the whites of their eyes.

"Take them, Caroline!"

The reins were in her hands and Charles's hat and boots on the floor before she understood what was happening. He stepped one stockinged foot up onto the corner of the wagon box and sprang from it into the creek. The wagon gave a terrible lurch behind him and—

Caroline's breath, her blood, stopped cold. The image of him leaping held itself [illegible] r. It was as though he [illegible] reg-ister [illegible]

But she [illegible] what happened next [illegible] the prin[illegible]

The [illegible] over his head.

[illegible] d itself as though he [illegible] were at all. [illegible] ged to Charles [illegible]

Caroline [illegible] the reins in her [illegible] her thr[illegible] eam, must not [illegible] not frig[illegible] hing in her had [illegible] pulled back [illegible] nd the reins tig[illegible] would hold [illegible] at this way until Cha[illegible] had to. [illegible] re but the pla[illegible] red.

[illegible] place, she thought [illegible] the same water [illegible] moving—creek [illegible] water and [illegible] nd somewhere [illegible] it or [illegible] The creek might [illegible] al-ready have [illegible] nd sweep him [illegible] eing.

[illegible] the left and she [illegible] ough Car[illegible] nothing solid be[illegible] oline pul[illegible] side line for balance [illegible] to the [illegible] ith it, yanked by the [illegible] collar did[illegible]

[illegible] d in the harness [illegible] belly ba[illegible] she could not be sure

Carolin[illegible] what to do. She could [illegible]—the bit [illegible] o deeply into [illegible]y's [illegible] could not [illegible] as had a firm h[illegible] erself in [illegible] r strength to ho[illegible] the [illegible] drag. The [illegible] beside Pet burst [illegible]

Charles [illegible]

Caroline [illegible] n spray from his [illegible] oplets

and her own lungs unlocked. He had grasped the traces and was hauling himself up along Pet's side. His shoulder plowed up a swell of water before him.

He took hold of Pet's throat latch. All Caroline could see of him were his head and his fist, tight under Pet's chin. His own narrow chin barely breached the surface; the creek had him by the whiskers. Then she heard him speaking. Not the words, but the sound of them, so light and calm, they buoyed Caroline just enough that she could begin to think more than one moment ahead.

The mustangs must not give in to their panic. Not with Charles in the water beside them. She could not steer. Her arms were no match for the push and thrust of the current. But if she held the reins up high and steady, Caroline thought, Pet and Patty might not have to struggle so to keep their heads above the water.

Slowly, Caroline began to feed the lines out straight. She heard a rustle behind her and her attention splintered. Laura had come out from under the blanket. When, she did not know. Caroline did not turn around. She could not take her eyes from Charles. Until he was out of that water, there could be no room in her consciousness for anything else.

"Lie down, Laura," Caroline said, and Laura did.

Caroline honed all her focus back into the reins. Slowly she lifted the lines, searching for the right height, the right amount of tension. Too much would signal Pet and Patty to stop. Too little and they would flail. Higher, higher—there. Just below her shoulders their heads leveled, chins parallel to the water. *Now, steady,* she told herself. She pulled gently, firmly, backward until the graceful curve of the mustangs' necks began to reappear. The roar of the creek fell away from her ears as Caroline concentrated. Her arms measured the ever-changing tension in the lines and matched the two sides to each other. With Charles encouraging her, Pet was pulling harder now than Patty. Caroline slid to the left end of the spring seat, cocking the reins to soften Patty's [illegible] swim ahead and [illegible] Suddenly both [illegible] hands. She wrapped [illegible] around her fists, [illegible] slack.

[illegible] anged. Caroline felt [illegible] y in the lines. [illegible] nds was no longer [illegible] It did not pull [illegible] balanced betw[illegible] team. She had [illegible] had regained control [illegible], and Caroline [illegible] them up the [illegible] They made no [illegible] inst the current [illegible] matter to Caro-[illegible] d stopped strai[illegible] that alone was [illegible] d for. All the po[illegible] fuel the mus-[illegible] d to their chests [illegible] charged stub-[illegible]

[illegible] re time than th[illegible] Again Caroline [illegible] mach. This time [illegible] lowered below her [illegible] de to side, unab[illegible] made her want to [illegible] seat and spread [illegible] the floorboards. [illegible] as moving in a way [illegible] before. Two [illegible] rattling, rocking [illegible] d this was both [illegible] deways sort of [illegible] t down the un-[illegible] on. *Like driving* [illegible] Caroline thought, [illegible] rd the middle of the [illegible]

[illegible] st to brace for. The [illegible] deways and ev-[illegible] ne's body snapped [illegible] boxes shifted [illegible] etbag on its hook [illegible] Just as quickly [illegible] Caroline did not [illegible] everything in her [illegible] ng toward her [illegible]. Only her eyes [illegible]

[illegible] cause. Nothing had [illegible] The water had [illegible] e more turbulent. [illegible] make out what [illegible] o the horses.

[illegible] Gee over, Patty."

Charles. He was trying to coax the horses away from the middle of the creek. Of course. That was why the wagon had teetered. It was too light to stand upright with its broad side exposed to the strength of the current. But the wagon must be turned to face the bank if they were to make landfall safely. There was no other chance. The thought of all that water heaving again at the sideboards whitened Caroline's knuckles. It would either turn them or topple them—right over onto Charles.

Caroline repelled the thought. She would not, could not allow that scene to unfold—not in her mind or before her eyes. There was not even time to think of such a thing. Once the wagon began to turn, those horses must swim faster than the water flowed or the current would overtake them. Charles could not do that alone, not up to his neck in the creek. Caroline coiled up her courage and hauled the reins sideways. As the horses' necks angled toward land, Caroline felt her weight begin to shift from beneath and knew the creek's hold on the wagon was tightening. She slapped the lines hard, again and again. One crackling spray of water after another shot up from Pet's and Patty's backs. The little mustangs jolted and the wagon swung.

Caroline watched nothing but Charles, clinging to Pet. The willows blurred behind him. Water smacked and splashed at the boards, the overspray leaping up to strike sharp drumbeats against the thin canvas walls. Caroline prayed with her fists clenched and her eyes wide open.

> *Therefore will not we fear, though the earth be removed, and though the mountains be carried into the midst of the sea;*
> *Though the waters thereof roar and be troubled, though the mountains shake with the swelling thereof.*

All at once the wagon and the creek ceased their grappling. The wagon moved as though it were a bullet careening down a rifle barrel.

"Haw!" Charles called out, and Caroline obeyed quicker than the team, quicker than thought, pulling the lines toward the western bank [illegible] out knowing why. S[illegible] saw [illegible] brown flat place a f[illegible] rods [illegible]. The break in the [illegible] be racing toward them. In- [illegible] threw the reins [illegible] Safe from capsizing, they must [illegible] cripple the horse [illegible] landing. She could [illegible] slow [illegible]eek, but she would [illegible] at little she could.

[illegible] iron tires struck [illegible] against the creek bed. Caroline [illegible] forward, then [illegible] Charles shouted, but Caroline did not hear what he [illegible] ground together beneath [illegible]. Everything from the [illegible] churn dash rattled. Then the [illegible] of wood scraping [illegible] tipped and it all s[illegible] [illegible] the tailgate.

Charles shouted again [illegible] rising, running, out of the [illegible]k—shoulders, back, [illegible] water.

The shock of the wheel [illegible] ground sent Caroline's teeth [illegible]ing down on her tongue [illegible] clamped shut against the pain [illegible] she opened them, [illegible] still. So still. The rushing and flowing and the roaring, [illegible] over. Charles stood panting [illegible] the shining wet [illegible] clothes clinging to himself in.

Caroline found herself [illegible] she could not let go of [illegible] reins. All the terror [illegible] time to feel still had hold of [illegible] everything that had [illegible] suddenly fanned out before her, [illegible] and terrible. Her [illegible] "Oh, Charles," and blood rose [illegible] her bitten tongue [illegible] Had she been able to move, she [illegible] have had him in her arms.

"There, there, Caroline. We [illegible]

[illegible] perhaps that she could not reach him, Caroline thought [illegible] she [illegible]ed and shook. There was [illegible] fulness in her to [illegible] him [illegible] just the other side of that, [illegible] of outrage. At him, at herself [illegible] had known—they [illegible] something was wrong [illegible] [illegible]use they could not [illegible] had gone into that creek [illegible] way. With no one else to [illegible] they had failed each other. There was no place in [illegible] for such mistakes, no [illegible] all, and so she only half listened to Charles trying to soothe them all with his praise of the tight wagon box and strong horses. Brushing aside her fear had nearly just cost more than she could pay, and she would not do it again now, not if it shook her apart.

"All's well that ends well," Charles was saying, and that was so. But it would not have begun at all, Caroline knew, if they had listened to their own good sense. Even with creek water streaming from his whiskers, Charles could overlook that part of it. He was always facing forward, that man. Never back.

Laura's fingers filled the spaces between the boards at Caroline's back. "Oh, where's Jack?" she cried as she pulled herself up from under the blanket.

Jack. Caroline's shaking halted all at once. Her conscience bulged up so hard and solid, she could feel nothing else. They had left him. *She* had left him. It was not Charles who told Laura the bulldog could swim. Caroline remembered how Jack had growled at the Indians on the street, yet did no more than scrunch his eyes shut to brace himself for Laura's mauling hugs. He had asked nothing of them but to be allowed to follow behind his ponies, and she had abandoned that steadfast creature to the creek. She could picture him standing on that shore just as plainly as though she had turned to look. But she had not.

They waited better than an hour while Charles searched, his whistle shrilling through the creek bottoms again and again after his voice would no longer carry. An hour with Laura so desperately hopeful that Caroline could not bear to look at her when Charles returned. Instead she saw Charles's face, saw him meet Laura's wishful gaze and know for the first time in his life he had failed his little Half-Pint. Caroline did not know how so much disappointment would fit inside one small wagon.

Charles said nothing to either of them. There was nothing to say. His clothes were dry, and there was no bulldog trotting behind him. It was past time for making camp. He climbed to the spring seat and flicked the reins.

IT WAS A was d ... e of them could eat, ye ... pushed at the fo ... as good as sand ... own looked li ... , all grit and muddy ... throat burned ... scraped the plates ... Even the scrap ... ithout Jack there to fi ...

God tha do ... 't ... rows won't leave a good dog ... the cold, Charl ... Laura when she begged for ... lowed into he ... ent soothed the chi ... ut ... solation to C ... ence throbbed all th ... of it: After al ... ayers for protection ... had left one o ... thout so much as a ba ... could ask for ... . Nothing but forgiveness.

"We'll ... two," Charles said when ... to the dishpa ... "I ... stay here. Good land, tim ... toms, plenty ... ing a man could want. Wh ... Caroline?"

Everything ... nt. Caroline's hands still ... cooling dishw ... man? Caroline did not da ... herself to ask ... She did not want to be insid ... did not want ... son who had been so sel ... day, it would ... simply to arrive.

"We might ... worse," she ventur ... asking.

Charles kn ... that. He waited for me ... her over the ... she scrubbed guiltily ... way, I'll look ... w," he answered whe ... "Get us some ..."

Caroline ... the dishcloth and wal ... bright ring o ... her hem rustled agai st ... she stopped ... oth to dry over the long ... Caroline look ... wide open darkness ... this the place ... moving toward? She ...

campfire with a roof and walls around it, the heart of a small house with Charles smoking and the girls yawning drowsily in the flickering light.

A howl wavered into the air, the sound cutting a thin line into the blank space around her. Caroline felt it slide through her, too, tickling the gaps between each bone of her spine as though she were no more solid than the sky. As she turned from the prairie to the campsite the darkness became palpable against her back. Caroline refused to let it make her shiver, or hurry. The girls must not see their ma flushed from the grass like a frightened grouse, not by a sound as familiar as thunder. Anyway, she was not truly frightened. Charles's rifle and pistol were loaded, and there was the fire just steps away. She only wished again for something thicker than a shawl to mark the boundary between herself and all that dark and shapeless space.

"About half a mile away, I'd judge," Charles said.

Mary and Laura looked at each other. Both of them knew well by now how little time it took to cover half a mile.

"Bedtime for little girls," Caroline sang out softly.

Her fingers were down to Mary's fourth button when Laura cried, "Look, Pa, look! A wolf!"

Charles had the rifle butt notched into his shoulder before Caroline saw what Laura was pointing to. Two molten globes hovering in the long grass where she had just been standing, each reflecting the firelight like the brass disc behind a kerosene lamp. Eyes. Creeping closer. She heard the click of Charles cocking the rifle and held her breath for the shot. None came. The animal had crept another step, then stopped still—a perfect target.

Charles did not fire. He lifted his cheek an inch from the stock and peered over the tip of the barrel at those motionless eyes. "Can't be a wolf," he said, "unless it's mad."

Caroline hefted Mary into the wagon without feeling it happen. She leaned down for Laura and Charles shook his head. His finger was loose on the trigger now. "Listen to the horses," he murmured. Caroline [illegible] but their teeth [illegible] grass. Nor was [illegible] alized. Her body [illegible] and yet she felt [illegible] alert, yes, and cautious [illegible] ough she kept [illegible] safely back, her mind [illegible] lean forward, [illegible] rd the riddle of what [illegible] might be. "A [illegible] ud.

[illegible] Charles said, picking [illegible] wood. "Hah!" [illegible] d it toward the sh[illegible]

[illegible] al should have bolted. [illegible] ropped to the [illegible] owe? Quicker than [illegible] ne put herself [illegible] animal as slowly [illegible] began to crawl [illegible]

[illegible] range. The animal [illegible] to scrape the [illegible] yes said. It was pitiful [illegible] ake her wince. [illegible] ld humble itself [illegible] sick or hurt.

[illegible] rd the edge of the [illegible] before him.

[illegible] Whether she meant [illegible] Caro-[illegible] darkness around [illegible] thin as it [illegible] the swirl of a shining [illegible] shape. Then [illegible] teeth, pointing straight [illegible]

[illegible] came from all [illegible] rles shouting, [illegible] ything moved in [illegible] Caroline [illegible] a and the creature [illegible] in the dirt.

[illegible] h, Jack!"

[illegible] her like a blow. [illegible] bedrag-[illegible] th glee. Caroline [illegible] as though [illegible] he shock, fearful [illegible] strength to [illegible] he could not speak [illegible] until all the [illegible] from her at the [illegible] mp tail. [illegible] to cry and could [illegible] The instant [illegible] g to her, nearly [illegible] He scrabbled [illegible] bent down to try [illegible] did not want petting. He licked and licked her wrists and palms and plunged his snorting nose into all the folds of her skirt until Caroline knew—it was her smell he wanted. Wanted to coat himself in it, so that he might never lose it again. Somewhere out on the open prairie he must have scented her, standing alone in the tall grass outside the campsite, and he had followed.

She had led him home.

Th[illegible]n

[illegible]MORNING BREEZE pushed [illegible]'s skirt to and fro as if she [illegible] school bell. The fabric hugg[illegible] and the small of her back [illegible] as Charles strode away a[illegible] grass.

[illegible]ught to have made her feel [illegible] on such a vast and empty [illegible]. Instead she felt a ful[illegible]ess th[illegible] to do with the outward [illegible] of her skirt. The wh[illegible]le day [illegible] before her, with no wagon [illegible] cutting through it. Besid[illegible] washtub stood full and [illegible] in the sun.

[illegible]hout woods or walls to par[illegible] space around her, the sense [illegible] word—*alone*—blurred. [illegible] between them might ex[illegible] until they lost sight [illegible] one [illegible] they were all in the same [illegible]. Or rather, *on* it. The prair[illegible] contain them, but held them [illegible] great open palm. Only th[illegible] small enough to [illegible] of the tall grass and disap[illegible] its surface. Their voices [illegible] up from the weed tops lik[illegible]els', and for the first time [illegible] could remember Caroline did [illegible] have them out of her sight. [illegible] need do to find them was [illegible] wagon box and watch for [illegible] rippling of the grass.

[illegible]oline's heels clicked lightly [illegible] floorboards and her tongue [illegible]ked the lively *tsk-tsk* of [illegible] low-splashed dickey birds [illegible] around her as she straig[illegible] boxes and slouching [illegible] One jig-like call ma[illegible] her [illegible] en with the half-ga[illegible]ed [illegible]thes in her hands. What m[illegible] who sang such a song look [illegible] vivid as a crazy qu[illegible] or [illegible] et? She finished st[illegible]pping [illegible]ens from the beds and dr[illegible] undle over the side of the wagon. There lay the fiddle box on the bare straw tick, muffled between the pillows. In all these weeks they had not once reached into that box for music. Only greenbacks. She would ask Charles to play tonight, she decided, and tucked the blankets neatly around it. If he were not too tired. It had been too long.

It felt both right and wrong to use the day for a washing. Thursdays belonged to the churn, not the washtub, but after rattling across all those many miles the wagon itself felt so much like the inside of a churn that Caroline could not think of taking up the dash and pounding away at anything so delicate as cream. And anyway, there was none to be had. So it would be the laundry instead.

Caroline looked tentatively over the rim of the tub at the flat circle of water. Her own face looked back at her, just the same. The slightly uneven widow's peak beneath the neat white parting of brown hair. The lower lip that seemed always mournful or stern, no matter how sweet the thoughts behind it. Whatever changes this journey had wrought in her, they had not yet broken her surface.

Pleased, she smiled at herself and quickly blushed at the way her face bloomed back at her. Suddenly Caroline did not want to look away. The unexpected sweetness of her own modesty held her captive. This must be the smile that made Charles's eyes twinkle so when he teased her. She could feel the familiar contours of it, but had never seen the rosy flush, nor the dark ruffle of lowered lashes. No wonder he showed her no mercy.

Now she was too much pleased, and the charm of the reflection faded. Enough of that, then. Caroline rolled up her sleeves and tucked her skirt between her knees. She dipped her fingers into the pannikin for a smear of brown soft soap and began.

First the great bundle of sheets and pillowcases. Her knuckles stung with cold as she plunged the fabric in and out of the water. With the handle of the rake she pried the yards of sopping muslin from the tub and wrung them out inch by inch before starting all over with the rinse water. The [illegible] white underthings [illegible] derthings. [illegible] the carpetbags [illegible] stacked th[illegible] inter clothes in [illegible] washtub.

The fold[illegible] shirts were stiff [illegible] of wear. C[illegible] own everyday br[illegible] ered it into [illegible] er crept hungrily [illegible] the caked [illegible] her hands deep i[illegible] and strum[illegible] hboard until the [illegible] appeared f[illegible]

Sweat ri[illegible] nd collar. In her [illegible] could sketc[illegible] le of grass pressi[illegible] never befo[illegible] uch pleasure in a [illegible] she worke[illegible] th the water ca[illegible] more itself[illegible]

She laid [illegible] like paper dolls [illegible] stood back [illegible] n their colors a[illegible] brown and [illegible] ry in shades of b[illegible] sprigged c[illegible] hade of red Car[illegible] Together a[illegible] he grass, so that [illegible] imprint of [illegible]

THE IMAG[illegible] y in her mind [illegible] were irone[illegible] hen Charles cam[illegible] the girls ra[illegible] im, the picture [illegible] They rose [illegible] nall billow of co[illegible] Charles wi[illegible], Mary skipping [illegible] smiled. La[illegible] ugh of her Pa.

A pang [illegible] How might thi[illegible] if this next [illegible] arles was not a [illegible] but there [illegible] softness in his [illegible] on someth[illegible] seen it kindling [illegible] days, as they drove across the prairie, and now she could hear it in his voice, telling Laura of all the bounty he had seen living in the grass and streams.

The game he carried did nothing to contradict his flourishes of excitement. Two fat fowl hung from his belt, and in his hand was a rabbit so outlandishly large its feet brushed the ground with every swoop of his arm.

Charles held up his catch to her and said, "I tell you, Caroline, there's everything we want here. We can live like kings!" The monstrous jackrabbit dangled from his fist, its long belly neatly slit. Where its vitals should have been, there was only a glistening cavern. A drop, then two, of rosy pink blood splashed the ground before her.

Caroline's viscera lurched. The dead rabbit loomed too large, a glory of waste and feast. She was thankful she had never seen it living. All the power and vibrance were gone from it, and what was left would feed them for no more than a day.

Be that as it may. Caroline shook the shudder of regret from her shoulders and took the rabbit by its ears. It was dead and they must eat. If she could not make the creature live again she would roast it up fine, wrapped in slices of fat salt pork, and they would take nourishment from every morsel.

CAROLINE SCRAPED THE bones from Charles's plate into the bake oven.

"Bet it weighed near seven pounds, field dressed," he said. Boasting, almost. She could not blame him. Not one fiber of the jackrabbit had gone to waste. Tomorrow there would be the good thick broth with dumplings for supper. The hide was pinned to the wagon box. She could hear Jack working over the head and feet beneath the wagon, and this once the rough sounds pleased her.

The sun nestled itself down into the horizon, tinging the water in the dishpan with shades of pink and orange. Caroline scrubbed slowly at the plates as the colors deepened. She was tired and sore from leaning [illegible] But it was not the same [illegible] had become [illegible] the indifferent [illegible] even the drain of [illegible] never fully left [illegible] could not harness [illegible] busy, always [illegible] At odd times she [illegible] ly, and that [illegible] conscious of the [illegible] flowing past [illegible] It was akin to [illegible] ngth rebuilding after [illegible] her thoughts we[illegible] ving her a time [illegible] d.

[illegible] a vigorous sort of [illegible] from doing, and [illegible] ng of muscles [illegible] under the sun, and [illegible] it with ma[illegible] gr[illegible].

[illegible] he heard the fa[illegible] tal clasps. She tur[illegible] pan and found [illegible] dle box open on [illegible] ey-colored [illegible] warm in the fir[illegible] the tin plates [illegible] sat down by the [illegible]

[illegible] rings twanged [illegible] found their ste[illegible] ure notes [illegible] tiniest twists of [illegible] sweetened the [illegible] had never yet lea[illegible] hose sounds [illegible] ves. They carrie[illegible] esides and [illegible] ng-off dances rea[illegible] ack to the [illegible] the banks of the [illegible] r heart ros[illegible] them at last. So [illegible] he played, [illegible] ing out first in we[illegible] than anything [illegible] e.

[illegible] to hold the [illegible] em, and so it rose [illegible] higher and hig[illegible] note seemed to [illegible] oline wished [illegible] out into the de[illegible] it. Something [illegible] all her own. Th[illegible] ut her voice, [illegible] ne her low co[illegible] et the stars.

[illegible] oosening [illegible] d the strings.

Until the music began to release it she had not known that she had been holding on to anything at all. A space opened inside her as she listened, widening with each long note. Coaxed by the fiddle, she was opening herself to this place, for Charles's songs were not strutting out at marching tempo. They ambled and danced, not reaching beyond the horizon, but wheeling upward within it.

At last, then, he was settling. Caroline's throat swelled so fast the gladness nearly choked her. She pulled in a cool thin breath and held it. The song and the night air swirled through her, indistinguishable from one another. Nothing but the fiddle had spoken to her, and she was overcome. And Charles? He had eyes only for the strings, rocking so gently in time with the music that his contentment was unmistakable. Did he choose such melodies deliberately to match his spirits, Caroline wondered, or were his hands so connected to his heart that his mind did not enter into it at all? She watched his hands, now. The lightness of his fingers on the strings sent little tendrils of warmth through her. There was nothing in the world he touched more delicately, not even her own face.

All around them the blue-black bowl of sky throbbed with stars. The bow caressed the strings so softly they seemed to whisper, and Charles's voice, deep and mellow, melded with them:

None knew thee but to love thee,
Thou dear one of my heart . . .

Caroline lifted her eyes from his hands and found him gazing at her in the same way he had gazed at the fiddle strings. Delight bloomed all through her. She had no strength for modesty when he made his feelings so plain. She might hold her pleasure within herself, but she could not keep the effort from showing. The spread of her lips and the rounding of her cheeks gave her entirely away. And anyway, who was there to see? To have such a man, as content to hold her in his sight as in his [illegible]ros, and never in[illegible]lge [illegible] that would be a w[illegible]. Se[illegible] [illegible]en. Let him look [illegible] long [illegible] [illegible]en, Caroline deci[illegible], and [illegible] [illegible]ce let him savor [illegible] ple[illegible]

Laura gasped an[illegible] heir [illegible] d toward the sound, [illegible]akin[illegible] [illegible]ll. Caroline swa[illegible] d to [illegible] ent to kneel besid[illegible] er da[illegible] [illegible]rs. The girls had [illegible] th sl[illegible] [illegible] wagon tongue in[illegible] ired [illegible] [illegible]aps of calico in th[illegible] gras[illegible] Laura?"

Her blue eyes w[illegible] e wi[illegible] sky. "The stars w[illegible] sin g[illegible]," [illegible]ura whispered.

Under her skirt[illegible] nd st[illegible] d silent baby see[illegible] to [illegible] [illegible] a key turning, [illegible] if it [illegible] ing, all this time, [illegible] this [illegible] [illegible]d those words. [illegible] deep[illegible] kfulness radiated [illegible]ough [illegible] [illegible]dy before her m[illegible] d co[illegible] e words. Caroline bl[illegible]ked [illegible] [illegible]m her lashes as s[illegible] said [illegible] You've been asleep. [illegible] [illegible]dle. And it's tim[illegible] ittle [illegible] ed."

The firelight sh[illegible] e in [illegible] yes and blushed al[illegible] he[illegible] [illegible]d dimpled places [illegible] the [illegible] they crawled into [illegible] [illegible]sses. Such plum[illegible] and [illegible] girls. Anyone could [illegible] they [illegible] [illegible]er known a mo[illegible]nt's [illegible] readed the bottom [illegible] the [illegible] [illegible]rel as she once [illegible]d. P[illegible] e like this they n[illegible]r w[illegible] [illegible]aroline tucked th[illegible] int[illegible] eaving the canvas [illegible]n sp[illegible] [illegible]ght see the stars [illegible] the[illegible] d returned to the [illegible]e. Sh[illegible] [illegible]wn close beside [illegible]harle[illegible] words, and looked [illegible] int[illegible] [illegible]de open night. It [illegible]vas [illegible] agine that darkne[illegible] tret[illegible] [illegible] the way back a[illegible]oss t[illegible] hey had come. An[illegible] he [illegible] [illegible]g, low and rich [illegible]w, i[illegible] ving in an easy ba[illegible] and [illegible] [illegible]thm until the [illegible] ne t[illegible] the home they [illegible]uld [illegible] [illegible]ned within rea[illegible] of e[illegible]

[illegible]EITHER OF THE[illegible] ied [illegible] on cover. There w[illegible] no [illegible] [illegible]he night was plea[illegible]tly [illegible] undressed, and [illegible] oli[illegible] [illegible] desire to separa[illegible] hers [illegible]

Nor did Charles. He lay down beside her and unfastened the yoke of her nightdress, tucking it back so her bare shoulder stood out white in the moonlight.

"Charles," she warned.

"Shhh," he said. "Just this." His hand traveled across her skin, stirring the downy hair along the peak of her shoulder. The inside of his wrist came to rest along the slope of her breast, and his warm pulse reached inward to meet her own.

Only his thumb moved now, so lightly Caroline felt as though she were rising like cream through milk. She opened her mouth to quiet her breathing and closed her eyes. Her fingers found a soft little gully between the corded muscles of his neck. With her thumb she stroked the whiskers along his jaw. "Caroline," he whispered, and she felt the word with her fingers. There was no need to answer.

[illegible] Fourteen

ONCE MORE [illegible] the wagon, with the sun just [illegible] over the rim of the ea[illegible] of them looked ahead now—[illegible] Charles—watching as i[illegible] that was to be theirs would [illegible] greet them. Charles [illegible] one tune after another as [illegible] trotted briskly through [illegible] swishing yellow grass. Away [illegible] it was tall enough to [illegible] their bellies.

Caroline [illegible]ing, her heart fluttering [illegible] was different. Each one [illegible] down to the horses knew [illegible] stretched before them [illegible] that they strive ahead. [illegible] harnessed to the [illegible] own line, Caroline thought [illegible] as Pet and Patty [illegible] used to the wagon. [illegible] of trudging eve[illegible] lifted, and she felt such [illegible] nothing pressed them [illegible] weather nor the time of day [illegible]—nothing but [illegible] eagerness. They hurried, [illegible] only for the joy of [illegible]

Before the [illegible] had begun to wear off, C[illegible] on the reins. “H[illegible] Caroline. Right here we’[illegible]”

Here. Caro[illegible] at the suddenness of it. [illegible] weeks and miles, [illegible] syllable.

The other [illegible] jar. Down Mary and L[illegible] bare toes [illegible]ing [illegible] kes of the wheels. “Rea[illegible] up his hands for [illegible] always did. Caroline [illegible] as though [illegible]e. The house was not [illegible] yet she had the unr[illegible] of crossing its threshold [illegible] his hands [illegible] her [illegible]ing her to the ground.

No matter where the wagon stopped these last few days, there was always the feeling of being at the very center of the world. And now this would be their center, their world. It was beautiful, this pale, bright country with its blue-white sky, as beautiful as anything they had seen along the way.

Caroline turned slowly, looking all around her for something to mark this plot of ground off from the boundless land around it—something to fix in her memory and recognize as their own if she ever needed to find this place again, as the two big oaks and the sumac along the fence back home had done.

Here there were no marks upon the land itself. No fence or road, no hedge or furrow. Only bluffs rising to the north, an endless span of grass unrolling to the south. Between them, the rumpled line of a creek. Even the path the wagon had made through the grass was already melding back together.

For a moment she was adrift in the sameness of it all. There was nothing but the wagon to fasten to, and a wagon could never be trusted for such a task. Caroline swept her eyes across the breadth of the horizon. East to west, west to east, and back again. The more she looked, the more she steadied. No one thing had grasped her sight. It was everything at once, the whole contour of the view—the particular curve of the creek, the rougher edge of the bluffs against the sky—and the emerging knowledge that none of it could look quite the same from anywhere else. She could learn to recognize those lines the same way she recognized a familiar line of handwriting. It would only take time.

They unloaded the wagon right then and there, everything onto the ground with the canvas to spread over it. Then the wagon box itself came off the running gear and rested beside its freight. Goodness, it was small out in the open, all bare and swept and only a little more than knee-high in the tall grass.

Then, perched on the running gear, Charles rattled away toward the creek bottoms with his ax.

[illegible] the next two w[illegible] le but the sound of [illegible] [illegible] pping, hewing. [illegible] of the bark and [illegible] away from the p[illegible] each log as he squa[illegible] Th[illegible] were lovely to [illegible] stacked and waiting to [illegible] together. The sun wa[illegible] logs and every [illegible] smell the smell [illegible] would become, imag[illegible] her. But she di[illegible] to begin feelin[illegible] the sun rose a[illegible] sides of her bed. G[illegible] [illegible] ed up by the ho[illegible] water came fr[illegible] clea[illegible] sweet creek. A[illegible] unutterable luxury [illegible] of poles with a [illegible] eat.

[illegible] daily movemen[illegible] into the land— [illegible] necessary, the [illegible] basin, and around [illegible] wing stack of lo[illegible] Laura had their paths [illegible] e little hills an[illegible] the grass parted, the[illegible] d [illegible] t until at last it [illegible] dirt and was trampled [illegible] t.

[illegible] and the week [illegible] customed shape. Th[illegible] re the churning [illegible] ght to have been, [illegible] fill[illegible] with the bland [illegible] tions for the child. [illegible] linen and paint [illegible] linseed oil to m[illegible] then fashioned [illegible] them—one for [illegible] ek to guard the [illegible] king diapers. To pro- [illegible] s she oiled rou[illegible] d to fit her breasts [illegible] ith linen. Then [illegible] for filling, so th[illegible] oper pad to ke[illegible] the birth from soa[illegible] Mo[illegible] e oilcloth [illegible] ver for that purp[illegible] the wagon cov[illegible] ght better of it. [illegible] seed oil and pa[illegible] tablecloths inst[illegible] g she found ple[illegible] to double her suppl[illegible]

[illegible] e small tasks d[illegible] way from the land [illegible] yet strangely nearer it, for the child she prepared for would be a Kansan. Indeed, it already was so. Every time Caroline looked up from her work she could see the square Charles had paced off for the house, and inside that square was the place where the child would be born. Charles and the girls must work at making the land their own, but the child would emerge belonging to it.

IN ONE DAY Charles built the house as high as Laura's head. Two dozen logs, notched and hoisted and fitted. After supper they leaned their elbows on the short walls, admiring the neat square space. Charles pointed out where the door and windows and fireplace would be, while inside Mary and Laura ran gleeful circles. Jack barked and wagged outside, trying to lick at them through the chinks. Caroline ran her hands across the topmost log. Good oak, just as their house in Wisconsin had been, but younger, slenderer. A youthful little house.

IN AND OUT went the needle. In and out and in and then the ax struck wood and she was looking up at Charles again. He stood halfway up the wall with his boot toes wedged between the chinks, chopping a notch into the topmost log. *Look, look, look,* the ax seemed to say each time it bit into the wood. *Watch, watch, watch.* Caroline pulled her needle through the flannel. In the time it had taken him to raise that log, she had sewn no more than a half dozen stitches. Perhaps if she sewed in time with the ax she could manage to keep her eyes on her own work. *Chop*-and-stitch and *chop*-and-stitch and *chop*-and-*whizz!* came a little chip of wood sailing down to land at her feet, and there she was, watching again. She forced her eyes back into her lap. Rags. Flannel rags she would not need for months yet. Impatience crackled in her elbows and all up and down her back. She could not do such tedious work. Not with the whole house going up ten feet from her face. She would fly apart. Caroline jabbed her needle into the half-finished pad and dropped it into her work basket.

Out of the scrap ag [illegible] curtain made of [illegible]
ad fashioned [illegible] quarters, it would lik[illegible]
curtains for the w[illegible] e [illegible] ngered the pr[illegible]
itching along the [illegible] ist match her che[illegible]
he rummage [illegible] and came up w[illegible]
nippings from La[illegible]'s [illegible] alico. Enough, p[illegible]
ain ties—if s[illegible] moothed the p[illegible]
p and smile[illegible] at [illegible] red and white [illegible]
reshly hewn [illegible] ak [illegible] lls [illegible] ould fly so much [illegible]
naking somet[illegible] ing [illegible] Charles's ax. B[illegible]
neasure and [illegible] t [illegible] tai[illegible] s that did not ex[illegible]
ttle fabric to [illegible] par[illegible] Ca[illegible] olded the calic[illegible]
ether and tuc[illegible] ed [illegible] scr[illegible]p bag. She too[illegible]
ad again and [illegible] er [illegible] fr[illegible]stration.

Always, th[illegible] sca[illegible] of [illegible] dwarfed her ow[illegible]
ook him to b[illegible] ild [illegible] re, she might knit [illegible]
pound of bu[illegible] ter [illegible] vital than the [illegible] r;
ot build or pl[illegible] nt [illegible] Charles knew th[illegible]
id and never fail [illegible] new shirt or a [illegible]
o have a han[illegible] in [illegible] ng that would no[illegible]
vorn out, ou[illegible] gro[illegible] gr[illegible]nd as a house [illegible]
ean against t[illegible] at [illegible] to come and kn[illegible] hat
elped put it t[illegible] ere [illegible] at [illegible] he thought.

But it was [illegible] ard [illegible] en for Charles. [illegible]
lay before. C[illegible] roli[illegible] ck and should[illegible]
wift exhale a[illegible] he [illegible] d. Yesterday hi[illegible]
he brunt of t[illegible] e [illegible] squat down, [illegible]
nd of the log [illegible] an [illegible] again. Today [illegible]
alf the task. No[illegible] the [illegible] lls demanded [illegible]
is arms to h[illegible] ist [illegible] pace had slo[illegible]
ven the girls int[illegible] finally wande[illegible]
Ip went one [illegible] nd [illegible] corner where [illegible]

Then, tentatively, the other rose as he worked, shuffling and grunting, to bring the whole timber level without dislodging the first end. One nudge too far and the wood lurched from its place, bumping its way down each of the logs beneath it. Charles staggered back, dropping his end without a word. He whipped out his handkerchief in a flash of red and swiped his face.

Caroline was beside him with the dipper and pail before he'd stuffed the handkerchief back into his pocket. "Let me help, Charles," she said as he drank. His eyes popped up from the dipper. One, then two drops of water trickled through his beard. Charles put down the dipper and wiped his chin in the crook of his elbow, still looking at her. Her empty hands reached for each other, then fled behind her back. She could not fold them before her as she usually did without drawing attention to her belly. There was no hiding it these days, but nor was there any need to proclaim it, either. Perhaps with no other women in sight he had grown accustomed to her shape. Perhaps, if she stood quite still and made no mention of it herself, he would not take it into account.

He considered so long her fingers began to wish for the needle and thread, if only to keep from fidgeting. She felt like one of the children, standing there so earnestly. Caroline watched the corners of his eyes narrow with thought and knew he was wondering how to accept without making more work for himself, as she did when Mary and Laura begged to lend a hand in her chores. She ought to have treated him to a jug of ginger water and sat back down to her sewing instead of trying to elbow in.

"I won't have you lifting logs," he said at last. "But do you think you could brace them while I lift the other end and square the join?"

Caroline did not say one word. All her childish excitement would spill out if she opened her mouth to say so much as *Yes, Charles*. She simply nodded and followed him to the west wall.

The logs that formed the northern corner jutted toward her like oversized pegs. Charles lifted the end of the fallen timber onto the highest [illegible] it [illegible] th the heels of [illegible] ha [illegible] way. Don [illegible] h [illegible] lift the other [illegible] move som [illegible] side—just lean [illegible] ol ne plan [illegible] la [illegible] ed her body forw [illegible] es de his. [illegible] n the wall under [illegible] slid- ing [illegible] nt to the south [illegible] other end. [illegible] ile I fit this into [illegible] cked, then [illegible] l squarely into pl [illegible] erself back [illegible] e did her end slid [illegible]

Charles [illegible] s on his hips and [illegible] roval. "Th [illegible] it [illegible]

[illegible] lt [illegible] e house one log [illegible] Each time [illegible] wn and took the [illegible] ands, leve [illegible] with a thrust of [illegible] nt his kne [illegible] hoisted the end [illegible] o ine nev [illegible] -the swoop of h [illegible] n the ball [illegible] ip of his palms a [illegible] n. He grin [illegible]

[illegible] e was like some [illegible] man, too [illegible] fully real. With [illegible] when life [illegible] arger than them [illegible] talked of [illegible] ad caught glimp [illegible] cur- ren [illegible] h purpose and [illegible] could acc [illegible] d on this blank [illegible] e end of [illegible] his part, she di [illegible] in a wo [illegible] what made him [illegible] as tho [illegible] e had sung, come [illegible] little to i [illegible] ong anyone coul [illegible] d be aki [illegible] g as commonpla [illegible] ilk.

[illegible] what happened [illegible] lt pass thr [illegible] own her elbows [illegible] d sud- de [illegible] down toward he [illegible]

She hitched herself sideways, going up on tiptoe to boost the log from beneath with her shoulder. Her foot caught in a hollow and one knee buckled. The log's weight shifted toward the notch of her neck, pressing her down. Caroline's thigh muscles surged upward. Too late—her knee could not straighten under the load. Her shin threatened to splinter like a matchstick. Every hinge in her body wavered as though it were on the verge of melting.

"Let go!" Charles called. "Get out from under!"

It was not a matter of letting go. Her hands bore none of the weight. It was her shoulder. She could not lift it from her shoulder. Her only hope was to throw her body down faster than the log could fall. Caroline let both knees buckle fully and thrust her hands up against the wood, hurling herself outward.

All the points of her body struck the ground—knee, hip, elbow, shoulder.

She lay waiting for the crack, expecting to be split like a pitcher and feel herself spilling out onto the grass.

No crack came. Only the steady weight of the log on her foot, and, smothered somewhere beneath that, pain. She was not sensible of the pain itself, only a strange sensation pushing hard against the log, impatient to be felt.

"Caroline!" Charles was beside her, and Laura.

"I'm all right." Her voice was a gasp, the words nearly a lie. She was hurt, that was certain. How badly she could not tell. But she would mend or manage without; Caroline knew that already. Nothing vital in her had broken.

Charles lifted the log free. Pain bulged up into the space it left behind, so large for an instant she feared her shoe might burst. Caroline pulled herself tight. If she could hold her body tightly enough, she thought, she could shrink the pain down small enough to fit back inside her.

"Move your arms," Charles demanded. "Is your back hurt? Can you turn your head?"

C[illegible]ne did not want to move a[illegible]. Simply exhaling sent flames [illegible] and cold racing through her [illegible]. But she had never seen such a [illegible] on Charles's face. Not even w[illegible] rising nearly to his ears [illegible] looked so horrified—whit[illegible]ling, and hardly an inch [illegible] tears. Gingerly she moved [illegible]. He looked to her middle, [illegible]ghtened to ask aloud.

[illegible]line pulled all the awareness she could muster away from her [illegible]bing foot. If anything had go[illegible] with the child she could not [illegible]. The log had struck nothing [illegible] she was sure of. The rest [illegible]nted to no more than a stu[illegible]. She tried to smile for him [illegible] managed mostly to wince.

“[illegible] God,” Charles said. H[illegible] one arm behind her shoul[illegible] and another across her belly [illegible] helped her sit up. He looked at [illegible] and his face seemed to shrink [illegible] the effort of holding his relief [illegible] check.

Caroline laid a hand on his a[illegible]. “I'm all right, Charles,” she said [illegible], her voice far from steady. “[illegible] my foot.”

With shaking fingers he strip[illegible] her shoe and stocking and [illegible]ed into the raging flesh to f[illegible] length of every slim bone and [illegible] each joint. “Does it hurt mu[illegible]”

“Not much.” A bald-faced lie, [illegible] compunctions. Anything to [illegible] him stop.

“No bones broken,” he said. “[illegible] a bad sprain.” The pro[illegible]ing [illegible]ed, but his eyes did not leave [illegible]. He stared at it, puffed and [illegible]ling in his palm—for once i[illegible] come by what might have [illegible]. He ran his other hand over [illegible] and up through his hair [illegible] was shallow through [illegible] open mouth.

“Well, a sprain's soon mended[illegible] so upset, Charles.”

“I blame myself. Should have [illegible]. He still held her heel in one [illegible], his head in the other.

She could not sit on the groun[illegible], or Charles would [illegible] the [illegible] to break. That was something [illegible] must never see. Caroline put her palms to the ground and pushed. Without a word between them Charles's arms were right where she needed them to be. Caroline felt him bracing for her weight and knew he would carry her, but she did not need Laura to see that, either. She pressed herself forward until his arms began to lift with her. Only a little wobble and she was upright on her good foot. Caroline stood still a moment, panting. Then she bent her grimace to resemble a smile and said, "Please bring my shoe and stocking, Laura."

Fifteen

THERE IS [illegible] world but the weight—pulling, [illegible] dragging down. No [illegible] hands, but her own belly [illegible]. If she lets up, it [illegible] tearing her dress, her [illegible] Barefoot, [illegible] prairie for help. In one cabin, only [illegible] Indians. [illegible] breasts weigh like sacks of [illegible] begin slipping [illegible] other. Then the sound of ripping [illegible] of cloth or flesh?

Caroline [illegible]. Nothing had split apart but [illegible] weight was only Charles's arm hugged down into the [illegible] valley between her belly [illegible]. Caroline lay awake, feeling [illegible] of her pulse against [illegible] and about her ankle. Her [illegible], making [illegible] dark. Charles pinned under [illegible] log instead. The [illegible] she must cross to reach help [illegible]. Caroline [illegible] shut. The pictures changed [illegible]. She saw [illegible] belly, and the empty [illegible] of a [illegible] from between [illegible] drawn-up knees. The place where [illegible] should be. "Oh, [illegible]," she [illegible].

Caroline [illegible] a deep breath as she could [illegible] Charles's arm and willed herself to relax. That she could not [illegible]. Her foot hurt, and [illegible] no longer smelled of home. [illegible], and prickly [illegible] the new straw Jacobs had given [illegible]. Caroline tried to shift [illegible] without rousing Charles [illegible]. A jerky little [illegible], as though she'd startled it.

She was [illegible] between them. Sandwiched [illegible] without and within. [illegible] she laid her arm over his, [illegible] trusting across the soft curling hairs that belied the firm muscles beneath. How different it must feel to be a man: built solid through, with everything beneath the skin belonging solely to yourself. Did he ever envy what she could take into herself, how much she could contain? Could he comprehend all it meant for a woman to hold herself open for her husband, her children? For all it demanded of her Caroline knew she would not trade the depth of those open spaces, those currents of life passing through her. No man could encompass another life so fully as a woman, except perhaps in his mind. Perhaps that was what made Charles clutch her so close now as he slept. He had felt her slip through his fingers this afternoon. It was providential, he had said, that her foot had not been crushed. She had not told him that the same hollow that saved her foot had caused the fall.

CAROLINE LOST COUNT of how many days passed before she could wear her shoe again, never mind lace it. Her instep swelled until the skin shone taut and yellow. Beneath the joint itself the side of her foot looked as though it were pooling with ink; a streak of black and blue and purple marked a line along the sole of her foot. Bands of greenish-purple ringed the base of her toes. The deep rosy smudges running up her calf seemed almost pretty in comparison. The smooth white fibers that joined muscle to bone in the stringy drumsticks of rabbits and fowl, these she could feel now in her own leg, and it was there that the pain lingered most stubbornly.

In the meantime she hobbled, and the house waited. Charles hewed out skids, and they leaned against the unfinished walls like a pair of crutches until the day he came up from the creek bottom calling, "Good news!"

An upward rush of hope surged through her and then leveled. He had not been to town—it would not be a letter or a paper.

"A neighbor," Charles said. "Just two miles over the creek. Fellow's a bachelor. Says he can get along without a house better than you and the [illegible] me build fi[illegible]st. [illegible] his logs rea[illegible]y, [illegible] do you like tha[illegible] Ca[illegible]

[illegible] ridiculous th[illegible]at [illegible] sh[illegible] seven hund[illegible]d [illegible]kled by the [illegible]isc[illegible]ery [illegible] She smiled, [illegible] [illegible]aning to, an[illegible] Ch[illegible]les [illegible]. It was fine ne[illegible]s, [illegible]

[illegible] before the [illegible]rea[illegible]st [illegible]ped—tall a[illegible]d [illegible] of a man. [illegible]is [illegible] [illegible]ker even th[illegible]n [illegible]ame's Edwa[illegible]ds, [illegible]out waiting [illegible]o [illegible]nd bowed s[illegible] lo[illegible] tha[illegible] coonskin c[illegible]p [illegible]nd. He loo[illegible]ed [illegible] way a wom[illegible]n [illegible]ing her in a[illegible] at [illegible]owledging t[illegible]e [illegible]regnancy w[illegible] hying from [illegible]t. [illegible] had told him [illegible] Pe[illegible]aps [illegible]e had come [illegible]o [illegible]

[illegible]nt he bent do[illegible] [illegible]ake her han[illegible], [illegible]ake her eyes [illegible]ro[illegible] [illegible] a wildcat fr[illegible]n [illegible] her, and sh[illegible] wa[illegible] him, too, b[illegible]t [illegible] she shouldn't Ca[illegible] looked at [illegible]is [illegible] watched h[illegible] e[illegible] [illegible]ure of awe a[illegible]d [illegible] spit a stream [illegible] corner of t[illegible]e [illegible] tongue.

[illegible] admit, if [illegible]nly [illegible] had never se[illegible]n [illegible]posefully. With [illegible] like emptyi[illegible]g [illegible]less brown stre[illegible] st inches fro[illegible]n [illegible] took aim eve[illegible] lips and sent a [illegible]aight towar[illegible] his [illegible]

[illegible] was to tame Ed[illegible] [illegible]mper and pe[illegible] [illegible] to bring h[illegible] for Christma[illegible]. [illegible] Edwards, [illegible] and swing a[illegible] [illegible] flew faster th[illegible]an [illegible]

CHARLES AND EDWARDS worked together like brothers, so fast and sure that it was bewildering to see. Caroline watched them singing and joking, riding the rising walls together and felt envy seeping into her gratitude. It had not mattered so very much yesterday when Charles had said their neighbor was a bachelor, but now Caroline longed for a Mrs. Edwards. Her girls helped, and eagerly, but it was not the same as working companionably alongside another woman.

And Edwards, who was he accustomed to working beside, back home in Tennessee? The way his movements harmonized with Charles's made it plain that he was used to being part of a team, and a good one, too. She and Charles could never have raised the walls in a single day. For that matter, neither could Charles and Henry, back home.

They would have dumplings with the stewed jackrabbit for their supper, Caroline decided. Never mind that there was no milk, no egg, no butter. White flour would show Edwards what his day's work meant to her. She dipped up a small cupful of broth and mixed it with bacon drippings, salt, and sugar. Then the soft, snowy flour, a full pint of it. She had not even opened the bag since . . . Christmas? Her eyes smarted at that, and Caroline shrugged one shoulder up to swipe her cheek. No use in summoning up thoughts of Christmas with Eliza and Peter.

CHARLES STOOD BESIDE the newly fashioned doorway, grinning. The house was just as he had said, just as she had pictured it: a little more than twelve feet square, with windows east and west and space for a fireplace at one end.

But looking at it did not feel the same as imagining it, not even with the homey smell of a company supper wafting in. Her mind had limned the image with warmth and softness, as though it would become home the moment it existed. The reality was simply a house—fresh and welcoming, yet surreal in its blankness.

She had felt something very like this before, Caroline remembered, the first time Polly put Mary into her arms. All those months waiting for the[illegible] baby, [illegible] their son or daughter [illegible] was an infant. [illegible] till overpowered [illegible] that moment. [illegible] arms, astoundingly [illegible] and as [illegible] though Polly had lifted [illegible] instead of Caroline [illegible].

Shyly, C[illegible] and touched the [illegible] doorway [illegible]. She would sweep [illegible] sleep in it, [illegible] dress in it. Come [illegible] a child with [illegible] likely one day [illegible] midst of [illegible] the place would shi[illegible] without her [illegible] to pinpoint the mome[illegible]

Pois[illegible], she pressed her finger [illegible] bare w[illegible] de. A notion had [illegible] foolish [illegible] rm to brush aside. [illegible] *introduce* [illegible]

THEY A[illegible] ire, halfway between h[illegible] spectful [illegible] made Caroline wo[illegible] cretly [illegible] the house acquaint[illegible] perhaps [illegible] anted to sit back a[illegible]

Edwards [illegible] the ground, her [illegible] his narrow [illegible] Charles played the fidd[illegible] Edward [illegible] and Mary and Laura [illegible] Charles' fac[illegible] the white flash of t[illegible] were pl[illegible] of swirling couple[illegible]

Caroline [illegible]. *This,* she thought [illegible] how it had [illegible] selves at home in [illegible] lars were [illegible] ds kicking up his h[illegible] still too [illegible] house only an outl[illegible] the glow of [illegible].

Caroline [illegible], to the empty hou[illegible] of its ro[illegible] he sky. Tomorrow [illegible]

Sixteen

WALLS, STRAIGHT UP and down, and a ridgepole too high to touch. Caroline had not realized how much she missed the simple shape of a room. Her eyes could not get enough of the lovely squareness of the corners with their sturdy intersections. It did not matter that there was no door, no shutters, no curtains. Even with sunshine pouring through the chinks and the open roof Caroline felt sheltered, truly sheltered, for the first time in months. All this time she had held herself half-hunched against the elements, always ready to cock one shoulder against wind or rain or whatever else the sky might hurl at them. What a delight to turn her back almost defiantly to the sky as she swept the last of the chips from the floor.

Above her, Charles wrestled with the wind, stretching the canvas like a skin over the skeleton of roof poles. All those onerous yards of stitches had held so well that the wagon cover could serve as their roof until Charles raised a stable. That in itself was so immensely satisfying that the idea of a cloth roof did not dampen the pleasure Caroline took in the house. Already the space it enclosed belonged to her in a way the inside of the wagon never had, for the wagon never held the same space—it only flowed through a place, borrowing as it went.

A beguiling, radiant sort of shade fell over her. It was the canvas, suffusing the bright sunlight overhead. Caroline stilled the broom and pushed back her sunbonnet to watch Charles work. The wind was giving him fits, billowing and snapping the canvas and blowing his hair and whiskers every which way. He snorted and blustered so, she wanted to laugh at him. He would have that wagon cover lashed down in a jiffy.

...f he did not. Caro... into place
...bare tent poles to... first thing
...nside the house w... plumped

...barked at the canva... "S... and be—"
..., her arms full of...
..." He blinked sweet... Caroline,
...was going to say?"
...e cried. "You scala...g."
...n the outer corne... ed up his
...ke he'd crawled ou... e bush.
...ld back earlier turn... grabbed
...triumphant. The ras... he world
...et herself enough to... a school-

...snug house?" Ch... er close
...y could both look...
...logs, topped wit... looked
...the soft blue sky. ... tell him
...ll be thankful to g...
...well here, Caroline," C... teasing
...oice. "This is a grea... ntry I'll
...n the rest of my life...
...used for an instant. Th... o those
...ard from him befo... hen it's
...ured, scarcely dari... rim to

...against his chest w... when
...nised, and leaned ... head.
...and close the neigh... never
...that sky!"
...might come with... chains

to mark the necessary range and township lines, but they would never square the curve from the sky.

EVERYTHING WENT WHERE she wanted it—the broom in one corner, the churn in the other. Charles's gun over the door, of course, and the beds against the back wall, leaving space between them for the fireplace. Every decision belonged to her. Charles and Mary and Laura would not put one thing down without looking first to her for approval, as though the map of the inside of the cabin existed in her mind alone.

So she pointed out places for pegs to hang their clothing, the dishpan and dish towel, and Charles drove them into the walls. He hewed out narrow slabs for shelves and wedged those in between the logs in the corner that she designated as the kitchen. Caroline could have spent the afternoon admiring those plain, serviceable shelves. No longer would she have to bend double for a scoop of flour or cornmeal from a sack on the ground. Nor would her neatly packed crates be jumbled and jostled into disarray. She had accommodated so many trifling inconveniences over such a long time that she had not felt their accumulating weight. Now, so many lifted all at once that it seemed she might rise from the floor. If not for the inevitability of cooking supper over the campfire, she might have.

But the campfire itself was more pleasant, too, because of the house. Because of the house, *outside* and *inside* had become distinct from each other once more. It was a rich feeling, sitting outside after supper for no better reason than because they wanted to. There was something absurdly delightful in the knowledge that behind those walls their beds lay ready and waiting, with the nightclothes hanging neatly on their pegs. Nothing need be dismantled or rearranged.

A warm, nectary scent glided by on the breeze. "I wonder," Caroline said, "if the cherry tree back home is budded out yet."

"I wonder what Polly will do for her cherry preserves if the Gustafsons don't share the fruit with her," Charles answered.

Carol[illegible] Sh[illegible]ould [illegible]st imagine Polly [illegible] her [illegible] share of [illegible] Perhaps she would [illegible] the child[illegible] basket [illegible] as she'd always [illegible] suspecting [illegible] their door to find thre[illegible] Charlotte [illegible] Wouldn't that be just lik[illegible] Peter's family [illegible] red by now," Caroline [illegible] hands [illegible] She was still not so big [illegible] when [illegible] niece or nephew, Caroline [illegible] stillborn [illegible] Eliza would be wondering [illegible] No, Caroline [illegible] ng—she had not told [illegible] left, [illegible] Charles.

"I [illegible] ready to post when we stop [illegible] dence," [illegible] she [illegible] been able to think ab[illegible] any news [illegible] h. The home folks wo[illegible] to have [illegible] snowfall. *Write,* Eliza [illegible] morning [illegible].

"I'll [illegible] into town one of these days [illegible] the roof, [illegible] our stable and Ed[illegible] raised, [illegible] and take them [illegible] room in [illegible] the letters you want to send [illegible]

Caroline [illegible] more weeks, but [illegible] At least [illegible] at the end of their bed, [illegible] her lap [illegible] pulled [illegible] en any time she pleased.

She [illegible] that trunk after [illegible] bed, [illegible] the [illegible]ace. Moonlight [illegible] a soft [illegible] Caroline knew she would miss [illegible] Charles [illegible] with wooden slabs.

"Come [illegible] Caroline, and look at the moon," [illegible] softly. Caroline [illegible] under the quilt [illegible] for a [illegible] spring seat, arms op[illegible] line sat [illegible] settled in against him. Ch[illegible] heel of [illegible] ground, bobbing the spring s[illegible] beneath them almost like a rocking chair. His thumb caressed her upper arm in slow harmony.

Caroline looked at the round white moon hanging free in the sky. Without trees or clouds to frame its light, there seemed to be no end to its reach, no end to anything at all. Darkness had melted the horizon; only the faint border of stars made it possible to separate earth from sky. Caroline closed her eyes and all of it melded together—the sphere of the child floating inside her, the circle of Charles's arms around her. Bounded and boundless.

Sev[illegible]

[illegible] CHARLES called "C[illegible] [illegible]hat Pet has [illegible]

[illegible]ed them to the [illegible]ttle [illegible] distance. Sh[illegible]
[illegible] be, but she had [illegible]
[illegible] was still glistening the [illegible] so new. The
[illegible] the cool morning ai[illegible] [illegible]he afterbirth
[illegible] oblivious, having e[illegible] [illegible]re's delicate
[illegible]ears. Caroline coul[illegible] [illegible]erment, but
[illegible] of it. The sigh[illegible] unruffled,
[illegible] filly standing on the [illegible] twin sister
[illegible] Caroline all slack[illegible] [illegible]almost. For
[illegible] she found herself wi[illegible] Charles and
[illegible] the stable in a single [illegible] the night
[illegible] filly had been waiting [illegible] be built—
[illegible]ing was ready to [illegible] [illegible]n stepped
[illegible] very next moment.

[illegible]simple when her time [illegible]
[illegible] the cabin finished [illegible] [illegible]e. There
[illegible] and a hearth and her [illegible] curtains
[illegible]s well before summer [illegible] [illegible]ne, Caro-
[illegible]ather lie on the floor, [illegible] [illegible]or and a
[illegible]ly could be there with [illegible]

[illegible] a thing when Charles [illegible] [illegible]d set off
[illegible]as not that she wanted [illegible] [illegible]he open

prairie under that hot white sun. Given the choice she would much rather spread a quilt on the grass in the shade of the house and have a Sunday school with her girls. It was only that he had these chances to unhitch himself from everything, and she did not. There was never the extravagance of an afternoon all to herself, to do no more than sit down with her desk in her lap and write a letter to Eliza without a single interruption. Envy, pure and simple, and nothing she said to herself would snuff the resentful flicker in her throat. If she spoke aloud Charles would hear it, too, and so she only waved as he trotted away. No sense in marring his pleasure simply because she could not partake of it.

"WHAT'S THE MATTER with Jack?" Laura asked.

Caroline looked up from the bake oven. The hair on the back of the bulldog's neck was bristling. Pet ran a nervous circuit and whickered for her foal.

It was as though a wind passed, touching only the animals. Caroline had felt nothing, not the least stir of unease. That in itself sent a little shiver across her arms. "What's the matter, Jack?" she asked. He seemed to raise his eyebrows at her. Caroline turned a slow circle. Nothing, as far as she could see. Nor a sound. She watched Jack's nose quiver into the wind. A scent, then?

Her first thought, always: *Indians?*

Could Jack's and Pet's noses perceive the difference between one race and another? More likely they could scent the dead things the Indians adorned themselves with—the skins and feathers, teeth and bone. Caroline had not seen an Osage since that day on the street in Independence, but she remembered the tufts of hair that fringed their leggings.

All this time in Indian Territory, Caroline thought, and not one Indian. Even Charles had not seen them—only their deserted camping places. When she asked why, he had answered in that careless way of his. *Oh, I don't know. They're away on a hunting trip, I guess.*

And wh… they … Caroline wondered? … at the thou… Ch… had not pai… ce… no proper claim … have papers … even filed on it … Indians? W… the … ge—what weigh… been before … his house standing … There wa… their rent as the … rifle, and th… already on gua… had been pu… Caroline could … but that was … so a … her mind answ…

The pony … from the bottoms … straight for th… Ca… not see the rider— … hunched low … straining neck. … the ground, a… her backbone … She did not ha… time … and rider tore … saw that it was … Charles. Patty's … slash in the gr… to a stop just … The pony shud… dripping with sweat. … down and spun … bluffs.

Caroline tu… horizon, too, … arty with arro… but the wind … rass behind hi… "Wh… said. "Why did yo… at?"

"I was afraid … come here," Charle… everything … "Wolves!" she … "Everything's … he said. "Let … breath."

Everything co… not with the way … shaking as he mop… back of his ne… under his whiskers …

It was all I coul… Charles panted.

Caroline, the biggest wolves I ever saw. I wouldn't go through such a thing again, not for a mint of money."

Caroline wanted to fold her ears shut, to pretend it was anyone but Charles describing how that pack of buffalo wolves had surrounded him, how he'd forced Patty to walk among them as they frisked and frolicked like dogs. If anything had happened to him, if just one of those wolves had taken a mind to— The thought loomed so large, she could hardly see around it. Widowed and pregnant like her own ma, his child a living ghost in her belly. Her whole life Caroline had carried the memory of how Ma had dropped where she stood at the news of Pa's shipwreck, as though the weight of that fatherless baby had yanked her to the ground.

"I was glad you had the gun, Caroline," Charles was saying. "And glad the house is built. I knew you could keep the wolves out of the house, with the gun. But Pet and the foal were outside."

Caroline bridled so suddenly the fear fell right out of her. Why had he gone off at all if he had reason to worry about the stock? Did it never occur to Charles that it might behoove them all to worry about himself now and again? "You need not have worried, Charles," she said, holding her voice exactly level. "I guess I would manage to save our horses."

"I was not fully reasonable at the time," he apologized, and some small part of herself Caroline hardly recognized was satisfied that he had been scared out of his wits. Perhaps he would remember that the next time he took it into his head to trot off toward the horizon.

"We'll eat supper in the house," she said.

"No need of that. Jack will give us warning in plenty of time."

If they ate inside there would be no need of warning, but she did not bother saying so. That sort of logic held no sway with Charles.

"CAROLINE." CAROLINE FELT her mind stir, then sink back toward sleep. "Caroline. Wake up."

His voice made no sense. She could hear Charles breathing heavily beside her, yet the words came from above. She lay in the near silence,

...tening to that rhyth...
...areness.

Caroline's eyes spran... ope...
...s wolf, the sounds ... its...
...h... logs.

...arles stood with ... ri...
...m all around the ho...e," ...
...le... and half-cocked. The...
...er hand and leaned i...
...h...mbers were full. C...rles...
...to stand beside the ...
...table. She could hear ...
...ly Caroline crept ... the...
...lf from the floor. F...
...d of her trunk and pu...led...
...olves' breath so near ...
...lance. Another shov... aga...
...ndowsill.

...oline paused to look ...ro...
...r hand became no m... me...
...t once, could do a... ne...
...gger wolves in his ... bu...
...ey looked like bears ... ou...
...n of them before the ... ng...
...the revolver she and ... ha...
...s ...l. If that pack set ... n...
...hought did not frigh... b...
...ted to come inside, C... oline...
...r aside and devoure... l f...
... Until they did all sh... ...
...protect themselves.

...he sat down on her ...nk...

...until something pric...ed...

...Charles panting besid... her
...h leaking between the ... hin...

...bent arm. "There's a... ng...
...red. "Take this. Caref... . It...
...roline took the wa... to...
...ight to see the cyl... A...
...toward the west windo... and
...oline knew he was wa... ing
...orting and pacing

...raw tick and begar ... ise...
...n she laid her free han... on
...er knees. With the sou... of
...her fingers into the ch...ks
...rought her eyes leve... th...

...llow hole and the revo...er
...a popgun. Those wol...s,
...Charles had said he'c ne...er
...atures were so imposs...y
...l wolf skins. She cou...d
...f her sight. Between ...
...able to discourage the...
...ning the cabin, it wou...
...ontrary—if the wol...
...ey would have nosed ...
...in their sleep. But the...
...uld do was signal the...

...her shawl from its peg

She propped the revolver's barrel on the windowsill, pulled back the hammer to full cock, and slipped her finger inside the trigger guard. So long as the wolves sat still, Caroline's thoughts kept still, suspended in an aura of calm. If the wolves came nearer, she knew her finger would squeeze the trigger before her mind formed the command, and so there was no need for her thoughts to go straying ahead.

The wolves made not a move, as though they sensed how near they could come without provoking a reaction. They sat, neither welcoming nor threatening, more acknowledging the boundary between them. Even Jack did not advance, did not so much as put his nose beyond the quilt hanging in the doorway. All of them silently watched one another. The moonlight glinted on the wolves' shaggy coats and made their eyes glow deep and green-gold. What part of her, she wondered, did the animals fix their gaze on? What feature most proclaimed her human—her clothing, her hairless skin? More likely her hands, Caroline decided, and the gun they held.

From the west side of the cabin came a long, smooth howl. As Caroline watched the wolves outside her window showed their white throats to the moon and a circle of sound rose up from them. The sound enveloped the cabin, reverberating all the way into the soft marrow of Caroline's bones until she felt it might lift her away. Was it music to them, she wondered, or prayer, the way it ascended into the sky?

Before she could rebuke herself for thinking something so profane Laura was up—straight up, clutching the quilt so tightly Caroline could see the little points of her knees and toes beneath the taut fabric.

At the sight of Charles with his gun Laura's grip on the bedclothes loosened.

"Want to see them, Laura?" Charles asked.

Laura nodded and went to him. Caroline knew she ought not take her eyes from her window, but she could not help it. The tableau of Charles lifting Laura to the windowsill captivated her in a way the motionless wolves could not. The child believed so wholeheartedly that

... her as long as he ... ar all but ...

... be, Caroline ... d hardly ... a feeling. She ... the last ... pa. Looking back ... terrible ... rocking beneath ... s death ... that came before the ... n sank. ... smooth metal seam ... ith her ... moved past her ... ad be- ... he could trust ... s first ... then to Charles, ... lread- ... after she lived ... e that ... could protect her ...

... another night, Charles ha... r the ...

... was gone, helpi... ouse ... with the girls ... per, ... beside her and ... the ... was only two mi... feel ... was out all day ... nd. ... separate labors were ... en- ... rles brought her ... ro- ... shade his neck ... in ... from that harves... nd ... "The House That Jack ... engaged in some ... ot ... Not one bit. If no ... y ... ent the night ... back-and-forth ... d ... no doubt she and Cha...

That was not the trouble. That was not what made her thoughts dreary and her smiles limp, even when the wind carried the sound of his approaching whistle up from the creek bottoms.

Caroline did not know quite what it was until after supper the second night, when Charles said, "Bring me my fiddle, Laura, I want to try out a song Edwards sang."

His eyes twinkled mischievously as he felt for the notes. It was a catchy melody with a good strong beat, well-suited for an accompaniment of swinging axes and hammers. Likely she would find herself humming it over the butter churn one day.

"What are the words, Pa?" Mary asked.

The bow gave a little squawk, and Charles colored ever so slightly. "Well, you know, I don't seem to remember any more than the tune," he said quickly.

Caroline knew from his grimace that the words were not fit for mixed company. That in itself was no great shock. She could imagine Charles and Edwards indulging in the occasional oath or bawdy song, just as there were things women would speak of only if there were no men within earshot.

Caroline rested her folded arms across the shelf of her belly. There, she thought. That was what she had been missing while Charles was away. Not her husband's company, but the chance to share her own. The girls had their games and giggles, the men their brash hijinks. Caroline had only herself.

BEFORE THE ROOF, before the floor, came the fireplace. Charles might have dug himself a well first and saved himself hauling water from the creek to mix the mud for plastering between the chimney stones. Instead he built the chimney and hearth, so she would not have to tussle with the elements to keep her cookfire going. That was the sort of husband Charles Ingalls was.

Caroline sat in the shade of the north wall, turning scraps of red calico into curtain ties [illegible] stones while the child tu[illegible] have discovered its limbs [illegible] akin to a spoon sti[illegible]ng [illegible] the past several weeks. [illegible] room it gave the bo[illegible] of t[illegible] her spine like a ramrod al[illegible] The straw tick, with noth[illegible] help at all.

Truth be told, what Caro[illegible] Not an upturned crate or lo[illegible] and arms. She would look [illegible] a chair to ease her weary b[illegible] rocker, and she smiled wis[illegible] was building her a fireplac[illegible] hurry to please her, lifting s[illegible]

He stood back, squinting [illegible] and setting it all askew [illegible]

"You look like a wild ma[illegible] your hair all on end."

"It stands on end anyway, [illegible] his back beside her. "When I w[illegible] no matter how much I slicked [illegible]

He had tried, she remembe[illegible] Mary swept her back to their [illegible] filled the room with the sme[illegible] combed her fingers through th[illegible] her younger brother and siste[illegible] *Rosemary Ingalls coming to call?* [illegible] so high, all by yourself," she [illegible] fingers.

His forehead shifted beneath [illegible]

[illegible]ing Charles stack [illegible] chimney [illegible]ly beneath her ribs. [illegible] seemed [illegible]ents more purposeful [illegible] now, [illegible] the tentative wing [illegible] flutter [illegible] she held her back [illegible] the [illegible] muscles were tired of bre[illegible] Her corset helped [illegible] so m[illegible] dirt floor beneath [illegible] did[illegible]

[illegible]almost in that house [illegible] as a [illegible]on, but a true chair, [illegible] th a [illegible] summer long, if only [illegible] there [illegible]upper. Her mind str[illegible] to [illegible] Charles, in his thoughtfulness, [illegible]ly wearing himself [illegible] t in [illegible] hauling water and clay [illegible] mu[illegible] from his forehead [illegible] his [illegible]

[illegible]," she teased. "You're standing [illegible]

[illegible] he said, flopping down flat [illegible]ing you, it never would [illegible] down, [illegible] grease."

[illegible]ly. The slightest whiff of ros[illegible], when every doff of hi[illegible] hat ha[illegible] herb-scented grease [illegible] Carolin[illegible] own mass, rememb[illegible]g how [illegible] old their noses and [illegible]ease, [illegible] well to build that chimney [illegible], twiddling a lock [illegible] between [illegible]

[illegible] as he lifted his eyebrows to [illegible]

smile up at her. Just for a moment, Caroline let herself conjure a picture of the pleasurable diversions they might take, right here on the quilt, if there were not two little girls romping in the grass nearby. A sweet, warm current coursed through her at the thought. Caroline closed her eyes and turned her face to the breeze, letting the soft wind whisk it from her.

ALL OF THEM waited before the new mantel shelf while Caroline went to her trunk and lifted the lid. Beneath the brown paper bundle that was her delaine, nested snugly between the good pillows, sat the cardboard box she had packed most carefully of all. She burrowed one hand deep into its center of crumpled newsprint until her fingertips brushed something cool and smooth. *Please,* Caroline prayed. If it were not in one piece—Caroline blinked away the thought. She would not cry over such a thing, not with Charles and the girls looking on. Gently she pressed the paper wrapping back, hollowing out a path until a glint of golden china hair peeped out. Once again Caroline tunneled down, wrapping her fingers protectively around the narrow china neck and waist. Up through the rustling papers, all in one piece, came her china shepherdess.

Caroline's heart gave a happy lurch. No matter that the painted lips could not speak, nor the tiny molded hands return the warm embrace of Caroline's palm. She was so bright and beautiful, so small and delicate, Caroline had never been able to get enough of looking at her. She flushed a little, feeling Charles and the girls watching. Here she was a grown woman with two dear girls of her own, and still she had as much affection for that china lady as Mary did for her rag doll.

Caroline wiped the dainty figure carefully with an apron corner, half cleaning, half caressing the smooth porcelain, then stood the china shepherdess right in the center of the mantel shelf, where she belonged.

Two words settled themselves comfortably in her mind: *Welcome home.*

[illegible]Eightee[illegible]

IF C[illegible] ome a prairie chick[illegible] she would [illegible] hearth and fry it [illegible] he hum[illegible] half waltzing to th[illegible] The logs [illegible] lay with their pale [illegible] up to her [illegible] walk across them [illegible] new and [illegible] d of her heels on th[illegible] wish of th[illegible]

She [illegible] the broom handl[illegible] ade of th[illegible] ine missed the glo[illegible] d known [illegible] s a welcome relief [illegible] to close [illegible] m wind and sun. [illegible] at [illegible] de her a[illegible] r skin. It was too [illegible] so const[illegible] oline gazed up at [illegible] silent[illegible] ds for the half keg [illegible] so tha[illegible] ttle pegs to secure [illegible] There [illegible] before to consider [illegible] each [illegible] rt from the occasi[illegible] made [illegible] s, their house had [illegible] was [illegible] oline harbored a [illegible] the sh[illegible] the chinking betw[illegible]

Eve[illegible] nail inched them [illegible] place. [illegible] nment opened a [illegible] the lan[illegible] settled, and as se[illegible] first ri[illegible] on the quarter s[illegible] That was [illegible] ors and railroads m[illegible] people who lived and worked on the land. The more she and Charles improved the land in the meantime, the more solid their claim, for the law had declared that a man's sweat contained as much worth as his pocketbook—more, even. Caroline looked out at the roll of prairie sloping off toward the creek. This time next year there would be a field of sod potatoes and another of corn taking root. Right beneath the window, a garden green with unfurling sprouts. This time next year, there would be a child clinging to her hip, sucking its fist and fussy with teething.

Outside, Jack growled. Caroline turned toward the open door. "My goodness!"

Two Osages stood in the doorway, their tufted scalp locks brushing the lintel. A narrow belt of colored wool held up their breechclouts. Above that, their lower ribs pressed faintly against their skin. Caroline flushed at the sight of so much bareness.

At each hip hung a knife and a hatchet. Her muscles tensed, as though she might spring at them if they came toward her, but she knew she could not move. A horse hair roach, black at the tips, made a ridge from their scalp locks down the back of their shining skulls. The broad base was a color so vivid Caroline had no name for it—neither red, nor pink, nor purple.

One of them went straight to the crate of provisions. The other looked at her so steadily in the face, it felt indecent. Caroline folded her hands tight against the crest of her belly, hugging her sides with her elbows. She prayed they would see and leave her be.

Outside, Jack's chain rattled and snapped against its iron ring. Caroline had never heard him so savage.

All at once the air seemed to shatter. She could not hear Mary and Laura—had not heard them since before the Indians came into the house. Alarm sluiced past her elbows and knees.

She could not look out the window without turning her back to the Indians. If anything had happened to her girls, Caroline told herself, she [illegible] ave heard their [illegible] had not made a sound herself [illegible] not even call [illegible] her heart drumming [illegible] er throat.

[illegible] rst man set the [illegible] n the checked table [illegible] em. Then patted [illegible] from the sound. T[illegible] a low ripple of [illegible] shook her head. She [illegible] where one would [illegible] began. The other [illegible] ack, pointing i[illegible] h. [illegible] nderstood, but [illegible] e the meal from his [illegible] forced herself to [illegible] the table.

[illegible] nd pivoted back [illegible] hands meas[illegible] e cornbread of [illegible] She had been wearing her [illegible] gged calico the [illegible] man walked in [illegible] took the pe[illegible] the vase beside t[illegible] Caroline could [illegible] g away with tho[illegible] imes gazing back [illegible] air. More vibrant [illegible] the [illegible] eyes was the [illegible] groan when they [illegible] as had disapp[illegible]

[illegible] e sound was [illegible] nting against the [illegible] of [illegible] tone as her w[illegible] with the effort of [illegible] and Laura. She [illegible] palms into the to[illegible] jerked back. [illegible] her fingertips. She [illegible] ese men the s[illegible] s of her hands. That [illegible] y to Charles. [illegible] grains of meal bri[illegible] and dropped t[illegible] the bake oven. T[illegible] ed into place.

[illegible] KED AT every[illegible] hed the loops of [illegible] away from th[illegible] they probed throu[illegible] rles's tobacco [illegible] into one brown [illegible] had no more [illegible] china shepherdess [illegible] might take anything and she would not move, if only they had left her daughters untouched.

The Potawatomis had stolen only feathers, she reminded herself, not her baby brother. While the rest of the family watched the Indian decorate his hair with their peacock plumes, the little boy had toddled out of sight into the corn patch. She prayed these Osages might be as vain, that Mary and Laura were sheltered by Providence as Thomas had been.

But this was not Brookfield with its woods and corn patches. Through the window she could see clear to the willows along the creek—clear to the bluffs beyond—but she could not see her daughters. If she called their names, the fear in her voice would point the Indians straight to them. The baby thrashed against her bladder. Caroline's jaw clenched with the strain.

Suddenly Jack erupted into such a fury the Indians went to the window. Caroline could hear the bulldog lunging against the chain, scrabbling at the dirt. With each charge the metal links clattered and thrummed.

In a flash of calico the girls darted into the house. Caroline's relief frothed up like saleratus. Laura ducked behind the slabs Charles had left propped in the corner for the bedstead. Mary skittered barefoot across the length of the house and clung to Caroline's sleeve. The instant she felt Mary's hands around her wrist, Caroline closed her eyes and offered her thanks heavenward. Now she only wanted Laura's tangled brown hair under her fingers.

The Indians' eyes traced her gaze across the cabin, where half of Laura's face peeped from behind the slabs. They peered at her, bending down so that their hatchets dangled from their hips. One man spoke, and the other said, "Hah!" Laura jolted, cowering tight against the wood with nothing but her little white fingertips showing.

Caroline pulled Mary to the hearth and yanked the lid from the bake oven. "It's done," she announced. The Indians turned. Caroline thrust a finger t[illegible] ar[illegible] ves and stepped back. The[illegible] fist dare[illegible] he [illegible] Laura again.

The[illegible] low on the hearth, t[illegible] ir [illegible] pins. Si[illegible] tly [illegible] ent re loaf of the hal[illegible] ake[illegible] every d[illegible] p [illegible] the floorboards. By [illegible] Mary's t[illegible] s [illegible] her sleeve.

The I[illegible] ians [illegible] shorter of the two pointed [illegible] and said [illegible] Mi[illegible] ner man smirked and [illegible] malice s[illegible] ted t[illegible] sions. Instead they looked a[illegible] they had [illegible] co[illegible] hing so plain they expected [illegible] and join[illegible] irs.

She w[illegible] ld [illegible] thing. Caroline shi[illegible] ed [illegible] through [illegible] r body. The lid to the [illegible] ake [illegible] her hand[illegible]

The [illegible] faces leveled. Without a w[illegible] their bac[illegible] and [illegible] The lid dropped fro[illegible] Ca[illegible] rolled on [illegible] ck of slabs.

Laura [illegible]

Caroli[illegible] sat [illegible] on the straw tick, n[illegible] ly [illegible] with her. [illegible] lie[illegible] d through her.

"Do yo[illegible] eel s[illegible] Mar[illegible] asked.

"No," [illegible] mo[illegible] welled in ever[illegible] oint [illegible] quivered. [illegible] the[illegible] 're gone."

"We th[illegible] ght t[illegible] hur[illegible] you," Mary said.

"We lef[illegible] ck [illegible] he[illegible] ," Laura interrupted.

Carolin[illegible] up [illegible] eks with her palms an[illegible] cra[illegible] against her [illegible] ou[illegible] ave little girls," she sa[illegible] their near[illegible] s, [illegible] rick[illegible] ed, weeping war[illegible] fle[illegible] into her ch[illegible] ise[illegible]

THE TABL[illegible] AS [illegible] esh mixing of cornme[illegible] in t[illegible] Charles ca[illegible] w[illegible] gh the grass. A jack[illegible] bi[illegible] hocks at his belt, and he swung two headless prairie hens in one fist. The girls nearly toppled over each other in their scramble to tell him the news. Caroline was glad for their zeal. She did not want to recollect the Indians' visit any more than she must.

"Did Indians come into the house, Caroline?"

She held her voice even as a line of print as she told him about the tobacco and how much cornbread the two men had eaten. "They took the meal straight from the crate with me standing there. The way they pointed, I didn't dare refuse." The memory swelled her mind. "Oh, Charles! I was afraid!" Her chest constricted; she had not meant to tell him that part of it. Nor the girls, for that matter.

He assured her she had done right, that it was better to sacrifice a few provisions than make an enemy of any Osage, but she was not comforted. "The cornmeal was already running short," she added. It was petty; she had seen their ribs.

"One baking of cornbread won't break us." Charles lifted his fistful of game. The prairie hens' blunted necks wagged at her. "No man can starve in a country like this. Don't worry, Caroline."

She did not know what she had wanted him to say, but it was not this. He had not even looked at the sack of meal. Nor was he the one who would have to make it stretch. Her chin stabbed out like a child's. "If that's so, I don't know why they can't make do without our cornmeal. And all of your tobacco," she added, hoping to pry something more out of him.

Charles waved a hand. "Never mind. I'll get along without tobacco until I can make that trip to Independence."

Independence. The irony needled her. Two days she and the girls would be stranded on the high prairie while he went to town to replace what the Indians had taken. Maybe three. Three days with those men free to wander in and demand whatever else they liked of her.

"Main thing is to keep on good terms with them," Charles went on blithely.

[illegible] urned throug [illegible] sene. She could [illegible] he was saying unt [illegible] hing dev—" [illegible] pped up. Car [illegible] together and je [illegible] The straighte [illegible] self, the harder [illegible]

[illegible] Mary and Laur [illegible] voice was so brig [illegible] if the words had [illegible] We'll skin that [illegible] the prairie hens [illegible] bakes. Hurry! [illegible]"

[illegible] down on a cr [illegible] to do but col [illegible] the heels of her [illegible] perspiration f [illegible] her hair. She [illegible] rabbit's leg to the [illegible] peeling the sk [illegible] Mary and La [illegible] chatter about [illegible] lowed only the [illegible] Charles's voice [illegible] the ax. "Did yo [illegible] urning Jack loose?" [illegible] struck the same [illegible] fell straight t [illegible] hat might she h [illegible] me raging in [illegible] and by and wa [illegible] the dog. That [illegible] moment she had [illegible] revolver. What [illegible] men have don [illegible] pistol and cocked i [illegible] tremble agai [illegible] she could use to [illegible] her daughters [illegible]

[illegible] ave been trou [illegible] "Bad trouble." [illegible] said it, at least [illegible] edgment left he [illegible] d to Charles [illegible] wished she cou [illegible] om the air. T [illegible] so cavalier wi [illegible] with Mary an [illegible] . In Pepin the [illegible] ttons in the [illegible] could not expe [illegible] nd the hazard [illegible] ry.

[illegible] ld and no har [illegible] Charles decla [illegible]

One objection after another crowded Caroline's throat. The girls did not understand. She could hear it in the shrink of their voices even as they whispered, "Yes, Pa." They were bewildered by his anger, and that was all.

Charles had not seen their fear, Caroline reminded herself. He had not felt Mary's tears soaking his sleeve, nor watched Laura try to press herself invisible behind the stack of slabs. He had only seen them boiling over in their eagerness to share the news of their encounter with the Osages.

But he was turning them in the wrong direction. They had not set the bulldog loose, and they had not been wrong to be afraid of the Indians, nor to want to protect her. Instead of being reproached, they ought to be praised for following their instincts. In a place like this, there could be no room for blind obedience. It was all the more dangerous to render them more wary of upsetting their pa than of the Indians. Their fear would guard them—if only Charles would leave them free to obey it.

Caroline swallowed all her protests back. She could not interject. Contradicting Charles would only muddy the girls further. She rose and went to the window for a breath of air. Alongside the woodpile, Charles had one of the prairie hens pinned by the wings under his boots. He pulled slowly upward on the thighs so that the bird began to stretch apart. The feathers shuddered, then the whole of the body tore free to leave the breast, pink and glistening, between the crushed wings.

CHARLES NAILED THE provisions cupboard to the wall, to keep the Indians from making off with the whole thing. Caroline's shoulders flinched with every smack of the hammer. She could hold her thoughts in check or her body, not both. If she felt entitled to her anger, she might have turned it loose, but she did not. The fact that Charles had devoted the very next morning to building a cupboard complete with a padlock proved that he shared her concern over their supplies. But he would not sa[illegible] not know why she nee[illegible] plain enough[illegible]

In went t[illegible] sugar and flour, coffe[illegible] flapped the li[illegible] a padlock through the [illegible] into the woo[illegible] and held out the key. [illegible] a shoelace or [illegible] wear it where the India[illegible]

"Wear it?" [illegible]

Charles no[illegible] f they take it into the [illegible] the place, the[illegible]

Caroline s[illegible] ould just imagine stan[illegible] key dangling [illegible] ts while those bare b[illegible] through the c[illegible] Charles," she said.

"No sense i[illegible] tch the key from me [illegible] to do your co[illegible] e key a little toss, fur[illegible] when she did [illegible] asked.

"That stand[illegible] aid, and reluctantly pu[illegible] accept it.

Caroline w[illegible] sket and retrieved a [illegible] chet cotton. If [illegible] he thing, it would not [illegible] shoelace. The[illegible] it must not be so fa[illegible] attention. So s[illegible] ary chain stitch with [illegible] until the strin[illegible] long enough to let the [illegible] behind the ste[illegible] rset.

It would be [illegible] between the Osages a[illegible] with the key a[illegible] retending to be una[illegible] How much eas[illegible] nce to simply put do[illegible] refuse. Then a[illegible] want to provoke then[illegible] them. So a lie i[illegible]

The first few[illegible] felt the scant weight o[illegible] her neck, felt it[illegible] when she bent or lean[illegible] after she becam[illegible] press of the cool me[illegible] her flesh, the br[illegible] print like a brand on [illegible]

Nineteen

HOW OFTEN THE world seemed to bend for Charles, Caroline thought as she watched him crank the windlass, in a way it did for no one else. When they were mired along the Missouri, Mr. Jacobs had ridden up out of the trees to trade horses. The log fell on her ankle, and along came Edwards to finish raising the cabin and stable. Even the ride that had ended with Charles's terrifying encounter with the wolf pack had brought them, in a roundabout way, the man who now shoveled at the bottom of their half-dug well.

He was a round, squinting fellow, his fair skin scoured to peeling by the sun. No shirker, though, for every morning at sunup Mr. Scott was at the door, calling out, "Hi, Ingalls! Let's go!"

Scott was pleasant enough, but he was not convivial like Mr. Edwards. After a polite "Morning, ma'am," he hardly seemed to notice her, or the girls. He swore mildly but absently during his spells down in the shaft, and Caroline tried all day long to keep Laura from straying near enough to hear the short blasts of execration echoing up out of the dirt walls.

At night, Charles was tired. Work with Scott was ordinary work—the bite of the shovel and the crank of the windlass. Occasionally a bark of laughter, but no rhythm, no real harmony between them.

Still, she was thankful for his work. Thankful even before the morning Charles said, almost in passing as he headed out the door with his shovel, "Scott said he spoke to his wife and she'll come for you. When it's time."

A flush crept up her neck to think of the men speaking together of such things.

[illegible] think him?"

[illegible] nodded.

[illegible]. It was done, ho[illegible] A space had cleared [illegible], as though the [illegible] her corset strings [illegible] would come. But [illegible] eady mind wanted [illegible] Mrs. Scott's voice [illegible] many children she [illegible] her hands were [illegible] things Caroline did not [illegible] ask her own hus[illegible] ying apprehensio[illegible] business intruding [illegible].

[illegible] would come, C[illegible] herself. That alone [illegible] thing about the [illegible] leave her own claim [illegible] to attend a lying-in [illegible] had were weaned. [illegible] an older girl, [illegible] the housework and [illegible] She had voluntee[illegible] much was almost [illegible] would picture M[illegible] his wife over supper, [illegible] the Ingalls famil[illegible] a carpenter and his [illegible] little girls, and [illegible] ily way. A man who [illegible] and wind—how[illegible] woman's presence [illegible] so reluctant to sa[illegible] he reckoned.

[illegible]?" asked the [illegible].

[illegible] would shake his h[illegible] why she had asked?

[illegible] them I'll com[illegible]

[illegible] voice strayed into [illegible] Scott? Scott! Scott! A[illegible] come quick!

[illegible] have scoffed at th[illegible] deed. Nothing she [illegible] these days. The soun[illegible] thing else altogether. [illegible] never heard his [illegible] billowed up around [illegible], everything el[illegible] sheets from her hands [illegible] from her mi[illegible] flew outside.

[illegible] down on all [illegible] hole, peering into it. [illegible] or something [illegible] "I've got to go do[illegible]

"Did you send down the candle?" Caroline asked.

"No. I thought he had. I asked him if it was all right, and he said it was."

She had seen Mr. Scott shaking his head at the way Charles lowered a candle down the well to test the air each morning. *Foolishness,* he'd said. At once Caroline knew that blustering, impatient man had not done it. He had shimmied down the rope into who knows what kind of miasma while Charles finished his breakfast. She shaded her eyes and squinted into the hole. Not a glimmer of light, nor a glimpse of Mr. Scott's sun-bleached hair.

What shall we do? The words never reached her lips. Caroline looked up to ask, and Charles was tying a handkerchief over his nose and mouth. "Got to get the rope around him or we can't pull him out."

No. Her whole body pulsed with the word. *No, no, no.* "Charles," she said almost tentatively, as though her voice were backing away from the idea, "you can't. You mustn't."

The triangle of handkerchief puffed out with each word. "Caroline, I've got to."

The wide black throat of the well gaped silently at his knees. Cold tingled in Caroline's belly at the thought of its depth. "You can't. Oh, Charles, no!"

"I'll make it all right," he promised. "I won't breathe till I get out." Caroline stood so still, the world seemed to quiver around her. What made him think he could promise such a thing? He could not climb back up that rope quickly enough to guarantee his own safety without someone to crank the windlass and draw him out of the earth like a bucket. For weeks, Charles had not let her carry so much as a pail of water from the creek. Now he asked this of her. No, did not even ask. She was so big she could no longer lift Laura onto her lap, yet he never considered for an instant that she would do anything but leap to the crank to help him save a man she hardly knew.

"We can't let him die down there," Charles said.

[illegible] declared. Better one [illegible] both of them. Th[illegible] arithmetic. "No [illegible] said again. Caroline [illegible] struck, as he slice[illegible] free and tied the rope [illegible] as if she had not sa[illegible] vow of obedience [illegible] held no power over h[illegible] matter whether she [illegible] Mr. Scott, Carolin[illegible] dizzying rush, be[illegible] stepped into the [illegible] not one fiber of he[illegible] refuse to strain [illegible] ring her husband ba[illegible] ed because she had [illegible] panic spurted into C[illegible] ling hot and sy[illegible] of her arms and be[illegible] can't let you. [illegible] for help," she pl[illegible]

[illegible] "There isn't time." [illegible] for the rope and le[illegible]

[illegible] pull you up—[illegible] down there and I c[illegible]—" The way he looked [illegible] earnest and determi[illegible] voice.

[illegible] to."

[illegible] lowed him up, [illegible] Caroline dropped t[illegible] her the windl[illegible] unspooling its la[illegible] turned to a sudden [illegible] straight and [illegible] k. He was at the b[illegible]

[illegible] ed. *Dear God.* [illegible] reached. There w[illegible] n to fasten to [illegible] walls of the pit. S[illegible] her, sounds so [illegible] ied by their long a[illegible] ld not make them out [illegible] If he did not shout [illegible] rope within ten h[illegible] hat? Turn the [illegible] *Twelve. Thirteen.* T[illegible] d twitched. Caroli[illegible] her fingers around i[illegible] of movement [illegible] As long as it was [illegible] romised herself. [illegible] So long as it was moving, she would not let go of that rough jute, no matter how many breaths passed. *Eighteen, nineteen.*

Suddenly the rope twanged to the center of the well.

Caroline pushed herself from the ground. She took hold of the crank and yanked. It spun three-quarters of a turn and stopped so short, her shoulders jolted. She pulled again, wrenching the skin of her palms against the wooden handle. It wobbled but did not budge. There was not strength in her arms, nor the whole of her body to pull that crank.

I won't breathe till I get out. The last breath Charles had taken would be pressing behind his teeth by now. Caroline shook the image away. There had to be a way—Charles was not so gallant that he would have gone down unless there was a way out. Frantically she searched her mind, calling up a blackboard charted in her own hand with wheels and axles, pulleys and weights.

Caroline ground her heels into the dirt until her almost-healed ankle was a welter of old and new pain. She refastened her hands to the crank and heaved, leaning backward so the weight of her belly swung her nearly to the ground. The windlass creaked, following. Caroline's throat bulged with grunts she would not release as she propelled the leverage of her body up into the peak of the turn. Not one particle of energy would leave her unless she could direct it into the crank.

The crank reached the apex and continued moving—one full turn, then two, three.

Every strand of muscle in her arms burned. If they snapped or frayed before Charles reached the top— *No,* Caroline commanded herself. Only a few more turns and he would be out of reach of the fumes, high enough to risk a breath. Nothing mattered before that. Only give him time to breathe. So long as he could breathe, it did not matter how long it took to bring him to the surface. She could even stop to rest, once he breached clean air.

Caroline did not stop to rest. Her thrusting thighs and heaving back knew better than to surrender their momentum. She could picture his

[illegible]ace, hear the [illegible] of [illegible] [illegible]lling Laura: *By jinks* [illegible]
little French h[illegible]

Lit-tle . . . Fr[illegible] *. . . French . . . horse,* [illegible]
[illegible]uscles chant[illegible] [illegible]ge[illegible] [illegible] [illegible]nk turned over ar[illegible]

The load li[illegible] fr[illegible] [illegible] abruptly, Carolin[illegible]
[illegible]hought it had [illegible] pe[illegible] [illegible] he weight redoubled, [illegible]d [illegible]
[illegible]vith a new fu[illegible]

In the same [illegible] on the ground [illegible]
[illegible]he leg of the [illegible] [illegible] heart seemed t[illegible]
[illegible]ibs, brimmin[illegible] [illegible] deep into her bel[illegible]
[illegible]harles spill h[illegible]elf [illegible] beside her. He slu[illegible]
[illegible]nees, gaspin[illegible] [illegible] over the edge [illegible]
[illegible]he crank and [illegible] her [illegible] back, feeling the [illegible]
[illegible]f him. Abov[illegible] [illegible] squealed and spun. [illegible]
[illegible]ullet came a [illegible]

"Scott," Ch[illegible] [illegible] tried to pry himsel[illegible]

"Sit still, C[illegible]es," [illegible] He had not caug[illegible]

She could [illegible] [illegible] He staggered to t[illegible]
and panting. [illegible] and took hold [illegible]
Together it w[illegible] [illegible] spool of thread. [illegible]
and, lolling [illegible] [illegible] Caroline brac[illegible]
Charles hefte[illegible] [illegible] Scott lay there, [illegible]
as if the fum[illegible] [illegible] Charles put tw[illegible]
wrist, then a[illegible]

"He's brea[illegible]ing," [illegible] "He'll be all right [illegible]
shiver rattle[illegible]n, [illegible] dropped beside S[illegible]
and eyes clos[illegible]

Caroline [illegible] [illegible] The quivers [illegible]
muscles, the [illegible] [illegible] her limbs, t[illegible]
relief—all o[illegible] [illegible] from her. She b[illegible]
lay there, so[illegible] [illegible] The question [illegible]
nearby, a pu[illegible] [illegible] her mind as it [illegible]

"I'm all right, Caroline." The words rushed out on a sigh. "I'm plumb tuckered out, is all."

The tips of her fingers began to tingle. Her palms burned where the grain of the windlass handle had bitten into the skin. "Well!" Caroline said, and a hot torrent came whirling up out of her. "I should think you would be! Of all the senseless performances! My goodness gracious! Scaring a body to death, all for the want of a little reasonable care! My goodness! I—" The child kicked, and the wobbly, watery sensation shattered her fury. Caroline snatched her apron to her face and sobbed.

NAKED, SHE LIES in the grass, the well a gaping hole between her splayed legs. A rope runs out from somewhere deep within her, down into the well. From the pit, the plaintive sound of Charles's fiddle rises. With each note the rope vibrates, as though it is strung across the neck of the instrument. Fibers of jute chafe her thighs, scour the delicate channel leading to the rope's source. She strains at it, the rope a writhing umbilicus between them, but Charles's head does not emerge from the hole.

A long, high wolf's howl melded with the wail of the note rising from the pit, and Caroline found herself awake. *Another dream,* she soothed herself as she twined her ankles together and tugged her hem back into place. Her nightdress had hitched itself halfway over her belly. *Only another dream.*

But the feel of it lingered. The sense of being tethered to that dreadful pit coiled around her in the dark. And the nakedness, calling her shame back to the very surface of her skin. What spiteful logic dreams dealt in: she would have been less ashamed to show her bare flesh than let Mary and Laura and Charles see the way she had abandoned herself to wailing and sobbing the moment all danger had passed. Worst of all was Mary offering her own dry hankie in place of Caroline's sodden apron. Fresh twists of shame wriggled through her at the memory, at the tentative pity on her five-year-old daughter's upturned face.

Caroline considered whether to close her eyes again. In daylight she [illegible] ket [illegible] om the well and her [illegible] noth-ing [illegible] ore [illegible] eeping the w[illegible] from [illegible] shoes. Nig[illegible] s, the [illegible] that dreadf[illegible] morning [illegible] differ-ent [illegible] ays, [illegible] thing more gr[illegible] tesq[illegible] ity.

[illegible] between the folds of [illegible] not be co[illegible] mories themselves, Ca[illegible] d, but ins[illegible] ed [illegible] into such ur[illegible] ly in [illegible]

[illegible] it, too, were dis[illegible] comf[illegible] ghts. Ca[illegible] ine [illegible] around the n[illegible] of [illegible] essed, hug[illegible] ng [illegible] palms. Poor t[illegible] ing. Not [illegible] ready it [illegible] sha[illegible] of [illegible] r most fearful m[illegible] omen[illegible] t have felt when [illegible] terror went [illegible] ing [illegible] id the sa[illegible] chill [illegible] flood its buc[illegible] limb[illegible] ced at th[illegible] ough[illegible]

[illegible] it. *No more.* [illegible] omis[illegible] hope to [illegible] ep. S[illegible] po[illegible] to seal hers[illegible] f off fro[illegible] than she could [illegible] happiness. If [illegible] ot[illegible] ng e[illegible] ddenly ch[illegible] d he[illegible] resolve to st[illegible] p her m[illegible] ng the w[illegible] of [illegible] night after night. H[illegible] lip[illegible] hought of [illegible] owin[illegible] h the store of fi[illegible] thin[illegible] in her he[illegible] the [illegible] e'd begun packing her trunk [illegible]

[illegible] aroli[illegible] er [illegible] s and imagined her ro[illegible] *swish-sw*[illegible] of th[illegible] the floor, the gen[illegible] tle c[illegible] against he[illegible] ack [illegible] lt the soft embrace of [illegible] s ends tu[illegible] ed ar[illegible] dl[illegible] bundle. The chi[illegible] l's fa[illegible] t form in[illegible] arms summoned up [illegible] armth ag[illegible] st he[illegible] future, twir[illegible] ed t[illegible] geth[illegible]

IN [illegible] ine [illegible] shioned a snug li[illegible] tle h[illegible] enter-in[illegible] each [illegible] the dearest of h[illegible] r me[illegible] hild to fe[illegible] o h[illegible] mother's blueberry c[illegible] cheese pi[illegible] The [illegible] of pinks in the sa[illegible] or's [illegible] ad, all the way back in Brookfield. Her first week's pay as a schoolteacher, two dollar bills and two shining quarters. The cornhusking dances in Concord—the rich green swirl of her delaine skirt, the sound of Charles's fiddle, the feel of his hands on her waist as they danced. Their first night together in their own little house in Pepin. Eliza. Henry. Polly. Ma and Papa Frederick. These memories ached, but softly, so that the ache itself became a pleasure. The ache hurt less than the blank places she had carved out by trying not to remember.

Nights passed, and Caroline found she did not need to reach so far back to find a memory that would unfurl into something so bright and warming that she thought surely the child must be sharing in her contentment. The child, after all, had been there, floating in the center of her every moment: Their first piping hot meal after the miring storm. The sky reflected in Laura's eyes the night she said the stars were singing. Supper with Edwards, with the newly built house outlined against that same starry sky. These recollections were not edged with wistfulness. They burned cheerfully, leaving no dim corners for darker thoughts of the creek, the Osages, or the well to congregate.

Then came the night after Charles finished the bedstead, when she could not think of one thing more comforting than the feel of that bed against her back. If she had not filled it with her own hands, Caroline would not have believed she lay on the same straw tick. The prairie grass beneath her was finer than straw, with a warm, golden-green smell somewhere between hot bread and fresh herbs, and it enveloped her like broth welcoming a soup bone. Her hips and shoulder blades, which always seemed to sink straight to the floor, floated above the rope Charles had strung between the framing slabs. She shifted deeper, and the rope sighed and the grass whispered. "I declare, I'm so comfortable it's almost sinful!" she said and closed her eyes, the better to savor every inch of the sheets cradling her body.

Twenty

AT THE S[illegible]T [illegible] two cowboys leadi[illegible] out of the [illegible] Caroline thought she [illegible] soft bed, d[illegible] down on the [illegible] window [illegible] waiting for the fire [illegible] the corn[illegible] the midsummer [illegible] sleep. Caroline [illegible] to sift the few frag[illegible] what she [illegible] a stretch to make hers[illegible] truly had [illegible] their claim, that the [illegible] Charles [illegible] longhorns out [illegible] of Edwards or [illegible] else in Montgom[illegible] it was, [illegible] itself—a day's w[illegible] piece of [illegible] a dream even as [illegible] hands for [illegible] her eyes and str[illegible] waiting [illegible] and refashion in[illegible] the roof [illegible]

Caroline op[illegible] instead there [illegible] animals [illegible] stable and shaking ha[illegible] boys. "W[illegible]?" [illegible] through the w[illegible] not answ[illegible] et from his saddl[illegible] The bee[illegible] *th*[illegible], Caroline thought[illegible] She felt [illegible] out of her, heard [illegible] great ru[illegible] it was not a dream at [illegible]

Of cou[illegible]. It could be noth[illegible] beef, a c[illegible] extravagant, even [illegible] *And* a calf[illegible] repeating it to hers[illegible] been a word so impossibly big as that *and*. A cow and a calf. Both rangy and unruly but goodness, milk and butter. Perhaps, Caroline thought, the hand of Providence had only been passing over them, on its way elsewhere with these fine gifts, and had somehow dropped them.

BUT THE LAND continued to burgeon with gifts for them. Yellow-orange plums small enough to scoop up with a spoon. Walnuts, pecans, and hickory nuts still in their green husks, plumping for autumn. A queer purple flower with a turnip-like root that Edwards called Indian breadroot; Caroline could not get enough of its crisp, white flesh.

"Close your eyes," Charles said as he came through the door. It had become a game with him, bringing home little surprises to plop into their open palms. If not something to eat, then something to marvel at—a kernel of blue corn, a speckled green prairie chicken egg. "Now open your mouth."

Caroline hesitated. Last time it had been a sunflower seed, from the Indian camp. Charles had cut one of the great yellow flowers from its stalk and pegged it up on the side of the chimney to dry. She did not like to wonder what the Osages would think to see it dangling there, no matter how many times Charles told her the camp surrounding the crops was deserted. The idea of the Indians leaving their corn and beans and sunflowers to the mercy of weather and wild animals was nonsensical.

She could feel Charles waiting, daring her not to trust him. Caroline opened her mouth.

She smelled the juice on his fingers before it touched her tongue. A blackberry, hot and sweet from the sun. Caroline sighed as she crushed it against the roof of her mouth. The rapture of its smoothness, the burst of flavor like a pinch to her tongue. Nothing had tasted so bright since last summer's tart cherries.

"All along the creek," Charles said. "The fruit just about brushes the ground, the brambles are so heavy. You couldn't pick them all in a week."

[illegible] salivated an[illegible] things she could do wit[illegible] [illegible]berry pie. B[illegible] . Blackberry jam. Drie[illegible] [illegible], stirred int[illegible] ca[illegible] [illegible]sty pudding, or ste[illegible] [illegible] fire. If she gath[illegible] the baking-hot sun[illegible] [illegible] enough to dry [illegible] [illegible]py smell would brighte[illegible] [illegible] all winter long [illegible] if [illegible] and more prairie chicke[illegible] [illegible] Caroline thought, [illegible] [illegible]rries in Ma's blue[illegible] [illegible] She would [illegible] [illegible]rds, and to Mrs. Scott [illegible] well, she de[illegible] [illegible]borly again, for [illegible] [illegible] would be as [illegible]

[illegible] morning sh[illegible] [illegible]aura in their oldest [illegible] [illegible] handed them [illegible] [illegible]led around her, chasin[illegible] [illegible] dickcissels a[illegible] [illegible] creek. Caroline di[illegible] [illegible] up. The ho[illegible] [illegible] feel dry and taut, as [illegible] too suddenly m[illegible] [illegible] though there were [illegible] [illegible]ling inches of [illegible] [illegible] the sides of her ma[illegible] [illegible] she had not been [illegible] [illegible]creasing size lately. Th[illegible] [illegible] not so much [illegible] in[illegible], so that most of what sh[illegible] [illegible] was the accum[illegible] [illegible] straining of her body t[illegible] [illegible]. And with be[illegible] [illegible] to wait, Caroline calcu[illegible] [illegible]ing a little. T[illegible] [illegible] would spend both thicker[illegible] [illegible] thinning, expan[illegible] [illegible] her own flesh stre[illegible] [illegible]wed itself to m[illegible] [illegible]. The sensation made he[illegible] [illegible] for her corset's [illegible]

[illegible] Ma!"

[illegible] had not exa[illegible] [illegible] great, fat berries [illegible] [illegible] black in the s[illegible]

[illegible]oline and [illegible] to a tangle of bramble[illegible] [illegible] mosquito[illegible] [illegible] down to crouch on th[illegible] [illegible] pierce the skin [illegible] [illegible]ped tongues.

[illegible]atch." Sh[illegible] [illegible] how to tease the dark [illegible] from their s[illegible] [illegible]hout bursting the [illegible] black globes. “Put them gently into the pail,” Caroline said, reaching all the way to the bottom before opening her hand. “The red and purple berries are not ripe enough to pull free.”

Caroline watched them a moment. Mary picked just as Caroline had shown her, but Laura’s pail would have to be made into preserves, or put into a pie. In her eagerness, Laura pinched the berries, then let them bounce by the handful onto the bottom of her pail. Caroline smiled in spite of herself. She ought to teach Laura how to keep from crushing the fruit, but Laura was having such fun. Already her short fingers were stained purple to the cuticles. There was little that pleased her more than helping, and blackberry jam was no less valuable than blackberries dried whole.

Caroline turned her attention to her own two pails and began to pick. It was lazy work, barely work at all with so many berries at hand, and heady with heat and the murmur of insect wings. Her belly snagged against the briars as she leaned to reach another cluster of fruit. A cloud of mosquitoes rose up sullenly at her approach, then crowded back in. They buzzed drunkenly, hardly aware of her fingers. Determined to pluck every berry within reach, Caroline stood in one place so long that her dress made a tent of heat around her. Sweat glossed the skin at her temples, dribbled between her breasts and down the backs of her knees. The key to the provisions cabinet clung to her damp skin, so warm that she could smell the tang of the hot brass. Mosquitoes pricked the back of her neck, her wrists, and even her ears. Purple smears streaked the girls’ legs and ankles, marking the places they had swatted.

Breakfast wore thin as the sun climbed the sky, yet Caroline did not indulge herself with mouthfuls of berries as the girls did. Hunger made a welcome pocket in her middle, and she did not hurry to fill it. As a child she would not have thought it possible that the empty rumble could be pleasurable, but now, brimming as she was, the feel of that space as it opened was a momentary luxury. Now and then she found

a blackberry t[illegible] the touch, and th[illegible]se [illegible]
mouth.

If there ha[illegible] bee[illegible] [illegible]ackberries in [illegible] [illegible]ick[illegible]
banks of the co[illegible] [illegible]line mused to her[illegible]elf, [illegible]
brothers [illegible]nd [illegible]ter[illegible] [illegible] have feared winte[illegible] [illegible]
picking h[illegible]d be[illegible] a[illegible] [illegible]ity as a treat in [illegible] da[illegible]

With a sm[illegible] she [illegible] [illegible]ttle Thomas, s[illegible]ent[illegible] sc[illegible]
berries fr[illegible]m [illegible]rth[illegible] [illegible] a serving spoo[illegible] he[illegible] [illegible]
the house [illegible] an[illegible] [illegible] [illegible]hen Martha fin[illegible]y [illegible]eal[illegible]
could not [illegible] [illegible] [illegible]onest, Martha," he [illegible]aid [illegible]
upturned for[illegible] [illegible] fingers'd be a[illegible] ju[illegible] [illegible]
berries," he re[illegible] on[illegible] [illegible] eyes, not [illegible]ow[illegible]ng [illegible]
ple tongu[illegible] co[illegible] [illegible] word. Martha wa[illegible] ma[illegible]
whip him and[illegible] [illegible] [illegible]ther. Thomas's co[illegible]eup[illegible]
all night [illegible]ong, un[illegible] [illegible] forth to the neces[illegible]ry. [illegible]
bled them all [illegible] [illegible]en, but now, watch[illegible]ng [illegible]
daughters fille[illegible] the [illegible] [illegible]lly, almost ind[illegible]ffe[illegible]ntl[illegible]
smile slum[illegible]ped [illegible] T[illegible] [illegible]ent a winter [illegible]
crumbled into [illegible] [illegible] perhaps he w[illegible]uld [illegible]ot [illegible]
himself. I[illegible] was [illegible] t [illegible] fiercely now, [illegible] am[illegible]
greed whe[illegible] he [illegible]ad [illegible] plenty. One co[illegible]ld [illegible]
the other. Chil[illegible] en [illegible] [illegible]y and Laura ough[illegible] [illegible]ver [illegible]
bellies gna[illegible]ving [illegible]

"My pa[illegible] is [illegible] "Can I go back[illegible]o[illegible]e? [illegible]
voice peak[illegible]d [illegible] a

"May I, Ca[illegible] in[illegible]

"May I, Ma[illegible] St[illegible] straw-colored [illegible]air [illegible]
the sweat [illegible]lon[illegible] the [illegible] [illegible]bonnet. Her fa[illegible] [illegible]ow[illegible]
cross. Had th[illegible] [illegible] [illegible]roline would n[illegible]t h[illegible]ve
was less th[illegible]n a [illegible] [illegible] the cabin. Mar[illegible] c[illegible]uld
lose her w[illegible]y fr[illegible] [illegible] the tall prairie gra[illegible]s. [illegible]
did not ans[illegible]wer. [illegible]he [illegible] the east, towar[illegible] [illegible]nd

was not that she did not believe what Charles had told her. If he said the camp was empty, it was empty. It was that he could not be sure where the Indians had gone, nor for how long.

"You may help Laura finish her pail," Caroline said, "and then we will all go home together."

The next day Caroline laid a tarpaulin full of blackberries out in the sun beside the cabin and let Mary stay behind to guard it from birds and insects while Charles built a paddock for the stock. The drying fruit seemed to draw the mosquitoes up out of the creek bottoms and across the prairie. Long after the berries were picked and put up for winter, the insects lingered, indifferent to the smudges of damp grass Charles lit to smoke them from the house and barn. No amount of coal tar oil and pennyroyal rubbed into the skin discouraged the mosquitoes from biting. All day long the crock of apple cider vinegar stood open on the table, so they might dab each new pink welt the moment it began to itch.

Caroline could not say by any stretch that she was thankful for the mosquitoes. She could not be thankful for a pestilence that found its way under the sheets to prickle her unreachable feet with bites while she slept. Though she could not speak of it, there was a measure of reassurance in their nettlesome clouds. The land had become so bountiful she was almost wary of it. Here at last was proof that it was not too good to be true.

Twe[illegible]

[illegible]W, and early. [illegible] when Caroli[illegible] [illegible]ming ache behi[illegible] [illegible] levered herself fro[illegible] [illegible] went to the d[illegible]or. [illegible] up, yet already t[illegible] [illegible]nd warmed her fac[illegible] [illegible]efoot into the ha[illegible] [illegible] followed, pertur[illegible]

[illegible] broke just outsid[illegible] th[illegible] [illegible] Caroline stood [illegible] [illegible]h, thankful it had[illegible] [illegible] new bedstead. Th[illegible] [illegible] soaking into t[illegible] [illegible]er thrill high in [illegible] [illegible]ead of her ribs. T[illegible] [illegible]ltogether differ[illegible] [illegible] the family chamb[illegible] [illegible]oads of Iowa an[illegible] [illegible] been a papist, s[illegible] [illegible]sed herself. Jack [illegible] [illegible]iff at the puddle a[illegible] [illegible] That was all [illegible] [illegible] needed, and s[illegible] [illegible]usiness.

[illegible]er at the cabin [illegible]

[illegible]?

[illegible] she must look—[illegible] [illegible] hair unpinned a[illegible] [illegible] gown wet and li[illegible] [illegible] best go ask for M[illegible] [illegible]day. I should th[illegible]k [illegible] have need of he[illegible]"

[illegible] fear and excit[illegible] [illegible] It's sooner than y[illegible] [illegible]?"

[illegible]ile. "Only by tw[illegible] w[illegible] [illegible]e." Perhaps even fo[illegible] [illegible], Scott'll be up [illegible] [illegible]ime I get there."

[illegible]?"

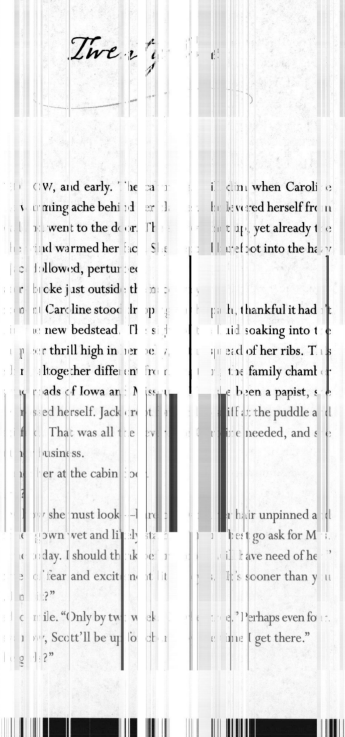

He nodded, shrugging into his suspenders. "I'll think of something to keep them busy."

ALL THROUGH THE morning, the pain stretched steadily upward, tightening the hammock of her belly. By the time she'd cleared the breakfast dishes, it was cresting beneath her ribs. Under the waves flowed a tension that never eased. The dull heat of it rose upward until her throat was rigid from cinching back the sounds of her discomfort. Determined not to groan or whimper in front of the girls, she tried humming a little over the dishwater and found a sort of harmony in letting her voice drift above the drone of clenching muscle.

"One little, two little, three little Indians," Charles sang, pointing at Mary's and Laura's tanned faces, then wagging his finger in the air. "Nope, only two."

"You make three," Mary said. "You're brown, too."

Caroline had never cared for that song, but the pulse of the melody pleased her now. As long as she hummed, she did not have to remind herself to exhale.

"How would you girls like to go with me to see the Indian camp?" Charles asked. Laura danced up onto her toes, clapping. Even Mary dropped her dish towel and dashed to Charles's knee.

Caroline went cold. "It's so far, Charles," she said, clambering for words that would not show her fear. "And Laura is so little. She can't walk so far in this heat."

Laura's heels drooped to the floor.

"Then she shall ride Jack," Charles said. The lift of his eyebrows begged her not to press further. "Camp's been deserted for weeks," he added. "Not a whiff for Jack to trouble himself over."

Caroline nodded and turned back to the dishpan. There was nothing else for it; the girls must be away all day. She fetched the comb and sat down on the tallest of the crates with the small of her back pressed against th[illegible]able. [illegible] you must be com[illegible] dian camp [illegible] not, [illegible] ve [illegible]ou going out with [illegible]

The smo[illegible] ng [illegible]ver and around h[illegible] her—suc[illegible] st [illegible] what was happen[illegible] While La[illegible] h[illegible] knees, Caroline [illegible] against th[illegible] La[illegible]ra spun around, [illegible] again, M[illegible]"

"All do[illegible]" C[illegible] sh[illegible]ping her along. "M[illegible]ry's [illegible]

She tie[illegible] their [illegible] nder their chins [illegible] off to Ch[illegible] es, [illegible] fra[illegible]ed in calico. Her [illegible] wanted so [illegible] up into her lap [illegible] but she [illegible] ul [illegible]nd followed them [illegible] the [illegible] lifted La[illegible] onto [illegible]. C[illegible]roline smiled a lit[illegible] reached [illegible] r b[illegible]re toes.

"Now [illegible]'ll all [illegible] to[illegible]ether," Charles sai[illegible]

Mary t[illegible]ned [illegible] ya[illegible]. "Ma?" Her blue [illegible]yes [illegible] very near[illegible] under [illegible]

Carol[illegible] soft[illegible] e [illegible] best she could an[illegible] nod[illegible] open prai[illegible]. "[illegible] pa[illegible]" she said.

A trem[illegible] of [illegible] ed [illegible]aroline's throat a[illegible] he [illegible] oped Ch[illegible] and [illegible] Th[illegible]re was not a sou[illegible] n a[illegible] the swish[illegible] of [illegible] nd [illegible] rising whir of in[illegible]cts. [illegible] without e[illegible] the [illegible] An[illegible] this cabin was no[illegible] fully [illegible] the chin[illegible] sheph[illegible] dir[illegible] on the mantel. [illegible]e la[illegible] beneath h[illegible] belly [illegible] ed [illegible]erself. Her mothe[illegible] wi[illegible] before T[illegible]mas's [illegible] no[illegible] been so forsaken a[illegible] this.

Carol[illegible] blin[illegible] e memory. There wa[illegible] not [illegible] such thin[illegible] No[illegible] Sc[illegible]t on her way, and work [illegible] before sh[illegible] rrive[illegible]

SWEAT [illegible] ME[illegible] h[illegible] as she rubbed he[illegible] nigh[illegible] washboar[illegible]. She [illegible] elp feeling misplaced[illegible] ean[illegible] bucket at this hour on mending day skewed the rhythm of the week. If she could not be near Eliza or Polly or Ma this day, Caroline wanted to be busy with her work basket as she knew they would be. But her soiled nightdress must be washed. It ought to have been done sooner if it were to dry in time, but she had not known how to explain the stain to the girls.

Much as she concentrated on her task, Caroline could not rinse nor wring the images of her kin from her mind. She paused to wipe a wet cuff along her hairline as a pang took hold. There was no sense in missing Eliza and Ma, she scolded herself as she squeezed the water from the nightdress. Neither of them had ever lived near enough to attend her deliveries. Yet with every stricture of her womb the stretch of the seven years since she had last seen her mother seemed to broaden. And Eliza. The thought of her sister nursing her own little one in the rocker they had left behind watered Caroline's eyes.

The twisted nightdress creaked before she realized her elbows were trembling. Caroline shook the garment free of itself and stood a moment, letting the rising wind snap the last droplets from its hem. One still morning, Charles had pointed out the smoke from the Scotts' cabin to Laura. Now the blowing grass leaned toward the neighbors' claim, its thousands of bending fingers leading Caroline's eyes ever eastward. The air carried a hearth-like smell of hot clay and browning grain, but not a sign of habitation breached the horizon. Her low voice sidled shakily into the wind:

Come to that happy land, come, come away,
Why will ye doubting stand, why still delay?

Eyes combing the prairie, Caroline hummed through another spasm. The drone of the cicadas cut in and out of the melody. She scanned the blue-white edge of sky once more, then hurried inside to strip the good quilt and muslin sheets from the bedstead. The gray blanket and the old oilcloth [illegible] k, if only she [illegible] between [illegible] First, she fold[illegible] cloth ar[illegible] [illegible]rything Mrs. [illegible] linen and [illegible] swaddling, a[illegible] f[illegible].

All th[illegible] eavy and musc[illegible] pulled a[illegible] child had roote[illegible] spine. [illegible] ne to the doo[illegible] Carolin[illegible] g a little, she [illegible] blotted [illegible] n of the gray b[illegible] the open [illegible]

The [illegible] as a barrel, [illegible] with a f[illegible] ed her. Again [illegible] and the [illegible] swells of her [illegible] dabbed [illegible] with her apron.

"Good [illegible]" said.

Caroline's [illegible] response, echoi[illegible] Luke: [illegible] *of thy salutation* [illegible] *babe lea*[illegible]

"Mrs. [illegible]

Caroline [illegible] oat. "Good morning."

"I am [illegible]

"I am [illegible] caught again. "[illegible] Mrs. Sc[illegible]."

"We[illegible] "Looks like I [illegible] too soon [illegible] trade that apr[illegible] leave the [illegible]

Caro[illegible]

While [illegible] with the blank[illegible] peeled [illegible] her damp [illegible] She poli[illegible] isions cupboar[illegible] before [illegible]

"Wh[illegible] Mrs. Scott said, [illegible]

bedstead. "It's good to see more of our own kind of folks settling the place up."

In the bed, Caroline's mind had nothing to attend to but heat and pain. The hearth crackled behind her in spite of the steamy wind barging through the open windows, for the fire must be kept high enough to scald the knife. Every crease of her body pulled the nightdress closer.

Amiably as she spoke, Mrs. Scott's voice crowded the cabin, while outside the insects' cry ascended without end. The sounds held Caroline teetering even as the clench of her laboring muscles released.

"Been here the better part of a year and I've never seen a one of those Indian women," Mrs. Scott was saying as she fitted the yellow flowers into a mug of water. "The men have so little modesty abroad, it makes a body wonder if the women wear anything at all in those huts of theirs. I don't blame you for locking up the foodstuffs with the likes of them prowling all over the countryside."

With the next spasm came a pressure so insistent, all Caroline wanted to do was scrabble backward out from under it. She pressed the heels of her hands against the straw tick and drew in all the breath she could hold. She did not want to push; she wanted only to put something between herself and that feeling. A picture of sausage-making filled her mind, how the filmy casings suddenly bulged and shone with each twist of the grinder.

She had forgotten this part of it, how the pain metamorphosed. With Mary, it had taken nearly two hours.

"Oh, Mrs. Scott!" Caroline cried.

"Yes?"

Caroline could not answer. She did not even know what she wanted.

The big woman clucked and nodded. "I was near about your age when I had my first. Yelled like a wild savage. Wasn't much quieter for any of the next four, either. Go on and shout if it does you good."

Caroline shook her head. She could not let go of herself, not with the whole world tilting and nothing else to hold on to.

[illegible] her next brea[illegible] [illegible] enough for [illegible] [illegible] child had loo[illegible] Caroline could [illegible] round it, an [illegible] mother cry [illegible] her [illegible] ed down her [illegible] same. She tri[illegible] [illegible] faltered.

[illegible] ott sat dow[illegible] bedstead and let [illegible]

[illegible] is a happy la[illegible] fa[illegible]
[illegible] saints in glor[illegible]
[illegible] hear the ange[illegible] King,
[illegible] His praises [illegible]

[illegible] surrendere[illegible] [illegible] ether they sang [illegible] [illegible] loudly than [illegible] st. [illegible] final chorus [illegible] [illegible] ease." Her v[illegible] only part of her [illegible] [illegible] over.

[illegible] verse to the [illegible] of [illegible] my Banks I S[illegible]" [illegible] song quick[illegible] Scott asked, "S[illegible] [illegible] Mrs. Ingalls?

[illegible] The pain was [illegible] itself downwar[illegible] [illegible] Caroline parted [illegible] gown over her [illegible] [illegible] to see.

[illegible] delight my [illegible]
[illegible] no longer st[illegible]
[illegible] Jordan's waves [illegible]
[illegible] launch away[illegible]

[illegible] man nodded [illegible] Any minute."
[illegible] joined her fo[illegible] topping the quilt [illegible]

pillows from Mary and Laura's bed behind her until Caroline was nearly upright.

She was full to quivering with the press of the child's head. Her nerves boiled and crawled around its shape, her flesh unable to cringe away. Desperate for movement, Caroline gripped her knees like the two handles of a plow and began to push.

With the hardening of her muscles the frisson ceased. Caroline's mind cleared as all at once she released herself into the pain. Breath by breath, she filled her chest with air and pressed it down against the bulge of her womb, down through her flanks to the end of the bed where Mrs. Scott sat coaxing. The force of each thrust bowed her spine and bunched the cords in her neck.

At the crowning, when it seemed as though the sun itself were boring its way out of her, Caroline lay back and held herself still as the seam at the base of her body unlaced, bracing for the snapping of the finest outer fibers. The hot squeeze of her heartbeat ringed the head and she felt herself stretched tighter and tighter until with a twist of lock and key the child bloomed into Mrs. Scott's hands.

For a moment she lay poised and panting. Her hips and knees were trembling and watery; her pulse thrummed between her legs. There was a tug and a sinewy slice as the cord was severed. Then the splutter of the infant's cry. It echoed deep into Caroline's own lungs and Caroline gloried in it, lifting her thanks to God.

Suddenly freed from the crush and strain, she went all but blank inside as Mrs. Scott tended to the child. The grip around her began to unknot, making Caroline's body her own again. She had not fully taken hold of the change before Mrs. Scott was laying the toweled infant across her chest.

"Here we are," Mrs. Scott said. "A fine little daughter, Mrs. Ingalls."

And there it was before her—the face her mind had been unable to conjure for all these months, so close Caroline felt the moisture of

[illegible] inhaled, tasting [illegible] led
[illegible] ted senses to gli[illegible] even
[illegible] ing the scent of [illegible] in,

[illegible] ne's body, the b[illegible] nd
[illegible] kin glowed red[illegible]
[illegible] her finger into [illegible]
[illegible] mpled into a squa[illegible].
[illegible] bserved with a smi[illegible] t
jer[illegible] uked.
[illegible] bot[illegible] ver the hunched [illegible]
stea[illegible],” she said as th[illegible]
in a [illegible] d's eyelids unbuckle[illegible]
and [illegible] chest, they rode [illegible]
vital[illegible] th. Caroline let [illegible]
much life [illegible] lungs, the bird [illegible]
W[illegible] ce barely larger [illegible]
night[illegible] Caroline unbut[illegible]
mouth [illegible] e baby nudged t[illegible]
the w[illegible] in small ripples, [illegible]
the lit[illegible] Even before the[illegible]
Caroli[illegible] ine grains of for[illegible]
As t[illegible] r eyes and took [illegible]
at the [illegible] stroked the line [illegible]
kerchie[illegible] legs folded tig[illegible]
a faint [illegible] its wisp of tar [illegible]
womb [illegible] Within a few [illegible]
smell of [illegible] terbirth slicke[illegible]
it outside [illegible] s. Scott tied it into [illegible]
Lying [illegible]
skin. He[illegible] Caroline no longer fe[illegible]
[illegible], thrusting her [illegible]

herself, as though its vibration melded with all that touched her. Every inch seemed to breathe and taste. Caroline soaked in the silky essence of the child nuzzled against her, the straw tick sighing beneath her, and reached for more. Putting a hand to the wall, she let the fibers of wood snag her fingertips, then smoothed them against the cool chinking. She turned her eyes to the rafters spreading overhead like open arms. All that sheltered them had been pulled, living, from the land. The whole of the house was a cradle of grass and timber and clay, proffered by the prairie and joined by the labor of Charles's hands. Caroline listened to the bite of the shovel and the fleshy thump of the afterbirth dropping into the ground. After all they had taken from it, it seemed fitting that this most raw and nourishing part of her should be swallowed by the land.

The strange flavor of that thought still wafted in Caroline's mind when Mrs. Scott came in to sponge her clean. With each cooling stroke Caroline's consciousness settled more deeply back into herself. Between daubings, she closed her eyes and waited for the singing of the droplets against the bowl. This water she so savored, Caroline realized as Mrs. Scott lifted the dripping sponge from the basin, had nearly cost both their husbands' lives. Her thankfulness that she should be beholden to her neighbor for this day and not the other flowed like her milk, so free and warm Caroline could not bind it into words.

It made no matter; there was no space between them that wanted for talk. To Caroline it seemed as though drawing the bucket from the gullet of that well had subdued Mrs. Scott. For all the earlier stridence of her voice, she spoke only with her hands as she guided the band of linen around Caroline's middle and pinned it firmly in place. Mrs. Scott squared the heaviest pad of flannel-covered oilcloth beneath her to take up the bleeding, then evened the nightdress over Caroline's knees as neatly as Caroline might have done herself. All the while she worked, Mrs. Scott kept her face turned steadily to her tasks, as though she understood that this birth had uncovered more of the meat of Caroline's soul than of her body.

[illegible] SKIRTING th[illegible] [illegible] Charles and th[illegible]

[illegible] Mrs. Scott [illegible] and Mary [illegible] the doorway, [illegible] pink from th[illegible] Laura cried. [illegible] [illegible]est stirred t[illegible] [illegible]ough her affe[illegible] [illegible]t was nothin[illegible] *Ma*, but the s[illegible] [illegible]er now, and [illegible] sight of her [illegible] [illegible]dle of the d[illegible] [illegible] the hearth, [illegible] [illegible]ary had not [illegible] [illegible]ove between [illegible] [illegible] shine of h[illegible] [illegible]oline feel shy [illegible] Scott stand[illegible] [illegible] tucked her fa[illegible] [illegible] touched th[illegible] [illegible] but Caroline [illegible] [illegible]dth of her s[illegible] [illegible]rew near. He [illegible] [illegible] of the bedst[illegible] [illegible]he child coil[illegible] [illegible]rm. One tin[illegible] [illegible]pon Carolin[illegible] [illegible]ion of pink [illegible] [illegible] her skin. [illegible] [illegible]ver the back [illegible] [illegible]and, then lea[illegible] [illegible]cheek. The [illegible] [illegible] eyes touched [illegible] [illegible] the empty b[illegible] [illegible]uttered.

[illegible]at Ma has for [illegible] [illegible] Laura.

[illegible] the girls m[illegible] [illegible] back the sh[illegible] [illegible]ok. Mary's li[illegible] [illegible]me, bringing [illegible]

[illegible]s's elbow Lau[illegible] [illegible] back. She pe[illegible] [illegible] bundle of bla[illegible] [illegible] laughed. "An[illegible] [illegible]arles twinkled [illegible] [illegible]ardly return [illegible] [illegible]he trembling [illegible] [illegible] of apprehe[illegible] [illegible]her to this spar[illegible] [illegible]e had not sa[illegible] [illegible] and now eac[illegible] [illegible]ough to brus[illegible] [illegible] before anoth[illegible]

[illegible] gone down on [illegible] gazing at her [illegible] sister as though she were a stick of candy too sweet to lick. "Such a tiny, tiny baby," she breathed.

"Hardly bigger than a prairie hen," Mrs. Scott agreed.

Caroline's passion flared. Mrs. Scott's every word about this child seemed too vibrant with meaning, but Caroline checked herself before speaking. *Least said, soonest mended*. "She will soon be big enough for you to play with," she assured her daughters instead.

"We'll call her Caroline, for you," Charles said. "Carrie for short."

Caroline recalled how this baby had twirled inside her that night on the prairie, the night Laura told her the stars were singing. Her spine tingled with the memory. "Caroline Celestia," she said.

"Carrie can have my beads," Mary said.

Before Caroline could ask, Charles reached into his pocket and drew out his handkerchief, knotted at both ends. Two pools of Indian beads glittered inside.

Laura stirred her portion slowly with her finger. "And mine too," she offered, not taking her eyes from them.

"That's my unselfish, good little girls," Caroline praised them, though her chest blossomed with sympathy for Laura. Mary was always so quick to show off her goodness. It was hardly fair to expect such a little girl to keep up. But Laura must learn. "Give them a strong thread, Charles, and they may string them." She touched Laura's cheek and felt the burn of the child's disappointment. "There are enough to make a little string of beads for Carrie to wear around her neck," she said. Laura was not consoled, but she nodded politely and went to join Mary.

Caroline closed her eyes, veiling herself from all of them as best she could. Not one fleck of emotion had entered the cabin without leaving its print upon her, and she thirsted for a space out of reach. Beside her in the bed, the soft movements of Carrie's breaths shifted and settled like whispering embers. In her newness, and her nearness, Carrie did not yet seem a separate creature unto herself, and Caroline welcomed the small animal comfort of her.

Carolin[illegible] ite [illegible] of the cabin t[illegible] sleep—the [illegible] ringing their b[illegible] tling "Dais[illegible] an [illegible] end the stock, [illegible] chain. Mrs. [illegible] n and mixing [illegible] steady. Ber[illegible] ly strummed [illegible] name.

THE SMELL [illegible] er was still in [illegible] line woke. [illegible] ght as a bud be[illegible] Laura were [illegible] small bed, th[illegible] hair lustrou[illegible] ow cases. He[illegible] open. There [illegible] ressing inside, [illegible] feel where t[illegible] re and the pa[illegible] inch of it hu[illegible] of the pain w[illegible] to be almost [illegible] ook a deep, [illegible] treating her [illegible] ly stretch in [illegible] not a thing i[illegible] ted.

"I'll sleep [illegible] as saying. He l[illegible] room. "Wher[illegible]

Mrs. Scot[illegible] ing," she said.

Charles [illegible] lt down by th[illegible] hand like a bo[illegible] His thumb rov[illegible] black hair as i[illegible] finer than any [illegible] The look in h[illegible] o meet; even [illegible] ound space i[illegible] oom in Carol[illegible] ffection he w[illegible] rd, he squeeze[illegible] nd kissed her [illegible]

"Come wa[illegible] ything at all," [illegible] cott. The do[illegible] Scott did no[illegible] ring.

Caroline clo[illegible] to the sounds [illegible] essing: the c[illegible] eased her fee[illegible] corset strings sighing through the eyelets, the click of the metal busk unfastening. Then Caroline felt Mrs. Scott crawl up over the foot of the bed, settling into Charles's accustomed place by the wall.

They lay alongside each other, politely still. Only Mrs. Scott's voice moved toward her, softer yet than Caroline had heard her speak. "My Robert . . . he told me how you helped Mr. Ingalls pull him from the well," she said. "My family and I—we're much obliged."

Guilt sliced through Caroline like a scythe as her own panicked voice reverberated in her memory: *No, no, Charles! I can't let you. Get on Patty and go for help. If I can't pull you up—if you keel over down there and I can't pull you up . . .* She could not bear to hold such selfishness alongside Mrs. Scott's gratitude. "Please," she started. "It wasn't—"

"Don't say a thing," Mrs. Scott said. "Please. I don't have words deep enough to thank you as it is."

The words Mrs. Scott would not let her speak bulged Caroline's throat so that she could not swallow. Silently she prayed for forgiveness, though she knew it could not come swiftly enough to keep the guilt roiling behind her breasts from tainting her milk.

Caroline smiled grimly at the ceiling. If Mrs. Scott would not allow her to beg pardon, there was no choice but to make do with the consolation of penance. Tired as she was, she must lie awake and make certain her shame had wholly subsided before the child next woke to feed. Suckling on such agitated passions would likely give a newborn convulsions. A fitting punishment, Caroline thought with rueful admiration. The more she fretted over what she might have cost Mrs. Scott and her family, the longer she endangered the blameless babe asleep beside her.

MRS. SCOTT STAYED for two days.

Caroline kept quietly in bed, letting herself reknit outside and in. When she sat up to sip a mug of Mrs. Scott's velvety bean soup, long threads of soreness flared through the muscles beneath her ribs. Inside, Caroline felt as though she needed a good tidying up. Everything had

o leaning aside … that the
l been still rem… ed. … n. It was
ot unlike the s… en … n after a
re pushed aga… th … Carrie
ng warmth to i… ke … g. Caro-
e no matter ho… til … passed
swollen flesh … ate…
hild nuzzled at her … t a few
ed fluid at a … e. … Caroline
ary and Laura … a … them.
her. *Just like* C… es, … ying of
of Laura's snub… ose … the set
s vexed was enough … think,
eone like Mrs. … t … t years
Laura was sim… La… eager
to impulsive… w… genial
or images of ea… ot … d: the

lation. Proud a… rst … aid the
without being a… d, … notice
ays within Mrs. Sco… rked.
line so often sa… Bu… raded
was suddenly … th… much
helping. The fl… Mary
rds, glancing … Mr… more
l pang, Carolin… ea… help-
household task… he … ingly.
for Caroline's … pro…
ed the hem of … s she
g out before her … flat … ble of
tt might have … rai… ush of
ot up Caroline's neck … own

mistake: in trying to keep Mary unconscious of her beauty, Caroline had instead marred it with another kind of conceit. Her eyes retreated to the little one in her arms, unwilling to watch her eldest daughter grope so openly for admiration. Likely Mrs. Scott had seen Mary's performance for what it was right away and did not care to applaud it. Every swish of the broom in her ears swept the blush further across Caroline's skin. She could see it as well as feel it now, spreading down her chest toward Carrie. *It must not reach the baby,* she chided herself. Her embarrassment did not feel strong enough to put the child in peril, but all the same Caroline would not risk tarnishing her. But she could not stop it at Mary's expense. Caroline herself had cultivated Mary's pride with her unstinting praise. Showing her approval now, with Mrs. Scott looking on, would only worsen it. Yet at the same time Caroline could not bear the possibility that the bulk of Mary's pleasures had become secondhand, her smiles from others' satisfaction rather than her own delight. Anything less than a compliment, no matter how gentle, would cut the child bone-deep. Caroline's chest tightened as she fumbled for a solution, and she knew Carrie should not take one more swallow.

Caroline slipped a fingertip into the corner of Carrie's mouth and broke her lips from the nipple. "Mary," she said as Carrie's mouth worked in confusion, "would you like to hold the baby?" The broom stilled. Mary's face went round with awe. Caroline propped Charles's pillow into the corner beside her and patted the mattress. Mary came scrambling so fast, Caroline almost laughed. Mary arranged herself with her feet jutting straight out and her elbows bent, palms up, as if she were about to receive a stack of planks.

Caroline laid the baby across Mary's lap. Mary sat stone-still, as though so much as a blink might make Carrie cry. Paralyzed with wonder and terror, Caroline thought, just as she herself had been the first time Polly laid Mary into her arms.

Bemused, Mrs. Scott came to stand over the bed with her fists sunk into her hips. "Well?" she asked Mary. "What do you think of your baby sister?"

[illegible] heavy," Mary said.

[illegible] felt her cheeks dimple. [illegible] a scant five [illegible],
[illegible] but for a child accustom[illegible] made of co[illegible] and
Carrie's heft was considera[illegible] and looked [illegible]
a small baby, but Mary [illegible] though there were too
[illegible] to see all at once. [illegible] nkled, then p[illegible],
gave a cry that struck the [illegible]

[illegible] now," Mrs. Scott said, [illegible] the bed for the baby.
[illegible] put her face beside Carrie's [illegible] ear and whispered,
"Shhhh." Carrie [illegible].

[illegible] Scott chuckled. "She [illegible] mother her[illegible]
said, and Mary glowed.

[illegible] WOULD have stayed [illegible] supper and help with
[illegible] baths, she said, but [illegible] her with a [illegible]
rabbit and insisted [illegible] time to roast it for [illegible]
can manage the supper [illegible] Charles promised
[illegible]. He fitted a spit into [illegible] turned two [illegible]
[illegible] on it until the skins [illegible] juice ran hissing [illegible]
Then he carefully carved [illegible] the bones and [illegible]
[illegible] on a plate, alongside [illegible] Indian bread [illegible]
blackberries bobbing in [illegible] and Laura [illegible]
the dishes while Charles [illegible] the washtub [illegible]
to boil.

[illegible] watched him [illegible] towel, then [illegible]
water and dip his elbow [illegible] the pan [illegible]
and came to the side of [illegible] to shift the baby
[illegible], but Charles reached [illegible], into the [illegible]
the meeting of the wa[illegible] and brought [illegible]
[illegible]. He opened it and [illegible] wrapped packet [illegible]
[illegible] you and Carrie," he said.

[illegible] turned back the soft [illegible] Inside lay a [illegible] cake of pressed soap, pale and smooth as butter. The faintest whiff of roses brushed her nostrils. Her lips parted in wonder. "Charles, where did you ever—"

"On our way through Independence."

Months ago. She saw herself sitting on that wagon seat outside the store, wary of the Indians, wishing that Charles would only hurry. And all the while he had been inside, picturing this moment in his mind and choosing something small and fine to mark it. With all his worries over prices and land offices, he had thought of this—of her. She looked up at him, her eyes welling. "Oh, Charles." It was not much more than a whisper. He rubbed at the back of his neck, sheepish and pleased, then bent to gather up Carrie for her bath.

Carrie squalled until she vibrated with fury, perfectly incensed by the touch of the water. Mary and Laura scrunched up their shoulders and covered their ears. Charles was not perturbed. He bathed Carrie with the sweet white soap, toweled her dry, and folded her into a clean flannel blanket, humming as he worked. "Clean as a hound's tooth," he pronounced, fitting the baby back into the hollow of Caroline's arm.

Caroline touched her lips to Carrie's fine black hair and breathed in. The scent of pollen still tickled her nose, but the raw newness of it was gone, shrouded by the smell of the store-bought soap. She kissed the baby's head, smiling over the pinch of disappointment in her throat. "Thank you, Charles," she said.

When the girls had had their turn in the washtub—they'd splashed more than they'd scrubbed, but Charles made sure to soap their hair and kept the suds from their eyes—Charles refilled the tub and draped the wagon cover between the bedstead and the mantel, screening off the hearth for her.

Caroline stood gingerly, her feet wider apart than usual. Between her legs it felt as though there was not enough space for what had always been there. One foot, then another went into the washtub. She gripped the rim and crouched slowly into it.

[illegible]he water [illegible], it felt like part [illegible] bre[illegible]thed, m[illegible] [illegible]ckling fire. [illegible] ute [illegible] letting [illegible] [illegible]ine unpinned th[illegible] Mr[illegible]. Scott [illegible] [illegible]ay Carrie was bo[illegible] her[illegible]elf. Her [illegible] [illegible]lounce, the [illegible] nav[illegible]l. She [illegible] [illegible]ed in tissue in th[illegible] of t[illegible]e bed w[illegible] [illegible]or for month[illegible] tho[illegible]ght—th[illegible] [illegible] a dress in [illegible] her[illegible]elf tenta[illegible]ly [illegible] her the soap [illegible] sm[illegible]ll the wa[illegible] [illegible]s newborn s[illegible] the cloth an[illegible] [illegible] pink.

[illegible]arrie's [illegible] [illegible]her side of the [illegible] felt the tingl[illegible] [illegible]ent it ran in [illegible] wr[illegible]nkled be[illegible] [illegible]w, white eno[illegible]gh wh[illegible]re it drip[illegible] [illegible] in her breas[illegible] sur[illegible] so grad[illegible] [illegible] it had barely re[illegible] gaz[illegible]d fondly [illegible] [illegible]re could be [illegible] no[illegible]. It was [illegible] [illegible]cried, and Carol[illegible] lik[illegible] a moiste[illegible] [illegible]orb the child ba[illegible]

[illegible]aroline [illegible] [illegible]er the wago[illegible] per[illegible]ched at t[illegible] [illegible]aying forwa[illegible] the baby as [illegible] [illegible]hair to rock [illegible] cha[illegible]nted. "H[illegible] [illegible]ming; Ma's co[illegible] she can." Ca[illegible] [illegible]om his assura[illegible] gra[illegible]velly an[illegible]

Unbutto[illegible] [illegible] Caroline whis[illegible] her[illegible]self. He [illegible] [illegible]. She nodde[illegible] Ch[illegible]rles did [illegible] [illegible]own and put [illegible] Ca[illegible]oline sa[illegible] [illegible]h her head [illegible] wo[illegible]nan wou[illegible] [illegible]hands aroun[illegible] ing held tigh[illegible]

His hands [illegible] [illegible]le body. One [illegible]

the tempest subsided. The baby hiccoughed and blinked, as if shocked by her own contentment. Caroline smiled to herself, knowing the feel of those hands spanning her waist. A flicker of envy warmed her skin at the thought of what it would be like to fit entirely within them.

She stood, pressing the towel to her breasts, her feet reluctant to lift from the water. Carrie would wait, cozied up that way on her pa's bare chest. With luck the baby might even fall asleep. But Caroline did not sink back into the tub. Moments ago she had wanted to stay in that warm, soft water, to pull it over her like a quilt and soak until morning. Seeing Charles and Carrie together, Caroline wanted only to be beside them.

She slipped her nightdress over her damp skin and fitted her body back into the hollow it had left in the straw tick. Between them was the little peak she and Mrs. Scott had made, lying so deferentially side by side. Caroline leaned across it and pillowed her head on Charles's shoulder. She could not see his face lying this way, but as they gazed at the baby she began to see his features reflected in Carrie, as though Carrie were a little mirror tilted sideways. His narrow chin was there with no whiskers to hide behind, and his high hairline.

"She has your eyes," Charles said.

She did, poor thing. "Newborn babies always have eyes like slate. They'll brighten in time. Mary's and Laura's did."

Charles's whiskers brushed her forehead as he turned. She could feel him looking quizzically down on her. "Is that what you think of your eyes?"

"Ma always said they were gray as the December day I was born." His were like a woman's, such a delicate blue as she'd only seen painted on fine china.

He traced her brow bone with his thumb. "Your ma was wrong," he said. "Your eyes are gray like flannel, and there's nothing half so warm and soft in the world as flannel."

Caroline's eyes flickered up, then her face ripened with a smile as the co[illegible] her. She presse[illegible]d as [illegible]ulder.

[illegible] shyness, rumbli[illegible]ie cri[illegible]

[illegible]hem made, his ba[illegible]d be[illegible] pulse burgeo[illegible] a fr[illegible]rned the path [illegible]r.

[illegible]ed herself as [illegible]as th[illegible] the child gr[illegible] to sp[illegible] she said and unco[illegible]"

[illegible] baby from hi[illegible]ty cr[illegible]e's lips butto[illegible]ed as[illegible] of Carrie's jaw s[illegible]

"Ca[illegible] a wonder."

[illegible] child, drawi[illegible]ce thro[illegible]man in the wor[illegible]e, b[illegible] his wonder [illegible]es co[illegible] wood and too[illegible]ad fo[illegible]eature of brea[illegible]ing b[illegible]n begun with a[illegible]en th[illegible]milk.

[illegible] window and t[illegible]a m[illegible]," he said.

[illegible]oney. She saw it a[illegible] did, [illegible]ss, h[illegible] running cree[illegible]ow i[illegible] They had ne[illegible]me i[illegible] land was diffe[illegible] its a[illegible] to suckle free[illegible]ing c[illegible] seeds to the g[illegible] rich [illegible]and w[illegible] would becom[illegible] *me* [illegible] *test us . . . ,* she th[illegible]ght, [illegible] the pl[illegible] *[illegible]it of it.*

Twenty-Two

"YOU BE MA and I'll be Mrs. Scott," Mary said to Laura. "My rag doll will be the baby."

Caroline's cheeks ached from holding back her smiles. The new center of Mary's world lay nursing in Caroline's arms. Overnight Mary had become a miniature nursemaid: earnest, attentive, and entirely unconscious of how darling she was as she bustled about the cabin. When she could not fuss over her new sister, she practiced with her doll. It would only be a matter of time, Caroline supposed, before Mary tried to suckle that poor cotton baby. Caroline's lips twitched at the thought. All day long, she wanted to let the delight tumble out of her, but she could not let Mary realize that her grown-up airs only made her more childlike.

Laura was braced against the doorjamb, having a tug-of-war with Jack over a stick of firewood. "I don't—want—to play—inside," she said, as though Jack were jerking each piece of the answer out of her.

"I'll let you hold my rag doll," Mary promised.

Caroline's eyebrow arched. That was a sacrifice, coming from Mary. Laura was tempted, and her grip faltered just as Jack's playful growl changed. He let loose the stick, and Laura plopped onto the ground. "Jack!" she cried as the bulldog turned from her, his throat rumbling. Then, "Oh! It's a man coming, Ma!"

"You mustn't shout, Laura," Caroline reminded her. "Is it Mr. Edwards?"

Laura shook her head. "A new man."

Caroline shifted to look outside. A bay dun, mounted by a sandy-haired man, was trotting up the path from the creek. Sunlight glinted off [illegible] spectacles, giving the [illegible] k [illegible] a schoolteacher. [illegible] into a fury of barking, an[illegible] hi[illegible]. Charles's voice [illegible] off Jack and hallooin[illegible] from the stable. [illegible] to soothe her rag doll fr[illegible]. Caroline tugged a[illegible] [illegible]dice, trying not to dislod[illegible] from her feeding. The [illegible] a poor shield. "Clo[illegible] the [illegible] Laura," she said.

[illegible]!"

[illegible] stay outside if you keep w[illegible] way. Close the door [illegible]."

[illegible] again for her rocking cha[illegible] resettled herself ont[illegible] [illegible] with her back against the w[illegible] rocked to the win[illegible] [illegible] wind seemed to blow the [illegible] the men's words, s[illegible] [illegible] only where one ended [illegible] began. The tempo [illegible] [illegible]rsation was absurdly clipp[illegible] from the stranger, [illegible] Charles, another from the [illegible] more from Charles. [illegible] man spoke no English, C[illegible]led. She gave up mak[illegible] [illegible] it and returned to the ta[illegible]

[illegible]'s attention had drifted, [illegible] were closed and her [illegible]ked lazily at the nipple, [illegible] of warmth trai[illegible] Caroline's hips, to the pla[illegible] to begetting a[illegible] Caroline tickled under Ca[illegible] remind her, and the [illegible]ps resumed their muscul[illegible]. Neither of her older [illegible] taken to idling at the breas[illegible] baby did. She suckled [illegible]urts, tugging at the nippl[illegible] times, then slacken[illegible] [illegible] to make a meal of each [illegible] Caroline in mind of [illegible] way Mary sipped at the ti[illegible] with Laura, but it [illegible], too, that a child so new [illegible] willing to make do with

"Take your fill, baby girl," [illegible]

[illegible] not speak to the baby by [illegible] the others did. To Car[illegible] [illegible] was a word whose meani[illegible] ing. The child her[illegible] [illegible] her body, but was still s[illegible] as to seem a part of

Caroline—a cutting grafted back into her side. Sharing her name with the baby only blurred the lines further.

Mary, being the first and only child in the house, had been *Mary* straightaway, though after the five years it had taken to become *Ma,* Caroline had loved even more to hear herself say *the baby, my baby, our baby,* as though saying it somehow made it truer than holding Mary in her arms. This child was spending her first days as Laura had—an anonymous little creature, barely beginning to peel away from the mold her sisters had left behind.

For now, Caroline contented herself with looking at the child and thinking *Caroline Celestia,* as though it were the Latinate name for spindly, black-haired baby girls native to the Kansas prairie. Even if such a taxonomy existed, she mused, it could tell her only so much, for although a seed called *Ipomoea purpurea* would always unfurl into a morning glory, it was anyone's guess whether the blooms would be pink, purple, or blue.

Mary came to stand beside them and peeped over Caroline's elbow. "Ma?" she said. Caroline knew what the question would be. She had promised Mary could mind the baby when she'd finished feeding. *Minding* meant little more than sitting on the big bed, watching her sister sleep, but Mary reveled in the responsibility.

"Is Baby Carrie full?" Mary asked. She said the name as though it were a single word: *Baby-Carrie.*

Caroline tried it for herself. "Baby Carrie is nearly finished." She liked the bridge it made so well, she said it again to herself. *Baby Carrie.* "You may fetch a clean flannel and lay out a fresh diaper while you wait."

Laura came scampering in with Jack trotting behind her. Charles followed. "He had a great big book, Ma," she said, breathless with the news, "and he wrote my name in it, and asked me how old I am, and put that in, too. He's going to send it all the way to Mr. Grant in Washington."

"My goodness," Caro[illegible] said to Laura. "That sounds very [illegible]ant. What is all this, Charles?"

"Census taker," Charles [illegible] his forehead with his hat. "[illegible]ble enough fellow," he said with a nod toward Laura. "Funny [illegible] though—he didn't mark [illegible] down for property value. [illegible] column's left blank."

Caroline raised Carrie [illegible] shoulder and leaned her cheek against the top of the baby's head. [illegible] fit [illegible] neatly as a teacup into a saucer. "We don't own it, Charles," she said gently.

"Not yet, but that doesn't make it worthless."

Twenty-Three

CAROLINE KNEW THE moment the sickness touched her. It had been all around her—first Mary and Laura, then Charles, all within a single afternoon—but the moment it breached her own body was different.

"Oh," she said, and sat down on the end of the bedstead. She was panting. Her nose tingled with something more than the smell of scalded broth, and her eyes were warm beneath their lids as they roved over the disheveled room.

The chamber pail needed emptying, the water bucket had to be filled, the soup pot must be emptied and scrubbed before she could begin supper again, and Caroline knew—knew with her whole body—that she could do precisely one more task. She pushed herself up, and her shoulders rattled with a chill. *Sit,* she told herself. *Get a minute's rest, then try.* She had hardly sat for two days.

Charles had still not taken to his bed, but Caroline was not fooled. He had not so much as lifted his gun from its pegs. Not even in the depths of a Wisconsin winter had he huddled by the fire making bullets in the middle of the afternoon, much less for two days straight. She'd seen the sheen of cold sweat on his brow in the firelight and watched his hands tremble. It had been all he could do not to spill the molten lead onto the hearth. She did not know how he was managing to keep the stock fed and watered.

Caroline looked again at their own water pail. From where she sat, she could not see past the brim to gauge what little was left. They must have more. To drink, to make more broth, to sponge the perspiration from Mary's and Laura's fevered limbs, to rinse the baby's diapers and her [illegible] p[illegible] Just [illegible]e sight of the pa[illegible] wa[illegible] by the door made her [illegible] with unease. Charles had [illegible] out to fill whe[illegible] as he always did. That [illegible] was not well. [illegible] if she could ask him [illegible] with the [illegible] im so long.

C[illegible] hk. How long [illegible]? The girls had [illegible] eantime, she could not [illegible] guess. Their fever [illegible] cided. One was [illegible] cold. She had [illegible] of their small [illegible] lt, so that [illegible] ulling and kicking [illegible] . That, at la[illegible] enough so they [illegible] ffled in h[illegible] ging away from the s[illegible] of a sheet. Charles [illegible] in the house during [illegible] have save[illegible] ing.

I[illegible] the middle of the b[illegible] an to snu[illegible]

"[illegible] begged. "Please don['t] wak[e] [illegible] sisters. Here." She [illegible] ut the fastenings [illegible] rsing cor[illegible] Her fingertips felt [illegible] come to h[illegible] thought, but that was [illegible] orked slow[illegible] ing for somethi[illegible] st but not [illegible]

[illegible] onto one elbow [illegible] toward the [illegible] till working at [illegible] "Shh-sh[illegible] I'm coming. Ma's [illegible] moved on[illegible] was on the verge of [illegible] ld see he[illegible] all the points of her lit[illegible] g. She wo[illegible] e. Caroline lay down [illegible] ting as mu[illegible] ugh the gap as p[illegible]

[illegible] awkwardly under [illegible] r, but Ca[illegible] to move. Carrie was feed[illegible] eeding and the girls were asleep, and all was quiet. There was so much that needed tending to, before the girls woke again and needed her most of all. *Rest,* she told herself. *Rest until Charles comes back from the stable.*

DARKNESS, WAVERING LIKE a dream all around her. Hot hands, hot fingertips tingling. Hot breath curling over her lips from nostrils like stove holes. She'd never felt such heat—heat that made her skin crackle and shiver. The soles of her feet were papery, as though they'd been peeled down to dry bone. The darkness advanced and receded, expanded and contracted, as though the thick black air meant to crush her, or inhale her. Caroline closed her eyes and the world went mercifully, mercifully still.

A SLIVER OF gray light. *Twilight or dawn,* Caroline wondered muzzily. The air around her had thinned and cooled, stopped its pulsating, but her limbs, her head, her very eyelids might have been filled with sand for all that Caroline could move them. She felt a scrabbling between her body and her arm, and knew it was Carrie who had woken her. Caroline turned her head to look. The effort made her gasp, made the room reel. Her breast still protruded from the half-opened corset flap, but sometime in the fevered night she had shifted, and Carrie could not reach. The baby had fastened herself to a button on Caroline's open bodice and sucked until she'd pulled the calico into a pointed wet teat. Carrie tugged and batted at it, confounded.

Tears blurred Caroline's eyes. "Carrie," she said, but there was no sound. Her throat was like bark. Caroline prized a quivering hand from the straw tick and managed to loosen the hard twist of fabric from Carrie's mouth. Carrie instantly raged. Caroline whimpered at the shock of the sound striking her ears and at their own mingled frustration. She gripped the side of the bedstead and pulled. A chill shook her so fiercely, her joints rattled. She pulled again, and her body spasmed. The

momen[illegible] sideways to meet C[illegible]rie, [illegible]
lay, gasp[illegible]ng [illegible], [illegible]ile Carrie took her [illegible]ll.

SHE [illegible] f filth rising up from the [illegible]
Carr[illegible]e. [illegible] n the stable, and [illegible]
whir[illegible]ed [illegible] zzed under her cor[illegible]t, [illegible]
wasp sti[illegible]? Ca[illegible] ve a little pull, and [illegible]
Caroline [illegible] lization. Pinned bet[illegible]een [illegible]
slab, Carrie [illegible] ly from the left brea[illegible], wh[illegible]
filled, [illegible] eels. The weight of i[illegible]
yearne[illegible] ck, but she did not [illegible]
the [illegible] ned over. She could only [illegible]
bedstea[illegible] ithin Carrie's reach.

A [illegible] newhere beyond the bed. [illegible]ink of
water, I [illegible] ater."

Mary. He[illegible] y, begging. Caroline's eyes [illegible]
tears [illegible] no moisture to spare fo[illegible]
olou[illegible] ump and a shudder [illegible]
her [illegible] that Charles was [illegible]
tryi[illegible] ents sent a cascade of [illegible]
Eve[illegible] air probed painfull[illegible]
clos[illegible] l her teeth. She wo[illegible]
cou[illegible] d tend to Mary. [illegible]
agai[illegible] l, howled. Then all [illegible]
voic[illegible] dry, Caroline could hear [illegible]
at M[illegible] dles of milk dampened th[illegible]
cors[illegible]et.

Car[illegible] ad up, just enough to se[illegible]
arm [illegible] seemed to flicker in[illegible]
awa[illegible] and yellow, a tired [illegible]
Laura [illegible] ing back at her. "Laura," C[illegible]
"can yo[illegible]"

"Yes, Ma," Laura said.

Caroline dropped down beside the baby. Sounds moved back and forth across the cabin. Jack's nails on the floor. Dragging, dragging, dragging. A rattle and splash. Then nothing. She could not tell whether Laura had done it, or collapsed trying—only that Mary stopped crying.

Thirty-Four

[illegible] E WOKE SO[illegible] So so[illegible] was exquisite[illegible] ill[illegible] [illegible] er skin. Her to[illegible] brush[illegible] sheets and she [illegible] smile[illegible] [illegible] to herself. [illegible] ot[illegible] g had [illegible] as that cris[illegible] [illegible] r skin. For [illegible] ake herself u[illegible] sta[illegible] [illegible] felt so sing[illegible] differ[illegible] g was as it alw[illegible] wa[illegible] [illegible] y on one sid[illegible] r, [illegible] Caroline turned he[illegible] [illegible] her side an[illegible] fo[illegible] . . . [illegible] stared, unabl[illegible] [illegible] the space wh[illegible] e bab[illegible].

[illegible] ng but her m[illegible] uld [illegible] dden speed of it [illegible] [illegible] sheets, her nig[illegible] dress [illegible] of [illegible] omfort itself—a [illegible] of it [illegible] ng. Her me[illegible] found Mary [illegible] ng [illegible] [illegible] e sound asw[illegible] eat and inert[illegible] [illegible] ent and thi[illegible] —not [illegible]

[illegible] emories sto[illegible] so sh[illegible] mind seeme[illegible] to [illegible] [illegible] xious to dis[illegible] el [illegible] her eyes to [illegible] [illegible] up the yok[illegible] of [illegible] round butto[illegible] Th[illegible] [illegible] s and their [illegible] for her thoug[illegible] ts, wh[illegible] [illegible] eeping up o[illegible] e voi[illegible]

[illegible] had becom[illegible] er corset? Ha[illegible] [illegible] the sobs a[illegible] howl[illegible] g in her brea[illegible] and [illegible] shimmerin[illegible]? Ha[illegible] that nightma[illegible] [illegible] d at all? Ca[illegible] conc[illegible] yet on the s[illegible] as another r[illegible] ion [illegible] of the void. *[illegible] happened, C[illegible] ou'ld [illegible] ty space beside [illegible]* [illegible] ered. A pin[illegible] of fea[illegible] n white-hot, [illegible] belly. Deep inside her head, a thin specter of a voice dared to whisper: *Was the baby herself even real?*

Caroline's heart stuttered, too weak to pound. "Carrie?" The word was a creak. Her mouth tasted bitter and shrunken.

Suddenly Mrs. Scott's face was over hers. "Don't fret yourself, Mrs. Ingalls. The little one's asleep in the washtub. Snug as a bug, next to the fire."

The dreadful thoughts released her so suddenly, Caroline felt as if she were floating.

Mrs. Scott brought a mug of cool water and held it for Caroline to drink. The water rippled as it touched her trembling lips. She lay back on the pillow and her body continued to vibrate, softly, steadily. Not the ague, Caroline thought. Fear. It had lasted only an instant, but it had permeated her entirely. She could feel it melting away now, passing through her skin and lifting, harmless, into the air as Mrs. Scott used her knuckles to brush the matted tendrils of hair from Caroline's forehead.

"Now you're awake and the fever's passed, let's get this straightened out," Mrs. Scott said. Her big nimble fingers coaxed the tangled hair pins loose as she talked, until she had Caroline's long braid unfurled across her lap. "There's fever and ague all up and down the creek," she said, "all from watermelons, of all things. Some fool settler planted watermelons in the bottoms, and every soul that's eaten one is down sick this very minute, with hardly enough folks left standing to tend to them. I've been going house to house day and night, but yours is the worst case I've seen. It's a wonder you ever lived through, all of you down at once. Dr. Tann—he's a Negro, doctors all over this side of the county, settlers and Indians both, heaven help him—was headed up to Independence when that dog of yours met him and wouldn't let him pass. And here you all were, more dead than alive!"

"How long has it been?" Caroline asked.

"Couldn't say for certain. I've been here since yesterday, and Dr.

Tann stay[illegible] day[illegible] [illegible]e I came." H[illegible] [illegible] braided s[illegible] [illegible] way to the s[illegible] [illegible] long you [illegible] [illegible]at. Dr. Tann [illegible] stock we[illegible] [illegible]ed another d[illegible] [illegible]

Three da[illegible] at [illegible] t[illegible]ied again to [illegible] tion. The[illegible] Laura's face [illegible] crawling [illegible], and the next [illegible] she was [illegible] [illegible]llness. In be[illegible] abrupt as [illegible] she had nev[illegible] her own [illegible]

Hidde[illegible] [illegible] were all the [illegible] Mrs. Sco[illegible] [illegible], Caroline t[illegible] them, d[illegible] [illegible]at state the[illegible] time the [illegible] not like to [illegible] set to rig[illegible] [illegible]nel between [illegible] tick was [illegible]

Carol[illegible] [illegible]overed her [illegible] heard th[illegible] [illegible]n Caroline's [illegible]

"Now[illegible] [illegible]mbed her ha[illegible] hair, "th[illegible] of."

But [illegible] She was [illegible] throbbe[illegible] [illegible] not have as[illegible] own blo[illegible] [illegible]ne for her. [illegible] repaid, [illegible] [illegible]e itself.

Mrs. S[illegible] [illegible], not untang[illegible] Carolin[illegible] [illegible]es. To think [illegible] in her t[illegible] [illegible]he had alrea[illegible] too swe[illegible] [illegible] no strength [illegible] wrung [illegible] [illegible]nside and out

Most [illegible] [illegible]arrie, but sh[illegible] To ask [illegible] [illegible]ing that she [illegible] notion [illegible] [illegible]ver-addled [illegible]

Scott had told her the baby was safe, and Caroline did not doubt it. Yet her body was unsatisfied. Her arms begged for the reassurance of the weight and shape of the child, the perfect fit of her, belly to belly and cheek to breast. She felt the insistent press of her milk—Carrie's milk—against her upper arms and took what comfort she could from its undeniable link with the baby.

While she waited for Carrie to wake, Caroline swallowed the powdered bitters Dr. Tann had left behind, puckering like a child at the way it drew every atom of moisture from her mouth. She lifted the mug for more water, but Mrs. Scott brought a spoonful of cream instead. "Don't swallow it right off. Hold it in your mouth a minute." Caroline obliged, and her entire face relaxed at the touch of that thick cream. It was silky-sweet and sank into the roughened surface of her tongue as softly as a kiss. Caroline's eyes rolled up blissfully to Mrs. Scott, who burst out laughing. "My mother's trick," she said. "Never fails. Most folks put their dose of quinine right into a mug of milk, but it's not nearly the same."

The laughter stirred Charles, who roused long enough to down his bitters and roll over. Presently a thin complaint rose from the washtub.

With the prick of the child's cry came a gentle bursting behind Caroline's breasts, and two warm, wet spots bloomed on her nightdress. She craned her neck, and there was Carrie, curled on Mrs. Scott's bosom like a little pink snail. Caroline's whole body seemed to smile as her eyes fell across the baby.

Mrs. Scott laid Carrie in her arms and helped her with the buttons. Caroline touched Carrie's wan little cheek with a fingertip. Carrie reached toward it, her lips poised in a taut pink oval. She briefly mouthed Caroline's finger, then found her proper place and sucked so hard and fast, Caroline hardly recognized her.

In the time it took for their shared astonishment to register, Carrie's face buckled. Her tongue darted in and out as she spluttered. Caroline wiped the milk from Carrie's chin and tickled the child's lips with [illegible] pple. Carrie [illegible] then arched ba[illegible] [illegible] ed.

"[illegible]at'll be the [illegible]," [illegible] ed. "I imagine [illegible] dose of bitters [illegible] Ingalls."

C[illegible]roline pressed [illegible] forehead, stroking [illegible] rieked. Carrie [illegible] ment too big for [illegible]. At the touch [illegible], a tremor ro[illegible] ine's chest. A [illegible] of fever, she [illegible] aby's cries w[illegible] roline felt as thou[illegible] ving into them [illegible].

"[illegible]ou'll be squal[illegible] drain some of [illegible] Mrs. Scott remark[illegible] haven't already [illegible] a case of bad b[illegible] ing else. My sister [illegible] ge leaves to ta[illegible] there won't [illegible] se parts for a[illegible]."

[illegible]ger crackled b[illegible] so abruptly, she [illegible] n sharp heat. [illegible] simple as a cabbag[illegible] l never have [illegible] struck with fe[illegible] isconsin. None [illegible] Henry and P[illegible]

"[illegible]hy, Mrs. Ing[illegible]!" [illegible] ed. "You loo[illegible] again."

"[illegible]'s only—" Ca[illegible] her head. She [illegible] more than she [illegible] too much," [illegible] ything." She [illegible] Carrie, then a[illegible] ned to ask alo[illegible] back again. [illegible] ne thing Caroli[illegible] laughter.

[illegible]rs. Scott unde[illegible], if not why [illegible] d scooped Ca[illegible]," she said [illegible] ms. She gave [illegible] ing squeeze. "[illegible] of the cream [illegible] t you waste [illegible] ying." Carolin[illegible] only that her[illegible] unspeakably b[illegible].

"I DON'T KNOW how I can ever thank you," Caroline said to Mrs. Scott. It could not be done. Both of them knew that. Caroline refused to so much as contemplate what sort of misfortune would have to befall the Scotts before she could repay her debts to them. Two more days Mrs. Scott had stayed. Even after Charles staggered up from the bed, she insisted on getting the meals and spoon feeding the baby in the wee hours so they both might rest through the night.

"Pshaw!" Mrs. Scott scoffed. "What are neighbors for but to help each other out?"

Caroline nodded. It was so. She had not fully known it, living alongside family most of her life. Caroline thought of embracing her, as she would have embraced Polly or Eliza, but did not know how to do it. Instead she contented herself with imagining the momentary feel of her heart pressing its thanks against the big woman's chest.

Caroline leaned against the doorway, thankful for its support as she watched Mrs. Scott go. She raised an arm to bid a final goodbye, and her pulse guttered like a candle flame. She had made too much of a show that morning, making up the bed and laying the table and wiping the dishes to convince Mrs. Scott it was all right to go. The bed ought to have waited, Caroline silently admitted. She was not fully well, none of them were, but she was well enough to do the things that must be done. That much and no more, she reminded herself.

Caroline sat down on one of the crates beside the table and surveyed the cabin. The wash was ironed and folded, the milk strained and the pan scalded. Mrs. Scott had given the floor one final sweep before leaving. Carrie lay freshly diapered in the center of the big bed. Caroline pondered a moment over what day it was. Wednesday. Carrie was five weeks old, and it was mending day. Both thoughts overwhelmed her. She smiled weakly at the scrap bag as if in apology, dazed at the realization that even so much as threading a needle required a precise sort of energy and focus she had not yet regained.

"Will you set one of the crates by the fireplace, please, Charles?" she as[illegible] and walked [illegible]er [illegible]it. [illegible] a pillow into the [illegible] laid Carrie in i[illegible] so that C[illegible] not move from the [illegible] her. And there Carolin[illegible], tending the [illegible] had put on the [illegible] dinner and supp[illegible]

THU[illegible] AND Saturday [illegible] slats of those [illegible] against her thigh [illegible] sitting, standing, or lying [illegible]. Standing fo[illegible] an[illegible] queer finding [illegible] her limbs, as though [illegible] her strength [illegible] she sat to help [illegible] dress, to mix the [illegible] the table and [illegible] the baby and chang[illegible]

A[illegible] doses of bitt[illegible] conceded to nurs[illegible] time Caroline put her [illegible] Carrie's small black[illegible] furrowed with con[illegible] before settling in[illegible] could not [illegible]ness. She had tast[illegible] herself, and while [illegible] she'd feared, there [illegible] metallic cast to [illegible] the child shrie[illegible] when her fee[illegible] upon the quinine [illegible] might [illegible] with kerosene. Th[illegible] to down [illegible] least likely t[illegible] as soon as the bab[illegible] laid down to nap[illegible] appetite seemed to [illegible] efforts.

"[illegible] hungry now," C[illegible] close to a whi[illegible] though it was plai[illegible] Carrie's mouth and [illegible] try that Carrie [illegible]. She could still taste [illegible] of quinine, t[illegible] tongue where it was [illegible] lodge. She un[illegible] resigned herself [illegible] action.

C[illegible]. She scowle[illegible] with her small sharp [illegible] med that th[illegible] in the same place not an hour before must still be there. Such a flood of warm sympathy filled the space behind Caroline's breasts at the sight of Carrie's consternation as would have drenched the child, but Caroline could not communicate it, except perhaps through the milk Carrie would not take. Defeated, Carrie threw back her fists. Her face flushed and her chest spasmed with a silent scream. The tiny body in Caroline's arms seemed to beg for movement, but every speck of Caroline's energy was rationed, with none to spare to walk the floor with her daughter. Again Carrie cried and Caroline's milk answered, wetting the both of them.

"IT'S AN ILL wind that doesn't blow some good," Charles called from the dooryard.

Her impulse was to hiss at him to hush, that Carrie was asleep, as anyone with the consideration to look before hollering out that way could see. Caroline looked up from her mixing bowl and saw him backing through the open door, carrying what seemed at first glance to be a strangely graceful armload of willow kindling. Charles stopped in the center of the room and put it down. "Didn't have the strength to cut firewood, so I sat myself on a stump behind the woodpile and built this for you instead."

A chair. A rocking chair.

Caroline could not speak. For a terrible instant, she thought she might burst into tears. She had never asked, never complained of leaving anything behind, yet he had known, and made her the thing she longed for most. And she had nearly scolded him for it. Now and again she had heard the sounds of his ax and hammer, and thought nothing of it.

"Should I show you how it works," Charles teased, "or are you happy enough just looking at it?" She was, nearly. It was such a lithe-looking thing, its frame a single swooping curve, its back and seat good plain wickerwork. Caroline reached out to touch the narrow willow arm. No further. She would make herself feel as lovely as the chair itself before sitting in it, she decided.

t, she smoo ed er h ff her apron, as ugh
ntary flicker ger he could strip fro
he went to t her gold bar pi
r collar. Cha es Mary and Laura
ir, and drap wh with their small red
Then Charle Ca and and led her to
the girls pranc g pup

ugh the pill ne strips cradled her
the chair's ea thought of the coo
g like hoop Caroline closed
Charles, I hav en since I don't know
well he kne shap en she rested
ocker's arm th did lders upward.
recisely mat ed small of her ba
her knees. e d to rise to mee
orward sw ven rocker she had
time had not well.
hair Charle ha fash ut of awe as
polishing u had worthy of the
n his mind wif be. Empty, it had
thing to lo a
hair was an ears had passed, and
w he had n er her. Indeed, he
ore closely. bered—how sh
, the way s elbows from its
houlders as those memories
chair that he h pitcher holds wate
ne it by me than his gaze.
s lifted Car reached for
eady curvin welcome. Wh
hed, it was kiss.
leaned back into the curling

the chair. All the crosspieces of her body seemed to loosen. With a sigh she looked at Carrie, and the child smiled up at her. Caroline's breath hitched. Carrie's eyes were still so big in her peaked little face, but her cheeks had shown a flicker of roundness. A feeling like a spreading of wings brushed Caroline's womb and she pulled Carrie closer, rocking deeply now, as if the motion might keep all that she felt from spilling over.

WITH A THUD, the floorboard bounced beneath her feet. Caroline nearly spilled the dishpan. She whirled toward the sound and saw a watermelon rolling just inside the doorway. Charles sank down beside it.

"Charles! Are you all right?"

"Thought I'd never get it here," he said, slapping the melon. "It must weigh forty pounds, and I'm as weak as water."

A strange mixture of dread and desire fluttered Caroline's stomach. "Charles," she warned, "you mustn't. Mrs. Scott said—"

He only laughed. "That's not reasonable. I haven't tasted a good slice of watermelon since Hector was a pup. It wasn't a melon that made us sick. Fever and ague comes from breathing the night air. Anyone knows that."

Caroline tucked her fingers into her palms. They itched to spank that fat melon as Charles had, to hear its delicious green thump. In her mind she could already taste watermelon rind pickles, with lemon, vinegar, and sugar; cinnamon, allspice, and clove. Her thoughts seemed to cartwheel over each other, she was so eager to talk herself into it. She only half believed Mrs. Scott's proclamations about watermelons and ague, and Charles's logic could not be denied. None of them had so much as laid eyes on a melon since Wisconsin. Caroline glanced at the girls, and all her eagerness fell flat. The very fact that they were playing quietly indoors on a day such as this reminded her of all the ague had cost them already. The consequences were more than Caroline dared chance. "This watermelon grew in the night air," she countered, then bit her lip. The argument was so weak, it had the ring of a joke.

"Non[illegible]" [illegible] "[illegible] eat this melon [illegible] me chil[illegible] [illegible]

Caro[illegible]. [illegible] would be no p[illegible] believe [illegible]

He h[illegible] onto the tabl[illegible] knife to th[illegible] green skin. He [illegible] hand and l[illegible]ward until his k[illegible] oilcloth. [illegible] and lay rock[illegible] and spar[illegible] of its flesh looke[illegible]. With his [illegible] ized a perfect [illegible] center a[illegible]

Caroli[illegible] "N[illegible], thank you, Charl[illegible] And [illegible] girls, eit[illegible]

"Aw, Ma[illegible] r.

Caroli[illegible] They were so dis[illegible] not stan[illegible] er in her life had [illegible] good, fr[illegible] the sound of [illegible] much as a [illegible] a risk."

Charl[illegible] dribble of juice [illegible] he popp[illegible] into his mou[illegible] and mad[illegible] keep the juice [illegible] sound of [illegible] bite was more [illegible] bear. "Ta[illegible] arles. It isn't fair [illegible] He went [illegible].

The g[illegible] y, but they were [illegible] it, not qu[illegible] they could [illegible] as she co[illegible] behind the wo[illegible] braced o[illegible] a giant cre[illegible] no one w[illegible] the seeds, glee[illegible] stopped [illegible] watering. Anothe[illegible] she'd be [illegible] Laura. She [illegible] the image away, finished the dishes, then mopped the puddles of juice from the table and wrung out the dishcloth. She picked up Carrie and went to her rocker.

It was hard to feel bereft of anything in that chair, with the baby in her lap. Caroline pressed her thumb into Carrie's palm and rubbed a slow circle. It was a trick she had learned early on, when she could not get enough of touching Mary's silken hands and feet, that made all of her babies go limp with pleasure. But now Carrie grabbed hold of Caroline's finger and pulled it to her mouth. She gripped fist and finger with her gums, testing the strength of her jaw. Then her eyes widened and her toes splayed. She gave a little chirrup and sucked and sucked at Caroline's fingertip.

"What in the world?" Caroline wondered.

Mary came running. "What is it, Ma? Is Baby Carrie all right?"

"I declare, your baby sister is sucking my finger as if it were a stick of candy."

Mary offered her own waggling fingers, but Carrie would not be distracted. She was still at it when Charles came back, wiping his chin with his handkerchief. "The cow can have the rest of it," he announced. He kissed her, and Caroline tasted the sweet juice on his mouth. She licked her lips. So sweet after days and days of bitter quinine, she shivered. And then she knew. It was the juice from the dishcloth that Carrie tasted on her fingers. Caroline looked again at Carrie and saw that she was happy. Happy, perhaps for the first time in her life.

SHE WAITED UNTIL after supper, excusing the girls from wiping the dishes so that she might slip a spoon into her pocket unnoticed. Without a word, Caroline went outside. First to the necessary. No one had asked where she was going, and this would render their assumption true; no need for questions meant no need for lies.

From the necessary, the woodpile beckoned irresistibly. The voice in

... entirely her ow... ...ispered at her ... ...ing, wheedling ... ...every thought ... seen the conte... ...girl's face.

... *fever and ague.* ... *idn't. Carrie ... of bitters withou... ...if Charles must ... could have nothin... ...nd ague. And ... eady tasted the ... ...? If Charles ... w, and they drank ... ...ference then if ... and Carrie drank ...*

... re on the stump ... ..., just as Caro- ... pe. Charles had ... ...exact center ... e. Ants cluster... ...and drippings ... ts, feeding on th... ...Three yellow ... ...tly with their ... ...edges of rind. ... e them away. ... ...ase smarted; ... heir fill was the ... ..."No great loss ... gain," she murm...

... he sheared a th... ...the rind, so ... pink scroll. She ... ...waited, as ... ke her then and ... ...course—only ... fear and the foo... ...ly warring ... roline thought ... ...ous face, of ... realization that ... ...offer than ... mfort, and pres... ...the roof of her ... bbled into the ... ...tongue. It was ... the sweetness ... ...*of medicine,* ... , and swallowe... ...her spoon- ... en Carrie's bitt...

... ght to the faint... ...drowsily Caroline ... ark, she could ... ...he felt the ... ard the rhythm ... ...that was all. It should have been enough. The child had not fed so easily in weeks. But Caroline had so looked forward to watching the baby's knitted brows soften, seeing her eyes pinch shut as her cheeks bulged greedily. Carrie's hands pressed lightly as she fed, almost patting, the way Caroline patted Carrie's bottom when she lifted the baby to her shoulder. The feel of it made her want to try to smile, but Caroline could not quite manage it.

Be thankful for what is given. Caroline heard the words in her mother's voice. *No matter if it is not enough, be thankful.*

"I am," she whispered to Carrie. But gratitude, Caroline had learned in childhood, was too often the feeblest of pleasures; gratitude was nothing like what she had been waiting to pass between herself and her daughter. Carrie gave her another squeeze, and this time Caroline smiled softly into the darkness in spite of herself. And then there was another, larger hand. Charles. He fitted it over her free breast and stroked softly, the way she would finger a fine length of silk. Drops of milk beaded up on the nipple. He caught them with a fingertip and brought it to his lips. "Sweet," he whispered to the curve of her neck, and kissed her shoulder. A lump bobbed hard in Caroline's throat. *Sweet.*

[illegible]ty-Five

THE WIND W[illegible]IPPE[illegible] [illegible]trings of Caroline's sha[illegible] agai[illegible] [illegible] bows as she st[illegible]d wa[illegible]ti[illegible] [illegible] the wagon to disappea[illegible]. [illegible]ehi[illegible] [illegible] whined and p[illegible]ed at [illegible]n. The pressure against [illegible] it was time to wake t[illegible] [illegible] for [illegible] morning feed, b[illegible]ore [illegible] and woke Ma[illegible] and [illegible] Caroline would no[illegible] [illegible]rn [illegible] the wagon.

Forty mile[illegible] to [illegible] [illegible] better measure[illegible] [illegible] distance. A [illegible] and [illegible] two days to get there[illegible] [illegible] morning to tr[illegible]e. [illegible] n. Charles could n[illegible] [illegible] less than four [illegible]ys. [illegible] way around it. [illegible] enough provi[illegible]ns [illegible] [illegible]ortably through [illegible] as repay Mr. [illegible]war[illegible] [illegible] had lent to finish [illegible] be bought in [illegible]weg[illegible].

She could [illegible] her [illegible] [illegible]ding as the wa[illegible] [illegible] sight, much a[illegible] had [illegible] Mary had learned to cre[illegible] [illegible] and Caroline [illegible]d [illegible] the perils of the st[illegible] the washtub. [illegible]st as [illegible] [illegible]elf daily betwe[illegible] the hazards [illegible] the [illegible] yard. Charles stood b[illegible] and everythi[illegible] be[illegible] [illegible] of their claim. [illegible] away, Caroli[illegible] be[illegible] [illegible] of that greater [illegible] ing for sound[illegible] from [illegible] [illegible] the path to the [illegible] house. Anyt[illegible]g th[illegible] [illegible] from an Indian [illegible] a [illegible] hailstone---w[illegible]ld [illegible]

So when J[illegible]k b[illegible] [illegible] before milking time [illegible] so that Carol[illegible] [illegible] the snap of his teeth fro[illegible] [illegible] her eyes darted from the bowl of cornmeal in her hands to the pistol box, high up on the ledge above the bedstead. Wood clattered and the bulldog's chain rattled. Someone yelped—a man.

"Call off your dog!" At the sound of English, Caroline exhaled. Another clatter of wood.

"Call off your dog!" the man yelled again, and Laura shouted, "Mr. Edwards!"

Caroline dropped the bowl and dashed out the door. Mr. Edwards indeed, crouched atop the woodpile, scrabbling backward from Jack and scattering stove lengths onto the ground. "He's got me treed!"

Caroline grasped Jack's chain as best she could with her meal-dusted hands and reeled the snarling animal toward her until she could reach his collar. "No, Jack," she said with a jerk that cut his wind. The slant of the bulldog's brow seemed to challenge her judgment, but he obeyed. Resentfully. "I'm so sorry," Caroline said to Edwards as Jack continued to grumble. His collar vibrated beneath Caroline's fingers so that she did not trust letting go. She twisted awkwardly to try to meet Edwards's eye. "I declare, Jack seems to know Mr. Ingalls isn't here. He's gone to town. Oswego," she added.

"Yes, ma'am, I know. Mr. Ingalls passed my claim this morning and asked me to come by these next few days and see that everything was all right. If you don't mind, I'll see to the stock for you while I'm here."

"Mind?" was all she could say. Caroline was so taken by surprise, Jack seized the opportunity for one last half-hearted lunge at Edwards.

Edwards grinned, dancing backward from Jack's teeth. "I didn't suppose you would."

THE NEXT DAY the knock came just as she was finishing the dinner dishes. Caroline's heart bobbed, lifting and sinking almost simultaneously. Because Edwards was not Charles. And, if she was entirely honest with herself, because he had come too early for the milking. *Of all things!* she scolded herself. Caroline took a moment to smooth her face i[illegible] no right to s[illegible] Mr[illegible] peck of d[illegible]pp[illegible] [illegible]ouble, no matt[illegible] wh[illegible]

O[illegible] opened the [illegible] Caroline th[illegible] [illegible]ack hadn't tre[illegible] [illegible]odpile. M[illegible], and Caroline [illegible] out of b[illegible] right?" Caroli[illegible] horizon c[illegible] [illegible]aim.

[illegible] and. "Just win[illegible] Thought I [illegible] you folks was [illegible] up and s[illegible] look well, Mrs[illegible]

[illegible] as though the [illegible]ure. A w[illegible] [illegible]ked nearly thre[illegible] than t[illegible] "[illegible]ome in," Carol[illegible] and let m[illegible] water."

[illegible] blend of ease [illegible] thought a[illegible] gar, and ginger [illegible] or h[illegible] [illegible]haved as thou[illegible] Caroline h[illegible] pain or feve[illegible] [illegible]om her t[illegible] [illegible]ber pail, neve[illegible] knowl- e[illegible] [illegible]meated their [illegible] for they k[illegible] [illegible]e of each othe[illegible] level g[illegible] [illegible]y comfort Ca[illegible] Scott [illegible] lavender sun[illegible] door to i[illegible] new willow-[illegible] Caroline the g[illegible]n.

"[illegible] since I saw her [illegible]t," [illegible]over [illegible] pail of blackb[illegible]s."

"[illegible] Mrs. Scott?" Lau[illegible]

"[illegible] murmured, with [illegible] head that s[illegible]s.

[illegible] eyebrow at La[illegible], "Oh, [illegible] as heavy as a [illegible] Caroline the said, "My husband's people raised cotton in Kentucky. Mr. Scott and I tried our hand at it in Missouri. We kept ourselves quite comfortable for a few years. Up until the war, anyway. After that there wasn't money in it anymore," she added. Pointedly? Caroline wondered. Or was that her own ears, hearing more than what was said where the virtue of the Union was concerned, as she was so apt to do after her brother fell at Shiloh? The sound of Mrs. Scott's voice dimmed as Joseph's soft smile, so much like her father's that she could no longer distinguish between the two, appeared in Caroline's mind. How strange to think she was older now than her eldest brother had ever been. Or ever would be. She had long ago become accustomed to his absence, but not to these odd reminders of her lifetime eclipsing his.

"Mr. Scott reckons he'll try planting a few acres here, too, if the Indians ever clear out," Mrs. Scott continued, oblivious. "No telling what they'd do if they came across a field of cotton. They've just got no sense of personal property. The way they come in and out, it makes a body feel as though you didn't own the place."

"It was different in Wisconsin," Caroline ventured. "In Pepin the Chippewas kept to themselves. When I was a girl in the eastern counties, even the Potawatomis weren't so bold as the Osages."

Mrs. Scott's brow furrowed. "Pepin County? How far were you from the Minnesota massacre?" she asked, continuing without an answer. "I've heard the stories. Like to scare me to death. My brother wrote me how they—"

Caroline cleared her throat, cutting her eyes toward the girls.

"Anyway, I hope to goodness we won't have trouble with the Indians," Mrs. Scott said. "I've heard rumors." She raised her eyebrows to show that she would not speak of them in front of the children and gave a smart nod.

JACK WOULD NOT lie down. His fur bristled and flattened, as though the wind were blowing inside the house. He circled and paced, sniffed [illegible] ndows and whir[illegible] at the [illegible] hen Caroline opened it, [illegible] go out.

[illegible] afraid of something, Ma[illegible]

[illegible] not afraid of anything, [illegible] declared.

[illegible] Caroline admonished [illegible] ting, she wondered [illegible] them was right. [illegible] Jack frightened, but the [illegible] he was uneasy. [illegible] The girls were [illegible] Every minute Charles [illegible] disappointed [illegible] counted four long days [illegible], eager for the first [illegible] they could begin to [illegible] All the care Caroline [illegible] all day long to say [illegible] time they [illegible] be home tonight [illegible] the sun began [illegible] the horizon. Insensible to [illegible] Mary and Laura [illegible] shoulder to shoulder at the [illegible] down the creek [illegible] intensity that might have [illegible] grass.

[illegible] her own eagerness, Caroline [illegible] keep from watching [illegible] as though he were [illegible] tangible something [illegible] trying to smooth [illegible] house. Perhaps, [illegible] they both were [illegible] apprehension [illegible] circled in the [illegible] ring around the [illegible] terms of Mrs. Scott's [illegible] "Indian trouble" [illegible] many shapes; [illegible] Caroline felt as though [illegible] were clouded with smoke [illegible] and shifting [illegible] ally along the edges of [illegible] so persistently [illegible] unlocked the [illegible] supper, she did so [illegible] glance out both windows [illegible] was a comfort [illegible] both. Any man or beast [illegible] harm would have to [illegible] twenty rods [illegible] to avoid being seen. [illegible] was Jack so restive? [illegible] Caroline wondered. Perhaps [illegible] some far-off scent only [illegible] detect, as it had [illegible] outran the wolf pack. [illegible] Caroline child [illegible] *king of the wolf pack.*

Jack kicked up a clamor of barking, and all of them jumped. "Someone's knocking," Mary said over the racket. Caroline hesitated. Jack's nose pointed to the roof and the force of his baying had lifted his front paws up on tiptoe, yet his tail waggled and he did not snarl. It could not be Charles, for the latch string was out. Caroline had not made up her mind before the door flapped open and there was Edwards, thrust across the threshold as though the wind were shoving him forward.

"You snuck up on us, Mr. Edwards," Laura scolded. "We've been watching the creek road for Pa all afternoon."

Edwards's answer came so readily, Caroline wondered if he had rehearsed it. "I was out hunting jackrabbits for my supper, and came up the Indian trail instead."

"Did you get any?" Mary asked.

"Nope." He shifted his eyes toward Caroline, adding, "Didn't see anything big enough to aim at."

The way he said *anything*—with a tweak of emphasis that made it seem a sentence in itself—Caroline felt a tingle at the back of her neck. Nothing on the Indian path. Likely he meant to reassure her, but the knowledge that he had felt compelled to look there made her wonder if she ought to coax the girls from the window and bolt the shutter.

Edwards shook himself almost like a dog. "That wind!" he said. "You might be bundled up tighter than a sausage in its casing and it'll still find a way through."

"Warm yourself a minute, Mr. Edwards," Caroline said. He took no more than that before trudging out for the chores, pushing back into the wind with his chin tucked to his collar. Caroline went out behind him to draw an extra pail of water for the night. The instant she passed from the lee of the house, the wind submerged her. Like the current in that terrible creek, Caroline thought with a shudder. Her shawl whipped around her, pulling as the wind pushed. When she turned back to the cabin after tussling with the pail and the rope, she could feel the wind splitting across her face as though her nose were the blade of a plow.

Edwards w[illegible] [illegible]et the pail of m[illegible] [illegible]nd stooped d[illegible] [illegible]ng his palms [illegible]

"I wish I co[illegible] [illegible]d some of th[illegible] [illegible]you," Carolin[illegible] [illegible]f you to do th[illegible] [illegible] Ingalls is away."

Edwards d[illegible] [illegible] nod and did no[illegible] [illegible]embarrassed [illegible] No. She coul[illegible] [illegible]ing, turning [illegible] [illegible]d as though d[illegible] [illegible]bring it out in[illegible]

"The Osag[illegible] [illegible]helter of the [illegible]s," h[illegible] length. "The [illegible] of there when I [illegible]toms." Caroli[illegible] to react. She [illegible]ly [illegible]words, as tho[illegible] [illegible]e could force th[illegible] [illegible]occupied to [illegible] [illegible]e room and eve[illegible]hing disturbed. Ed[illegible] [illegible]ast. They seem[illegible] He spoke aga[illegible] [illegible] tone or volume [illegible] his v[illegible] you have a gu[illegible]?"

"I have M[illegible] [illegible]e answered.

Edwards [illegible] stay close in c[illegible] this."

"Yes," Ca[illegible] [illegible]ould make it s[illegible]

A furrow [illegible]rds's brows. "I [illegible] right comfo[illegible] [illegible]ble. I'll stay the[illegible] say so."

Did he kn[illegible] [illegible]line wondered, [illegible] that she mus[illegible] [illegible] at the childr[illegible] brightened a[illegible] [illegible]rds staying al[illegible] had made M[illegible] [illegible] eyes were me[illegible] if she were c[illegible] [illegible]t to be scare[illegible]

A little m[illegible] [illegible]ould do Laura [illegible] line's first, [illegible] [illegible]cepting Edwar[illegible] offer be teaching [illegible] [illegible]ul inside their [illegible] the door latched and the pistol on its shelf and the bulldog keeping watch—simply because Indians existed? If they realized their ma was not certain she could protect them as their pa did—what then?

Caroline had no choice but to make the words brisk and calm. The way he had asked her about the gun, Edwards would surely understand. "No, thank you, Mr. Edwards, I won't put you to that trouble. Jack will look after us. I'm expecting Mr. Ingalls any minute now."

He looked at her long enough, Caroline wondered for an instant if she were making a mistake. Mary and Laura and even Carrie trusted her implicitly to keep them safe, without regard for how she accomplished it. Was it a peculiar strain of vanity that made her insist upon doing it herself?

"I don't guess anything will bother you, anyway," Edwards said, standing.

"No," Caroline answered.

He crossed the room and put his hand on the latch, but he did not open the door. Caroline did not know him well enough to make out what he was thinking now. By his outward appearance alone she would never have suspected what kind of a man Edwards was. Tobacco stained the corners of his lips. His hair looked as though he'd been cutting at it with his razor rather than a pair of shears. It was long and fine and inclined to snarl, a lustrous golden brown halfway between Mary's and Laura's. He had been towheaded as a boy, Caroline reckoned, and not so terribly long ago. She rubbed her finger and thumb together, imagining the feel of it.

"Mr. Edwards?" She paused, sure of her intentions, yet unable to gauge how he would receive such an invitation.

"Ma'am?"

"Mr. Edwards, I know it is quite some time off, but I wonder if you would consider having your Christmas dinner with us. Our family would be proud to have you."

She saw how the words touched him, how he wanted to smile but

[illegible] himself to do it. H[illegible] swal[illegible] before speakin[illegible]
"[illegible]," [illegible]dwards said. So[illegible] The [illegible] corners of h[illegible]
[illegible]nce. "I should [illegible] at ve[illegible]
[illegible] the door behin[illegible] and [illegible] latch string.

[illegible]te for Charles [illegible] was no sense [illegible] all for him to dr[illegible] late [illegible] and the wind. [illegible] be camping som[illegible]re, s[illegible] oline was eve[illegible] as the girls had [illegible] to go [illegible] so, even. [illegible]ttered in the wi[illegible] self from turni[illegible] ch string again. [illegible] pul[illegible] not laid a fing[illegible] ing Edwards out. [illegible] ters were bolt[illegible] ween the lintels, [illegible] hold. There w[illegible] fe[illegible].

[illegible] only the wind, [illegible] was [illegible] thing to be afr[illegible]d [illegible] Laura woke, frig[illegible]d, C[illegible] d tell them so, [illegible]d [illegible]e. The wind its[illegible] facts remain[illegible]: [illegible] blowing, and C[illegible] e wa[illegible].

[illegible] touched the ho[illegible] slap[illegible] snatching at [illegible] [illegible]ling the shutter[illegible] to get insid[illegible]— [illegible]l not help thinki[illegible] r standing i[illegible] sound. If anythi[illegible] ing [illegible] way, she wo[illegible]ld [illegible]utside to assuag[illegible] Caroline tho[illegible]ht [illegible]st crashed again[illegible] sh[illegible] matter how m[illegible]ny [illegible]ed herself that [illegible] unds [illegible]g. Every ner[illegible] [illegible]ted to them, ins[illegible] that [illegible] as amiss. [illegible]ocked in her chair, [illegible] ment, and tra[illegible]ed [illegible] he fire. One by [illegible] she [illegible] ges of the th[illegible]ng [illegible]d bring back wi[illegible] sa[illegible] d oil, sacks of [illegible] beans, a keg [illegible] ls [illegible] wards, perha[illegible]s [illegible] for herself. O[illegible] se, [illegible] be a treat for [illegible] squeal over. Sh[illegible] pictur[illegible] and Martha [illegible]

Henry and Polly reading the letter she had sent, and felt her face soften momentarily.

But the pictures were no more than a haze; Caroline could not hold them before her for even a minute without the thing she did not want to think of showing through. Her eyes strayed to the shelf that held the pistol, and she closed them. *There is no need,* she told herself, rocking deeply. *Only stop thinking about Indians.* But her mind would not obey. It rubbed and rubbed at that thought until it shone too brightly to ignore.

Caroline went to the bed. For a moment she stood, watching Carrie sleep. Her little fists lay flung open on either side of her head. *Anyone with sense would stop fretting and climb into bed beside that baby girl,* she thought. But the baby was not what Caroline wanted. She put one hand on the mantel shelf, stepped onto the bed rail, and reached up over Carrie's sleeping form. Her fingers touched the cold metal barrel first. Then the stock, polished smooth with use. Her thumb found a scratch in the wood she had not noticed before.

Caroline did not look at the gun. She did not need to. She went back to her rocker and laid it in her lap, half-cocked. Its barrel she pointed toward the fire. The weight of it seemed to draw her shoulders down where they belonged. At the same time her eyes lifted, found their way to the china shepherdess, and settled.

The fear was not gone. She had only made a place for it, invited it to sit alongside her. That was less wearying than refusing to acknowledge its presence. For a time she was aware of nothing but the gun in her lap and the shepherdess on the shelf. Both of them cool, still, and shining. Both of them a kind of assurance.

The wind wailed long and high, and Caroline rocked, letting the sound pass through her as though she were an instrument. She thought of how the fiddle screeched on those rare occasions when Charles struck a wrong note and wondered if it felt the way she did now.

Something gasped, something inside the house, and Caroline's fingers were around the pistol's stock, her thumb poised over the hammer.

[illegible]as Laura, sitti[illegible] strai[illegible] [illegible]d. Mary lay be[illegible] [illegible]er, [illegible] [illegible]pen. Caroli[illegible] [illegible]ze. [illegible] [illegible]eant for the c[illegible] [illegible]n the gun in [illegible] ap. [illegible] [illegible]e at all like the [illegible] [illegible]les with his [illegible] She [illegible] [illegible]ura's eyes follo[illegible] [illegible]p and down th[illegible]pisto[illegible] [illegible]el. It was the[illegible] [illegible] [illegible]d she had no[illegible]zen [illegible] air still rocke[illegible] [illegible]itself.

[illegible] be afraid.

[illegible]oline could [illegible] [illegible]er only comfo[illegible] [illegible] [illegible]e her own fea[illegible].

"[illegible] down, Laura, and g[illegible] [illegible] managed inst[illegible]d [illegible]i[illegible] of a quaver.

"[illegible]hat's that how[illegible]?"

[illegible]ltter of pan[illegible] [illegible]rced [illegible] [illegible]lly. Could the[illegible] [illegible]ing, how he[illegible] [illegible] struggled to a[illegible] [illegible]coiled her fin[illegible]s fro[illegible] [illegible]k and flattened th[illegible] [illegible] *Don't frighte[illegible]*, Ca[illegible] [illegible] herself. She im[illegible] [illegible]ice needed [illegible] [illegible] the words. G[illegible] [illegible]. Firm enoug[illegible] [illegible]tions. "The w[illegible] [illegible]ne told her. "[illegible]"

[illegible]ra inched bac[illegible] [illegible]d Caroline ref[illegible] [illegible] china shep[illegible]ss. [illegible] smile back at t[illegible] [illegible]d felt a stran[illegible] [illegible]or being unabl[illegible] [illegible]ooked and loo[illegible] [illegible]lue eyes, and [illegible] [illegible] the shepher[illegible] [illegible] them if she h[illegible] [illegible]. The single [illegible] [illegible]nd night, wit[illegible] [illegible]gh the ope[illegible] [illegible] Caroline win[illegible] [illegible]ps her paint[illegible] [illegible]vard instead, [illegible] [illegible] different a[illegible] [illegible]self. The fara[illegible] [illegible]pied, in Det[illegible] [illegible] Henry Quine[illegible] [illegible]ry home to [illegible] [illegible]-old daughter. [illegible] china woman remember what Caroline herself could not—did she recall the moment Pa had placed her in Caroline's hands?

Caroline nearly smiled then and began to sing softly. To herself, to the shepherdess, to the children, still wide awake behind their closed eyes.

There is a happy land, far, far away.
Where saints in glory stand, bright, bright as day.

THE JOLT AGAINST the door ought to have frightened her, rousing Caroline as it did from a fretful doze. But she recognized the sound as surely as if Charles had called out to her. The instant she heard it Caroline wondered how she could have taken the wind's purposeless clattering for anything human.

"Didn't you think I might have been an Indian, Mrs. Ingalls?" Charles's voice scolded as she flung open the door.

He was teasing—she could hear the twinkle in his eyes even if it was too dark to see beneath the brim of his hat—but Caroline's mouth dropped open at the thought of her own foolishness. "No," she said just as suddenly, and bold as brass. "Jack wasn't growling. He knew it was you, too."

Charles grabbed her up in his arms and laughed. His coat was stiff with cold. Clumps of frozen mud dropped from his boots and iced her toes. She did not tell him she had been afraid; the half-cocked pistol lying on the seat of the rocker spoke more freely of that than she ever would.

Charles knew. He would not speak of it any more than she would, not with the children suddenly awake and eager to claim their places on his knees, but Caroline heard it in his cheerful boom as he told Mary and Laura about the wind and the rain and the freezing mud that had seized the wagon wheels and slowed Pet and Patty to a crawl. *Everything*

is al ... *ig* ... ying, even as Car ... is
and ... id ... lf without a word ...
And ... house was full ...
fille ... fee bubbling on th ...
hus ... sight of all the pr ...
the ... bl ... vy sacks. Cornme ...
tea, ... es and lard. Ever ...
and ... with a smirk a ...
pou ... d ... gar, as if Charles ...
his ... pendence. Carol ...
keg ... ting the way she ...
afte ... and dried black ... t
wo ... ld ... see them through ...
... *ou* ... a ... even yet tired of ...
wo ... ld. ... d been too grand ... t
ber ... yi ... Ma had had occas ... *l*
be ... *ou* ... just barely true, ... s
mo ... d itself.

Op ... ge," Charles said ...
... w ... y, with its crisply ... t
of ... thought was of a ... –
ex ... sense. She lifted ... d
he ... en book was not s ...
Be ... on't drop it."
... er, of delight and ... d.
It ... "Oh, Charles," sh ...
pe ... se ... id it back down ... of
da ... ag ... side.
"O ...
Ca ... ng and folded back ... of
wi ... dc ...
The ... figures from cha ... er

mind. Eight panes of glass could not be less than twelve dollars back East. But here—a place where white sugar went for a dollar a pound? No, she assured herself. That was why Charles had driven forty miles to Oswego. That was why she and the girls had spent four days alone on the high prairie. He had saved the overland freight, at least. Still, the cost amounted to no less than the equivalent of nine and a half acres. The single square pane in her hands represented more land than it took to hold the house and stable and well. It was a foolish, frivolous thing to do with so much money.

But gracious, it was beautiful, that glass. Clear and cool and smooth, and ever so faintly blue, like ice. Caroline lifted the top pane to the firelight, and the edges seemed to glow. She put a hand to her chest, to keep from floating away. Four panes for the east, four for the west. He had bought her sunlight and moonlight, sunrises and sunsets. She would be able to see clear to the creek road and the bluffs beyond, all winter long. Come spring she could look out at her kitchen garden and see Charles working the fields of sod potatoes and corn.

He should not have done it. Every cent he had saved by going to Oswego had surely gone into this glass. Caroline could not get air enough into her to properly thank him.

Twenty-[illegible]

H[illegible] SH[illegible] [illegible] many Indi[illegible] [illegible] those
w[illegible] [illegible] thought as [illegible] tra[illegible]
fo[illegible] [illegible] that day, she m[illegible] [illegible] t. She
tr[illegible] [illegible] at it was only [illegible] ght the
gl[illegible] [illegible] e aware of [illegible] s, but
th[illegible] wa[illegible] [illegible] ie[illegible] She told he[illegible] hat [illegible] wit-
o[illegible] [illegible] glancing askan[illegible] [illegible] othing
to[illegible] [illegible] at did not feel [illegible] like [illegible] They
m[illegible] [illegible] their hea[illegible] [illegible] d their
e[illegible] [illegible] ward. *I refuse to* [illegible] ned
[illegible] ent thing to [illegible] n [illegible] did.
N[illegible] ied, she could [illegible] differ-
e[illegible] that trail clai[illegible] —Jack
p[illegible] Indian pass. [illegible] barked
a[illegible] his chain, unt[illegible] with
s[illegible] nearly drag [illegible] he was
s[illegible] the trail ungua[illegible]
[illegible] him," Caroli[illegible] "[illegible] re get-
t[illegible] here that I can [illegible] up [illegible]."
Cha[illegible] at the wind[illegible] almost
t[illegible] before anglin[illegible] to [illegible] ouldn't
[illegible] so close if I'd [illegible] it [illegible] d like
[illegible] months when [illegible] use it,
[illegible]
Car[illegible] ot say that she [illegible] nor se

in complaining, either. “That can’t be helped now,” she said. She put a bowl of jackrabbit vitals on the floor for Jack, then dredged the remaining pieces with flour, salt, and pepper. The lard in the skillet had begun to crackle. She turned, lifting the plate of meat, and nearly dropped it.

An Indian stood in the doorway. “Goodness,” she gasped. Jack looked up from his bowl and lunged. His jowls were bloodied with jackrabbit, his teeth bared. Charles leapt forward and snatched the dog back by the collar. The Indian had not moved one step, but Caroline saw him draw himself up, his chin and chest both lifting in a kind of internal backing away. “Ho-wah,” he said.

“How!” Charles answered.

The Indian seemed to smother a smirk at Charles’s reply and stepped into the house. He was tall, taller yet than Charles, so that he reached up to gently bend back the feathers on his scalp lock as he crossed the threshold. He walked the length of the house and squatted down beside the fire as though he’d been invited. Charles pulled his belt from its loops and used it to buckle Jack to the bedpost by his collar. Then Charles squatted down alongside the hearth. The two men said nothing. Behind them, the melted lard gave a pop. Mary and Laura sat on their little bed with their backs against the wall, watching.

Caroline stood completely still for a moment before she realized that she was not frightened. She was not entirely at ease, but she was not afraid. In fact, she thought, having the Indian in the house was not so very different from sitting down to milk a new cow for the first time. Caroline had the same sense now of being nominally in charge and at the same time acutely aware of her own physical disadvantage. If the man poised on her hearth had a mind to, he could spring up and harm any one of them. Yet if he had a mind to, he gave no indication of it. The silence between Charles and the Indian seemed almost amicable, and gradually Caroline understood that if she did not carry on with her task, her hesitation would tip their tentative accord out of balance.

So she picked up the plate and a fork and strode to the fire. One by [illegible] pieces of rab[illegible] [illegible] Everyone watched. [illegible] the frying meat [illegible] They watched her [illegible] up golden brown [illegible] to five plates. She [illegible] and one to the [illegible] Mary and Laura [illegible] as though they [illegible] every day of the [illegible] picked up [illegible] and held the [illegible] while she ate one [illegible] No one spoke.

[illegible] finished eating [illegible] legs and took his [illegible] paper of tob[illegible] mantel shelf. He fill[illegible] offered the pack [illegible] who did the same. Th[illegible] smoke rose up [illegible] Caroline wished th[illegible] out the [illegible] puffed at the to-b[illegible] were hazy [illegible] empty. Then the In[illegible]

[illegible] head in surprise. [illegible] nothing like the tw[illegible] come into the house [illegible] sounds were so s[illegible] they seem[illegible] word. *French?* she w[illegible]

[illegible] his head. "No speak," he [illegible]

[illegible] a hand in ackno[illegible] more was said.

A[illegible] stood and walk[illegible] pulled against th[illegible] him to the bedpo[illegible] with his nose a[illegible] not growl.

[illegible] gracious," Caroli[illegible] Carrie's back ag[illegible] as though it were [illegible] comforting.

[illegible] no common [illegible]

[illegible] around the cabi[illegible] boxes of flour and salt [illegible] on the table [illegible] door to the pro-vis[illegible] stood partway op[illegible] of bulging sac[illegible] The Indian had not [illegible] Caroline had no re[illegible] had not seen [illegible] keep themselves to [illegible] she said, "and we [illegible]

"There's nothing to worry about," Charles said. "That Indian was perfectly friendly. And their camps down in the bluffs are peaceable enough. If we treat them well and watch Jack, we won't have any trouble."

Caroline agreed, but she did not say so. She did not know how to explain to Charles how she could be thankful they were friendly and still not want them inside her house. It did not seem a thing that should need explaining.

"MA, BABY CARRIE'S hungry."

Caroline did not argue. Mary knew. She had set to learning her baby sister's signals by rote and could decipher them nearly as well as if Carrie were her own. This once, Caroline was grateful for the interruption. Her fingertips ached from pushing the needle through the rabbit skins. Mary and Laura could hardly wait for their caps to be finished. Each time Caroline laid aside her sewing, they came to kneel beside the work basket and stroke the fur. She herself favored the beaver pelts. Their rich brown underfur was deeper than the lushest velvet; you might sink a finger to the first knuckle into its improbable softness. But those pelts, along with the mink and wolf, they could not afford to keep—not if they were to have a plow and seeds for planting.

Charles had done well, so early in the season. The stack of pelts reached nearly to Laura's knees. If Charles's traps kept yielding this way, all the cash in the fiddle case might go toward proving up on the claim.

Caroline stood and stretched and went to stand a minute in the doorway. The air was pleasantly brisk, yet lacked the familiar scent of leaves bronzing in the sun. Autumn here had a golden, grassy smell, dry and soft, like a haymow. She reached for her shawl—its red the color of a sugar maple at full blaze—and pulled it comfortably about her shoulders. This was the welcome stretch of weather that turned the fireplace into a boon companion. Soon enough it would become a ravenous to feed. For ... ded little in re[turn] for the ... it gave.

... nd her, the ... fuss ... her. Carrie h... near... out of her ... ine enjoyed ... e voice that ... between the ... Next autum[n] ... ure, not with ... s to pick, an[d] ... autumn, Carr[ie] ...

... NE TUCKE[D] ... pin ... er of Carrie's ... roke the ba[by] ... The little mouth ... e eased her ... bow to another ... e sound of ... up, expecting ... ting his smil[e] ... rocking chair ... would swee[p] ... er neck and ... e.

... ious!" she c[ri]ed ...

... rown men ... hey headed stra[ight] ... ed cupboar[d] ... of flour and lard ... off the prair[ie] ... toned up. Her f[in]g... smatching th... es. ... see the key on ... aby was on[ly] ha[lf] fed ... ed and squirme[d] ... rs, her appet[ite] ... Caroline put her ... mouth. Car[rie] ... Caroline felt th[e] tri[ck]l[e] ... ilk letting ... as the stain ... her bodice ... he slipped an arm ... nd the baby ... and against her ... leak steady.

... njustice of it ... must withhold ... from ... to protect ... hers.

... st the child ... this time, wit[h]in reach ... e girls were ... side ... rag doll—Car[oline] ...

not know how or when she had gotten it—and Laura clutching her half-finished fur cap. She heard a quick hiss of pain from Laura and knew that the needle she had left poised in a seam had stabbed her daughter's palm. Laura did not make another sound.

One Indian, the one wearing a dingy green calico shirt above buckskin leggings, lifted the corner of the dishtowel from the pan of cornbread on the table. Green Shirt motioned to the other man, who came over and snatched the towel away so sharply it cracked against the air. He laid it out and tied the loaf of cornbread in it, to take. The Indian's dusty hands snagged the fabric as he knotted it to his belt.

Caroline swallowed hard. Mother Ingalls had given her that towel, its corner embroidered with a pine tree that had once been green. It was so threadbare now it was good for nothing more than screening leftovers from the flies, but she did not want to let it go this way. *If that is the most valuable thing they take,* she promised herself.

Caroline did not finish the thought. As she watched their eyes probed every niche of the house. She saw them study the mantel shelf, the windowsills. Green Shirt squatted down to reach into her work basket. Mary and Laura skittered backward. One by one he inspected every one of her crochet hooks and knitting needles. *Looking for the key,* Caroline thought, and hugged Carrie closer. They had not seen it on her neck, she realized. If they were looking for it, it was because they did not know where it was.

Before she could feel any relief, Green Shirt made an exclamation and held up a triumphant hand. Caroline jolted at the sight. The key to her trunk.

"Oh," she said without meaning to. The Indians' faces lit up as her hand flew to her lips. Without a word they set upon the lock of the provisions cupboard.

The key would not fit. The shaft was round instead of flat. The tip would not reach far enough inside to give them even the satisfaction of a hopeful jiggle. Towel Thief smacked the padlock so hard the hasp rang out. Green Shirt [illegible] sound that sounded like [illegible] *they swear,* Caroline [illegible] herself wondering [illegible] mind, *in another language [illegible] a heathen god?*

Green Shirt turned, the key pinched in his fingers. [illegible] hole that it would fit [illegible] raised his eyebrow [illegible] pivoted in the air. Back and forth, back and forth [illegible]

If she so much [illegible] in the direction of [illegible] to it. Caroline lifted [illegible] point her eyes [illegible] *I will bake them a cake,* she thought. *A cake with* [illegible] *a roast prairie hen* [illegible] *they will not open* [illegible] turned, following her gaze. She saw their attention [illegible] pegs over the door, and watched their lips [illegible] derstood that Charles [illegible] was not in the house. [illegible] though a bead of [illegible] rolling down the [illegible] might take anything [illegible] now.

Green Shirt gave [illegible] a violent flick. The key [illegible] the basket, and [illegible] against the toes of Mary's shoe [illegible] and ducked [illegible]. Carrie screeched and [illegible] ach chilled with [illegible] that her grip on [illegible] so hard, she could feel [illegible] thigh bone.

One of them—Towel Thief—picked up the [illegible] of [illegible]

No. Caroline [illegible] feet. She did not step [illegible] speak, only let the [illegible] the thought vault [illegible] billow from her [illegible] until it filled the room.

Carrie stopped crying. The men stopped [illegible] what sounded like [illegible]. Towel Thief shook his head [illegible] struck his palm with [illegible] of one hand, swiping [illegible] brushing away [illegible] Towel Thief glowered. Green [illegible] finger in Caroline's [illegible]. The entire core [illegible] coiled as he spoke, his [illegible] motions she [illegible] pret. Towel Thief dropped the furs in a heap and [illegible]

"ALL'S WELL THAT ends well," Charles said when she told him what had nearly happened.

No, Caroline thought, *it is not.* She could not say so. If she opened her mouth, she would cry. Her every muscle was fixed with the task of holding the corners of her lips steady. The very sight of a man in green calico, even her husband, wearing a bright, clean shirt she had made with her own hands, made her almost dizzy. The only scrap of consolation was the absence of Charles's usual blitheness. But the resignation Caroline heard in his voice instead was no comfort. The Indians would come and go as they pleased. Charles would do nothing about it, because there was nothing to be done.

Caroline tried to imagine the scene as it would appear to Charles: the Indians had not hurt her, had not even touched her, nor made off with anything of value. On the surface the encounter did not sound considerably different from the first two men who had come into the house months ago.

But it was. She had been wrong to be afraid of those first men. Caroline could see that now. Everything that had frightened her that day had risen out of her own dread of what they *might* do, not from anything they had actually done. Her fear had blotted out the subtle expressions and gestures that ought to have signaled civility, and so she had not understood that they were asking, not demanding. Green Shirt and Towel Thief's behavior had been crude enough to violate not only her own standards but the Osages' customs as well. There was no one thing she could point to as proof, yet Caroline was certain. All the courtesy she had been incapable of understanding before was entirely absent in them.

"If you had seen the way they looked at everything," Caroline began. Charles's face stopped her. All the sympathy she had wanted so desperately after her first encounter with the Osages was there in his eyes and mouth. It was so genuine, it hurt, and all the more because it was misplaced.

[illegible] derstood: his [illegible] was [illegible] s, the way a chi[illegible] and she had bee[illegible] eft [illegible] rk.

[illegible] d no concept [illegible] mali[illegible] rveled. He wo[illegible] g, man or beast, [illegible] until [illegible] eason not to. [illegible] a sudden gust [illegible] nder [illegible] *es for granted* [illegible] *he Osages.* No wo[illegible] der [illegible] ould leave her [illegible] imperturbed b[illegible] the [illegible] ions. Charles [illegible] girls would do [illegible] them, and so [illegible] safe. The reali[illegible] tion [illegible] *Perhaps if* [illegible] oline thought, *h[illegible] ould* [illegible] harles Ingalls [illegible] a world that no [illegible] nger [illegible] a better one [illegible] the flicker of a [illegible] ile [illegible] ath hitched. [illegible] that was one of [illegible] best in him

[illegible] ld not compreh[illegible] d [illegible] heir mercy [illegible] walked into the [illegible] use [illegible] s like an- [illegible] here were wea[illegible] ns [illegible] would never [illegible] half-unbuttone[illegible], with [illegible] ed in one [illegible] t burning a hole [illegible] roug[illegible] s those men [illegible] e tasted acid in [illegible] ng.

[illegible] at scene out of [illegible] score her [illegible] p to pull hersel[illegible] ed her eyes [illegible] nothing—only [illegible] arkness be- [illegible]

[illegible] image, and tha[illegible] was [illegible] of every- [illegible] ined, thick and [illegible] t. A sort [illegible] without focus. [illegible] aim it at [illegible] nowhere else for [illegible].

[illegible] e spoke and mo[illegible] ough she'd [illegible] red not jostle he[illegible] The [illegible] began to [illegible] bedtime feed, h[illegible] picke[illegible] to spare [illegible] night further tr[illegible] ble [illegible]

[illegible] ked and patted. [illegible] ckle[illegible] g to her.

Carrie was tired to a frazzle. Caroline could hear it in the breathy whine before each cry. *Hweh, hweh,* Carrie whimpered. *Hweeeh-heh.*

Caroline closed her eyes, touched her fingertips to her forehead, rocked in her chair. Still, the baby fussed. *Leave them be,* Caroline urged herself. *Let him find his own way.* But Carrie. Carrie could not say more plainly what she wanted, any more than Caroline could pretend not to understand.

"She can't be hungry," Charles protested as Caroline rose from the rocker. "And she's bone dry." If he had seen the thumb-shaped bruise on Carrie's thigh when he diapered her, he had said nothing of it.

Caroline held out her arms. Charles seemed to shrug as he lifted Carrie into them.

Caroline nestled Carrie into the space between her breasts, fitting the little round cheek into her palm. The baby's ear lay over her heart. Caroline enfolded herself around her daughter, so that every soft part of her body pressed gently against Carrie's skin. "Shhhhhhhh," she whispered, holding almost still. "Shhhhh." Caroline began to sway, more gently than a breeze. The baby shuddered, panted, quieted. Out of the corner of her eye Caroline saw Charles's expression, his half smile betraying a medley of admiration and hurt. Caroline leaned down to nuzzle her own cheek against Carrie's hair and felt at once how the singular fit of their bodies excluded him. She was sorry for Charles, yet could not bring herself to separate herself enough from Carrie to open their tight circle to him. *Selfish,* she thought, *selfish and spiteful,* and closed her eyes so that she would not see if she had pained Charles further.

Into the long silence came the snap of the fiddle box's clasps. The bow glided through rosin, then there were the hollow woody plunks of the fiddle itself being lifted from the felt and into its place beneath Charles's chin. The bow sighed tentatively across the strings, then sang out.

"*Blue Juniata.*"

Oh, Charles, Caroline thought, helpless. And there she was again, [illegible]t the cornhuskin[illegible] dance [illegible] had looked out [illegible]ss hi[illegible] strings and seen [illegible] she [illegible] back at him—and [illegible] him [illegible] seen her face and [illegible] own [illegible] furtive, hopeful [illegible] had [illegible]en wasted. Carol[illegible] he laughter, the [illegible] m o[illegible] g feet swirling a[illegible] bered the blush [illegible] ning [illegible] cheeks and her p[illegible] fingers and toes. [illegible] his [illegible] hose twinkling, [illegible] were known on b[illegible] anks [illegible] Oconomowoc—[illegible] one. They might [illegible] have [illegible] eir marriage vow[illegible] re, Caroline had [illegible] ught [illegible]ter.

[illegible] notes could just [illegible] hands, the way t[illegible] mu[illegible]ched her. He was [illegible] have made it plai[illegible] nor [illegible] ncere, with his [illegible] did not know qu[illegible] what [illegible] apologizing for, [illegible] id not matter to [illegible] les. [illegible] ld not hold to an[illegible] ould not also have [illegible] r. [illegible] line let out a lit[illegible] est signal of def[illegible] and [illegible] sing:

[illegible] ld roved an Indian [illegible]
[illegible] flow the water[illegible]
[illegible] ong and true my a[illegible] quiver,
[illegible] ft goes my light ca[illegible]

[illegible] ng it his way, [illegible] mistakes she [illegible] so [illegible] ded him for tha[illegible] im sing it—*girl* [illegible] ne [illegible] *snowy* turned to [illegible] ust as he had wr[illegible] it [illegible] ittle poetry book [illegible] locked safely insi[illegible] er

[illegible] ords met his mu[illegible] d to form one se[illegible] ss

Twenty-Seven

IT SOUNDED, AT first, like the wind. High and long and wavering. Caroline had tugged the quilt over her shoulders before she woke enough to realize the chill that made her shiver was not from cold.

She sat up in bed. Charles stood at the door in his nightshirt, lifting his rifle from its pegs. A feeble gray light fringed the curtains. An hour or so remained until dawn.

"Is it wolves?" she whispered.

Charles shook his head. It was too early in the day for wolves.

Caroline drew her knees to her belly, gathered two fistfuls of quilt under her chin, and listened again.

The sound traveled on the wind, but it was not the wind. It was shrill, and arrow-sharp, as if it had been aimed at them. At intervals it was punctuated with bursts of speed and volume that made Caroline's shoulders jerk.

It was human, she realized, and female. Women. The pitch told her that, though she had heard bull elk reach notes as high.

"How far is the Indian camp?" she asked.

"Two, three miles northeast."

Two or three miles. How could they hold their throats open so wide that they could be heard at that distance, even with the wind to carry their voices? Caroline could not imagine what it would take to make her turn loose such sounds—what immensity of grief, or rage. Ma had not made sounds like that when Pa had drowned, nor when Joseph was killed. Yet it was not unbridled wailing. Each tone had been honed into a particular [illegible] Caroline could grasp [illegible] meaning, sh[illegible] there must be notes a[illegible] word[illegible]

If it were [illegible] semblance to any[illegible] call music. It [illegible] did not seem to p[illegible] and again Ca[illegible] caught a semblance [illegible] lowed no pat[illegible] with. This was [illegible] All she could [illegible] that the sounds di[illegible] women were [illegible] least.

Mary and [illegible] Charles standing gu[illegible] and soundless [illegible] big bed. Caroli[illegible] them, but it [illegible] strangeness of [illegible] held them and [illegible] the firm press of [illegible] kept her from [illegible] it was time for [illegible] shifted to mak[illegible] they stayed still [illegible]

At sunup, t[illegible]

"What was [illegible]"

Charles pro[illegible] against the wall [illegible] palm across [illegible] heard anythin[illegible] "Never even [illegible] ing like it."

IT BEGAN EAR[illegible] ing. Caroline fel[illegible] heard it. Her [illegible] the same high pitc[illegible] the quilt from [illegible] Carrie with her to [illegible] Charles sat wit[illegible] resting on the [illegible] dowsill. They [illegible] was nothing to say. [illegible] baby's head und[illegible] ould feel the rhyth[illegible] heart against h[illegible] her hand over C[illegible] Mary and Laura [illegible] for them. The[illegible] quilt and hunch[illegible] to hide their fa[illegible] harder she tried [illegible] her body tremble[illegible]

Her throat a[illegible] frustration. I[illegible] warning, a threa[illegible] how to heed it. [illegible]

ing or singing or yowling or wailing. And yet it was all of those things. It rose and rose, dipped for a merciful instant and then rose again so sharply that Caroline flinched. Even weeping had a cadence. This had none. Caroline closed her eyes and rocked, counting a deliberate tempo for each gentle sweep of the rockers across the floorboards.

One-two-three, *one*-two-three, *one*-two-three.

She dozed without any awareness of being asleep, for the sound penetrated her dreams. When she woke the sound had ceased. The vague fragments of her dreams evaporated as she blinked into the silence, but the count of the waltz, and the hot stricture in her throat, remained. *One*-two-three, *one*-two-three, *one*-two-three. As she braided Mary's and Laura's hair, stirred milk into the cornmeal, walked from the table to the fireplace. The rhythm circled her every movement until she was half-dizzy with it.

All day, her mind replicated the Indians' strange high notes at the slightest provocation. She heard them in the whinnying horses and the squeaking of the windlass and the ring of Charles's ax at the woodpile. Anything pitched above a whine snatched her entire focus, leaving her feeling foolish and lightheaded when she realized its source. Yet when Jack broke into a deep rolling growl, Caroline went absolutely still. She knew down to her bones that this sound—the opposite of everything her senses had been attuned to—signaled something actual.

Her eyes darted to the latch string, then to the girls. They had seen her look. If Mary and Laura had not guessed already they knew now that she was afraid.

But they shall not see the depth of it, Caroline silently declared, and resisted the impulse to take the pistol down from its shelf before going to the window. With her shoulder to the wall she peered out sidelong, so as not to move the curtains. Jack was up on his back feet, straining on tiptoe against the chain on his collar, snapping at the air. Charles had put down his ax and stood with his rifle pointing east. He was not squinting down the barrel yet, but his thumb was poised to cock breath fogged … ts as she

… le. Then anoth…

… n as two men … e's long
… pane as she … Ingalls.
… ls propped aga…
… roline said, 'a… Laura
… not be so bad … herself,
… wife and child… to the
… mps.
… not come into … ey rest
… the ground. … ide the
… was at once … Caroline
… e eastern hor… turned
… on, too. Edwar… nd the
… the window … ildren
… a waved, but … ok on
… wince than … e.
… arles called to … door.
… ive me a hand …
… Caroline's … ad of
… ews the men … said
… les," she answe… ease,
… will you pull … d me
… me back?" La… oline
… chest and went …
… the stable, wa… ck of
… moval act pass… Senate
… s were grante… f the

Kansas line. This land will be sold at $1.25 an acre, just as we were promised."

News they had waited months to hear. News that should have made Charles whoop and grab her up in his arms. Now he said it with a grimace.

"July," she repeated. And then, when he did not explain, "Why haven't they gone?"

"The Osages only just approved the act. They were late returning from the summer hunt and took five weeks to think it over."

That, too, was good news. Caroline peered at him. He spoke as though he were confessing a sin.

"Charles," she said. "Tell me."

"Fifty Osage warriors went into town a week after they'd approved the act. They stood in the middle of Independence and put on some kind of fancy garb and painted their faces." Caroline's skin began to creep as she pictured them undressing in the street, streaking their faces and heaven knows what else with slashes of red and black. "And then they danced," Charles said.

Caroline blinked. She could not adjust the scene in her mind to match what she had heard. "Danced?"

Charles nodded. "Scott heard it from a man who was there."

"What does it mean? Is that what they've been doing these nights?"

"I don't know. Neither did Scott. The Indian agent has called in troops."

"Thank heaven for that, at least."

Charles swallowed. He would not look at her. Caroline clutched her shawl closer about her neck even as her center filled with heat. Anger or dread would overtake her in a moment—she could not tell which.

"Charles?"

"Scott said their orders are to protect the Indians."

"The Indians?" Her voice was shrill. She spun so that he could not

ace and stood ... k. She would break ... art
e could feel it hap ... ing ... g ... ain of her was loos ... ng
to fly apart.
ine, we don't k ... —"
hrugged his hand ... r. "I have to get back ... the

E DID NOT un ... s th ... e craved the feel of th ... bar
ever slight, that ... tings and shoes m ... be
skin and the ... rati ... up in the rocking ... hai
harles squatted b ... e ... bullets. Her mind ... led
welcome thought ...
ad they come? ... y, ... ion of Indians m ... he
oil, had she con ... ed ... children to a place ... lled
rritory? Charles ... who made life s ... like
a song so sweet ... times failed to h ... it
But to think that ... foreseen something like
line would have ... had she been able.
ied instead to fe ... room for it. In a ... gle
ith two little girl ... ch every blink, ... cu
antry door to hid ... space for anyt ... like
ears. The only ... necessary, and ...
go out where t ... touch her.
nd again she wa ... stream of liquid lea ... low
bullet mold, th ... ater, hard and s ... g. I
could do just th ... ng thoughts into ... ght
ball capable of pi ... was most frighte ... of
he imagined h ... barrel of a rifle ... led
a bullet. To ... fire? Images ... we
Green Shirt ... erializing; she c ... nc
ture their fea ... s. ... ame into focus ... ad
ine jolted back ... tha ... hair creaked.

No. She did not want to take aim. She wanted only to fire, to feel the hard recoil of the stock against her shoulder as the anger and fear were propelled outward into the empty black air.

They sat up all that night without a word passing between them. When the first cry finally sounded, Caroline gasped, as if inhaling the sound. Carrie cried, too, and would not be soothed. The harsh union of Carrie's shrieks with the Indians' made Caroline tremble with the effort of holding her own voice at bay. She pressed her forehead into the heel of her hand and plunged her fingernails slowly into her scalp. The child was hungry, yet Caroline would sooner scream herself than unbutton her bodice. It was more than the habit of concealing the key while Indians were abroad. Even with the door latched and the curtains drawn, she still did not want to bring her bare breast out into the open. As though there were any real choice in the matter. The milk would come. Caroline felt the hot pricking, half pain and half pleasure, as it corkscrewed downward, and submitted.

THEY DID NOT recognize when it was over. The fifth morning came and silence rang in Caroline's ears. The sensation was oddly discomfiting. It was as though she could feel the space where the sound used to be—a space that now felt too large and open.

Caroline had been so intent on deciphering its meaning that she had lost sight of the one crucial piece of information the wailing-song had imparted: where the Indians were. Now, it seemed, they might be anywhere.

But they were not. For a day and a night she and Charles stood at the windows with weapons loaded and cocked, rebuking the children for the slightest whisper that might muffle an Indian footfall—and saw nothing. Jack paced and peered and sniffed, and did not find anything to growl at.

Near midday a quick burst of barking signaled the approach of something from the north, out of the creek bottoms. Caroline glanced first at the pistol, [illegible] that a bullet w[illegible] in [illegible] She closed h[illegible] eye[illegible] peering inward [illegible] co[illegible] looking out.

A rider. [illegible] was tied to the [illegible] which he wa[illegible] curls of golden-b[illegible] in the sun.

Edwards. [illegible] recognized him at the same [illegible] flung open t[illegible]

Edwards [illegible] inches from the threshold[illegible] gone," he ann[illegible]

"Gone?" C[illegible] asked together.

"Packed u[illegible] went there, to s[illegible]," he [illegible]

"Mr. Edwards!" [illegible] exclaimed. "They m[illegible] tongue hove[illegible] ping for the next wor[illegible] seemed to ha[illegible] They might have en[illegible] of the horro[illegible] these last several days[illegible] Plainly, they [illegible]

Edwards [illegible] couldn't stand it a[illegible] lo[illegible] like risking [illegible] sitting in my cabin, [illegible] tomahawk b[illegible] time a stick of [illegible] crawled on [illegible] hundred yards," he [illegible] arm. The di[illegible] into the fabric [illegible] like leather. [illegible] up the nerve to lift [illegible] the grass I [illegible] in my life. Hardly [illegible] ashes and su[illegible] gnawed-over buffalo bones."

"Where a[illegible] asked.

"South's a[illegible] said. "The tracks [illegible] Winter camp[illegible] reservation."

Caroline [illegible] afternoon sun. [illegible] she had liste[illegible] torn asunder [illegible] pened. Every[illegible] every atom of the [illegible] mained as she had left it. Nothing but the terror and the ire had been real, and all of it of her own making.

It was still there. Caroline could feel it within her, a thick, dark inner lining, suddenly stripped of its purpose. A tremor came over her, clutching her by the gut and radiating upward. Her breath tasted of acid. Her body, preparing to purge itself. Caroline walked to the necessary and emptied herself of it.

Twen[illegible]y Ei[illegible]

“IT H[illegible]’ Laura said. “It ha[illegible]o.”

Ca[illegible]ve[illegible] up polishing [illegible] gir[illegible] from the win-dow [illegible] br[illegible]ath misted the [illegible]ass [illegible] arrow streams that [illegible] ra[illegible]n falling just b[illegible]ond [illegible]

“[illegible],” Mary asked. “[illegible] find us, so far away [illegible] rri[illegible]ory? Ma?”

M[illegible] d[illegible]fferent wo[illegible]ds [illegible]ster[illegible] ay before, but it wa[illegible] qu[illegible]stion. *Patie[illegible]ce,* [illegible]arol[illegible] f. They would neve[illegible] ve [illegible]atience for ot[illegible]s if s[illegible] first be patient with [illegible] n't know,” she sai[illegible] “I ex[illegible] a way. Santa Clau[illegible] e [illegible] find my s[illegible]ock[illegible]g wh[illegible] m Brookfield to C[illegible] ad[illegible]ed.

“[illegible] East,” Laura [illegible]aid [illegible]s if [illegible] r country. And so it [illegible]

C[illegible] bl[illegible]d for a reply. “[illegible]ell, [illegible] first family to mo[illegible] Territory. You [illegible]'t s[illegible] e other pas and mas [illegible] re Santa Cla[illegible]us [illegible]ldn't [illegible]s to their little boys [illegible]

C[illegible]ed up from h[illegible]r [illegible]rk, [illegible] them a buoy ant [illegible] set of narrowed [illegible]e ey[illegible] The difference am[illegible] width of a blade [illegible] gras[illegible] enough to put twi[illegible] sc[illegible]nce. Carol[illegible]ne [illegible]uirm[illegible] b[illegible]ers had neve[illegible] look[illegible] t [illegible]ay. Was it any[illegible]onde[illegible] erself, when al she [illegible] ers answers th[illegible]t [illegible]uld n[illegible]

[illegible] would find some c[illegible]entr[illegible]o, Santa Claus would not come this year. He would go to the Big Woods and find them gone, and bring all their presents to Kansas next year. But Edwards. Caroline could not discount the slim possibility of Mr. Edwards. He still had the nickel Charles had given him over a month ago to buy Christmas candy for the girls in Independence. What he did not have was a horse.

"You'll tell us if you run short of anything," Charles had said when Edwards came to warn them to lock their stable. Edwards had not even heard the horse thieves. He could not say whether they might be Indians or white men, though his missing saddle pointed away from Indians.

"Anything we have, you're welcome to," Caroline added.

"I'm well provisioned," Edwards assured them. "And I can still get to town so long as my boots hold out," he'd said, knocking one heel against a fencepost. None of them had given a thought to anything so trifling as Christmas candy.

Now, though, she and Charles had room in their minds for nothing else. Caroline gazed out over the girls' heads at the blurry gray morning. She longed for snow almost as much as Laura; there had never been a Christmas Eve so leaden. If the rain did not let up, it would not matter whether Edwards had fetched the girls' Christmas treats from town. Twice this week Charles had tried to reach Edwards's claim, and the rising creek had held him back.

THE RAIN STOPPED as if by magic. Mary and Laura bit their lips and grinned at each other. Then Caroline opened the door to the sunlight, and their faces fell. The wild *whoosh* and tumble of the flooded creek, inaudible over the rain, now filled the room. They had not considered the creek a barrier. Of course they hadn't. Winters in Pepin, the frozen Mississippi River became the smoothest road in the county.

When Charles came in bearing a great wild turkey, Caroline looked past it to his pockets, searching for a telltale bulge.

"If it weighs less than twenty pounds I'll eat it, feathers and all," he announced.

T[illegible] was unmistak[illegible] was [illegible] his coat. "My g[illegible] said, [illegible] the turkey. It[illegible] glist[illegible] [illegible]s watched, dis[illegible] rain[illegible] beneath the bi[illegible]

"[illegible]" Mary asked.

[illegible] abandoned the [illegible] he a[illegible]

[illegible] fast. No Christ[illegible] No [illegible] turkey. Caroline [illegible] of [illegible] too pleased to sm[illegible] din[illegible] im[illegible]eating his ba[illegible] Ch[illegible]

[illegible] "A man would [illegible]

tha[illegible]

[illegible] hands, Mary an[illegible] an[illegible] wished they [illegible] up[illegible]es had gone flat[illegible] sm[illegible]d been hopeful.

[illegible]s," she said as [illegible] ru[illegible] good house[illegible] to[illegible] for your Christ[illegible] sm[illegible]ed farther yet.

[illegible]lack. The words [illegible] o[illegible] though they we[illegible] h[illegible]eful that her chi[illegible] w[illegible] felt the sort of [illegible] im[illegible] warmth and [illegible] s[illegible] her daughters' n[illegible] C[illegible] how to make them [illegible] t[illegible] ever to speak of, s[illegible]

[illegible]

THE FIRE POPPED and hissed into the stillness. The girls lay in their bed with their eyes to the rafters, obediently waiting for the day to end.

"Why don't you play the fiddle, Charles?"

He looked into the fireplace. "I don't seem to have the heart to, Caroline." His words might have been made of water, he was so sodden with disappointment.

Caroline could not stand it. "I'm going to hang up your stockings, girls," she declared. "Maybe something will happen." They looked at her with such wonder, Caroline's heart did not know whether to break or swell. She strode to the mantel and hung their two limp stockings beneath the china shepherdess. It was thanks to Edwards that she could do even this much, Caroline thought as she threaded the wool over the borrowed nails. Silently she wished him a happy Christmas. "Now go to sleep," she said to Mary and Laura. "Morning will come quicker if you're asleep." Eager now, they squinched their eyes shut and tunneled deeper into the quilts. Caroline lingered there with her fingertips still on the mantel. Her thumb brushed the head of one nail as she looked down on her daughters. It was so easy to forget, now that there was Carrie, how little Mary and Laura still were. Quickly she bent and kissed them good night a second time and returned to her chair.

Caroline heard herself humming faintly as she rocked. She gave no thought to the tune. Her mind scoured the cabin, pondering what sort of Christmas she might patch together. It must be something new and fresh, or Mary and Laura would not be fooled. Nothing from the scrap bag or the button box. Paper dolls might lift a rainy afternoon, but she could not expect them to bear the weight of Christmas morning. There could be no molasses candy without snow, nor vanity cakes without eggs.

Charles's voice was hardly a murmur. "You've only made it worse, Caroline."

Caroline's stomach seized at the thought of them waking to empty stockings tomorrow morning. She had been careful to say *maybe*, but by stockings … ise, no mat

l. Someth … the power

girls, her … o little girl

on might … hing as sim

es," she sa … "There's th

er with wh … ur she wou

te patty c

at a hang … in both di

safe place … ught of C

went to O … "I took for

e for anot

he said. H … on his face

roline felt … when Carri

manage," … sion eased

at the sam … ude. That

r all his lo … rles had fai

yes did no … aroline coul

e. But she … shelter the

sight.

r, white … atus, and

white flo … Caroline

anded unt … as her own

a thick c … e, then nea

with the … knife she cu

edged the … ey glittered

t. Quietly … in the bot

aid the he … nto the pie

plate into

extravaga … d flour. An

e ought to … d cookies,

d sugar ca … e sat vigil

oven. Swedish crackers, vinegar pie, dried apple pie. The cabin should be heady with brown sugar and clove, and the rich velvety scent of beans and salt pork lazily bubbling in molasses. At the very least, a dried blackberry pie. Even without a cookstove, Caroline knew she could have contrived to make some of it.

We have left undone those things which we ought to have done.

Caroline's skin prickled at the gravity of the words. *An empty cookie jar is not a sin,* she assured herself. But still her throat grew hot and tight. Charles had been merely remiss, while hers was a disregard so sly she had been unable to recognize it. It was as if she believed she could keep Christmas from coming, Caroline thought, pressing an apron corner to her nose, as though without the sweet smells and tastes to remind her, she would not think to miss Eliza and Peter, and Henry and Polly. Or, she thought with a deep-belly resonance that signaled the greater truth, it was as if she believed the special things they'd so enjoyed together should not be enjoyed apart.

Caroline Ingalls, what nonsense! That's what Eliza would say. Caroline could hear her sister's incredulous laugh, see her starry-black eyelashes blinking back tears at the very idea. And Polly—Polly would be too heartbroken even to scold at the thought of such a bereft Christmas. Caroline shook her head, thankful that it would not occur to either of them to imagine what she had done. For oh, how it would hurt them to see her like this.

I'm sorry, she thought to Eliza and Polly, and to Charles and the girls. *I'm sorry.*

SILENTLY CAROLINE UNLOCKED her trunk and pulled out the blue tissue paper she had saved from the cake of store-bought soap. A trace of rose scent still clung to it. She teased the two thin layers apart and laid one patty cake in the center of each, taking care to keep the surface that had touched the soap to the outside as she wrapped them. The paper would rip when the girls pulled their gifts from their stockings, no ma[illegible] were. She was n[illegible]

cou[illegible] into the sto[illegible]

Car[illegible] tips to the frai[illegible]

[illegible] hairs at the [illegible]

shru[illegible] sensation awa[illegible]

wha[illegible] his grumbli[illegible]

to [illegible] someone passi[illegible]

so[illegible] scrap of salt po[illegible]

befo[illegible] But the bulld[illegible]

into a[illegible] hatever was ap[illegible]

gav[illegible]

[illegible] girls were alr[illegible]

ing[illegible] snatched up a [illegible]

the [illegible]

[illegible]

[illegible] and Charles. Hi[illegible]

wi[illegible]

[illegible] ith his boot and t[illegible] There

st[illegible] fairly jingling [illegible] hair

c[illegible] dice.

[illegible] ards!" Charles [illegible] What's

ha[illegible]

[illegible] rly, as though [illegible] st.

"[illegible] my head—[illegible] he

ga[illegible]

[illegible] open. That icy, [illegible] at

th[illegible] d water rushing [illegible] did

n[illegible]

"[illegible] as I get some h[illegible]

"[illegible] nd ran for the [illegible]

[illegible] d. He was still [illegible] ring

[illegible] "It was too big [illegible] cap-ing the fire with fresh wood. "We're glad you're here, but that was too big a risk for a Christmas dinner."

"Your little ones had to have a Christmas," Edwards replied with a cock of his head. "No creek could stop me, after I fetched them their gifts from Independence."

Caroline's heart stopped beating. If he were joking about such a thing, she would not know how to forgive him.

"Did you see Santa Claus?" Laura shouted. She was up on her knees in the bed, like a dog begging.

Caroline stilled every thought, trying to imagine how she might absorb the words from the air if Edwards's answer was not what her children needed it to be.

"I sure did," Edwards said, matter-of-factly. Mary and Laura erupted into a flurry of questions. "Wait, wait a minute," Edwards laughed. He opened up his coat and brought an oilcloth sack from an inside pocket. Caroline took it dumbly. The stiff fabric was creased with cold. Then Edwards sat down cross-legged on the floor beside the girls' bed, and leaning forward with his elbows on his knees, he spun Mary and Laura a tale tall enough to rival the likes of Mike Fink and Davy Crockett.

Caroline opened the mouth of the sack and everything else melted from her consciousness. Two gleaming tin cups. Two long sticks of peppermint candy as big around as her thumb. And winking up from the bottom of each cup, a new copper penny. Her throat burned and her eyes swam. How many months had it been since he'd seen Mary and Laura sharing their single tin cup, and he had remembered. The sudden burst of affection she felt toward Edwards was too big for her heart, too big for her chest. She filled the stockings with shaking fingers, then sat down on the edge of the big bed and scooped up Carrie. Carrie's warm body filled her arms. Caroline held the baby close, pressing gently, gently, with each grateful thud of her heart.

"We shook hands," Edwards told the girls, "then Santa Claus swung up onto his fine bay horse and called, 'So long, Edwards!' And I watched [illegible] s way down the Fo[illegible]t [illegible] and his pack [illegible] around a be[illegible]d.' Ed[illegible] with a smart [illegible] *There!*

[illegible] Laura regarded [illegible] they were not sure [illegible] A man who had spoke[illegible]—shaken [illegible] near enough to tou[illegible]h. [illegible] forgotten their [illegible]

[illegible] waited a moment, [illegible] faces before she [illegible] "You may look now, girls."

[illegible] passed before [illegible] they flew to the [illegible] of bare feet and [illegible] had never been [illegible] and laughing. Right away [illegible] to feel and taste [illegible] her gifts. She [illegible] her empty cup, [illegible] peppermint stick, nibbled [illegible] of her patty cake. [illegible] each object with utter [illegible] to touch their [illegible] much and mar their [illegible] only stood, [illegible] by the brilliance [illegible] her: the cool [illegible] the twirling red stripes [illegible] sugar.

[illegible] Edwards watched the [illegible] yet subdued, [illegible] as if he were [illegible] than the ones [illegible] Jim—made C[illegible] little boys [illegible] where in Tennessee [illegible] Edwards this [illegible] her mind [illegible] could not [illegible]. Silently she thanked [illegible] and nephews, [illegible] for the loan of him.

[illegible] your stocking [illegible] asked just when [illegible] had begun to dwindle.

[illegible] at her—all of them [illegible] Charles. Caro- [illegible] toward the stocking [illegible] Laura obediently [illegible] hands down to the [illegible] the puzzle- [illegible] the girls' faces [illegible] brushed smooth, [illegible] they froze, wide eyes [illegible] each other. Both of them knew what it must be, yet could not believe it. Even as the coins emerged pinched between thumb and forefinger, they could not fathom possessing such a thing. They held their pennies wonderingly in the palms of their hands, as if the coins might melt like snowflakes if they dared turn away.

Caroline smiled so broadly, her temples ached. Who but a bachelor would think to give two little girls a penny apiece? Only a man without children would think so broadly, unhampered by any limits as to what kinds of things could come out of Santa Claus's sack. At the Richards brothers' dry-goods store in Pepin, those cups could not have cost less than four cents each. What he had paid for them in Independence, and the candy besides, Caroline did not want to suppose. And yet it was the pennies that dazzled them. After all that she and Charles had fretted, believing they had nothing worthy of their daughters' Christmas. It was like a parable, acted out before her own hearth.

Laura plunked her penny into her cup and jingled it round and round. Mary studied hers, making out the numbers stamped on its face. "One. Eight. Seven. Zero," she read, triumphant. Caroline nodded her praise, happy beyond speech.

They would never, never forget this Christmas. None of them. Already Caroline could feel the morning embedding itself in her own memory. Her mind was bottling it whole, so that it would remain fresh and glistening as a jar of preserves.

Charles gave a little cough that was not a cough at all. He pumped Edwards's hand up and down, broke loose to give his nose a quick swipe with his cuff, and took Edwards's hand again, holding it so firm and steady that Caroline could feel the gratitude passing between them. She stood to offer her own thanks, and Edwards's hand disappeared into his coat pocket. Out came a sweet potato. Then another, and another, each one a full handful. Caroline did not have arms enough to hold them. Edwards piled them into her apron until the knotted ties at her back strained with the weight. Nine fat, knobby sweet potatoes.

There was no time for [illegible] for Edwards then. She h[illegible] felt this way tow[illegible] any [illegible] husband, her brothers. There [illegible] reason in the world fo[illegible] have been so generous. N[illegible] her life had [illegible] been [illegible] so rich.

"Oh," Edward said, [illegible] his shirtfront. Som[illegible] partway down. [illegible] and drew out two en[illegible] said simply. [illegible] went [illegible] the other he held [illegible] to C[illegible]

At the sight of Eliza's [illegible] the envelope, Caroline [illegible] crumple. S[illegible] could [illegible] breath; she was [illegible] ears. The paper [illegible] as w[illegible] envelope so fat it co[illegible] circulator. Eliza [illegible] Pet[illegible] Papa Frederick. H[illegible] Martha and Cha[illegible]. Al[illegible] put their hands [illegible] Caroline pulled [illegible] hairpi[illegible] open the enve[illegible] good.

Ma had begun [illegible] letter [illegible] did: *Dear Child* [illegible]

The words [illegible] her [illegible] person at least [illegible] a child in this w[illegible]. *Oh* [illegible] thought as comfort[illegible] her. Caroline's [illegible] flutte[illegible] the first lines [illegible] as ever, for [illegible] writi[illegible] sooner—holding [illegible] between laughter [illegible] d tea[illegible], Caroline u[illegible] *n't spoil; don't g[illegible] your* [illegible]. Only she could [illegible] without treati[illegible] herself [illegible] of Eliza's sec[illegible] she saw there se[illegible] a wa[illegible] through her, as th[illegible] news had reached [illegible] it and [illegible] inch of her s[illegible]

"Eliza and Pet[illegible] had a [illegible]," she told Charl[illegible] your father."

"That's fine [illegible]," Ch[illegible] held a twenty-d[illegible] in his hand. "First [illegible] ayme[illegible] ation," he expla[illegible] the third of Septe[illegible] er." [illegible] since they'd left, [illegible] had sent what ar[illegible] a month. [illegible] nipped at her, th[illegible] as her eyes retu[illegible] news. *Lansford Ne[illegible] 5, 1870.* Caroline [illegible] fingertips to the baby's name, imagining a boy with Eliza's bright eyes and Peter's gangly limbs; the soft Quiner mouth, the untamable Ingalls hair. She looked at the date on Eliza's portion of the letter and marveled at the passage of time. The nephew in her mind was only a few minutes old, yet by now the real Lansford Newcomb Ingalls must be crawling.

The dipper jangled in the water bucket—Laura, trying out her new cup. Caroline blinked once before realizing that of course she was still in Kansas. For the briefest flicker of consciousness, she had been wholly elsewhere. Not so far away as Wisconsin, Caroline was too far grown for that sort of make-believe, but someplace both high above and deep within, where distance was of no consequence. That was as much a gift as the letter itself.

She turned to Edwards, ready to lavish him with thanks. His face, both wistful and sated, stopped her. She could not escape the sense that it was he who was trying to repay them for kindnesses already given. Had a plate of white flour dumplings and a half dozen fiddle tunes by the fireside meant so much? Caroline regarded her neighbor more thoughtfully, recalling how he had settled his shivering self right down on the floor alongside the girls and launched into his Santa Claus tale without taking a sip of hot coffee or turning his palms toward the fireplace. That alone gave her cause to believe that Edwards wanted no more than to feel at home with family. To laud his generosity and enthrone him as a guest of honor now? That would almost certainly spoil his pleasure.

It was a guess, and one she was willing to hazard aloud. "Charles," she said, "why don't you and Mr. Edwards see to the stock while I warm the stew and set the breakfast table for five?"

Charles looked at her as if she'd blasphemed. But Caroline saw the happiness soak Edwards straight through. He buttoned up his coat, loped to the milk pail, and called, "C'mon, Ingalls!"

CAROLINE COULD NOT remember the last time she had been so full. Of food, of affection, of gratitude. The cabin was redolent of tobacco, pe[illegible]rmi[illegible] st[illegible]d[illegible], [illegible]av[illegible]y and browned s[illegible]et [illegible] S[illegible]e had al-lov[illegible] Edw[illegible]rd[illegible] t s[illegible]ction of gallant[illegible] refus[illegible] cha[illegible]r, and [illegible] she [illegible] her lap while [illegible] table wit[illegible] their [illegible] at what remai[illegible]

[illegible]hat's [illegible] town, Edwards[illegible] Cha[illegible]

[illegible]ward [illegible] ary and Laur[illegible] [illegible]sleep, ma[illegible]n?"

[illegible]rolin[illegible] was snuggled [illegible] with [illegible]

[illegible] there[illegible] C[illegible]les asked.

[illegible]ward [illegible] "U[illegible]p in Cherry Tow[illegible]hip[illegible] fro[illegible]n Pen[illegible]sylvan[illegible] [illegible] half-breed an[illegible] Fel-la's [illegible] G[illegible]ss he's part C[illegible] whi[illegible]e wo[illegible]m. E[illegible]ars, even raise[illegible] k ago yes[illegible]day [illegible] posse ordered [illegible] chi[illegible]d out [illegible] their [illegible]nt and torche[illegible] d the lot [illegible] the[illegible] he yard while [illegible] ards's eye[illegible] ine. He drop[illegible] hea[illegible]r Mr[illegible] Mosh[illegible] way."

[illegible]wing[illegible] d across Caroli[illegible] us" she[illegible] d.

[illegible]s, ma[illegible] turned a turke[illegible] poke. "M[illegible]hed [illegible] into the woo[illegible] Those Ca[illegible]bells [illegible] tened him som[illegible]

[illegible]e the [illegible]

[illegible]ear [illegible] enough to re[illegible] e In-dia[illegible] oard[illegible] t I don't rightly [illegible] the[illegible], and [illegible]er hal[illegible] was torn down.

[illegible]e new[illegible] with all that [illegible] Caro-line [illegible]ould [illegible] for it to lodge [illegible] tside of h[illegible], like [illegible] had happened [illegible] own-ship [illegible] north [illegible] seemed asham[illegible] king and [illegible]ward[illegible] [illegible]ey scraped silen[illegible] unt[illegible]l

Charles asked with a note of cheer so deliberate it was jarring, "Did I ever tell you about the time my father took a sow sledding on the Sabbath?"

"Twice," Edwards said. Caroline burst out laughing.

"I'm sorry, Charles," she said, then buttoned her lips between her teeth so that they could not smile.

Charles grinned and shook his pipe at her like a schoolmaster brandishing a pointer. "Caroline Ingalls, you are not the least bit sorry."

"Did I ever tell *you* how I got the coonskin for my cap?" Edwards countered.

Charles shook his head.

"Well," Edwards said. "I wasn't but eight years old, and I treed a fat old daddy raccoon one Saturday night at twilight, right in our own front yard. My mama said it'd be a sin if I shot and dressed one of God's creatures on the Sabbath, so I asked her for my blanket and my catechism and sat under that chestnut tree all night and all day Sunday, studying the sacraments and waiting to shoot that varmint. I kept the Sabbath and the raccoon, both." Charles leaned back against the wall and chuckled. "He was so big, Mama made me two caps—one boy-sized and one man-sized. When I outgrew the one, she lopped off the tail and sewed it onto the other."

Caroline watched the smoke from the men's pipes twine together as they all laughed. She blew out a long, silent exhale, envisioning how the smoke of her breath would meld with the tobacco smoke were they sitting outside before a campfire instead of under the good roof Charles had built with Edwards's nails. It was moments like these that she had envied when Charles had gone to help build Edwards's house, moments when the thread of one story joined into the next, forming a lattice of shared memories. The thread extended toward her now, well within reach, if she dared unlock her store of memories to grasp it.

"I remember—" Caroline ventured. The men turned toward her, the lift of their brows encouraging. "It was the year we were married,

...s and Papa ... ving on the big ma...
... the riverbank ... she explained to ...
... must have been ... It was a perfect pla...
... smothered ... ar, you felt as if ...
... aight over it and ... opposite bank." ...
... t place wafted thr... and silvery and d...
... llow sun. "W... ca... hough the big b...
... ed it just as mu... that every one of ...
... en years older th... complained, until ...
... he cows decided to ... ls face twitched. ...
... her, to see if he we... line went on with...
... embellishment. "T... o the plank seat, ...
... et through, and she ... dn't walk more th...
... before the swing ... she didn't know h...
... Oh, how that ... norted with laughte...
... s, who knew ... did. She might ha...
... re but the men ... ed to be stretched ...
... h. Lottie just ... a back. That was t...
... life ... saw Papa ... ning. It winded h...
... zed like a broken ... he laughed. Thom...
... he ropes to get the ... d and cried. She c...
... ouldn't drink ... has fixed the swing ...
... his head and sh... Caroline feasted ...
... g that he would ... ght of campfires an...
... ears to come.

... day ... Caroline ... he felt it tapering ...
... before Edward po... ced resignedly ...
... et me at least ... line offered.
... his palms ... ger than I ought ...
... said, rising, "and ... kely to be. Once ...
... ed, it won't ... blaze, coat and all ...

Caroline winced. She had forgotten the creek. The water would be black, its cold surface like a blade against the skin. The moon was no more than the width of an onion skin.

"You know you're welcome to stay," Charles said.

Edwards shrugged into his coat. "And I thank you."

"You'll come back if the current is too high," Caroline added. He wouldn't, she knew that, but it bore saying.

Edwards touched his mittened fingers to Carrie's belly and gave her a jiggle. "Next year it'll be your turn for a treat from Santa Claus, little miss," he told her. He looked at Mary and Laura, content in their beds, and nodded to himself. Their happiness bolstered him, Caroline mused, as if they were his own.

Had he been Henry, or Peter, Caroline would have taken hold of his arms and leaned her cheek against his then. Instead she laid a hand on his sleeve and pressed, gently. "Merry Christmas, Mr. Edwards," she said.

His long, flat smile all but cut his face in two. "Merry Christmas, Mrs. Ingalls," he replied.

Thirty-Nine

THEY PREPARED [illegible]R the [illegible] the plow, both [illegible] and Charles as though it were [illegible] impo[illegible] When they ate from their first harvest, it would [illegible] in the [illegible] and, not unli[illegible] Mary had joined them. H[illegible] existen[illegible] them in a way they could not otherwise achieve, even w[illegible] lives were linked one with the other. So it would be with [illegible] the prairie. The blade would cut the soil, so [illegible] it could be [illegible] seeds. As soon as the crops had put down roots and [illegible] up out of the ground, there would be no mistaking to [illegible] quarter section belonged. After that, the papers [illegible] the fil[illegible] reality.

Every pelt nailed to the [illegible] scraped clean, the work of before the fire was [illegible] stacked up against the purchase. All winter long, the[illegible] little else. While they worked, they spoke of the seeds Charles [illegible] buy, not only this year but the next and the next, and of [illegible] of earth would best suit each variety. Charles had every [illegible] out in his mind, and he could twist and turn his [illegible] kaleidoscope. Hearing him talk night after night of [illegible] patterns, Caroline savored the knowledge that the plow was [illegible] bring Charles to the land. From time to time he [illegible] hunt [illegible] the planting, watering and hoeing required [illegible] he stay [illegible] of the cabin. With luck, Caroline promised herself, [illegible] girls might never be alone with the Indians again.

There was no time for [illegible] season. Instead there was the rhythmic slop and [illegible] of br[illegible] onto dried hides. Charles brought her the brains, which she screwed into canning jars until they were needed. If it was cold enough, they were put out to freeze. When it was not, she put the jars in a pail and lowered them down into the cool shaft of the well.

Once a hide was scraped and stretched and dried and soaked, Caroline heated a bowl of water on the hearth until it was just warm enough to bathe a baby. Then she unjarred a brain and kneaded it into the warm water, grinding the soft bits between her fingertips to form the milky slurry that Charles would rub into the rawhide to tan it.

With the head of a dulled hoe, Charles scraped the moisture from the brained hides until they were barely damp. Jack sat beside him, waiting to lick up the accumulated scum of liquid rawhide that Charles wiped from the blade every so often. Finally he wrapped the hides around the bedpost and worked them back and forth—as though polishing the toe of a shoe—to turn them smooth and supple.

All winter long, the house smelled of brains and skins and sweat. Caroline took to looking out the east window as she worked. There would be her kitchen garden. She could see it as clearly as Charles could see his fields of corn and sod potatoes: cucumbers, tomatoes, and onions, squash and carrots and beans, all drenched in the morning sun. In the afternoon, the cabin would shade the plants from the harshest heat. She would plant them as she always had, so that the rows of colors would meld from one to the next in a living rainbow. All those seeds had come from home. Wisconsin seeds bred in Kansas ground. Like Carrie, Caroline thought, and smiled. Alongside Polly's cucumbers there would be sweet potatoes, from Mr. Edwards, for she had saved one back from Christmas dinner. As soon as the ground softened and the sunlight grew less watery, she would bring in a few spadefuls of earth and start the sweet potato in a flat before the window. Perhaps when Charles went to Oswego for the plow, she could busy herself and the girls for an afternoon with that small task.

THE [illegible] een giddy the da [illegible] s [illegible] go. Gid [illegible] oline had a case o [illegible] ted ever [illegible] ale to kiss her go [illegible] in surp [illegible] m that jostled he [illegible] elf brea [illegible] es kissed Mary [illegible] ces and [illegible] our ma!" They ju [illegible] wn with [illegible]

T [illegible] ll and muddy, but [illegible] ge in th [illegible] rm breath had bee [illegible] eve- ning [illegible] ls came in rosy [illegible] eat dam [illegible] ath their woole [illegible] he lines [illegible] ares Caroline had [illegible] m the [illegible] alized with fros [illegible]

T [illegible] sed easily. On the [illegible] ke pock [illegible] s of every minute [illegible] ur days [illegible] n the fifth morn [illegible]

"[illegible] on the fourth nigh [illegible] en five," [illegible] er.

La [illegible] she'd been tricked [illegible] ns Pa ha [illegible] y,' she declared. C [illegible] to dissu [illegible] ld be home or he [illegible] id woul [illegible] pointment if he did [illegible]

N [illegible] nd that her own a [illegible] d high [illegible] ay passed. Every f [illegible] p from [illegible] chicken Mr. Edw [illegible] y befor [illegible] e creek road. The [illegible] l. Not [illegible] l plow and the see [illegible] r, sugar [illegible] oline thought of sa [illegible] at had [illegible] er lips. That woul [illegible] r so mu [illegible] . She had not aske [illegible] f. Ther [illegible] rticularly wanted [illegible] r. With [illegible] low, there migh [illegible] r extras, though she hoped for Mary's and Laura's sakes that there would be. Surely a stick of penny candy, at least. Charles never forgot his girls.

As she admired the pictures in her mind, Caroline found herself humming without regard for where the tune had come from. When she realized, she swallowed and stood still, listening, to be sure.

Indians.

It could not be. Their camps had been empty since before Christmas. But it was. There was no mistaking that sound. She let go of the fistful of feathers and wiped the sweat from her palms. Was that why Edwards had come calling the day before? She had been so pleased by the prairie chicken, she suspected nothing but neighborliness.

Caroline felt as she had the night on the prairie when they had lost Jack and Charles had nearly shot the bulldog by mistake as he approached the campfire. Her body had poised itself on the edge of fear, but her mind was not yet fully afraid. Her mind wanted to know more. She went to the window and listened again.

It was music, at least. The melody was unlike any song she had ever sung, but Caroline could find the pattern in it. The beat was choppy, like the sound of the girls jumping in and out of their hopscotch squares. Perhaps that was why she had not recognized its source sooner. This song was the opposite in every way of the sounds they had heard in the fall. Even as she cautioned herself that she could not be sure, Caroline ascribed joyfulness to it.

What sort of song would they sing after killing a man?

Caroline stepped back, bewildered. That thought had come from her, as if her mind had no concern for the consequences of its thoughts. "Stop that," she said, as though one of the children had talked back to her. It had no business asking such questions of its own accord, questions she did not want asked, much less answered.

A LITTLE MORE than two hours after that, Charles was home. Laura yelped and Jack whined, but Caroline did not let them outside to greet [illegible] one to help hi[illegible] ney hefted the [illegible] sible. Charles lo[illegible]

[illegible] s were still singin[illegible]

[illegible] ey'd gone," Ca[illegible]

[illegible] ed. He had expe[illegible] aroline could not [illegible] ation was comp[illegible] d. "So did I. W[illegible] e come back fr[illegible] one last time," [illegible] ian agent will le[illegible] new reservatio[illegible]

[illegible] elf calculating th[illegible] absolute measur[illegible] culated Charles [illegible] ple, not severa[illegible] eks, then. Twent[illegible] d allow them [illegible] complaint. Every[illegible] pray morning [illegible] departure.

[illegible] in all was smil[illegible] s had traded w[illegible] needed and mo[illegible] able, down to [illegible] otatoes. Instead [illegible] bought all man[illegible] a paper sack ca[illegible] ers and a jar of [illegible] Caroline's mo[illegible] ered at the sigh[illegible] gherkins bob[illegible] had been near[illegible] had asked him to[illegible] store in Indep[illegible] that time he had [illegible]

[illegible] the flour sa[illegible] oblong packa[illegible] er and tied wit[illegible] opped it onto [illegible] of slap and raise[illegible]. It could only [illegible] for a new spr[illegible] inched her lip [illegible] as she untie[illegible] es had only o[illegible] choosing a calic[illegible] t his indiffere[illegible] oprieties of fash[illegible] certain amount [illegible] d have bought yar[illegible] ant Turkey red [illegible] possessed the g[illegible]

[illegible] haled at the sigh[illegible] under ground, [illegible] lilacs, with a spray of feathery gray fern leaves. In the center lay a fat coil of narrow gray braid to trim the hem. Had there been a woman at the store to help him coordinate the goods? she wondered. They complemented each other perfectly: the trim, a few shades darker than the gray in the fabric, serving to accentuate the delicate pattern. The calico was Charles's doing, that was sure. Lavender was not a color she would have thought to choose for herself. It was a demure shade, fit for a little girl's Sunday best, and entirely impractical for an everyday dress.

Caroline loved it. Under the hot Kansas sun it would be gentle to the skin and refreshing to the eye. Already she could imagine how Charles would look at her when she wore it. He loved to see her wreathed in color.

"It's too much," she told him, as she always did.

His face told her it wasn't nearly enough, as it always did.

For the girls there were cunning little black rubber hair combs that fit like bandeaus, with a star shape cut out from the center and backed with ribbon. Blue satin for Mary and red satin for Laura, just as if Caroline had picked them out herself. The girls were enraptured. They gazed at each other, then swapped combs so they could see their own. Laura put hers on Jack and squealed with laughter at his dubious face, crowned by such finery.

"Charles, you didn't get yourself a thing," Caroline said. His eyes twinkled at her. Both of them knew that was not true.

CAROLINE STIRRE[illegible] of sugar into th[illegible] [illegible]d dried blackb[illegible] Charles would [illegible] [illegible]t at noon, in th[illegible] could hear hi[illegible] [illegible]ustangs: *Gee u[illegible] Straight and true* [illegible] Below his voic[illegible] went sighing [illegible] [illegible]. Caroline smi[illegible] [illegible]led that plow [illegible] [illegible] were another wif[illegible] owned such [illegible] [illegible]cted he had na[illegible] would send I[illegible] [illegible] him in for din[illegible] table, and th[illegible] [illegible]ed only to brow[illegible].

Caroline watche[illegible] and out of [illegible] [illegible] was so differen[illegible] at this age [illegible] [illegible]led knees and [illegible] furrows enc[illegible] [illegible]s and ankles. [illegible] a little jac[illegible] [illegible] Yet Caroline [illegible]turing the [illegible] [illegible] sharp heels a[illegible] beginning to [illegible] [illegible] hardy way.

[illegible]e sunlight di[illegible] Carrie lay pois[illegible] [illegible] to strike. Sl[illegible] toward her [illegible] [illegible]d with waiting [illegible] rows and m[illegible] [illegible] mouth, in hop[illegible] her surprise [illegible] [illegible]xed. Carrie g[illegible] sunbeam had [illegible] [illegible], melting into [illegible] to brighte[illegible] [illegible] Caroline stir[illegible], until it mig[illegible] [illegible]n instead of no[illegible].

"I do believe it's going to storm," she said to the girls. But the light was wrong. Rather than clouding, it had shrunken somehow, turned down like the wick in a lamp. Yet through the west window, the sky was clear. A dissonant twang sounded in her mind. Caroline put down the spoon and went out to look. Halfway across the room, she saw. To the south, the sky was black.

The smell reached the cabin at the same moment as Charles's shout: "Prairie fire!"

For one crystalline moment, it was beautiful. Like silk, like water. Orange and yellow, a perfect saturation of color writhing over the prairie. The great curve of flame caressed the earth, its long arms slowly undulating outward. The fire itself did not appear to move forward at all. The black spume of smoke billowed so high and wide, it seemed instead as if the landscape were surging forward, passing into it.

Her eyes feasted on the blaze, unable to deny its splendor, but Caroline's mind made no concession. The radiant vista before her did not simply burn; it consumed. It fed on all that was put before it with the indifference of a threshing machine. If they themselves passed through it, there would be nothing left on the other side but the empty chaff of their bodies.

Caroline ran.

Bucket after bucket of water. Up from the well, into the washtub. Burlap sacks snatched from the stable, pressed down into the tub. The burlap would not take the water fast enough. It bubbled up around her hands, tried to float, even as the water beaded over the coarse fabric. All manner of creatures fled past her as she struggled. Rabbits, prairie chickens, snakes, and mice, dashing toward the creek. From them rose a nameless sound, a frantic rush of panting and scurrying.

"Hurry, Caroline!" Charles cried. He was tying the team to the stable, plow and all. "That fire's coming faster than a horse can run."

Caroline opened the mouth of one sack and dragged it through the tub like a dipper, scooping the water into it. Then Charles was beside [illegible] up one hand [illegible] ther they stagg[illegible] [illegible] line. *Fa[illegible]er* [illegible] *still,* warned he[illegible] [illegible] in the world [illegible] direction, even [illegible] jackrabbit leapt [illegible] een them, fearless [illegible]

[illegible] gash in the [illegible] and yard. Tw[illegible] south from the [illegible] third joining [illegible] I couldn't plo[illegible] ere isn't time," [illegible] and dashed back [illegible] furrow. Fift[illegible] wall them off [illegible] torn sod lay [illegible] ots splayed in [illegible] Those fine [illegible] quick as hair, [illegible] She stood [illegible] n of smoke and [illegible] of its warmth [illegible] ar was such th[illegible] her sound, [illegible] ly the faintest [illegible] ticked and [illegible]. One furrow, [illegible] ter.

[illegible] s came out of [illegible] a stick of firew[illegible] candle in one fis[illegible] ed the small [illegible] over the furrow [illegible] grass. Behind h[illegible] ed.

[illegible] Charles set [illegible] ould have held [illegible] her hand. I se[illegible] element from [illegible] gulfed the horiz[illegible] not enough to [illegible] lapped [illegible] s within the[illegible] fence, oblivi[illegible]," she urged. [illegible] hough the big [illegible] hear and ob[illegible] lit another [illegible] began to hiss [illegible] one, the lit[illegible] and join hand[illegible] spread itself [illegible] *round the rosy,* [illegible] sang. *Ashe[illegible]* [illegible] current of [illegible] h, and the li[illegible] bowed down. Caroline watched as a clump of roots lit up. They looked like fine wires, all gold and copper. Like Charles's whiskers in the light from the hearth. Then the flames were on her side of the furrow.

Put it out.

With the swing of the wet burlap, Caroline felt her mind unhitching itself. *Shuuush* went the sack through the flaming grass. Again. And again. She heard the sounds of her own exertion as she swung and stamped, felt the heaving of her chest as she grunted. Her heels bit into the soil as she ran to the next fire. When it was gone, there was another—two more, three. Where her thoughts had been, there was only clean space. Beyond that space was an awareness that the fires north of the furrow must not be allowed to spread. The children were north of the furrow. And the house, and the livestock. The command hung suspended in front of her, where she could not lose sight of it. The fire could penetrate her skin with its heat and her lungs with its smoke, but it could not touch that edict.

A dickcissel, wing tips flaming, streaked to the ground. Breast to the sky, it flapped, spattering flames into the yard. Caroline's sack swooped down. The little bulge pulsed, heart-like, beneath the burlap. Caroline brought her heel over it and stamped. Beneath the crunch a single desperate squirm, then nothing. She ran to the next small blaze.

Her cheeks were dry and taut. Her feet were wet, and the hem of her dress. The line of sweat down her back met with the spray from the swinging wet sack. None of it had significance. There was only awareness. Each sensation briefly registered and then was dismissed. Only those things that might prevent her from beating out the next fire were retained. The lightening of the sack as the water evaporated. The blurring of her vision and the cough that cut her breath if she lingered downwind of the smoke.

The change did not sink in immediately. No more than one surface of her body had felt the approaching fire as it loomed up out of the south in a flat, pulsating wall. The heat intensified as it neared, but its shape never al[illegible] side of her body f[illegible] her squa[illegible] [illegible]eeks felt the heat [illegible] It crept [illegible] face, but her skin [illegible] the mea[illegible] mind until she be[illegible] waves b[illegible] [illegible]er temples at once [illegible]

Caro[illegible] the fire breaking i[illegible] white k[illegible] [illegible]s of flame. There [illegible] The two [illegible] [illegible]zen rods south of [illegible] sideway[illegible] [illegible]ce call. *Forward* [illegible] Two lin[illegible] [illegible]ating, and parting [illegible]

Two [illegible] [illegible]se on either side [illegible] stood i[illegible] [illegible]ellow. Above it, a [illegible] pale blu[illegible] [illegible]ed: "West!"

Caro[illegible] [illegible]b, doused a fresh [illegible] with it [illegible]. She beat and be[illegible] trample[illegible] [illegible]e bare roots with [illegible] That it [illegible] not matter. She w[illegible] no easy [illegible]

The [illegible] [illegible]r hair. Caroline ra[illegible] ered it [illegible] no pulse or squirr[illegible] ceased [illegible] More sparks, and [illegible] sky as [illegible] [illegible]e fire swept along [illegible] and an[illegible] [illegible]v to burn, yet ac[illegible] she co[illegible] [illegible]e ran and pante[illegible] around [illegible] something so de[illegible] her th[illegible] [illegible]ated and reached.

The[illegible] [illegible]k, but a ragged, [illegible] skin s[illegible] [illegible]istering.

The[illegible] [illegible] a rush of cold [illegible] like a [illegible] [illegible]e whirled.

Not[illegible] [illegible]all—the fire was [illegible]

so cool against her skin, she might have been naked. As she watched, the head of the blaze reached the plowed field north of the house and veered off to the west. Away.

Four or five small fires remained inside the furrow. Caroline walked to them and put them out. As she did so, each shred of muscle in her shoulders throbbed to life. She lifted an arm and pressed her closed eyes into the crook of her elbow. They were gritty with soot, and the sweat stung. Cool air seeped into a torn seam where her sleeve joined her bodice.

When she lifted her head the land smelled scorched, like burnt bread. Through the haze of smoke she saw Charles moving toward the washtub. A flicker of red caught her eye, and Caroline's body snapped toward the house, her sack raised. Red calico, and above it, two small white faces peeping round the doorway. As they moved cautiously forward Carrie appeared, dangling like a puppy from one of Mary's forearms; in the other Mary clutched her rag doll.

Caroline felt a swelling within herself. It pressed against every edge of her body, so light she was utterly weightless. Relief.

She crossed the yard to the house and went down on her knees before them. Her fingers touched their cheeks, but her hands, sodden and dulled with the sting of burlap, could not feel them. Caroline put her lips to each of their foreheads in turn, poised in the shape of a kiss. With her lips she felt their presence. When she pulled away she saw the smudges where her chin had brushed their noses. The slight lift of her cheeks as she smiled squeezed two fat tears past her swelling eyelids. "The backfire saved us," she assured the children. Her voice trembled as she said it. "And all's well that ends well."

Mary's eyes welled. "I let the dinner burn," she said.

Behind them Caroline saw the cookware on the hearth. The cornbread was charred, the pan of berries blackened beyond smoking. That was all they had lost to the fire. Her laugh came out a dry bark. It

... d watered her ... Mary close, ... er cheeks, and ... You didn't let ... she whispered.

... hand over the ... lick as she ... Charles or the ... her what ... could explain, but ... he opened ... out the Bible a... she found ... looking for.

... still small voice.

... pocket she drew ... narrow, its ... delicate curlicue ... walked the ... line of grass ... of kindling ... ght the backfire ... from it with ... Caroline laid ... so that it un- ... It would be impossible ... words without ...

... spoken all evening ... with a tap of ... her ... ching ... them. It ... the truth. Be... something like ... softly, and Ca... use it with ... she harbored ... and to her ... to remain wi... silent, holding ... the fleck of warm...

... closed the Bi... and slipped ... She felt the ... her brother ... children were ... everything ... through to her ... of the ... ng through h... had not no- ... notes betwe... the feeling ... each time the ... and the ... y that veil had ... though no one had passed through it, Caroline still sensed its nearness and its thinness.

The scent of smoke wafted upward as she stepped out of her dress and hung it on its nail. Likely that smell would never fully leave the fabric. She wrapped her shawl close around her nightdress and went to stand a moment in the doorway. The bare, burned prairie stretched out beneath the moon, all black and silver. Like an ambrotype, Caroline thought, and wished that her mind could preserve the sight as clearly. It was not a scene that would lend itself well to a pressed metal frame propped against a mantelpiece. In the dark the line that separated the brown earth from the black all but vanished. Yet to Caroline it was as perceptible as the outline of her own skin.

That was how near the fire had come. That close and taken nothing. Rather, it had left something. Caroline rested her fist against her chest. With each beat of her heart her consciousness of the burn line seemed to momentarily intensify, as if her own blood were pulsing through it. Quietly she walked out from the house until the grass beneath her feet became stiff and dry. She crouched down and touched her palm to the earth. Warm.

Caroline let go of her shawl and put both hands to the ground, as though her cool skin might soothe the burned places—as though the prairie were a fevered child, and she its mother. A small portion of the heat entered her hands, and Caroline felt her body soften, as it did when she held her husband or her children. When she stood, she did not brush the ashy soil from her palms. She balled her two fists together, knuckle to knuckle against her chest, and held them that way all the way back to the house.

Inside, she bent over Charles and put her hands to his face. He stirred, half waking, and murmured something indistinct. Caroline climbed into the bed beside him. The sooty, sweaty smell of the fire still clung to his whiskers. She ran a toe lightly, so lightly, along the sole of his foot.

A sound, something less than a syllable, passed through his throat—

the sound of every[illegible] else [illegible] toward her, slip[illegible] a han[illegible] low her breast. [illegible] bone[illegible] where he could fe[illegible] the f[illegible] Their feet slip[illegible] past [illegible] smooth places [illegible] crossing [illegible] into his whiskers. Charles ki[illegible] Each kiss wake[illegible] the tin[illegible] she thought.

He lifted hi[illegible] bo[illegible] der. She close[illegible] her eyes [illegible] brown whiskers sl[illegible] ing the bare sk[illegible] along th[illegible] the feel of his [illegible] and [illegible] she felt that s[illegible] nudged his way in[illegible] her. [illegible] it his diffuse. [illegible] to melt into a soft haze [illegible] gether it had b[illegible] one of [illegible]

That first t[illegible] she had expec[illegible] the surety that she [illegible] knew, would [illegible] gentle a[illegible] what she prep[illegible] weight ginger[illegible] could not kee[illegible] reminded herself [illegible] ever was his right [illegible]

Instead she fou[illegible] herself [illegible] ished to see what her bo[illegible] became like a [illegible] ful with pleasure. What [illegible]

softly from his [illegible] ribs, his thumb [illegible] apart than the [illegible] heart beating b[illegible] again and again, [illegible] shivers. Carolin[illegible] tips as they bru[illegible] by [illegible] warmth deep with[illegible] her. *[illegible]* she thought.

[illegible]ms framing her [illegible] burrowed into [illegible] hair [illegible] and collarbone [illegible] nightdress. She [illegible] ading her temples [illegible] st opening, ever [illegible] ed her eyes to [illegible] the [illegible] break, the way the stars [illegible]

From their very first [illegible] she relished mo[illegible] surprise, though [illegible] fully what to e[illegible] self to her husb[illegible] Ch[illegible] little fear of pa[illegible] ever intangible. [illegible] een one quick [illegible] of [illegible] m. *It is only Char*[illegible] still and trust hi[illegible] more.

[illegible]ginning to rock [illegible] to this man. On[illegible] and grateful, [illegible] only an indistin[illegible] much unpleasant as unaccustomed. Twice he moved just so and there were quick flickers of heat, glimmers of the brilliant flashes he himself seemed to be experiencing. The second of them had made her gasp at the delight telegraphing beneath her skin.

He'd stopped, drawing back as though fearful he might have burned her. "Are you all right?"

Caroline was panting softly. She could see it in the faint rise and fall of her breasts beneath her nightdress. "Yes, Charles." And then, "Go on."

He descended again, tentatively. This time the overwhelming sense was of enveloping him, of embracing him entirely, and all at once the last of her apprehensions fled. Her body yielded, a sudden ripening, welcoming him deeper.

Charles had sensed the change and his pace had quickened until he whimpered and shuddered. Caroline felt a hot spurt and then it was done. He shivered all over and sank down around her. Caroline lay still beneath the pounding of his heart, listening to the *luff-luff* of his breath falling into her hair. In a few minutes he raised his head to look at her, a little abashed, and she had ventured a smile.

"It was all right?" Charles asked. "I didn't hurt you?"

She'd wanted to tell him no. Nothing he had done had put his own pleasure above causing her pain. There had been a fleeting sting at the outset, but Caroline did not see how he could have prevented that. Likely he had felt it himself, so she shook her head. It eased him considerably, but there was still something pinched in his expression. If not for the fact that he was able to meet her eyes she might have mistaken it for shame. Perhaps, she'd thought as she studied him, she did not know Charles Ingalls well enough yet to decipher these ever-so-slight anglings of lips and brow. And then with a warm rush she recognized the shape his features made.

Beholden. He had looked for all the world as though he felt beholden to her. Caroline herself perceived nothing of the kind. He had taken [illegible] to have him [illegible] itself, [illegible] ever anticipat[illegible] to his [illegible] down onto [illegible] night-[illegible] combed his [illegible]

[illegible] him beache[illegible] sense [illegible] her until she [illegible] could [illegible] was a revelat[illegible]

[illegible] gainst hers, [illegible] plea-[illegible] ten years si[illegible] take all [illegible] the times w[illegible] Charles [illegible] her hungry [illegible] Caroline [illegible] him, she did [illegible] g. All [illegible] breach that pa[illegible] ween [illegible] fe she had forb[illegible] ng to [illegible] rself in her m[illegible] is as [illegible]

[illegible] [illegible] er chest flare[illegible] and as [illegible] e free. *It is no* [illegible] Ma [illegible] children to b[illegible]

[illegible], Caroline pr[illegible] the [illegible] ch of her thig[illegible] sire [illegible] h and nuzzle[illegible] eck [illegible] ured to him [illegible] his [illegible] dle strings, pl[illegible] ords [illegible] body. She fe[illegible] well [illegible] et go of herse[illegible] les. [illegible] ut the cadenc[illegible] ame [illegible] e could not e[illegible] was [illegible] With her eye[illegible] the [illegible] across the st[illegible] hat [illegible] er every nerv[illegible] est, keenest edge, the rhythm building until at the last her body trembled in a final vibrato.

When he had caught his breath Charles whispered, "None knew thee but to love thee, thou dear one of my heart."

The chorus of "Daisy Deane." She had not imagined it, then. The music had been in his mind and in his flesh. Caroline smiled broadly into the darkness, anticipating the memories her mind would conjure the next time he played that song. The day had consumed every ounce of her, yet Caroline could not remember the last time she had felt so vibrantly alive.

THE NEXT DAY was not washing day, but Caroline filled the washtub and brought out the clothes she and Charles had worn the day before. There were two small black-rimmed holes on the back of Charles's shirt, just at the shoulder blade, that she would have to patch. At the front of her own dress, the skirt was scarred with places where fire had eaten into the braided trim along the hem. Beneath that the calico itself was badly scorched. Caroline sighed. The trimming could not be salvaged. Nor could the dress be worn without fraying the remains of the hem further. And it was her new dress, made from the lilac calico Charles had brought back from Oswego. To mend the skirt properly would require more braid or ribbon—yards of trim she did not have.

Look at what you do have, her mind insisted mechanically. Her chest and throat tightened in resistance. *No,* said another part of her, equally frustrated that she could fall back so easily into that old habit.

Caroline made herself pause, the way she did before speaking to the children when they were at odds with each other.

Might it be possible, she asked herself, *to mourn the one while rejoicing in the other?* The loss of a dress was a small one. It did not compare with all the irreparable things that might have gone up in smoke. But it was a loss, and she would allow herself to feel it. She touched the charred er

...o break the ... new, she ... he pattern of th ... of ... across

...veet as it was ... ing ... rely ac- ... had passed. ... it has ... she set to work ... —lye soap, ... Wis- ... rubbed it in ... places. ... mured.

...urned from the ... squeezing ... e clothes. The ... especially ... sweat had mix ... through ... the garments ... ll and safe," ... Ed- ... wasn't touched ... the

...at. She held out ... the

..." ...ever felt a ... added, ... "that the In... off

...ettle, working ... she ... e washboard ... the ... e. "They've al... ...dipped up a bucket ... well. "I ... didn't say I bel...

...Likely he could ... The ... of the Indians ... from

for doubt. For all her kindness to her neighbors, Mrs. Scott had seemed to savor the thought of what depredations Indians—any Indians—were capable of, as though it vindicated her hatred for them. Caroline could not say whether she herself hated them any less, but she found nothing to relish in it. Nor was it a conviction she cared to cultivate any more deeply.

She sat back on her heels to look at him, her hands submerged in the cold rinse water. "If I am to live here, Charles, it cannot be under the cloud of what the Indians might have done, or may do." She said it without force. It was not a threat—only a fact. "I've seen enough that I can already imagine more than I care to."

He understood. Or rather, he agreed. He did not understand. Charles would never share her sentiments toward the Indians. He could stand before an Indian man without feeling his viscera clench and his bowels shudder, without the fine hairs on every surface of his skin rising up in a feeble attempt at protection. Caroline's body told her to be afraid, and she obeyed it; there need not be a reason. Charles's did not.

Caroline could not change his response to the presence of the Osages any more than she could change her own. Yet Charles was willing to abide by her condition. He had agreed with only a moment's consideration, without coaxing or scoffing. Warmth swarmed suddenly around her heart, and Caroline surprised them both with a smile. Charles smiled back without knowing why, happy, as always, to have pleased her. She would let that be enough. Caroline heard her thoughts and spared another smile, for her ma this time. *More than enough.*

"COME HERE, CAROLINE. And you, Mary and Laura."

Something to see, Caroline guessed. Perhaps an animal, by the way Charles called out to them—low and slow, so as not to frighten whatever it was away. Unless there were a bison grazing in the yard, she could not think what would make him interrupt her work. Caroline gave a scolding smile to the crochet thread in her hands. It was not work, really.

The [illegible] s [illegible] one, and the [illegible] [illegible] alloped lace she had [illegible] go in Wisconsi[illegible] ad b[illegible] ng, there at the bott[illegible] basket. So sh[illegible] end it could be used [illegible] burned hem [illegible] even though its patt[illegible] laborate for an[illegible] hands delighted in th[illegible] ments, so unti[illegible] wringing laun-dry [illegible] vexed each ti[illegible] d on the rough tips [illegible]. How long since [illegible] thing beautiful for it [illegible]

A[illegible] s voice was [illegible] her concentra-tion. [illegible] e realized the [illegible] e stitches. She set th[illegible] into the bask[illegible] g her back to a [illegible]. Let's go see w[illegible] s,' she said to Mary [illegible]

[illegible] e ahead of her, [illegible] board Charles ha[illegible] e doorway to [illegible] In the weeks [illegible] a begun creepin[illegible] lling with her hands [illegible] r knees along [illegible] uld be crawl-ing. [illegible] lowed her sister [illegible] then gripped the b[illegible] and mouth. "V[illegible] pa to tack a [illegible] edge," Carolin[illegible] hitched up her sk[illegible] Otherwise the [illegible] ff a mouthful of spli[illegible]

Car[illegible] o to shade her [illegible] n. When she [illegible] short. Her ha[illegible] At once [illegible] arles had calle[illegible] the girls. [illegible] seen so many [illegible] m, mounted [illegible] s and bundles [illegible]

"[illegible] es! See the [illegible] er, clapping [illegible] spotted one."

It wa[illegible] way the [illegible] the Indians [illegible] hoes, cookpot[illegible] ing behind.

"Mercy," Caroline heard herself say. She had not expected to watch them go—only to learn one day that their camps were empty, that they had fulfilled their agreement with the government and moved south of the Kansas line.

"Thank God," Caroline said. She meant it, but she did not feel it. Not yet. Here before her eyes was an answered prayer, and she could neither rejoice nor reflect, only witness its happening. Now that it was happening, Caroline wondered what she had supposed she would feel. Glad, relieved? She felt so little, she could not put a name to it. The moment flowed by without seeming to leave a mark.

Near the head of the procession rode the Indian agent, a white man of about forty, with a dark beard and eyelids that sloped gently downward at the outer corners. A ghost of a memory grazed Caroline's thoughts as he passed. Not so much a recollection, but a sensation, as though for a fleeting instant she inhabited the mind and body of a child who was accustomed to looking up into a face like that one.

Pa, she thought with a warm shiver, and her feet carried her to within a few yards of the procession. Not Papa Frederick, but her own father. In all the years he had been gone, she had never seen eyes so much like Pa's. Her brothers had inherited fragments of his smile, his hands, even his voice, but not one of them had his eyes. Had she known the agent's name, she would have called out to him, just to see those eyes looking down on her once more.

Instead the man rode on, and Caroline stood suspended in her memory as one Indian after another passed through the space he had occupied. For the first time Caroline felt safe enough in their presence to observe them with no other thought than to see what they looked like. The shape of their faces fascinated her. They were unmistakably different from her own. The planes were flatter, the lines straighter. Even the plumpest of cheeks appeared oblong instead of round. If their skin were white and their hair done up in curls, Caroline thought, she would still know the difference, just as she would know a spaniel from a bulldog.

was Mary … them. She gave … Caroline's … behind it as tho … bashful toddler … green calico shirt … crossed he … man who had … trunk at the … the lock of the … She remembered … it careened off the … and skittered …

At his knee … garters, woven … bags of green, blue … been wearing the … the cabin. Caroline … thing beyond his … movements of his …

He did not … did not so much as … direction. Caroline … back and thrust out … imagined that he … would look her … that she was not … did not. He rode … with his free hand … the man riding al … she felt as tho … ed. Was it possi … d happened inside … hold enough si … and put in his memory?

She scanned the … to see whether … to frighten her … ones who had com … before Carrie was … could recall nothing … laying silver ear … bones. A dozen … last night … of them looked … did not. Caroline … of them.

She turned her … Nothing the me … frightened her … the Osage women … autumn in the … own. Those endle … had come from … voices were so … did not seem poss … essed carved a ho … into Caroline … time, as Caroline … sisters and her mo … been the only w …

seen. Now, dozens. Sisters, daughters, mothers, grandmothers, none of them with the slightest link to her.

No, Caroline realized, that was not so. Some of them must be wives or mothers of the men who had come into the cabin. Was there one among them who had received a loaf of cornbread, tied up in a towel with a pine tree embroidered at the corner? Perhaps that towel was folded carefully into one of the bundles tied to the horses, or incorporated into a garment. Caroline studied the women individually as they passed. Their hair, so smooth at the parting it looked wet, was so enticing that Caroline put her hands into her pockets to keep her fingers from fidgeting over the imagined strands. Their clothing was an assemblage of deerskin and calico, in vibrant hues she had not worn since she was a child. Rich yellows, reds, and violets, decorated with beads, fringe, and ribbon work. Through the fabric Caroline could see the shape of their uncorseted breasts against their chests and the way they puddled on the women's laps. One woman, a little older than herself, lifted her blouse to nurse an infant, and Caroline could not avert her eyes from that bare brown breast. She had never seen a nipple so dark.

What did Charles think, looking at such women? Was he imagining running a hand over that sleek black hair, as Caroline herself was?

"Pa," Laura said, "get me that little Indian baby." Caroline turned in surprise. She had never heard such a tone from her daughter. Laura was not asking, she was commanding. Beneath the firmness, her small voice quivered with desire. Coming from a man's mouth, that timbre would mean avarice, or lust.

"Hush, Laura," Charles said.

She only spoke faster, her voice rising, "Oh, I want it! I want it! It wants to stay with me. Please, Pa, please!"

Laura did not look at Charles as she begged. Her eyes were fixed on what she wanted. Caroline traced Laura's gaze and saw an infant tucked into a basket that hung over the flank of a piebald pony. There was nothing to set it apart from the other Osage children, except that it seemed to [illegible] looking [illegible] at Laura. "I declare [illegible] I've [illegible] of such a thing," Caroline [illegible]

[illegible], [illegible] said again. "The Indian [illegible] keep her [illegible]."

[illegible] her voice cracked. [illegible] face and [illegible]

[illegible] what to say. Some [illegible] looking at [illegible] they think—what [illegible] might [illegible] they hea[illegible] Laura [illegible] what she had said? "[illegible]," she [illegible], and [illegible] immediately. Laura had [illegible]. The self [illegible] enough to sob [illegible] down besi[illegible] softly, "Why [illegible] ea[illegible] Indi[illegible]

[illegible] laughed before she [illegible] eyes [illegible] tered, looking pas[illegible] of t[illegible] more than coveting [illegible] it, too, and [illegible] tryi[illegible] Laura's cheeks [illegible] touc[illegible] grasp what Laura [illegible] did [illegible], she did not have [illegible] too [illegible] all she could not [illegible] it. [illegible] at Caroline [illegible] unde[illegible] knew the [illegible] had [illegible] Laura's misery was [illegible] feel [illegible]

"W[illegible], Laura," [illegible] suddenly she was [illegible] don't [illegible] have a baby, our own baby [illegible] words [illegible] she gestured toward the [illegible] the cr[illegible] of [illegible] head was visible above [illegible]

La[illegible] to agree. Then her [illegible] the ot[illegible]

Her outburst struck Caroline's face like a wind. She sat back on her heels, too bewildered to try anything else. "Well, I declare!" she said.

"Look at the Indians, Laura," said Charles. "Look west, and then look east, and see what you see."

Laura obeyed, and Caroline with her. The line of Indians seemed to rise up out of the grass to the east, then sink back into the west, as though they were as much a feature of the prairie as the creek and the bluffs. When Laura turned back, the black-eyed baby was out of sight. Caroline braced herself for a fresh surge of desperation and protest. Instead Laura accepted the blow as if she were grown. The expression slid from her face until her features were slack. Her shoulders jerked with jagged, silent sobs. However incomprehensible its cause, Laura's grief was real. The sight of it left Caroline staggered, as though something had been taken from her, too.

Caroline took Laura's hand and held it until the last of the Indians had passed. She wanted Carrie more, to turn her back to the Osage procession and take the baby up in her arms so that Carrie might feel how vital she was, no matter how many black-eyed Indian babies might pass through the dooryard. But it was Laura who needed her, not Carrie, though Caroline could think of nothing to do but stand by the child until Laura had absorbed the brunt of her loss.

"Are you ready to go inside?" Caroline asked when the Indians were gone. Laura shook her head. "All right. We'll sit on the doorstep awhile."

Caroline sat down with her back propped against the doorway and pulled aside the board that separated them from Carrie. The baby scooted out and found her place in Caroline's lap. Caroline's body eased some as Carrie settled back against her. Carrie knew perfectly well where she belonged. Caroline stroked Carrie's plump knee with her palm—round and round, as though she were polishing it.

It was time for dinner, and Caroline could not compel herself to move. "I don't feel like doing anything," she said to Charles, "I feel

not know how … any more th
re was no single … of the Indian
nce against the … d left her bla
ing she could fe … —the smoot
s knee under he … the baby's spi
t. "… et down," … ot it, but it w
ould manage.
ything but rest," … did not have
but her cheeks … had not spok
since she was pr …
it something, Cha…
, looking at Laur … ." He went to t
hitched the mu … he and Laura a
hungry, either. … hing the path t
rn across the yar … grass would gro
footprints and h … ould be no trace

Thirty-One

CAROLINE SET DOWN the pails and lifted the back ruffle of her bonnet so that the breeze could find the nape of her neck. Three rows remained to be watered: the carrots, the sweet potatoes, and the tomatoes. One thing never changed, and that was the everlasting heaviness of water. Pail after pail she pulled from the well and toted to her kitchen garden. Each dainty plant must have its dipperful if it was not to suffer during the long afternoon.

The soil here was sandier than she was accustomed to. It was warmer to the touch and easier to work, but did not hold water in the same way. Water splayed outward over the surface of the ground before sinking in, leaving only a thin layer moistened. Caroline had shown Laura how to carefully press a little dimple into the earth around each stem, so that the soil might cup the water long enough to soak the thin white roots. Twice a day Caroline bent double all along the length of each row, emptying each dipper of water where it could do the most good. Laura begged to help, but Caroline diverted her to digging a shallow trench around the perimeter, to ensure no rainwater fell out of reach of the seedlings. Careful as Caroline was with the dipper and pails, her hem was always damp and gritty by the time she finished. Laura would no doubt douse herself to the kneecaps.

Mary sat on a quilt spread over the grass, minding Carrie and sorting out remnants of calico from the scrap bag to sew her own nine-patch quilt. Caroline shook her head fondly, watching Mary arrange her favorites into pretty patterns. Five going on twenty-five, that child.

A gleeful squeal came out from under the sun canopy Caroline had [illegible]rived out of a p[illegible] two crates. [illegible] beads dangled [illegible] slats, and [illegible] side, jabbering at [illegible] beads. Caroline [illegible] rows of plants [illegible]. They would [illegible] minutes' time. She [illegible] edge of the qui[illegible] herself on an elbow [illegible] hair that had [illegible] black as soot had gi[illegible] den brown. H[illegible] knees and elbows w[illegible] apples. A smil[illegible]'s cheeks to see [illegible] to tinkle the [illegible] fingertip. Carrie fla[illegible] and squeale[illegible] hand to the bab[illegible] reached up [illegible]

"Letter for you, [illegible] voice called.

Caroline bounce[illegible] lightened with [illegible] ulator. "Mind t[illegible] as she smo[illegible] and strode out to th[illegible] Charles and [illegible] ting. "It's good [illegible] at the post [illegible] ards," she said.

"Just got back fr[illegible] night," he re[illegible] Charles the envelop[illegible] fresh. Th[illegible] post office said [illegible] a week or t[illegible]

[illegible] was addressed [illegible] hand she did [illegible]

Caroline felt fidget[illegible] Charles an[illegible] nged pleasantries [illegible] invitation to [illegible] fusal. Edwards ha[illegible] to head hom[illegible] [illegible] was holding [illegible] to slit open th[illegible]

"Who is it from, C[illegible]"

"Couldn't be any[illegible]

A single sheet of [illegible] then Caroline [illegible] turn to the top of t[illegible]. He said no[illegible]

"Does he send an[illegible]?"

Charles turned [illegible] looked inside th[illegible] n't know."

"Charles?"

Charles licked his lips. "He's reneged. Can't make the payments, so he's moving out—moving on. That twenty dollars he sent last summer is the last money we'll see from him. The property defaults to us."

No more payments. Caroline's mouth went dry. Every dollar and a quarter the Swede did not send was an acre lost. "How much is left in the fiddle box?"

"Not quite twenty-five acres' worth. Thirty-one dollars and twenty cents." He turned to the plow and slapped it gently with the letter. "Could have had forty acres for what this cost. Don't that beat all. Traded fifty dollars in furs for a steel plow and the only land I can afford to till is seven hundred miles away."

"The land office wouldn't have traded furs for acreage," Caroline said gently.

Charles whipped his hat down onto the freshly turned furrow. "Damn it all."

Caroline winced at the strike of his words. She glanced back at the girls. They were watching. Not scared yet, but alert that something was happening. Caroline moved so that they could not see Charles's face and lowered her voice. "If we raise a crop—"

"This ground won't raise anything but sod potatoes and sod corn until the grass roots have rotted out." Charles pronounced *sod* as though it were a vulgarity. "We can't raise anything of value in time to make payment."

"We've lived here a year without paying." Caroline trailed off, unsure where that feeble thought was headed.

He spoke fast, already impatient with the figures—figures she knew just as well as he did. "Government allows thirty-three months from the time we settle to make proof. That leaves less than two years to raise two hundred dollars beyond what we need to live. Plus two dollars just to file our intent to preempt. I don't see how we can do it. Thirty-one dollars isn't even enough to see us home, much less through two more years."

[illegible] rt of tremor throu[illegible] bone, [illegible] nded, suddenly [illegible]

[illegible] "I'll have to find wo[illegible] one [illegible] in's bound to [illegible] hand."

[illegible] a weathervane sla[illegible] wind [illegible] faced herself firmly [illegible] a sin[illegible] nor did she turn com[illegible] sneezed [illegible] his hand. "Takes six [illegible] word [illegible] sooner—" Ca[illegible] quiv[illegible] he moment for [illegible] spoke, [illegible] would snap.

[illegible] Her eyes linger[illegible] kitchen [illegible] the low fire in [illegible] had [illegible] ld of any of it [illegible] not [illegible] itself at the pa[illegible] line [illegible] hand into it. It was [illegible] though [illegible] herself with cott[illegible] and [illegible] approaching it as [illegible] of a [illegible] before crossing [illegible] stop[illegible] single room, sla[illegible] log [illegible] had been a mo[illegible] exist[illegible] presence encircli[illegible] weight [illegible] the sensation from [illegible] no [illegible] windows with [illegible] red [illegible] of creek stones. [illegible] bough[illegible] rose up in surr[illegible] into the [illegible] herself, eyes closed.

[illegible] Caroline heard [illegible] trying [illegible] see the beads? [illegible] Car[illegible] as Carrie prote[illegible] to jolly her with tones so fawning they made Caroline's jaw tighten. The baby was having none of it.

"Bring her here, Mary," she said.

Mary and Laura crept across the threshold together. Carrie was pushing her hands into Mary's shoulder and her knees into her sister's belly. She rarely consented to be carried now that she could crawl. Caroline took her long enough to kiss her, then set the baby down on hands and knees so that Carrie could move freely. Caroline closed her eyes and resumed her rocking.

"Ma?" Mary asked.

Caroline opened her eyes. "We're going home."

The girls looked at her, at the china shepherdess on the mantel, the rifle over the door, and finally at each other. Caroline understood without their asking. The meaning of the word had shifted for her, too. Like theirs, her mind no longer reached backward at the thought of *home*. "Back to Wisconsin," Caroline said. One dry, soundless sob clutched her throat, and then another. Caroline turned her face and drew her emotions inward, to the very center of herself. She exhaled, slowly, until her face relaxed. "Everything is all right," she told Mary and Laura. It was the falsest truth she had ever spoken.

CHARLES LAY IN the bed beside her, his eyes fixed on the ceiling. He had spoken only two and three words at a time since coming in for supper. Through the window, Caroline could see the plow where he had left it standing in the field. The gentle swoop of its blade shone out white in the starlight.

"Charles," she whispered. She touched his whiskers. He was mute. Likely fearing what might come out of him if he tried to speak, Caroline thought. So in need of comfort, and utterly unable to ask for it.

She could grant him his silence. Words could not be relied upon to soothe him. But she would not leave him embedded in his own grief.

[illegible] d to fac[illegible] him and [illegible] braid across her [illegible] the thick length [illegible] lo. With its ip, [illegible] is hand. He did no[illegible] s continued o [illegible] over the ceiling, a[illegible] ting and re-coun[illegible] ns and nails it had [illegible] of.

[illegible] d; but my beloved had [illegible] and was gone, Ca[illegible] to herself. *I sought [illegible] d him; I called him* [illegible] *no answer.*

[illegible] beneath his nightshirt. [illegible] narrow seam of [illegible] center of his belly, [illegible] ng the crease of [illegible] body had no choice [illegible] ard a small, del[illegible] and felt the sheet in [illegible] ba[illegible] l, as it began to [illegible] ned.

[illegible] was, meeting her [illegible] e bed. Their for[illegible] d, but his eyes wo[illegible] r collarbone. As [illegible] that happened to t[illegible] m [illegible] thing to be ash[illegible]

[illegible] in hooking her le[illegible] in [illegible] his knee and pul[illegible] His belly touched hers [illegible] m closer yet, until [illegible] feel his heartbeat against [illegible] embrace was wo[illegible] gh he dared not let [illegible] ns [illegible] t all Caro-line [illegible] es. The only thing [illegible] w [illegible] s a place for his [illegible] t.

[illegible] s she rocked him with h[illegible] and coaxing until [illegible] od, began to yield [illegible] s. She felt it pre[illegible] t were a solid thing [illegible] elt [illegible] ing at itself as he [illegible] g the pieces go. C[illegible] ne [illegible] per, whisper-ing [illegible] how you looked at me, [illegible] r first Kansas sum[illegible] teeth clenched and should[illegible] ath went rag-ged [illegible] y, but his mo[illegible] en [illegible] t of sobbing. Ca[illegible] nd rocked, milki[illegible] he [illegible] flesh.

He gave a muffled cry and she paused with her belly pressed to his, holding herself open for him while he spasmed.

If there were a child to come of this, Caroline wondered, would it bear a trace of the sorrow that had made it? Her heart throbbed softly at the thought of a small woebegone creature—a boy, perhaps, with Charles's blue eyes and long fingers. She surfaced from her thoughts and Charles was looking at her with those very eyes. The shadows at his mouth remained, shallower now.

"I'm sorry," he said.

It pained her to smile. "So am I," she answered.

He brushed the edge of her face with his knuckles slowly back and forth until they slept, joined.

ELIZA, HENRY, POLLY, Ma and Papa Frederick. Caroline said their names to herself over and over again as she emptied the cabin into the wagon. And there would be Eliza's new little boy. *Lansford Newcomb Ingalls.* To see them again in this world would be . . . what? Caroline knew no word to encompass it.

Then shouldn't the thought of their faces when the wagon arrived back in Pepin be enough to spur a smile? she asked herself once more. Caroline had a letter already written to drop at the post office on their way out, but there was every possibility that they themselves would arrive in Wisconsin before news reached the family. Imagine knocking on Polly's door, with Carrie in her arms, and asking to borrow a jar of pickles as though no more than a day had passed. Imagine Polly Quiner, speechless. That scene raised one corner of her mouth. It was all the joy Caroline could summon.

Think of the pantry, she told herself as she crouched before the little provisions cabinet to pack a crate with small bags of flour, cornmeal, coffee, and sugar. *Think of cooking on a stove again, with an oven and enough room to boil and fry and bake all at once. Think of cooking and eating in one*

...sleeping in a ...oth... All ... want to be happy...

...it on the w... Ch... she handed the...
...ailgate. "Se... n... it ... the way out." H...
...with the cra... e... s h... the inside of the...
...'s plenty of pa... her... ing the empty b...
...orner—th... sa... pla... just vacated.
...s shook his ... ea... Sa... rocking chair,"...
...ow she want... ed t... mi...
...line turned ... fro... til there was her...
She had neg... ect... to... ing. Though th...
...truly wilti... g ye... he... were beginning t...
...ves had a sof... loo... bo... like cloth. A f...
...they woul... be... mp... down each cent...
... She went t... th... ell... pail, then anoth...
...time for it, ... se... in... cruel. Tomorr...
...wilt again, an... t... w... ite.
...line could no... t... ers... derly she watere...
...weet potat... s, ... ca... ing a glance to...
... the cabin. ... les... asked, she woul...
...at the plant... ne... w... need them to un...
... than that. ... thr... she paused to l...
...ground she ... ac... ere... agged edges of th...
...were tilting g... tef... up... oline knew the...
...abandon th... se... its... the sun and the ja...
...she had car... ed... se... om Wisconsin.
...moved more ... qui... th... s, cucumbers, p...
...onions, m... e... cid... the time she had...
...she still ne... de... ac... sk. Then she we...
...the cabin, ... her... he... d to start the sw...
...od propped ... g... th... oline counted th...
...s along two ... edg... mu... ded. Room for...

plants from each row. By the numbers, it was not worth the effort. And her rocker was already straining the capacity of the wagon box. She dared not ask Charles to make room for one more thing. Caroline picked up the trowel, undeterred.

Hurrying around the corner of the house, she met Charles on his way to the stable. He carried a small coil of rope. If he took notice of the garden implements in her hands, he gave no indication. Perhaps he thought she was carrying them to the wagon, to pack. "If you don't object, I'd like to take the cow and calf over to the Scotts' claim," he said. "The mustangs will outpace the calf if we try to bring the cattle along. Maybe the cow, too." He slapped the rope against his thigh and said with a faint note of petulance, "Even if they could keep up we can't afford feed for all of them."

Caroline nodded. It was fitting, after all the Scotts had done for them. "That would be a fine thing, Charles. You'll give Mrs. Scott my thanks?" she asked. "For all her kindness. She has been . . . ," Caroline's lips tightened, tugged by a pang of loyalty to her blood kin. Yet it was true. Though the threads were of different fibers, her tie to Mrs. Scott was as firm as the knots that joined her to Eliza, and to Polly. However true, it was more than she could ask Charles to relay. "We'll always be beholden to them, cow or no cow," she finished.

"I'll thank her as best I can," Charles promised. "I want to offer Edwards the plow," he added. "I can't figure any way to pack it. The plow we left in Pepin ought to be there in the barn yet, unless Gustafson made off with it."

"Yes," Caroline said. "I would be proud for Mr. Edwards to have the plow. He'll want to pay you," she supposed.

"He will, but I won't let him." The challenge of compelling Edwards to accept such a gift seemed to buoy him so that he came within a fraction of smiling. "Can you be ready when I get back—say an hour or so?"

"I think so. Yes."

That satisfied him. Caroline waited while he went into the stable. He came out [illegible] long twisting horns. [illegible] untethered.

"An ho[illegible], [illegible] d. He grimaced [illegible] distinctio[illegible] re. Scott's a talk[illegible]."

"An hou[illegible], [illegible] He made no m[illegible] went over [illegible] king something [illegible] neck. Did [illegible] nded to do with [illegible] ter all? Su[illegible] and kissed h[illegible] off to the [illegible] behind.

Caroli[illegible] moment's bewilderment [illegible] task. Wit[illegible] round the hardie[illegible] ing care [illegible] if she could avoid it [illegible] loose and [illegible] into the small wo[illegible] by one sh[illegible] felt the tug and [illegible] visible fib[illegible] soil. When the [illegible] kitchen ga[illegible] d as a mouth full of [illegible]

She w[illegible] latched the tailg[illegible] her resol[illegible] nowhere, not e[illegible] stood the [illegible] ped it into a cre[illegible] shelf. Tho[illegible] every tangible f[illegible] the wago[illegible] r. Unopened ba[illegible] brought f[illegible] to the aisle, nar[illegible] Their w[illegible] ould not fit into [illegible] draped o[illegible] The displaced pro[illegible] on the se[illegible] ne put her hand [illegible] gave it a [illegible] replied with a sh[illegible] certing c[illegible] under the seat to [illegible] to be we[illegible] t willow runners [illegible]

"Oh," [illegible]

The sp[illegible] ners was empty. [illegible] frame fill[illegible] d Wisconsin pla[illegible] tween th[illegible] e rocker had bee[illegible]

BY THE TIME Charles came up the creek road, the empty coil of rope dangling at his side, Caroline had herself and the girls all freshly washed and braided, with their sunbonnets tied under their chins. "Come, girls," she said. "Pa's ready to go."

Charles held up a hand to slow them. "Edwards will be along soon," he called.

"For the plow?" Caroline asked.

Charles shook his head. "Not yet. Creek's still too high from the spring thaw to get it across, even for Edwards." He pulled a padlock from his hip pocket. "He gave me this, to put on the stable door so he can come for the plow when the water's gone down." Charles tossed the lock an inch or two into the air and let it drop heavily into his palm. "He wants to say goodbye. To you and the girls."

"That's kind of him," Caroline said. A slim strand of sympathy twined around her heart at the thought of how it would pain the children. She shifted Carrie to her hip and rested a hand on Laura's back. Mary and Laura both understood, in a way they had not before, how long and how far a goodbye might stretch. A year ago they had stood in the snow and kissed their cousins dutifully, without feeling the weight of it. Now the significance of the looming farewell made their faces long and sober.

"I'll hitch up," Charles said.

They waited in the shade of the wagon. The girls leaned against the wheels, holding the spokes as though there was comfort to be found in the smooth lengths of hickory. Caroline stood with Carrie in her arms, trying not to take it all in, trying to keep the freight of this single day from engraving itself upon all her memories of this place.

Jack growled so softly it was almost a purr. Caroline stepped into the sun to watch the creek road. The girls crouched, peeking under the belly of the wagon. A moment later, Edwards's long gangly shadow came loping toward them.

First he shook hands with Charles. "Goodbye, Ingalls, and good luck." Caroline knew from the jolly way he tried to say it that the men h[illegible] true goodbye. As [illegible]wards [illegible], she saw [illegible] eyes that belie[illegible] [illegible]rmined to [illegible] ould do the sa[illegible] [illegible] the chil-d[illegible] what Caroline [illegible] knew bet-t[illegible] e playacting fo[illegible] Charles and E[illegible] ding the childr[illegible] the [illegible]

[illegible]," Edwards sai[illegible] a genuine s[illegible] re will never for[illegible]

[illegible] Edwards. I don[illegible] have done w[illegible] sity," she answere[illegible] all the r[illegible] ed bright in her [illegible]

[illegible] ck little nod, a[illegible] jaw. Then E[illegible] own on one kne[illegible] hands as t[illegible] wn-up ladies. [illegible] Mary said, "[illegible] rds," as though [illegible] Laura, C[illegible] d not be able t[illegible] art was too m[illegible] ards's lips bu[illegible] Laura re-g[illegible] helpless.

[illegible] d meant to hi[illegible] imagine. W[illegible] hought to hers[illegible]

[illegible] -he had come t[illegible] his own a[illegible] e knew it was s[illegible] ppen, they h[illegible] their family tr[illegible] same. And r[illegible] him.

[illegible] so clear and st[illegible] question it. S[illegible] Charles and h[illegible] wagon to u[illegible] There in the c[illegible] was her r[illegible] e dozens of ti[illegible] up like s[illegible] se one sweet p[illegible] it into M[illegible] d tin cup. The[illegible] plants and c[illegible] dwards waited, s[illegible] though f-f[illegible] with dainties.

"My best seedlings," she explained. "Tomatoes, carrots, cabbage, beans, cucumbers, turnips, onions, peas." Her voice hitched. "And sweet potato." Her vision blurred, but she held her chin firm. "I'd thought to take them with us, but . . . ," Caroline trailed off. She could not say what she wanted to say: *They belong here.* "They would stand a much better chance if you would care for them," she finished.

"I'll miss your good dumplings and cornbread, Mrs. Ingalls, but come fall these vegetables will brighten up my jackrabbit stew just fine." He took the flat carefully, propping it against his hip like a baby so he could offer a free hand for her to shake.

Caroline took his hand in both of hers, clasping it for a long moment. "Mr. Edwards." She steadied herself and spoke the thought one piece at a time, so that her voice would not falter: "You have been—as fine a neighbor—as we have ever had." She gave his hand an extra squeeze at *ever*. "As we ever will have," she amended.

His thin lips fought for the words. "Yes, ma'am."

"Oh, Mr. Edwards," Laura cried out, "thank you, thank you for going all the way to Independence to find Santa Claus for us."

Caroline's chest gave an almighty heave. Edwards's hand broke from hers and he was away, striding through the long prairie grass.

Caroline put her hand on the lip of the wagon box and stood a moment, looking. The place itself tugged at her. All of it. From the bluffs and the creek road to the north, to the thin blue-white lip of the horizon to the south. It had never belonged to anyone before. It had not even belonged to them.

Eliza. Henry. Polly. Ma and Papa Frederick, her mind coaxed. *Lansford Newcomb Ingalls. A stove and a pantry and rooms with doors.*

Caroline climbed up and took her place on the wagon seat. Charles handed Carrie up to her.

Edwards, she thought. *Mrs. Scott. The smell of the grass on the wind, and the everlasting blue vault of the sky.*

Her heart was full and heavy behind her ribs, like a breast in need

ing. She pressed C... close ... ffuse its deep heat
boosted Mary an... ick.
her moment and Charles ... he reins in his han
d?"

he thought. *Never. And ... breaks me.* "L...'s g..."

want to see out." ... a, make it so I can
e again."

ine looked straig... ahead ... ouldn't and see t
d.

wagon lurched as Charles ... then shuddered w
... of the rope ... and Mary could p
... the wagon cov... was still. The Ca
... Charles's foot... of approaching. S
... herself to lo... looked back, ut
Laura and Mary ... ole Charles ha... m
... Past their h... the cabin was visib
... stood in the do... edge. He did not s
... stood with one ... other on the l...ch.
... she could see all ... oking at. Th...em
... The place beside ... willow-bough ...
... The glass wind...ws.

... could not wat... her cheek to Carr
... closed her eyes. ... ving the sme... of
... through the cl... n she felt the wag
... with Charles's weight, ... al. A small d...k
... the pink cal...o.

... latch string out ... might need shelter.
... nodded, grat... m that hid her v
... om him.

... rned to the ho... r face into the wa
... Before the fi... ould dry her ...ars

IT WAS TO be a piecemeal farewell to Kansas itself, Caroline realized as they drove northeast. That was a mercy. Mile after mile, the grass still rippled and the sky extended beyond the reach of her eyes. Tomorrow they would drive into the sunrise, across the same hills that a year ago had beckoned them west. The symmetry of it pleased Caroline in a way she could not account for.

"Something's wrong there."

Mary and Laura stood up on the straw tick and grasped the back of the wagon seat to balance themselves while they looked. "Where, Pa?"

"There," Charles said again, pointing with the reins. "Look right between Patty's ears. See it?"

It was a fleck. A pale, still fleck in a sea of swaying grass, perhaps a mile off. Caroline narrowed her focus and the shape became a wagon. A wagon, motionless by the side of the road in midday. No smoke meant no cookfire.

"Sickness?" Caroline guessed, keeping her voice low. Or worse.

A smaller, darker smudge gradually appeared at the stilled wagon's front as the distance closed between them. Where horses should be, yet too small to be horses. People. They were as motionless as the wagon.

Charles guided the mustangs off the road, approaching cautiously.

A man and a woman sat on the wagon tongue. They were young. Little more than twenty, the woman, perhaps less. Caroline could not see past the woman's bonnet brim to her face, but her milk-white hands were so profusely freckled, they could belong only to a redhead. Her dusty hem did not obscure the fact that the dress was new. It was an everyday work dress, but the sleeves were shaped in a fashion that Caroline had not seen before, and every line of the paisley pattern stood out crisp. A few months in the Kansas sun and the sage-green print would hardly be distinguishable from the fawn-colored ground. Both of them looked so morose that Caroline began planning what she might cook for their supper while Charles helped the man dig a grave.

"What's wrong?" Charles asked. "Where are your horses?"

"I [illegible] "I tied them t[illegible] and t[illegible]."

St[illegible] [illegible]usea trickled th[illegible] ach, [illegible]

"W[illegible] [illegible] Charles.

"H[illegible] [illegible]aid. He sounde[illegible] child [illegible] not having kno[illegible]

"W[illegible] [illegible]" Charles said, [illegible] not fully [illegible] r see them aga[illegible] for ho[illegible]

"Yes," [illegible]

Charles [illegible] [illegible]ard her. Caroli[illegible] plain[illegible] [illegible]er would be. S[illegible]

"C[illegible] [illegible]ndence," he off[illegible]

"N[illegible]," [illegible] [illegible]ot is in this wag[illegible] [illegible]

Charles [illegible] a punch to the [illegible] "W[illegible] will you [illegible] [illegible] may be nobo[illegible] Week[illegible]

"I [illegible]

"W[illegible] [illegible] he woman dec[illegible] back [illegible] to look at her [illegible] small [illegible] woman's folde[illegible] of a c[illegible] [illegible]aped posture?

"B[illegible] [illegible]. "You can com[illegible]

"N[illegible]," [illegible] e signaled an e[illegible]

Charles [illegible] lummoxed. Ca[illegible] gers t[illegible] his [illegible] es," she said. "I [illegible]

"T[illegible] [illegible] under his bre[illegible] onto [illegible] own, and no c[illegible] keep [illegible] horses with ro[illegible] head. [illegible] "Shouldn't be [illegible] the M[illegible]!

It stung to hear him speak so harshly, as though they had done him some personal offense. In a way, they had. He, who had done everything right, must leave the land he so loved, while they had shackled themselves to it out of pure foolishness. "Charles," Caroline said. Tenderly, as though they were lying side by side on the straw tick. He sighed and leaned back a little. "Whatever will become of them?" she ventured.

"I'll leave word tomorrow when we pass through Independence. Someone will have to take a team and go out after them."

They spoke no more of it. Charles drove until the mustangs' lengthening shadows leaned eastward. They had come seven or eight miles all told when he turned the wagon from the road to an overgrown trail. "I think this is the place," he said. "Doesn't look quite right, though. There's a good well a little ways off the road," he explained as the horses nosed through the brush. "A young bachelor from Iowa staked his claim right near here, if I'm not mistaken. I made his acquaintance on my first trip to Oswego." Charles cocked his head as he tried to align his memories with the landscape. "He'd just finished the well and was eager to show it off, so I humored him and stopped to water the horses. Nice enough fellow, talked a blue streak. Lonely, probably. He told me three or four times I was welcome to rest my team on his land any time."

A quarter mile down the trail, Caroline spotted a chimney. "There?" she asked.

"Must be," Charles said, "though I would have sworn the chimney was on the other side of the house."

The jagged outline of a burned claim shanty emerged around it as they approached, blackened and spindly against the sky.

Charles whistled a low note of astonishment. "Fellow said he was headed back East in the spring to fetch his sweetheart. Next time I passed by he was gone, but the house still stood. Shall we make camp here, or . . . ?"

Caroline considered. The ruined shanty lent the place a hollow feel-

attachment. Th ... an attempt
don't know wh ... water."
rcled the sha ... from the
at would bur ... cornmeal
water and ende ... ng about
ened to the pe ... here.
Caroline coul ... lieve they
out. Everythi ... uly little
he wind, the s ... surface of
with pink an ... nto their
agon box. Eve ... meward
the same. C ... pull had

to the fire she ... tin dishes
the sweet pot ... though,
around the mu ... *that feels*
this single tin
rt is. That was ... lled out
d threads. Bu ... where to
h it had moved ... chest.
oline," Charle ... wagon
ing what fur ... ting that

and deep and ... e had not
en a stab at fo ... ness and
er spot instead ... an echo
adage: *There is* ... n. Caro-
ob to subside. ... Charles."
ment, looking ... smile.
se her hurt, ... windled
his mouth cu ... we're
lian Territory

Caroline detected the sly undertone of a joke, but lacked the energy to guess where it was headed. "I don't know what."

"There's the mule colt. And Carrie."

Caroline's burst of laughter took them both by surprise, it was so out of proportion to the remark. He grinned at her, eyebrows cocked wonderingly. Caroline covered her mouth and shook her head. She could not explain. Only a man could miss the absurdity of such a notion. He had not felt the weight of a half-formed child sloshing in his belly as the wagon clattered over every rut and stone in seven hundred miles, nor vomited his breakfast into the ditches of five states.

Caroline wiped her eyes and found that he was gazing at her, his fist propped against his temple. The laughter had scoured her almost clean, and a soft, deep ache filled the space where the pain had been.

Charles leaned down and slid the fiddle box from under the wagon seat. He plucked the strings, coaxing the four familiar notes to their round, sweet centers, and Caroline shivered with a tremor of emotion too rich to name.

In that sound was the feel of her green delaine, whirling about her waist at the cornhusking dance; the scent of rosemary and pipe smoke and the shine of a crochet hook, flashing before a fire of stout Wisconsin hardwood. And now it was imbued with the first flutterings of a black-haired baby girl, and the unexpected delight of Edwards, dancing and whooping in the starlight. Caroline ached for all of it at once. The fiddle sang out high and sweet, as though it were pulling the notes from her chest, and Caroline remembered: It had been the sound of the fiddle that first awakened her heart to this country.

Now her heart seemed to spread, to peel itself open so that it could span the full breadth of the memories contained in those sounds, and Caroline marveled that her body could hold them all, side by side.

Her left hand slipped around her waist, her right settled over her breast.

Here, she thought. *Home.*

Author's Note

CAROLINE IS A marriage of fact and Laura Ingalls Wilder's fiction. I have knowingly departed from Wilder's version of events only where the historical record stands in contradiction to her stories. Most prominently:

- Census records, as well as the Ingalls family Bible, demonstrate that Caroline Celestia Ingalls was born in Rutland Township, Montgomery County, Kansas on August 3, 1870. (Wilder, not anticipating writing a sequel to *Little House in the Big Woods,* set her first novel in 1873 and included her little sister. Consequently, when Wilder decided to continue her family's saga by doubling back to earlier events, Carrie's birth was omitted from *Little House on the Prairie* to avoid confusion.)
- No events corresponding to Wilder's descriptions of a "war dance" in the chapter of *Little House on the Prairie* entitled "Indian War-Cry" are known to have occurred in the vicinity of Rutland Township during the Ingalls family's residence there. Drum Creek, where Osage leaders met with federal Indian agents in the late summer of 1870 and agreed peaceably to sell their Kansas lands and relocate to present-day Oklahoma, was nearly twenty miles from the Ingalls claim. I have therefore adopted western scholar Frances Kay's conjecture that Wilder's family was frightened by the mourning

songs sung b[illegible] Os[illegible] w[illegible] they grieved the l[illegible] and ancest[illegible] in [illegible] following the agre[illegible] instance, [illegible] lving the Osages[illegible] family's re[illegible] re [illegible] product of their [illegible] prejudic[illegible]

- Though [illegible] ily's departure [illegible] on "blaste[illegible] white squatters [illegible] Osage lan[illegible] issued over Rut[illegible] during the [illegible] e. Quite the re[illegible] only whit[illegible] s known as the [illegible] of Oklah[illegible] make way for th[illegible] Osages [illegible] Wilder mistake[illegible] her famil[illegible] rty—rather th[illegible] fourtee[illegible] ence, an error [illegible] the ficti[illegible] area affected [illegible] order.) Ra[illegible] decision to aba[illegible] was almost [illegible] for Gustaf Gust[illegible] default on [illegible]

The exce[illegible] ctional counte[illegible] historica[illegible] n to leave Wisc[illegible] in Kansas [illegible] ard one. Instea[illegible] eventual re[illegible] transactions t[illegible] the spring [illegible] Ingalls sold hi[illegible] property t[illegible] shortly therea[illegible] 80 acres [illegible] issouri, sight un[illegible] has been a[illegible] y certainty whe[illegible] whether [illegible] lly resided on t[illegible] scanty pape[illegible] that they actu[illegible] from Kans[illegible] again between [illegible] 1868 an[illegible] t is certain is t[illegible] February [illegible] had returned [illegible] his Chari[illegible] e Missouri lan[illegible] so for simplicity's sake I have chosen to follow Laura Ingalls Wilder's lead, contradicting history by streamlining events to more closely mirror the opening chapter of *Little House on the Prairie,* and setting this novel in 1870, a year in which the Ingalls family's presence in Kansas is firmly documented.

Acknowledgments

I AM INDEBTED TO:

William Anderson, for kindling my interest in Laura Ingalls Wilder by so willingly sharing a number of uncommon resources. Had that information not been so easily accessible, the idea for this book might never have fully germinated.

Christopher Czajka, for reading the manuscript with a keen eye for accuracy and an impeccable instinct for authenticity.

And to Little House Heritage Trust, for entrusting me with Caroline Ingalls. I have never been, and never will be, unconscious of that honor. My time with her, and my partnership with you, has enriched my life in more ways than I could have hoped to foresee.

P.S.

Insights, Interviews & More . . .

*

Sarah M... le...

...LLER began wri...
...e age of ten, and...
...decades work...
...tores. She is the...
...s historical no...
...ching Helen K...
...wn. Her non-f...
...Murders: Lizz...
...of the Centur...
...York Times as "...
...Law & Order." S...

Behind the Book Essay

In the middle of the night she sat straight up. Ma was sitting still in the rocking-chair by the fire. The door-latch rattled, the shutters shook, the wind was howling. Mary's eyes were open and Jack walked up and down. Then Laura heard again a wild howl that rose and fell and rose again.

"Lie down, Laura, and go to sleep," Ma said, gently.

"What's that howling?" Laura asked.

"The wind is howling," said Ma. "Now mind me, Laura."

Laura lay down, but her eyes would not shut. She knew that Pa was out in the dark, where that terrible howling was. The wild men were in the bluffs along the creek bottoms, and Pa would have to cross the creek bottoms in the dark. Jack growled.

Then Ma began to sway gently in the comfortable rocking-chair. Fire-light ran up and down, up and down the barrel of Pa's pistol in her lap.

When I heard Cherry Jones read those words from the audio edition of *Little House on the Prairie*, my entire mind jolted. A pistol? In Ma's lap? I didn't even remember that Pa owned a pistol. It had never occurred to me that maybe Ma is just barely holding it together in that scene. And really, why would it? As a kid—as an adult, even—you ▸

tru[illegible]t L[illegible] [illegible]. You know
eve[illegible]yt[illegible] [illegible], so long [illegible]
Pa'[illegible] rif[illegible] [illegible] Ma[illegible] chi[illegible]
she[illegible]phe[illegible] [illegible] because [illegible]
Lit[illegible]le [illegible] [illegible]use is always
saf[illegible] an[illegible] [illegible]
B[illegible]ut [illegible] [illegible]man in the
roc[illegible]ing [illegible] [illegible] the one
wh[illegible]'s [illegible] [illegible] everyone
else saf[illegible] [illegible] *[illegible]an was my*
age, I re[illegible] [illegible]nd not onl[illegible]
that it [illegible] [illegible] Ingalls
was pre[illegible] [illegible] child the
year he[illegible] [illegible] pull up
stakes a[illegible] [illegible] Kansas.
Can you [illegible] [illegible]on, I
coul[illegible]n'[illegible] [illegible] her life
had [illegible]eal[illegible]
W[illegible]he[illegible] [illegible]ndle[illegible]
this [illegible]way [illegible] [illegible]onfir[illegible]
with the [illegible] [illegible]ent.
That's h[illegible] [illegible] all of
Laur[illegible] In[illegible]lls [illegible] written
man[illegible]scr[illegible]ts, [illegible] then-
unpublis[illegible] [illegible] *[illegible] Girl*
and [illegible] [illegible]ographers'
resea[illegible]ch [illegible] and fiction
meld[illegible]d [illegible] [illegible] more,
I pon[illegible]d [illegible] [illegible]men
who [illegible]ad [illegible] [illegible]n in
the 1[illegible]00s [illegible] myself
collec[illegible]tin[illegible] [illegible] social
critic[illegible]sm [illegible] [illegible]ooks,
which [illegible] [illegible] many ways
(both po[illegible] [illegible] Wilder's

stories have embedded themselves in our collective consciousness and culture. That led to studying histories of the Osage Nation by John Joseph Mathews, Louis Burns, Willard Rollings, and Garrick Bailey, as well as the 1870 and 1871 annual reports of the Board of Indian Commissioners.

And then, because I'm what friends like to call a "method writer," I drove to Missouri, Kansas, South Dakota, Minnesota, Wisconsin, and Iowa, to see the sites of the Ingalls family's lives, where they were born and where they were buried. I learned to crochet so I could replicate a piece of Mrs. Ingalls's own lacework that I'd seen on display in Missouri, as well as a shawl I saw in South Dakota—both of which appear in *Caroline*. I made myself a calico dress. (I thought I could sew the whole thing by hand. I was so very wrong.) I bought—and wore!—a corset. I lent a hand in butchering livestock and wild game, rendered lard, fried salt pork, roasted a rabbit, and tasted head cheese. I haven't yet made maple sugar, but I intend to.

The more I learned about the realities of the Ingalls family's history, the more I realized that Caroline Ingalls was the glue that held her family together. Laura Ingalls Wilder herself admitted that Pa was "no businessman," as well as "inclined to be reckless." When Charles's schemes for a better ▸

the Book Essay (co

d. Caroline Inga
nd believe me, th
For years they s
disease, and the
le House series is
al comfort food
rs. How is that p
pect the answer li
tion that "the Lit
serenity. Their d
ristic is that they
re and hardship
Ma is the embod
How did she do
e to carry that re
ere the questions
d me, and the on
y hand at answer
e more facts I ac
mplicated my tas
who has read *Pi*
s, the Little House s
lica of Laura Ing
d. As she crafted
's fiction, Wilder
of unsavory circu
other, more palat
fabric of her nove
tions are simple.

———

ginia L. "Laura Inga
ks: A Personal Story
the Best in Childr
e, edited by Perry N
ette, Indiana: Child
, 1985.

things, like the utter absence of chamber pots and outhouses. Nobody so much as changes a diaper in Wilder's novels, for heaven's sake. Other gaps are matters of life and death—literally. In the world of Little House only animals are born or die, and even they never do so right before our eyes.

Consequently, in order to make Caroline's story as authentic to the real Mrs. Ingalls's experience as I wanted it to be, there were times when I had to muster the courage to contradict Laura Ingalls Wilder's version of her own life. Just as often there were times when I had to coax myself into loosening my death-grip on historical precision, rather than do away with fictional moments that generations of readers hold dear. I'm still not entirely sure which type of changes were more difficult for me.

These decisions represent a delicate balance between instinct and accuracy. I want Caroline's world to feel wholly familiar to anyone who has read the Little House series, and yet at the same time I want readers to come away with a new appreciation for the realities Mrs. Ingalls faced during her year in Kansas. Instinct tells me that no version of *Little House on the Prairie* would be complete without the fictional Mr. Edwards, while accuracy demands that I contradict Laura Ingalls Wilder's racist and stereotypical portrayal of ▸

the O... e N... and history. Lik...ew... Ca... ...ence of tha... is i... ...bout her pregn... y a... ...her third chi...d. ...tim... ...n I struck wit... elf ... ...ilder's fict...on ...ta... ...t create a fal... o... arm... ...n of reality.

Peo... ha... ...like Laura Ingalls ...ilde... ...g over my should... as I ... ...e I don't expect ... yo... ...e when I say tha... don... ...ndering what L... ra ... ...what I was doin... ...t it's ... ...did wonder— dai..., e... ho... ...—was what C... line ... ...thin... She was an ...ten... ...rian. There were th...gs I... ...ilder didn't lear... a... ...over...shed chil...ho... ...galls had die... A... he ... ...ing u... scen... ...chil... ...templating the ...nt...cies ...s—both em...tio... an... ...her hus...an...

S...ft-...oke... ..., an... trut...fu... lmo... ...ura Ingalls ...lder ...mother as a ...ar... ...ntury femi...ni... ...irt... ...reader Ma ...lso ...pe... ...passive ("W... ...r yo... ...Charles") and ...ft... ...com... ...thing of a killj...y (... lod... ..., Laura").

Don't be fooled, though. She packs the wagon again and again without a murmur of complaint, and never gives up reminding Laura to put on her sunbonnet, but at the same time, Caroline Ingalls was also quietly making sure that her daughters were as educated and self-supporting as their individual circumstances allowed. Watching her own widowed mother struggle to support six children under the age of ten likely had a profound influence on Mrs. Ingalls's views of a woman's place in the world. The concept of "strong girls" is probably too recent to graft directly onto her outlook; I think a desire to raise capable girls is more apt.

And she certainly succeeded. Mary went to college for the blind (Spoiler? Sorry!) where she learned to make beadwork, lace, hammocks, and fly nets. The other Ingalls sisters made their way in the world as homesteaders, journalists, and schoolteachers before marrying, at a time when marriage was still considered a woman's primary vocation. I find it endlessly intriguing that despite her own strict compliance with the manners and expectations of the day, Mrs. Ingalls somehow cultivated a strong streak of independence in each of her daughters—which fully blooms in her granddaughter, globetrotting journalist Rose Wilder Lane. There ▸

[illegible] Book Essay (co[illegible]d)

[illegible] been so much [illegible]
[illegible] placid faca[illegible]
[illegible]hen, it's not [illegible]
[illegible] imagine that [illegible]
[illegible] forgive me [illegible]
[illegible] intimate m[illegible]
[illegible] illuminating [illegible]
[illegible]h and resili[illegible]
[illegible]n and devot[illegible]
[illegible] love. I have e[illegible]
[illegible] all the hon[illegible]
[illegible] Mrs. Ingalls h[illegible]
[illegible]

Reading Group Guide

1. *Caroline* presents the events of Laura Ingalls Wilder's *Little House on the Prairie* from the perspective of Caroline Ingalls. How would the story be different told from the perspective of Charles? Of Mary? Of an Osage Indian living near the cabin?

2. Laura Ingalls Wilder's Little House books, as well as other works of historical fiction, tend to sanitize and simplify the past. In *Caroline,* Sarah Miller partially addresses how dirty, dangerous, and desperate life on the frontier really was. What instances and events brought the grittiness of frontier life alive for you? What surprised you about the challenges Caroline faced throughout the novel?

3. What is your favorite moment in Laura Ingalls Wilder's *Little House on the Prairie*? Does it correspond with your favorite moment in *Caroline*?

4. What aspects of Caroline Ingalls's life do you find appealing? Repugnant or distressing? Which aspects of her life do you wish we hadn't "lost along ▸

Guide (continu

technology,
cation, etc., hav
ed over the last 15

Ingalls, the act
has been romant
logized as the
ghter's Little H
nning televis
ess other adapt
ttle House and pi
th. She is freq
ized as submis
nt to her husba
ine maintain-
ective? How do
Ingalls of this n
or agency?

hoice, would C
ed in Wisconsi
? What would
o in her plac

ze Caroline's p
ge. Is her view
Why or why n

pect of the Inga
in Kansas is mos
ine? How has s
point of view
ed the way yo
experience?

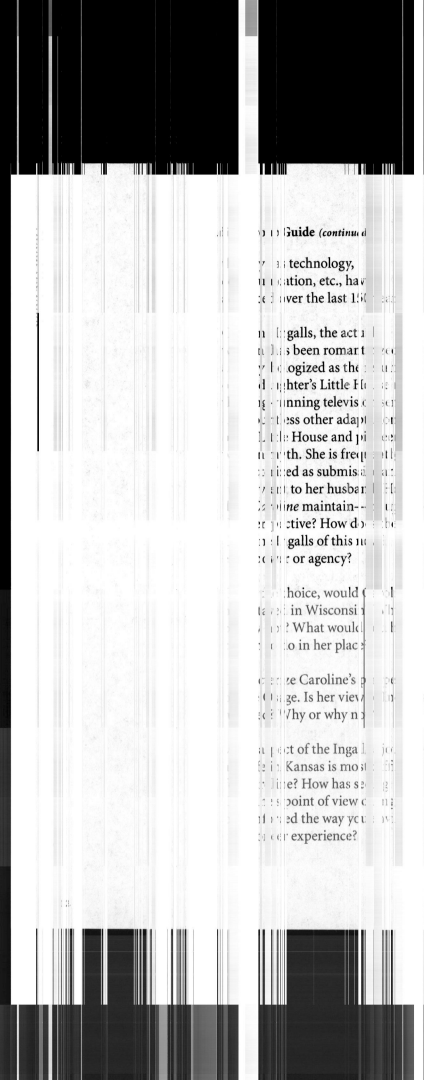

9. Does the Caroline Ingalls of this novel have a favorite child? Who? How would you characterize her relationship with each of her daughters?

10. What attracts Caroline to her husband? What faults, if any, does she see in him? Has the fictional Caroline's view of her husband affected your own feelings toward Pa Ingalls?

11. Ma Ingalls of the Little House books often comes across as the embodiment of nineteenth-century feminine virtue: gentle, composed, competent, and pious. By contrast, what faults does Sarah Miller's version of Caroline Ingalls see in herself? Are they the same or different from what you perceive as Caroline's weaknesses?

Furt[illegible]

For a c[illegible] lo[illegible] a
Caroline [illegible] knew
it, expl[illegible] and
films. (N[illegible] are
available [illegible] Google
Books.)

Books

Anderson, [illegible] *[illegible]un:
A R[illegible]
Laura [illegible]*[illegible]rk:
HarperCol[illegible]

———. *[illegible]unny:
The P[illegible] Ingalls
Wilder[illegible]* York:
HarperCol[illegible]

Bull, Thomas [illegible] *for th
Ma[illegible] the
Fer[illegible] Lying-
in R[illegible] Popular
Erro[illegible] se
Subj[illegible]ing*.
London: [illegible] Brown,
Green[illegible]

Burns, [illegible]
Osage [illegible]: The
University [illegible], 2004.

Child, Lydia Marie. *The American Frugal Housewife*. Boston: Carter, Hendee & Co., 1835.

———. *The Mother's Book*. Boston: Carter, Hendee and Babcock, 1831.

Fraser, Caroline. *Prairie Fires: The American Dreams of Laura Ingalls Wilder*. New York: Metropolitan Books, 2017.

Hill, Pamela Smith. *Laura Ingalls Wilder: A Writer's Life*. Pierre, SD: South Dakota State Historical Society Press, 2007.

Holmes, Kenneth L. *Best of Covered Wagon Women*. Norman, OK: University of Oklahoma Press, 2008.

Ketcham, Sallie. *Laura Ingalls Wilder: American Writer on the Prairie*. New York: Routledge, 2015.

Leavitt, Judith Walzer. *Brought to Bed: Childbearing in America 1750–1950*. New York: Oxford University Press, 1986.

Marcy, Randolph B. *The Prairie and Overland Traveller*. London: Sampson, Low and Son Co., 1860. ▸

Fur[illegible]her [illegible]

Mc[illegible]Dow[illegible] *[illegible] of Laura [illegible]ngall[illegible] [illegible] Landsca[illegible]es [illegible]Tha[illegible] [illegible]se Books* [illegible]ortl[illegible]d, [illegible], 2017.

Ril[illegible]y, G[illegible] [illegible] *[illegible]. Wom[illegible]n [illegible]nd [illegible] 1[illegible]5–1[illegible]15.* [illegible]lbu[illegible] [illegible]r[illegible]ity of N[illegible]w [illegible]Mexi[illegible] Pr[illegible]

Str[illegible]sser, [illegible] *[illegible] History [illegible]f A[illegible]* [illegible] [illegible]w York: [illegible]an[illegible]

Str[illegible]tto[illegible] *[illegible]e[illegible]: Voi[illegible]es [illegible]rom* [illegible] [illegible]ew York [illegible]ou[illegible]

Wa[illegible]ke[illegible], [illegible] *[illegible] House [illegible]Cook[illegible]* [illegible] [illegible]er & Ro[illegible]v, [illegible]97[illegible].

We[illegible]ner, [illegible] *[illegible]h[illegible]ldren on [illegible]he [illegible]* [illegible]n[illegible]isco: [illegible]Wes[illegible]

Wi[illegible]der, [illegible] *[illegible] Girl: T[illegible]e [illegible]Ann[illegible]* [illegible] [illegible]ierre, S[illegible]: [illegible]South [illegible] [illegible]r[illegible]cal Soci[illegible]ty [illegible]Pre[illegible]s[illegible]